ALSO, BY R.W. MARCUS

The Fate of Tomorrow: Tales of the Annigan Cycle
Book One

Shadow of the Twilight Lands: Tales of the Annigan Cycle
Book Two

Whispers from Nocturn: Tales of the Annigan Cycle
Book Three

Agents of the Void: Tales of the Annigan Cycle
Book Four

The Bane of Empires: Tales of the Annigan Cycle
Book Five

R.W. Marcus

The PRIDE and the FURY

A Tale of the Annigan Cycle in Three Acts

BOOK SIX

R.W. MARCUS

LAUGHING BIRD PUBLISHING
GALAX, VA USA

The Pride and the Fury

Copyright © 2023 by Jeff Morris

Published by Laughing Bird Publishing
Galax, Virginia USA

Visit us on the web!
https://AnniganCycle.com

Cover art by SelfPubBookCovers.com/ FrozenStar
Cover layout and design by Laughing Bird Publishing

Laughing Bird Publishing® is a registered trademark of Mark W Phillips

Manufactured in the United States of America
10 9 8 7 6 5 4 3 2 1

First Printing, 2023
ISBN 979-8-9877180-2-5

R.W. Marcus

Dedicated to the memory of
Edgar Rice Burroughs...
with a wink and a nod to
Philip José Farmer &
Quentin Tarantino

CONTENTS

ACKNOWLEDGEMENTS

It's important to note endeavors on the scale of this tome are hardly achieved in a vacuum. There are many who stand behind and support the person whose name adorns the cover.

First and foremost, my greatest appreciation and love goes out to my partner in crime, the woman I share my life with, Cheryl Pepper, who puts up with listening to my hair-brained schemes and ideas on a daily basis.

To Mark Phillips, my good friend and creative muse for over forty years, who has always been the perfect sounding board and the one with the ability to bump my work up to the next level of weirdness.

A big thanks to my awesome beta readers: Max Yirik Valentonis, Lynn Marie Firehammer, Dave (lather, rinse, repeat) Hollman and Ivy Maxine Elissa who help keep me on track with the story.

And not to be ignored is my growing army of technical folks. Jessica Pepper RN who humors my gruesome questions about doing harm to people. Physicist Keenan Pepper for informing mee about the laws of the universe before I break them. A double shout out to analytical chemist Dave Holman who also keeps me in line when it comes to science. A tip of the hat to the newest addition to Team Marcus, artist extraordinaire, Kilson Spanny.

Finally, Laughing Bird Publishing, who believed in this twisted little story I've got going enough to put it in print.

A big thank you to all. Let's keep this crazy train rolling!

WELCOME TO THE ANNIGAN

This mostly aquatic planet travels in a geosynchronous orbit around a small yellow sun. It's set far enough back in the solar system's Goldilocks Zone so that it maintains an atmosphere conducive to a wide variety of life.

Sentient creatures, terrestrial, marine or amphibious, share a hyper-fertility devoid of genetic boundaries. Any sentient creature may mate with any other and produce offspring.

Lumina basks in perpetual sunlight on one side of the Annigan. Humans dwell alongside many other sentient races thriving across its various continents and island chains. The fertility enriching rays of the sun, and the warmth of the Shallow Sea, support a vibrant and rich ecosystem.

Although life is abundant there, Lumina is hardly a serene place as you will see. Millennia of feuds, ruthless ambition and individual hatreds forged a fragile peace, barely sustained under the rule of the Great Houses.

Because of the incredible diversity of sentient creatures, all races, genders and hybrids in Lumina enjoy social equality, judging each as an individual based upon their own merits. Beneath the veneer of peace, however, dwells a hotbed of totalitarian torture, raider uprisings and a constant escalating cold war between the Great Houses.

Nocturn languishes in constant darkness on the other side of the Annigan. Only moonlight, starlight and bioluminescence illuminate the land of endless night. Without the warming rays of the sun, Nocturn's oceans froze over, but constant geothermal activity heats the land masses, creating a temperate and misty terrain teeming with exotic and predatory sentient races.

Imperialistic cat people rule aboveground and hive nations of humanoid mantises swarm beneath the surface. In the Ocean Deep, a race of sentient octopoids dwell in vast underwater cities worshiping the ancient ones of the abyss. You are predator or prey in Nocturn's despotic societies.

The Twilight Lands reside at the fringes of the Annigan and remain in constant gloaming. Here, warm and cold air currents clash, generating a perpetually stormy climate.

Ruled by the amphibian Bailian race, the Twilight Lands serve as a neutral zone for cultures from every corner of the Annigan. Many encounter the other races for the first time, and like the weather, their clashes can prove tempestuous.

Only the sun of Lumina keeps back the nocturnal predators of the dark side. Legends tell of a prophesied great eclipse stripping away all boundaries and igniting an apocalyptic war. Until then…

…these are the tales from the Annigan Cycle.

The Annigan stumbles.
Reeling from the blow.
A sudden aggression
Disrupting the flow
Of that which they covet
And others hold dear.
Uniting the world
Against an unholy fear.

ACT ONE

Rumblings

D olan Aramos was determined not to be cheated this time. He would take his rightful place as sovereign of House Aramos, *no matter how many people must die.*

It had been a full five cycles since his nephew Bartol's apparent suicide in the city of Zor, leaving the noble Human house in turmoil. Already the Bespoke Lords used their influence, pulling in any direction benefiting themselves.

That would end today!

When Dolan arrived in the city of Aris, he found the Aramos royal palace immersed in the planning of the former sovereign's funeral. The solemn event, scheduled to take place in less than two cycles, had bogged down with leaderless bureaucracy as usual.

He stepped from his coach, parked in front of the palace's ornately carved wooden doors, with his top general, Subay, six Black Talon elite soldiers and two Garf Sunal EEtahs in procession. Two hundred Forsvara Guards followed behind them, dispatched from their garrison up the coast in Sury, marching from the docks to hold positions in critical areas of the city.

Dolan watched the palace door guards snap to attention and salute as he drew near. *By the gods I will restore order to this house and city!* he decreed to himself, before stepping up onto the wide portico, and the guards flanking the entryway opened both doors.

"Wait here," Dolan ordered the two EEtahs.

He turned and crossed the threshold with the grey tunicked Black Talons following close behind. The tall, ornately decorated central hallway bustled with humans and Piceans moving in and out of various large rooms. All cleared out of the procession's path, staring as they passed.

Straight before them, at the end of the hall, stood the double doors to the throne room, but Dolan stopped at the last doorway on the left before the receiving hall.

He threw the door open without knocking and stepped inside. The intrusion startled the four men and two women seated around the table inside, but they quickly recovered upon seeing the stern-faced, senior Aramos.

"Lord Dolan," an older man in a yellow tunic greeted, rising to his feet, "so good to see you. You're obviously here for your nephew's funeral…"

"As far as I'm concerned," Dolan snapped, eyes boring angrily into the official, "you can shove that fat turd into an unmarked hole and forget he ever existed!"

Stunned, confused faces nervously glanced around the table at each other, unsure of what to do or say. A shared look of trepidation swept over them when the Black Talons entered and fanned out along the walls.

"Sir," the spokesman began, "we were just about to cast lots for the next sovereign…"

"Sit down and shut up!" Dolan snapped.

The man warily eyed the Talons and did as ordered.

"The Council of Lords," Dolan contemptuously addressed the nervous assemblage. "You people aren't worth a wet shit! I remember what happened the last time you voted for a sovereign. You bypassed me and put my inept nephew on the throne. Well, no more! I am here to assume my rightful place as head of House Aramos."

"Sir," the spokesman sputtered in surprise, "this is highly irregular and goes against thousands of grands of your *own family's tradition!*"

Dolan's eyes narrowed and his lips went taut. The spokesman swallowed hard under Dolan's virulent gaze and searched for support on his colleagues worried faces. He found none.

"This one tires me already," Dolan calmly responded. "Hang him."

The bureaucrat's face grew ashen, looking around wildly in disbelief. He started to protest when two Talons grabbed each arm and yanked him to his feet. Two more drew daggers and stepped over to him. One severed the sash around his waist and gruffly tied his hands behind his back. The other cut off a sizeable length of curtain cord and tossed it over an exposed beam in the ceiling.

Dolan intently watched the terrified looks following the pleading official being muscled to the front of the room. They watched one of their own hoisted into the air, legs kicking and flailing. Once the spokesman's eyes and tongue bulged, Dolan leaned on the table. When he heard the man's last gurgle before going limp, he slowly, with chilling effect met each one of their horror-struck gazes.

"Now that we better understand each other..." Dolan continued in a low malevolent tone, while the former spokesperson lurched behind him like a macabre, discordant marionette.

"Make no mistake, I *am* the new sovereign of House Aramos. Now, we're going to go around the table. You will give me your name and your respective duty, and if I deem it necessary, under my rule, you just might get to live."

Bo-Lah held the torch above his head and stared around at the twenty Human faces glowering at him. The Kan fog grew thin this particular evening, making the contempt on the river lord's faces clearly visible.

The most noticeable face belonged to Sani, Matka's only remaining child. She had tall and thin angular features like her mother, but her light brown complexion contained the glow of youth. A sneer pulled her normally pleasant features taut with suspicion and hostility. She stood beside her husband, Arn Volga, patriarch of House Volga, who also shared her contemptuous glare.

"On this Kan," Bo-Lah began, "we say goodbye to my beloved wife."

The white Tiikeri claimed this marriage with authority, even though he knew it to be a lie. True, she bore his child—which inevitably killed her—but they never wed. He paused for effect and listened to the rushing of the mighty Otoman River in the distance.

"Even though she is gone, she leaves me, and us, with a son to carry on the proud tradition as master of Staghorn and Otoman River Lord. She will be missed."

Feigning sorrow, he peered down mournfully at Matka's shroud draped body set atop a rectangular three-foot-high pyre of neatly stacked logs. Lowering the torch, he placed it at the base of the funeral structure and it immediately caught fire. Bo-Lah stepped back beside the wet nurse holding his son and watched the flames grow, bathing the entire area in the warm light.

Bo-Lah could clearly make out the mourners. All of the surviving Lords of the Western Fork were represented; Kenev, Volga, Annov, Vladof, Donyeb and Boshka.

His son now represented House Sorbornef and his foothold in the continent of Otomoria.

They carried on the silent vigil until the flames began to die and Bo-Lah, head bowed respectfully, led the procession back to the front of Staghorn Manor. He stood in front of the portico expecting a receiving line of the bereaved to form. Instead, everyone crowded antagonistically around him and Sani Volga stepped to the front of the mob.

"How is it I did not hear of my mother's wedding and my half-brother's birth?" she asked, sharply and critically.

The Tiikeri remained calm. "There was no time. Your family's males had been wiped out in that ill-fated campaign against the Dreeat. I was here on a trade mission. Your mother needed an heir. She came to me and I agreed to provide her one."

Sani leered at the Tiikeri/Human baby sleeping in the nurse's arms and scoffed loudly. "And it *killed* her!"

"I warned her of the dangers," Bo-Lah defended, "but she became obsessed with the next generation of Sorbornef."

"What did you name it?"

"We didn't have time to name it before your mother died," the Tiikeri explained. "As her only remaining child, I had hoped to confer with you on that."

"I don't care what you name it!" Sani yelled defiantly. "You and that… that… thing may, *by law*, be the new lord of Staghorn, but you will never be accepted as an Otoman River Lord! As far as we're concerned you two are filthy animals, just like the damn crocs!"

A murmur of agreement passed through the group and Bo-Lah realized the next stage of his plan would prove substantially more difficult.

With a slight adjustment to the flaps, Kumo began a slow descent when the Zorian skyline came into view.

"It's good to be back home," Mal said.

Zau, who sat beside her, nodded. "Still, it felt good to land an easy job after that excitement back in the Dark Waste."

Smacking her lips, Taleeka popped the last bite of the meat sick in her mouth and then bounded into a seat next to Zaad. The man-shark gave a satisfied grin when she snuggled up against him.

"Zaad," she asked, "how did you meet Mal and Alto?"

The Outer Clan EEtah looked down at the inquisitive face peering back at him and chuckled. "Well kid, I've known your mom longer than your dad."

Mal closed her eyes and sighed. Both Zaad and Zau referred to Alto and her as Taleeka's parents so often now, she gave up correcting them. The Spice Rat's reaction caused a chorus of smiles to pass through the cabin.

"It was about nine grands ago," Zaad said, reminiscing.

"Wow, that's almost as old as me!"

The EEtah flashed a knowing smile and tussled her hair.

"It sure is kid," he agreed, continuing. "Anyways, at the time I was working as a deck hand on a spice transport out of Tamil Island over in the Outer Zerians. One Kan, we were attacked by Rayth raiders just off the coast of Zer."

Taleeka sat up, her face filled with excitement.

"How many did you kill?!"

"I managed to take out a few," Zaad said with a boisterous laugh, "before they ganged up on me."

"Why didn't you used Bowbreaker on them?"

"It was before I got Bowbreaker. I wasn't even armed."

Taleeka sat on the edge of her seat, her face alight in wide eyed wonder. "What happened?"

"They took the ship, killing or capturing the crew and cargo. They tossed me over the side and left me for dead. I don't know how long I'd been floating before your mom's ship came along and they pulled me out of the water."

"Were you hurt real bad?"

"They dinged me up a bit, but you could tell they weren't used to tangling with my people. Mal's crew fixed me up and welcomed me into their ranks. I bought Bowbreaker with my share from my first job with your mom."

"What about Alto?"

"After the Unification War, quite a few of us Outer Clan were enlisting in the Valdurian Marines. At the time I was looking for a steady gig that wasn't quite so dangerous, so I left the crew of the *Regis* and joined. They shipped me out to Immor-Onn as an over glorified guard. I was bored out of my mind until your mom and dad showed up in this airship. I've been with them ever since."

"Well, I'm glad you came back," Taleeka said gratefully.

"Me too, kid. Your mom has managed to make us all a lot of money and kept things from getting dull. And, best of all, I got to meet *you*."

The young girl reached her arms as far as they would go around the EEtah's frame in a heartfelt hug. "I love you, Zaad."

The man-shark returned the embrace and gently patted her back. "I'm pretty fond of you too, kid."

Banavor knelt with head bowed, naked and trembling before Stryder. The young man found himself awash in mixed emotions. Both elation and a sense of dark power lived side by side within him.

A trickle of blood ran down his buttocks from the marks Stryder cut into either side of the base of his spine. He shifted in discomfort on the cold damp stone floor of the basement and fought to keep still.

"I feel unworthy lord," he said anxiously.

"Do not doubt yourself." Stryder said confidently. "You serve a mighty god. One who knows you are up to the task."

The runes across Stryder's black body stopped strobing and he motioned for his new acolyte to rise. "Consider the fact that you worked your way into the confidence of arguably the most powerful man in the Goyan Islands. That proves you are smart and resourceful. From your prior life in the brothels of Moras to your willingness to suck my brother's disgusting little cock, I know you're capable of doing what is *necessary*. With my mark, I gave you financial wisdom beyond your grands."

The young man, now on his feet, suddenly became aware of his rampant erection jutting out in front of him. Stryder assessed it with a salacious grin.

"Pa-Waga arouses strong urges when encountered," he explained.

The vicar of Pa-Waga reached over to a nearby stone table and picked up a small, pale pink crystal shard with red striations.

"This is the Etheria Rhodosite," he said, handing it to Banavor. "It increases the libido of you and anyone around you."

The moment the gem touched Banavor's palm, he felt his already erect organ begin twitching. He winced slightly when his balls began to ache. The veins running down his rigid member rose and pulsed. He started convulsing when the already engorged head grew even larger. His vision grew blurry and he cried out as several powerful ejaculations splattered a nearby wall five feet away, streaking it in white.

His knees buckled and he leaned on Stryder, semen continuing to flow and running down his leg. Stryder ignored the lewd spectacle and helped steady the naked man.

"You have all the tools necessary to serve me well," he assured, "but let's put your resolve, and your new abilities, to the test. A major obstacle needs to be removed before we

8

can begin to usher in a new era of prosperity. This will be your first task."

The Tiikeri Ministry of War occupies a nondescript building near the royal palace in central Hai-Darr. Normally, on any given luna, a steady stream of activity passes through its doors. On this specific occasion, however, the traffic grew especially heavy.

A group of ten mawls stood examining a huge map of the Twilight Lands laid out on a table in the operations center. Supreme General Jal-Pi, one of the few white Tiikeri present, glanced up from the map to his subordinates and gave a confident smile.

"Here is how I expect the operation to proceed. Commander Ansi," he said, addressing an older female Singa. "Your Sikari hunter-killer packs will travel with Commander Zabit's amphibious force and be dropped off in the Py-Shaa Bayou. There you will proceed along the north road of the Os'Tor Forest, harassing the hamlets along the way. It is important to keep moving, you are the distraction."

Jal-Pi placed a marker on the map then looked over at a younger male Singa.

"Zabit, once you drop off Ansi and her force, proceed south along the coast to the Bailian capital of Immor-Onn. You must take and hold it until reinforcements arrive. The Bailian's have no standing army. There is only a small peace keeping force of Human marines used as city guards. They should prove little resistance."

"I won't let you down sir."

The general placed a marker on Immor-Onn and indicated To-Nok to the rear of the group. The white Tiikeri spymaster stood with his hands clasped behind his back silently observing the briefing.

"Lord To-Nok will be with Zabit's amphibious force and will immediately begin setting up an intelligence network. He will also be in temporary command until the main force arrives."

Jal-Pi then addressed To-Nok directly. "Lord To-Nok, is everything ready in your Makatooa and Zorian operations?"

"Yes, General."

"You will be kept busy in Immor-Onn. Are you sure your direct control won't be necessary?"

"I'm certain, General. My operative in Makatooa is one of my best and the Diaemus Ash-Ta clan has never let us down before. All is ready in Zor."

"Excellent." The Supreme General then addressed two older Singas, with touches of gray around their whiskers and manes interwoven with multi-colored citation beads.

"Generals, your force of ten thousand are bivouacked on Gar-Yesh Point. General Ja-Wee, you will take half and march through The Barrens and secure any major fields of Etheria. General Baag-Tar, your half will cut through The Dark Waste. Secure and hold the three oases. Leave whatever force you deem appropriate. Instruct your forces that the lapidary's compounds are to be taken but left operational. Then both of you rendezvous in Immor-Onn, reinforcing Commander Zabit's force. He should have already taken the city by then."

Jal-Pi moved two markers across the map and joined them with Zabit's token on Immor-Onn.

Baag-Tar stroked his chin, surveying the map. "It is a bold plan."

"The Lord favors bold plans," a lone Yagur in black robes said. "I will assign an Adherent to each force as an advisor."

All looked at the Pa-Waga cleric suspiciously.

"We don't need any of your kind with us, *priest*!" Ja-Wee said, sneering. "It was because of your zealotry we lost valuable assets in Zor. The only reason you are at this meeting is at the King's insistence."

The Yagur gave the General a condescending look but remained calm. "Yes, the King is a believer. He has tasked me with the spirituality and the prosperity of the empire. I'm sure he would be greatly displeased if I were inhibited in expanding the empire's prosperity."

"Ja-Wee, Raa-Ja, enough!" Jal-Pi snapped. "One adherent per force, with the exception of Commander Ansi. Her Sikari will be moving too fast."

"Thank you, General," Raa-Ja said, smiling triumphantly at Ja-Wee at the concession.

The Supreme General pointed to the map. "Remember what this is about! Our primary goal is to secure and control the Etheria production, not plunder. There will be plenty of time to collect trinkets once we have established dominion. Speed and surprise are of the essence. The only thing that concerns me is that we have no Worrgs for communication. We will have to rely on Ash-Ta fliers and Duma runners to get messages back and forth. That could take up to two lunas, so stick to the plan. Does everyone understand?"

Everyone nodded silently.

"Excellent," he responded, "The Cub Prince is due to be born anytime now. King Kar-Gor wants to leave a legacy for the empire and his son.

"My brothers, we are going to deliver the greatest birthday present ever… the Twilight Lands.

"Operation Crystal Annex begins the moment you return to your forces. Good Luck to you!"

From the palace balcony, Queen Shula watched the moon sink below the skyline of Immor-Onn and sighed. The beautiful, blonde haired, Bailian queen let her eyes linger on the city's graceful snowflake spiers and flowing architecture. Raindrops glistened off the covered streets below, sheltering its citizens against the frequent inclement weather. The beloved monarch felt a touch of melancholy sensing her city, known across the Annigan as the Crown Jewel of the East, might be in peril.

"You're absolutely certain?" she asked over her shoulder.

"Yes, Your Majesty," Kai replied, standing just inside the double doors. "Reports say the buildup of Singas on Gar-Yesh Point has reached mammoth proportions. There are thousands of them."

"What are they doing?" the queen asked, stepping back into the room.

"Nothing at this point in time, but I don't expect that to last. You don't amass that many Singas in one place for a picnic. I fear they're planning an invasion, my queen."

"And we are all but powerless to stop them," Shula acknowledged with a forlorn sigh.

"If their target *is* Immor-Onn," Kia added, "the only consolation is they've got a lot of ground to cover and we'll have plenty of notice."

"Some consolation," Shula lamented. "Just when things were beginning to come together. We have the Avatar, the available regions are finally repopulated, the city is actually thriving, and now this."

A knock on the door preceded a Human Valdurian marine opening it. "Your majesty, the Tiikeri Ambassador is here."

"Show him in."

The Bailian Queen gave her spymaster a worried glance. "Let's see what he has to say."

"Your Majesty," Jo-Rakk thundered heartily, crossing the room. "How can this humble servant of the Tiikeri Empire serve you this moonless?"

"You can tell me what thousands of Singas are doing on Gar-Yesh Point, ambassador." Shula said formally.

The white man-tiger's demeanor instantly sobered. "I'm afraid you have me at a disadvantage Your Majesty. I don't know what you're referring to."

"Ambassador," Kai broke in, "we both know the Singa race is too fragmented and unambitious to mass in such great numbers. There is little doubt in my mind your king placed them there. We would like to know his intentions."

"You must believe me. I had no knowledge of this. Unfortunately, as ambassador I am sometimes placed in the precarious position of being intentionally uninformed."

"Like now," Kai said, sensing genuine surprise in the Tiikeri.

"Like now," Jo-Rakk confirmed.

"Get in touch with your king," Shula ordered. "I want an answer."

"At once, Your Majesty," Jo-Rakk said anxiously, before bowing and promptly leaving.

"Do you think he's lying?" Shula asked when the door closed.

"No, Your Majesty."

"Do you trust him?"

"Not when it comes to matters of state, Your Majesty. We may have fought together, and call each other friend, but you can never forget he is a loyal subject of the Tiikeri Empire."

The constant roar of the crowd grew deafening and the atmosphere throughout the entire stadium felt nothing short of electric. The exuberant rumble echoed outward, well beyond the city limits of the Tiikeri capital of Hai-Darr.

When the Singa gladiator entered the arena, ten thousand mawls erupted in cheers and applause. The huge male dressed only in a loincloth and sandals, saluted the king, and his party in the first row. Clearly a fan favorite, he worked the crowd with sword raised high above his head, roaring loudly. His long mane swayed elegantly and his scarred, bare chest spoke of many hard-won past battles.

After an appropriate amount of adoration, the doors on the opposite side of the arena swung open and three Dumas warily entered the colosseum. Along with simple round shields, each of the humanoid cheetahs were armed with a different weapon. One held a chain flail with a spiked ball at the end, one wielded a long javelin spear, and the last brandished a double-edged short sword.

Upon seeing them, the Singa hissed and his tail began to twitch from side to side. Reaching down with his free hand, he parted the front of his loincloth and exposed his penis extending from its furry sheath. He grabbed it, aimed, and let loose a long stream of urine, marking a line in front of him.

The crowds responded decidedly less enthusiastically to the Duma trio's apprehensive expressions, which spoke more about their hopes for a hard-fought contest, rather than partiality. The three cheetah-men tensely acknowledged the king, before cautiously maneuvering around the arena floor, ears twitching nervously while they attempted to surround the wily lion-man.

The Singa, who carried no shield for protection, stood defiantly behind his line in the dirt. He crouched at the ready, guarding any of the challengers from getting behind him.

The Duma armed with the flail lashed out first with an attempt to entangle. The six-foot-long chain wrapped around the lion-man's free hand and the spiked ball embedded in his thickly muscled forearm.

The gladiator bellowed in pain and hissed angrily. To the attacker's surprise, instead of attempting to pull away, the Singa grabbed the chain and yanked his attacker onto the tip of his waiting sword.

Using the impaled Duma as a shield, he angled his body in the path of the javelin wielder's ranged attack. The spear impacted the already impaled Duma, leaving him skewered from both front and rear. The Singa kicked the pierced Duma in the abdomen, pushing the body further back onto the spear to dislodge his sword.

The spear wielder frantically tried to extricate his javelin from the corpse, when the Singa split his skull in two with a powerful overhead strike. Adrenalin pumping, the snarling Singa squared off against his only remaining opponent.

The Duma's face was etched in fear at seeing his two comrades so quickly dispatched. With trembling hands, he laid his sword and shield meekly on the ground in front of him. He dropped down on one knee and bowed his head, chattering nervously.

The crowd now booed and hissed at the easy victory from the Duma's surrender. The victorious Singa swaggered over and stood beside his vanquished foe, looking up at the king for direction.

King Kar-Gor scowled.

"Coward!" he spat, before drawing a thumb across his throat.

The crowd resumed its boisterous cheering when the Singa placed the tip of his sword in the center of the kneeling opponent's back. Slowly, for painful effect, he inched the blade into the Duma's body.

The cheering made too much noise for the crowd to hear the tearing of flesh and cracking of bones, but they saw the drawn-out agony on the Duma's face and his flowing blood. They pointed and caterwauled when the sword tip exited the mawl's chest, pushing him into a forced bow. In a dramatic flourish, the ostentatious Singa swiftly yanked the blade out of the torso and brought it in a wide arc downward, severing the vanquished mawl's head with a single swing of his blade.

Picking up the still dripping head, he held it aloft on full display for king and crowd. The audience thundered its approval, their bloodlust almost satisfied after such a disappointing contest.

Kar-Gor was about to remark to his spymaster seated next to him when a mongrel runner reverently approached. Lowering his head, he went down on one knee and offered the monarch a folded piece of paper.

"This just came in for you, my liege."

Kar-Gor accepted the note with a disdainful side glance. The messenger scurried away and the king sniffed the memo for its olfactory message: *Operation Crystal Annex has begun.* He smiled and handed it to his white Tiikeri spymaster, before settling back to enjoy the games.

Gre-Norr always took his job seriously, even when the parameters of the task were ill defined. This is how he found himself in the sewers beneath Makatooa surrounded by dozens of angry Cul-Ta. Being able to think on your feet in unconventional ways was a distinguishing characteristic of the Rangatira, the elite, deep cover operatives working directly under Bo-Lah, the Tiikeri spymaster.

Much like all his assignments, they inserted him in the bustling seaport over a grand cycle ago to infiltrate and observe. It was imperative the Tiikeri presence in Lumina be kept secret. Only then could he begin his dual component directive. The first part of which, infiltration, had proved a rousing success when he won the favor and backing of the region's richest sentients, the crime boss, Lord Hanara.

Gre-Norr began the second part of the directive, sowing discord in the Annigan's second largest seaport, with the commencement of his empire's operations in the Twilight Lands. Now was the time, as the city of Makatooa still reeled from the fiery riots several quintes ago.

The process itself should be quite simple. He just needed to fan the flames of suspicion with envy and stir up buried prejudices. Specific situations made the process nebulous but one thing could be counted on, the weak-minded proved easiest to sway into the path of conflict... hence the Cul-Ta.

With the spring quinte of Derde ending, and the summer heat slowly building, the oppressive heat and humidity reminded Gre-Norr of his rainforest home in the Dasos region of the Land of Mists. The inhospitable conditions also served a more important purpose. Prolonged exposure to them made the sentients irritable.

Now, sitting cross-legged on the sewer's anteroom floor, he witnessed the heat's effect before his very eyes. The new ruling council of Cul-Ta chattered away and agitated rat-men crowded the Tiikeri operative.

"How long has it been since you've seen your cousin, Chu-Chu?" Gre-Norr asked their leader, Haa-Chu, as he paced nervously in front of him.

"Long time!" Haa-Chu replied, with a frustrated wave of his arm. "Ever since Chu-Chu went to rebuild city."

"How many of your people did he take with him?"

"Many, they no come back. They live up there now. They friend of humans now. They turn their back on us, they think they better than us!"

Gre-Norr played on the Cul-Ta's inability to count. Anything over two could be considered 'many' by them. He knew the number to be somewhere around two hundred.

Lord Hanara had commissioned the Cul-Ta to rebuild the damaged wharf and the burned section of town and chose

Chu-Chu to supervise the project. He ended up giving those two hundred Cul-Ta a section of the rebuilt city to call their own, as a reward for completing the project in record time.

This division played perfectly into the Tiikeri agent's hands. These disgruntled rat people just needed a nudge in the right direction and the second part of his directive would be well under way.

"You've been treated *very* unfairly," Gre-Norr agreed, mournfully shaking his head. "I will help in any way I can."

Haa-Chu stopped in front of the seated Tiikeri and looked him directly in the eyes.

"We need weapons, good weapons," he said, his face an indignant scowl. "Not like the kind we steal."

"I'll see what I can do," Gre-Norr said with a wicked grin, realizing the nudge proved successful.

Li-Erén knelt beside the freshly slain deer and offered up a prayer of gratitude to Toro-Za, God of the Hunt. He gave thanks for making his aim true and for the animal's swift death. He felt truly appreciative for the essence of this creature, whose body would now provide for so many.

The hunt had been good, almost too good, but the holy Os'Tor forest never failed to offer up its bounty. He already bagged three deer, a wild pig and several giant hares. This kill meant he could end the hunt early and head home to the Sodor-Ess Hamlet.

The Bailian Os'Tor huntsman removed the arrow, stood, and gave out a warbling call to his team at the hunting camp. He would stay with the body and wait for the game bearers to bring the carcass back to camp, where the butcher would skin, slaughter and salt down the body to be transported. He had learned his lesson the hard way many lunas ago when he didn't wait for the bearers and chose to continue to hunt. A pack of wolves claimed his prize and the unarmed bearers were helpless to stop them.

Li-Erén cleaned off the arrowhead, placed the projectile back in his quiver and wondered what was taking them so long. Everyone on the hunt team knew, once an animal had been brought down, time was of the essence.

After waiting for what he considered an ample amount of time, he felt certain something was amiss. He cut off a lengthy section of vine from a nearby tree, tied the deer's back legs together, tossed the other end over a high branch and winched the lifeless animal into the air.

He fought back a wave of anger setting off for the hunting camp. If the team began celebrating early there would be a price to pay. As archer, and senior member of the unit, he considered carrying the kill beneath his status. Hamlet life kept a strict caste system, everyone knew their place and societal task.

Approaching the temporary encampment, the huntsman noted the eerie stillness. Stealth being the operative norm, the camps were never noisy, but this was different. Nothing punctuated the usual chorus of birds and bugs. Then, there was the smell, a distinct pungent aroma of urine ammonia growing stronger the closer he got.

When he saw the first dead body, he unslung his bow and nocked an arrow. Slowly advancing into the hushed camp, he saw three tents shredded across the ground, along with various utensils and random items. The corpses of all five members of his team lay sprawled across the ground.

A closer inspection of the bodies found most clawed to death. Two also showed small puncture wounds to the head. All had been sprayed with the pungent urine. They even sprayed their kills, rendering the meat tainted and unusable.

A glint in the moonlight on one of the trees in mid-camp caught his eye. Investigating it, he found a small sickle-shaped, throwing blade lodged in the trunk. Whoever did this left a trail anyone could track toward the north road and the hamlet. The Bailian archer followed the broken limbs and trampled ground at a cautious, yet brisk, pace.

They are moving fast, he noted, rapidly approaching the agricultural fields surrounding his home. Just before the forest cleared up ahead, he heard the baying howl of a big cat amongst screams of panic.

He hid behind a bush and looked out over the acres of neatly plowed fields, now littered with dead bodies. A humanoid female lion, the likes of which he had never seen before, viciously rubbed her crotch on a dead body, spraying it with urine, and loudly howling in the middle of the field.

At least a dozen more attacked and ransacked the village. Balian bodies of men, women and children littered the ground. They threw open the doors to various dwellings and dragged their occupants out. Every corpse had their throats bitten out. Fire raged through buildings in the center of town and columns of smoke clouded the bright mid-luna sky.

Li-Erén scowled in rage and let an arrow fly. The bolt struck the Singa defiling the corpse on the side of her chest, catapulting her off the body. She fell dead between furrowed rows of freshly planted crops.

This compromised his position. Half a dozen frenzied Singas stopped and looked over at him. Giving an enraged scream, they charged.

The huntsman got off another shot, dropping the lead lioness, before he spun and bolted into the jungle. Although they were faster than him, he had a head start and knew the forest very well.

He could only think of running to Immor-Onn. They needed to be warned. The hamlets were under attack.

One of the main things Rafel appreciated about working with Colonel Zekoff was that the door to his office was always open.

Literally.

The Zorian spymaster gave the formality of a brief knock before whisking into the room. He closed the door behind him and plopped down in one of the two chairs facing the commander of the city guard's desk.

Zekoff glanced up from the report he was reading. He raised an eyebrow quizzically at the androgynous man with long dark hair staring wistfully off into space.

"Well," Rafel said, sighing deeply and locking eyes with the old colonel, "you can't say we didn't see this coming."

"Is there something you wish to share with me, Rafel?" Zekoff asked, pushing his papers aside.

"I just got this from Kai, the Bailian spymaster." Rafel tossed a confidential dispatch onto the desk. "As we speak, Singas are attacking the hamlets along the north road of the Os'Tor Forest."

"Have you contacted the Valdurians about this?"

"They're my next stop."

"Looks like we booted them out of town just in time" Zekoff said, reading the report.

"Singas can be aggressive, to be sure, just not overly ambitious," Rafel said with a shake of his head. "I'd bet my last copper piece the Tiikeri are behind this."

"And I would have to agree," Zekoff concurred, putting the paper down and sliding it back to Rafel. "I knew when we expelled those mawls from Tiger Town and their ambassador, we were headed down the road to trouble. Get with Gasata and have him put patrols on alert, especially the Kan patrols. Let's share that with the other houses too, not just the Valdurians. They may want to offer the Bailians some assistance."

Rafel nodded. "I have a feeling this is just the beginning."

"Yes, but of what?" Zekoff asked, getting to his feet and reaching for his jacket. "I can't imagine what the Tiikeri would want in the Os'Tor Forest. Keep me updated. I'm headed over to the university to see my new office and finalize a few details with the Board of Regents."

Blyth Calden couldn't help but stare in wonder at the new Valdurian air station. His eyes traced its wide entrance jutting out from the jungle covered cliff face at the mouth of the Makatooa inlet. The station replaced the jungle clearing which previously served as the landing field.

He had to admit that Lord Hanara came through on everything he promised. They rebuilt the burnt parts of the city back better than before and even expanded on them, but the new wharf pleased the former naval officer the most.

Like the renovated city, they expanded it into one of the largest seaports in the Goyan Islands, second only to the one in the High Holy City of Zor. The young mayor's mind reeled at the economic potential a modern wharf and air station could provide.

Of course, there *were* drawbacks. The hundreds of Cul-Ta laborers, which facilitated this metropolitan rebirth, now occupied a section of town all their own. The citizens of Makatooa *slowly* started to accept their new neighbors.

The renovations weren't the only reason he and the other city leaders gathered on the new wharf this morning. Chu-Chu, the Cul-Ta leader, was supposed to give them an official tour. Out in the harbor, the Turine rang thirteen bells snapping Blyth out of his musings.

"He's late!" Velitel snapped.

"A little patience," Hanara cajoled. "I have a feeling this is going to be worth it."

The commander of the city guards shifted his massive six-foot four frame and stroked his perfectly groomed white beard. "It had better be, a late curtain call is always a bad sign."

Kem shook her head at Velitel's constant theatre references, but the petite spymaster had long since grown used to them. She peered around and caught Blyth stealing a lustful glance her way. The remembrance of their lovemaking last Kan.

"There are times I regret not throwing that little shit right back in jail." Velitel said, wiping the perspiration from the dark brown bald spot on the crown of his head. "Ugh... summer's coming."

"Chu-Chu's been a big help," Hanara said, peering up the street busy with the morning bustle, "far more than if he were rotting in a jail cell. His involvement proved instrumental in recruiting and organizing his people."

Kem glanced over at the Hammerhead EEtah. "Lord Hanara, I understand you've been working with him about proper behavior outside of the sewers?"

"Yes, Mz. Lau is working with him. He's quite the quick study," Hanara replied, drawing their attention to the miniature coach approaching, "as you shall see."

The single lizard drawn coach rolled to a stop directly in front of the startled group. It stood no more than five feet high and eight feet long, custom painted bright red, blue and gold, with gems and gilding decorating its trim. A large chandelier crowned the top of the carriage, strung with dangling gems and baubles sparkling in the orange light. The brightly polished, independent, inner rim of the wheels continued spinning long after the carriage halted.

"I think the set designers went a little crazy," Velitel noted, unable to take his eyes off the ostentatious carriage.

Two Cul-Ta attendants, a driver and a servant, sat on an outer bench extending from the rear of the coach. Both wore expensive looking blue silk uniforms and riding boots.

"What in the name of the Goddess?" Kem asked, running delicate fingers through her short brown hair.

Once the carriage came to a complete stop, the servant on the rear bench picked up a small stepstool beside him and climbed down to the street. Walking around to the side door he placed it in front of the door and opened it.

They were not prepared for what they saw next.

A radically different Chu-Chu poked his head out of the buggy and smiled. Gone was the smelly, mangy rat-man in a filthy tunic. The Cul-Ta leader emerged meticulously groomed with yellow silken robes and a long Kel-skin cape trimmed in fur. He wore a floppy beret, and a monocle with a long tassel covered his right eye.

Chu-Chu regally stepped down onto the stool and Blyth got a good look at the interior. Garish red velvet covered the seats and gems encrusted the gilded walls.

"Ah, I'm glad you're all here," Chu-Chu announced in a squeaky but refined voice.

The servant who opened the door fell in behind Chu-Chu, holding the edge of his luxurious cape trailing behind him. The Cul-Ta leader greeted each of the attendees.

"Your honor!" he beamed, offering up his tiny hand to Blyth. "So good of you to make time from your busy day."

"Mz. Aleki," he said, taking her hand and kissing it. "Lovely as ever I see."

Velitel studied the rings on every finger when the Cul-Ta stepped over to him.

"Colonel Velitel, I know we've had our differences in the past," Chu-Chu admitted, "but I feel in the light of this auspicious occasion we should let bygones be bygones."

The commander of the city guards just leered suspiciously. Chu-Chu did not wait for a response but flitted over to the Palu Hammerhead EEtah.

"And what can I say?" the Cul-Ta clamored, extending his tiny arms. "*Lord Hanara*, the sentient who was the catalyst for this monumental project. Sir, we shall all be in your debt for ages to come."

A moment of silence passed as all but Hanara stood dumbfounded by the creature's transformation.

"Well, enough with the platitudes," Chu-Chu continued unphased, "I'm sure you're eager to get a look at what your money bought you. This way please."

Chu-Chu then took them on a walking tour of the rebuilt section of the city. The workmanship and details in the shops and various buildings, including a new bank, as well as the addition of the expanded sections of the city with enlarged living spaces, greatly pleased the mayor.

When they entered the Cul-Ta neighborhood, the humans condescendingly smiled at the pretentious exteriors of their brightly painted, miniature mansions with jeweled trim and ornately carved front columns.

Cul-Ta of every age, dressed in flashy finery indicative of recent wealth, happily waved at the official the entire way across the roughly five block neighborhood. Chu-Chu greeted each of them back colorfully, obviously relishing his star status.

The tour ended back on the considerably enlarged wharf and warehouse area already humming with ship trade.

"And that, is that!" Chu-Chu proclaimed, sweeping his arm across the cityscape. "I hope the reconstruction meets with your approval."

Lord Hanara and Mayor Calden launched into a congratulatory monologue, praising their work while Velitel and Kem held their suspicious demeanors.

"Well, I'm certainly happy this meets with your approval," Chu-Chu said, guiding the meeting to a conclusion. "I've taken up enough of your time, besides I have a flight to catch in a few deci."

"A flight, already?" Blyth said in surprise. "The air station was just completed."

"Yes, I know," Chu-Chu replied, obviously excited. "I've booked the debut flight out to Dryden. I've got tickets to the Grand Dryden Theatre. The Dryden Thespian Troupe is performing the Guru Ka Labaada."

At the mention of the play's name, Velitel's mood shifted from suspicious to intrigued.

"'The Master's Robe!'" he translated, barely able to contain his excitement. "I've not seen *that one* before. Will the Dryden Orchestra be accompanying?"

"But of course," Chu-Chu replied superiorly. "Colonel, if you wish, you may accompany me as my honored guest. It's not often you find a theatre aficionado in such a rustic local."

Everyone witnessed the internal struggle on the commander's face. The Cul-Ta had been a perpetual adversary for his entire career and now he had been given an offer difficult to refuse.

Finally, Velitel's face softened. "To refuse such a gracious starring role would be boorish in the extreme."

"Splendid!" Chu-Chu cheered. "Meet me at the air station at fifteen bells. Once in Dryden, we can catch an early supper and then settle into the balcony seats I've reserved. It should be a rousing evening of culture. Don't you agree?!"

It had been a while since Zekoff had seen Kasha and he almost didn't recognize her. The master linguist and head of the language arts Department at The University of Marassa had gained an incredible amount of weight. A wave of pity swept over the old colonel. Kasha obviously struggled coping with the loss of her boyfriend, Pa-Waga's possession, the kidnapping and rape by the Tiikeri. It amazed him she even returned to work at all.

He gently knocked on her open door and attracted her attention. She looked up from her desk and smiled.

"Colonel, good to see you. Come in."

When she stood to greet him, her obesity became obvious. Zekoff estimated she weighed almost four hundred pounds.

"I was in the neighborhood and thought I'd drop by."

"Yes, I heard you accepted a teaching position," she said, extending her hand.

"Had to come by and check out my new office and I'm meeting with the regents in a deci," he said, shaking her hand. "There was something I wanted to discuss with you."

"Sure," she said, offering him a seat.

"Actually, I've come to solicit your help."

"How can I be of assistance to the Zorian Guards?"

"It's about the Tiikeri and their damnable god."

The linguist fell silent and her pleasant demeanor evaporated. Zekoff noted the change and his tone turned conciliatory.

"I'm truly sorry for bringing up any painful memories."

Kasha shook her head. "No, it's okay. I'm just glad they got thrown out of town."

"About that," Zekoff said, sitting forward. "They caused that earthquake last quinte. They've brought Stryder back. From the reports I've seen, there's no humanity left in him. He's become an embodiment of that cat god he worshipped, allowing it to take him over completely and transform his body. To make matters worse, the Tiikeri are moving against the Twilight Lands."

Kasha sat staring intently, digesting the news. "I can't imagine what I could do to help. I'm a scholar, not a fighter."

"You were possessed by Pa-Waga. Your proximity to it makes you one of the most knowledgeable humans on their god and culture. We could use your insight."

Kasha nodded her head absently, deep in thought.

"You know," she said, "I've put aside every project I was working on to study our copy of that prayer book. I've made it my life's work to find a way to destroy that cat god... and maybe take out a few Tiikeri along the way."

"Well, it sounds like you're ready for some payback."

"They killed my boyfriend Tysonn in this very office. They kidnapped me and turned my lady parts into hamburger. *Whatever makes you think I'd want revenge?*"

Heads turned when Banavor stepped off the fog laden Zorian streets and into the upscale Amira Pub. Almost all the men, and more than a few women, cast a lustful glance his way. His gold embroidered red vest—worn open, revealing a thin, coffee-colored chest—complimented his confident bearing and slow sensual swagger. His sheer harem pants clearly displayed a firm bottom and gently swaying, semi-erect penis.

The former Morasian Puff Boy commissioned jewelers to fashion the pink and red Rhodosite Etheria Crystal into a belly button jewel, now decorating his flat, hairless abdomen. Sex was his expertise. He knew well it equaled power if wielded correctly.

Scanning the room, he quickly spotted his person of interest sitting at a small table by himself. The well-dressed man looked to be in his mid to late forties with an angular, clean shaven face and greying pompadour hair style. He stared thoughtfully into a tumbler of amber liquid and didn't notice Banavor's approach. He did, however, sense the young man's carnal presence and looked up into a seductively smiling face.

"May I sit down?" Banavor asked.

A look of muted surprise was replaced by a lecherous smirk. "Why not?"

To the man's astonishment, Banavor slipped onto his lap and wrapped his arms around his neck. "Your friends have hired me to make sure you have a very *satisfying* evening."

"I'm a banker. I don't have any friends, only clients."

"Well, you've got one now," Banavor said, cooing flirtatiously. "Besides, I know all about you Gyara."

"How?"

"I'm a pro," Banavor whispered in his ear before taking the lobe in his mouth.

Banavor immediately felt Gyara's cock stiffening beneath him and wiggled his butt enhancing the sensation.

"I've got a room at the inn next door," the young man purred.

Gyara quickly downed the remainder of his drink. "So, what are we still doing here?"

They exited the busy tavern with Banavor's arm around the much taller man's waist and Gyara's hand on Banavor's ass. Once outside, the cool Kan fog hardened Banavor's nipples. He reached over and rubbed Gyara's crotch.

Gyara grabbed Banavor by the waist and shoved him up against the wall of the alley behind the pub. He kissed him roughly and he slid his hands inside the back of Banavor's sheer pants cupping his ass cheeks. Pulling his ass cheeks apart, Gyara slipped a finger into his quivering hole. The digit easily slipped in up to the second knuckle and Banavor groaned with pleasure.

In a lust filled frenzy, the older man yanked the pants down and they fell around Banavor's ankles. Now naked from the waist down, Banavor broke from the embrace and dropped to his knees. Trembling fingers quickly unbuttoned the front of Gyara's pants and his rigid member tumbled out into Banavor's waiting mouth.

The young man greedily worked the shaft until a series of giggles interrupted the banker's groans of pleasure. Both looked over to see two prostitutes standing at the alley entrance transfixed in voyeuristic delight.

"Let's go get comfortable," Banavor suggested, rising to his feet.

With Gyara's grunt of approval, Banavor grabbed the wet cock jutting from the front of the banker's pants and led him into a nearby door. Once inside the single room, Banavor stripped off the vest and sat naked on the edge of the bed. While Gyara quickly slipped out of his clothes, Banavor reached over to a table by the bed and retrieved a small, delicate bottle of oil.

Gyara, now fully naked, stepped over in front of Banavor with his rampant erection directly at face level. Grabbing the sides of Banavor's head, Gyara shoved his organ at Banavor's face. Without hesitation Banavor opened his mouth and the hard cock slid in down to the balls. Holding his head firmly, Gyara began fucking his mouth.

The former prostitute easily took in the entire shaft, expertly deep throating the assaulting member. Gyara yanked it out of the younger man's mouth and Banavor looked up at him with lust filled eyes. Thick strands of saliva connected his mouth with the head of Gyara's member.

"I need you inside me now," Banavor breathlessly begged, coating the glistening cock in oil.

Setting the bottle aside, Banavor slipped up onto the bed on his back and spread his legs. Gyara jumped on top of him and tried to roll him over. Banavor gently put a hand on his arm, stopping him.

"No, I want to see your face when you cum," he pleaded, "and no pulling out."

"You're a slutty little thing," Gyara said, barely able to contain himself.

"You haven't seen anything yet. Now *fuck* me!"

Without any formalities, Gyara jerked Banavor's legs up, rammed the shaft into his waiting ass and began pumping away enthusiastically.

Gyara could hardly believe his luck. The beautiful young man writhing beneath him was truly enjoying himself. It wasn't the moans, all prostitute's feigned passion, Banavor's own erection betrayed a true exuberance for his role as a bottom. When he pleaded to be fucked harder, Gyara knew he couldn't last very much longer.

Banavor definitely knew how to fuck. He also recognized the older man neared release. As a finishing touch, Banavor wrapped his legs around the small of Gyara's back and ground his hips, matching the frantic thrusts. The change in pressure and motion proved too much and Gyara gave out a loud grunt. Banavor watched his face contort and felt the man's cock convulsing deep within him.

In mid-climax, Banavor quickly reached under his pillow and pulled out a small dagger. He sliced Gyara's throat open with a single rapid sweep. The look of shock on Gyara's face did not diminish the involuntary pumping of semen into Banavor's ass, and the young killer locked his legs tighter around his victim's back, milking every last drop.

Banavor tossed the dagger aside, grabbed both of Gyara's shoulders and held on. The hemorrhaging banker thrashed about violently, futilely trying to escape. Blood showered all over Banavor and the bed. Feeling himself being sprayed with the warm liquid, Banavor leaned his head back and cried out in genuine pleasure.

Unable to contain himself, Banavor's cock twitched and shot several powerful eruptions of cum in a hands-free orgasm. The ropy white fluid left a trail up to his neck, mixing with the dark red blood covering the satisfied youth.

When Gyara went limp in his arms, Banavor tossed him to the side of the bed and got up. Staring down at the naked corpse, he gave a breathless smile.

"That was fun!" he reveled.

Even though he enjoyed the sex, and surprisingly the kill almost as much, he had successfully removed a formidable obstacle from The Zorian Monetary Council. There now remained only one person who could stand in his way, Cedar Aramos, but he would address that soon enough. Most importantly, he proved himself to his Lord.

He chuckled at his blood and semen splattered body. *Crimson Rain, that's a good code name*, he decided.

With his grizzly task completed, a naked and bloody Banavor stepped out into the thick Kan fog and disappeared.

The *Attila* had only been airborne for a short time when Cha-Rod fell sound asleep, snoring loudly.

Demetrius intentionally didn't take the airship 'upstairs,' because a transport ship with one hundred Valdurian Marines followed directly behind them. A hundred, heavy, medium crossbows, along with thousands of bolts, loaded down his cargo area.

Their destination: Immor-Onn.

"You know I feel a little guilty for my part in helping put Kar-Gor on the throne," Demetrius said remorsefully.

"You couldn't have possibly known," Okawa said, sitting in the seat behind him. "Things change with time."

"Speaking of change, have you given any more thought to my proposal."

"Yeah…" Okawa leaned forward, put her hand on his shoulder and kissed him on the cheek, "but…"

"Look, I know it's a big step, but you spend most of your time at my place already, and we get along great. Why not move in together?"

"It's not that, it's…"

Demetrius turned, his face inches from hers.

"What then?"

The Valdurian agent peered wistfully out the window.

"It's the job."

"I thought we've been through this before. I know your job is inherently dangerous."

"That's not it either."

"Well, what then?"

Okawa paused and looked away for a long moment, before peering back at Demetrius.

"Look, I really think I have strong feelings for you."

"Hey, right back at ya. Wait a minute, *you think*?"

Okawa shrugged. "It's never come up before."

"Well, it hasn't for me either," he countered, "but I'm pretty darn sure, and I'm still not seeing the problem."

Okawa nervously bit her lower lip. "It's just that in the future, I may get an assignment that may require me to be intimate with someone, and I don't want that to screw things up between us. Living together just complicates an already complex relationship."

"I see," Demetrius said distantly, while trying to process what he had just heard. "Thank you for your honesty."

"Joc's already steering me away from those type of assignments," she added, "but you never know what the future holds. I wouldn't want to hurt you and I couldn't live with the guilt."

The pilot stared silently out the windshield for what felt like an eternity while Okawa fidgeted nervously in her seat.

"Demetrius, say something!"

Demetrius sighed deeply. "Well, it's not like you're out there sleeping around."

Okawa's mouth dropped open in surprise. "Really?"

"Oh, don't get me wrong, I'm not crazy about the idea. But like you said, it's your job."

"Demetrius, I… I had no idea that you, or frankly anyone would be so understanding."

"Two conditions," he said holding up as many fingers. "One, I definitely don't want to know about it."

Okawa smiled. "Those kinds of missions, I couldn't tell you about even if I wanted to. What's the second one?"

"Two, don't be bringing home any strange and potentially deadly diseases."

"Deal!"

"Okay, so now that we've got that cleared up, are you moving in?"

"That sounds wonderful," she said before giving him another kiss on the cheek.

Sitsa sat quietly in her navigator's chair listening to the exchange and finally turned to face the pair.

"I have closely observed Human relationships since I arrived," the Tinian said clinically, "and have come to the conclusion they require far too much effort to maintain."

Tuccar de Moet stared in panicked disbelief at the trading board from the hectic floor of the Commodities Exchange in central Zor.

"I'm ruined!" he said, his voice cracking with fear. "I mean, I can't believe it, the copper market just tanked and

Banavor makes a fortune. How does the little bastard do it, Sudagar?!"

Tuccar and Sudagar de Tass, an older man with receding gray hair, stared up as Banavor smiled triumphantly from one of the elite private balconies. His bright red, ruffled blouse contrasted with his light brown skin. The crotchless, tight fitting, Kel skin pants with elaborately carved codpiece and riding boots, conveyed hedonistic decadence.

"I've been doing this a long time and never have seen anything like it." Sudagar answered. "He's made a killing every cycle for the last three, but you're the first person I know of that he's actually bankrupted."

"That was borrowed money I just lost. I'm a dead man!"

"Word is, he was behind Cedar Aramos' prosecution and ouster from the Zorian Monetary Council." Sudagar said, glancing back at the board. "Well, that's it for me today."

"Not me. I'm going up there to give that smug little shit a piece of my mind!" Tuccar said, heading for the stairs.

Before the senior trader could talk him out of it, Tuccar angrily bounded up the stairs. When the brash young man made it to the balcony alcove, he found a small group of fawning traders congratulating the successful Banavor, who graciously smiled with each back pat and handshake.

"I don't know what kind of shit you're pulling!" Tuccar yelled, stepping into the room.

Everything came to a standstill and the revelry of the moment vanished. All attention focused on the angry trader who stepped up to Banavor.

Banavor calmly looked Tuccar up and down with a condescending smile. "I'm sorry, can I help you?"

"That little trick you've got going cost me big time today!" Tuccar yelled.

An amused grin played at the corners of Banavor's mouth. "I'm afraid I don't know what you're referring to. All I'm doing is efficiently seizing opportunities in the market, like you *should* be doing."

The insult set off a series of murmurs in the group and Tuccar's fists tightened.

"For three straight cycles you've been raking in a fortune. No one is that lucky!"

"I agree," Banavor replied. "Luck had nothing to do with it. It's called skill."

"Skill my ass, you've got something shady going on!"

Banavor kept the patronizing smile and shook his head. "A baseless accusation I'm going to let pass because you've obviously had a bad day."

"A bad day!? I'm ruined!"

Banavor mockingly nodded his head in contrived sympathy. "Well, I've come into a bit of money lately. I suppose if you got down on your knees and sucked my cock right here, I could see fit to perhaps give you a loan."

This set off a round of snickers and Tuccar could feel his restraint slipping away.

"You're a Morasian Puff Boy," Tuccar snapped. "Maybe you should suck *my* cock!"

"I don't suck poor people," Banavor replied smugly.

With this final insult, Tuccar lunged for the snarky youth. Two men in the crowd immediately restrained him and coaxed the enraged trader away with promises of getting him drunk.

"How droll," Banavor said haughtily, watching them lead Tuccar out the door and down the stairs.

Tuccar staggered up to the front door of his apartment and, leaning on it, he fumbled around for his key. His coworkers had plied him with copious amounts of alcohol as promised, with commiserations and assurances tomorrow would be better.

Now, as he unlocked his front door and stepped into his one room apartment, he caught a slightly familiar odor. He just had time to tap a light crystal, before being struck on the back of the head and falling unconscious to the floor.

He awoke naked, with his hands and legs tied securely to a chair. Directly in front of him, a free-standing full-length mirror revealed his precarious situation. In the reflection, he saw Banavor sitting casually on his single bed behind him, flanked by two large, scowling thugs.

"You know," Banavor said, standing up and stepping over to him. "The only thing worse than a loser, is a poor loser."

"What, what do you want?" Tuccar asked shakily.

Banavor ignored the question, slipped on a pair of tight fitting, leather gloves and picked up a small jar he had placed on a nearby table. He stepped in front of the bound man and held it up.

"This is Prowda Balm," he explained. "The Amarenians use it for the discomfort of childbirth."

He opened the lid and pulled out a large dollop on the ends of his gloved fingers.

"Normally we wouldn't have access to it, but we're trading with the Amarenians now."

Banavor began spreading the paste all over and around Tuccar's exposed penis.

"Hey wait!" Tuccar yelled. "What are you doing?!"

Once again, Banavor ignored the question and silently wiped his hands on the bed sheets. With a sadistic grin, he pulled out the hook bladed knife and Tuccar's eyes went wide in panic.

"Wait no, you don't need to do this!"

Banavor chuckled maniacally. "Need to? I know I don't *need* to. I just really *want* to."

Without further conversation Banavor reached down between Tuccar's legs and sliced off his entire member, including the balls.

Tuccar felt a slight tug, but no pain. In the reflection, he looked on in horror at the open wound where his penis once was pumping like a fountain. A torrent of blood immediately covered seat of the chair and floor in front of him.

When Tuccar cried out in shock, Banavor shoved the bloody, limp penis into his open mouth. He then leaned down until his face was right beside Tuccar's and peered at their reflections in the mirror with the same sadistic smile.

"Who's sucking whose cock now?" he whispered.

Tuccar felt weak from massive blood loss. In the mirror, he saw Banavor and his men unhurriedly walk out the door, leaving him to helplessly watch himself bleed out with his own cock lodged in his mouth.

Velitel looked down at the two dead guards and sighed heavily. He recognized one of them as Old Haris, whose retirement was scheduled for the next grand. The other—one of the new guys he hadn't really had a chance to get to know yet—lay next to him, face down in a pool of blood.

The commander of the city guards felt a touch of guilt. He had taken Old Haris off patrol and assigned him 'light duty,' as a stationary guard at the front gate of the city's armory. Now, he lay dead, throat cut, blood soaking and drying in his gray beard, while staring lifelessly upward.

"Sir," a voice called out from behind.

He turned to see two city guards coming off the street, heading in his direction. Both stopped before the two bodies and peered mournfully down.

"Damn shame about Old Haris," one said, shaking his head. "He used to always carry treats for the neighborhood kids. You were always popular when you went on patrol with him."

Velitel allowed them their moment of reflection before getting down to business. "What have we got?"

"Well sir, it looks like four distinct sets of boot prints tracked through the blood," one began. "Whatever they took, they loaded it into a wagon and headed off in that direction."

The guard pointed out the two, blood red wheel tracks leading into the city. "We lost the trail a few blocks away."

"Did it appear that they were heading towards anything in particular?"

"Unclear," the guard reported.

"All right," Velitel said, surveying the grisly scene. "I know it's a long shot but let's ask around and see if this tragedy had an audience."

"You wanna hear something strange?" Kem asked, exiting the armory's broken front door.

Velitel's raised eyebrow answered her question.

"They only took daggers and short swords.'

"Oh really?"

"Yep, and that's pretty strange seeing how they bypassed the newest model crossbows and some expensive, high-quality steel, not to mention a handful of really exotic weapons which could fetch a good price."

"Looks like someone's getting ready for some in-close fighting," Velitel noted.

Kem gave a suspicious scowl at her boss' assessment. "Or they were meant for small targets."

King Shom Eldor, naked and sweat drenched, toppled back onto the copious pile of pillows with an exhausted but contented sigh. Across the room, an equally naked, attractive and prominent Rophan couple bounded towards the baths. The husband made a name for himself as a successful silk trader and his wife beguiled the city's fashion scene as a highly regarded socialite.

Shom had wooed them for some time now and today his seductive patience paid off. Technically, the Eldorian king could have just ordered them into his bed, but where was the fun in that?

As always, Attina stood dutifully on guard at the head of the bed with a lustful gleam in her eye.

"Was it worth the effort and wait, Sire?" she asked, handing him a towel.

"Yes, indeed," Shom replied, running the strip of cloth across his face and neck. "There's just something about splattering a prim noble's face with cum that warms the cockles of my heart."

"It was an exceptional basting, Sire," she said, grinning lecherously.

"It looks like you enjoyed it too," Shom said, noting the bulge in the front of her cropped pants.

"I found it very exciting."

"So, I see," Shom replied drying off his chest. "There's something I've been meaning to ask you for a while now."

"Yes, Sire?"

"You stand guard, right there, over all my amorous misadventures... and you never get jealous?"

"Jealous," The Hill Sister and Seneschal to the King repeated, pondering thoughtfully for a moment. "I've only become familiar with that term since being stationed in the Goyan Islands. It is not a term used in Amarenia."

"Even though we share a bed, and for that matter, a life together? I mean, you're always around. There's no feeling of possessiveness?"

Attina shook her head and shrugged. "Free people can't be possessed, only slaves, and slaves have no say in the matter. And you are the king after all."

"Yes, so they tell me."

The Rophan couple emerged from the baths clean and fully clothed. After the appropriate good-byes, they passed Keuangan, the Minister of Finance on his way in.

The short, bald economist nervously watched the couple slip out of ear shot before speaking, "I'm sorry to disturb you, Sire."

"Quite alright, Keuangan," Shom said, getting to his feet and reaching for his pants. "Just finishing a quick mid-day pick-me-up."

"Uh... yes, Sire," the official said, peering nervously downward.

"So, what do I owe the pleasure?" Shom asked, closing the front of his pants and reaching for his shirt from Attina. "By the look on your face when you came in, there's obviously some calamity of coin afoot."

"Uh... yes, Sire," Keuangan repeated hesitantly, finally meeting his sovereign's gaze. "It's about the Otoman River Lords, Sire."

Shom gave a loud exasperated huff and threw his hands into the air. "By the gods, what now?!"

"Well, Sire, you know there's a new Lord Sorbornef?"

"Yes, I've heard the reports."

"Then, you know he's not Human?"

"Yes, what of it?"

"Well, Sire, the Lords of the Western Fork aren't taking it well."

"All of them?!"

41

"Uh… yes, Sire, especially Lord Sorbornef's neighbors."

"It sounds like a regional matter."

The minister's pudgy face scrunched with apprehension.

"I'm afraid it's more complicated than that, Sire. You see, the other houses refuse to trade with House Sorbornef's plantation now and House Volga refuses to let any Sorbornef barge pass down the part of the river they control."

Shom's eyes narrowed and his mouth drew tight. *Mal and her team had just finished bringing the river lords under control, now this!*

"It gets worse," Keuangan continued uneasily. "My people just finished running the numbers, and if this is allowed to continue, it will reduce total grain output for the continent of Otomoria by a full ten percent before the end of the quinte."

"The whole continent?!"

"Yes, Sire."

"Is there anything else?" Shom asked anxiously.

"No, Sire."

"I would think that would be enough."

Shom suddenly seemed to relax a bit. He watched Attina's expression become quizzical.

"Thank you, Keuangan, good work catching that," he said, effectively ending the briefing.

"Yes, Sire… thank you, Sire," the finance minister offered meekly, before bowing and scurrying out the door.

"Have the head scribe send one of his people to the throne room," Shom commanded with a resolute nod of the head. "I've had it with the Lords of the Western Fork!"

"I sure hope Cha-Rod will be okay back in Immor-Onn," Okawa said, watching the crystalline treetops of the Barrens pass swiftly below them.

'Why wouldn't he be?" Demetrius asked, checking the compass on the dashboard.

"That's right, you weren't at that meeting." Okawa answered, bringing her attention back to the pilot. "From what he told me and Joc', if members of his order get their hands on him, they'll put him on trial."

"In the name of the gods, why?!"

"Remember that incident in Air Station Three awhile back when you we're attacked?"

"That's one I won't soon forget."

"Well, his people apparently blame him for the ambassador's death."

"Now you got me worried," Demetrius said scowling.

"He did say he had people he could contact. I'm just hoping he finds them before he's discovered."

"Captain," Sitsa spoke up. "We are approaching the end of the Os'Ani Mountain range. I have successfully mapped this side to the horizon line. However, with the moon setting, charting the rest will be sixty-eight percent more difficult."

Demetrius glanced over at the humanoid moth and nodded. "Understood, do your best."

"Yes, captain."

"So why are we heading back to Gar-Yesh Point?" Okawa asked.

"I need another look at that Singa encampment. I've got a bad feeling."

"That feeling is about to get worse," Okawa said, pointing out the windshield towards the ground.

Rows of marching male Singas covered the entire strip of land as far as the eye could see. Packs of female Singas and several Dumas acted as advanced guard along the sides and in front of the army.

Demetrius and Okawa quickly put on their Etheria glasses and flipped down the orange, night-vision lenses.

"There's thousands of them!" Okawa said in disbelief. "Where are they going?"

"That's a heavily armed force on the march," Demetrius answered, now seeing clearly in the fading light. "Wherever they're headed, you can bet they're not going just to talk."

Something began pelting the craft, interrupting the conversation. Each thud grew in volume and rocked the *Attila*. Suddenly, furry faces with gnashing jaws filled with rows of sharp teeth covered the windshield.

"Chiro Ash-Ta!" Demetrius said, his voice raising a register. "I focused so hard on the ground that I didn't see them coming."

"What are we going to do?!" Okawa asked when the ship rocked again.

"We gotta get out of here fast. Even as small as they are, with their numbers they can take down this ship."

Humanoid bats the size of small dogs continued colliding against the hull, violently jostling the besieged aircraft.

"All right, you little creeps," Demetrius grumbled, reaching up to the overhead console. "Take off your glasses, I've had just about enough of this!"

Using two fingers, he quickly tapped either side of the embedded orange disk. Two fireballs erupted from the Trinilic rods under the ship, bathing the front of the craft in a blast of orange light. The blazing projectiles soared through the throng of circling man-bats, setting many ablaze. Their high-pitched squeals of pain filled the cabin and the erratic paths of living torches flooded the dark sky.

'Now that we've got some room to operate, hold on," Demetrius yelled, "I'm taking her upstairs!"

He yanked the wheel hard to the right and pulled down on the flaps. The *Attila* violently banked and rocketed upward.

"Sitsa, plot me a course back to Immor-Onn," Demetrius said, staring intensely out the windshield. "Okawa, get on

44

that communication crystal. Let the Bailians, the Valdurians and the *Haraka* know the mawl army is on the move! Make sure they know they're coming with Ash-Ta air support!"

Oro' Korra walked slowly down the windswept streets of Immor-Onn with his hands clasped behind his back. By now, the old general had grown used to the windchime's constant melodic jangling. He initially hated them when the new queen put them in, but now he barely noticed.

The passage of time had a way of fostering acceptance, he silently mused. So much had changed in the past eight grands.

None of it good.

The new queen however, had been merciful to the vanquished in the Black Pearl Revolution. She could just as easily have fed him, and all of the old guard, to the Do-Tarr army. The old queen, *his queen,* certainly would have.

He paused by the window of a bakery, enjoying the warmth radiating through the glass, and studied his scarred, pockmarked face in the reflection. His skin tone was a slightly deeper shade of blue than those Bailian's passing around him.

He inwardly bristled at what he considered an inferior trait being bred into the gene pool. Under the old queen and the Racial Purity Movement, this would not have been allowed, but there was nothing that could be done about it now. The smoke was out of the bottle and he knew it would never go back.

"Hello, old friend," a familiar voice to his right broke him from his contemplative trance.

The reflection revealed an older Bailian, with much the same skin tone as his, and a bushy white moustache. He leaned on a cane with an ornate handle, smiling pleasantly.

"Cha-Rod!" he said, clearly surprised. "What are you doing here?"

Cha-Rod opened his arms, "Oro' Korra, is that any way to greet a fellow comrade in arms?"

The two enthusiastically embraced and then held each other at arm's length.

"I never thought I'd see you again," Oro' Korra said, releasing his grip and stepping back.

"Neither did I, old friend, neither did I."

The old general's demeanor quickly changed from friendly to cautious and he glanced around warily.

"You know it's not safe for you to be here?" Oro'Korra said in a low voice.

"Were my mission not dire, I would not have taken the risk."

Oro' Korra's expression went from cautious to concerned. His former junior officer was not prone to exaggeration.

"What is it, my friend?" he asked.

"The forces of Nocturn threaten our land. As we speak, they are attacking the hamlets of the Os'Tor Forest. I greatly fear they have their sights on Immor-Onn."

The old general grimly nodded and then indicated the shop they stood before. "Let's get out of the wind. I want to hear more about this. You can buy me one of Usho's sweet cakes and give me the details."

When they stepped inside the warmth of the bakery the odor of fresh baked goods wrapped them in a blanket of familiarity and solace. Two sweet cakes and hot tea later, the two older Bailians found themselves seated at one of the few small tables.

"Who are the ones attacking us?" Oro' Korra asked after taking a sip of tea.

"Cat people from the Land of Mists," Cha-Rod replied solemnly.

"We have some of the tiger people living here. They're filthy creatures. As far as I'm concerned, the new queen has allowed too many foreigners to take up residence here. She has a good heart but is too soft to rule effectively."

"Not like the old days my friend, eh?"

Both sat silent for a moment sharing a sad smile of recollection.

"Let's say you're right," Oro' Korra said, breaking the reflective mood, "and their ultimate goal is Immor-Onn. What can be done? The queen, fearing another coup like the one which allowed her to ascend to the throne, abolished the army exposing our soft underbelly. The Human marines she employs as city guards are too few to be effective against an invasion."

"We may not be able to repel an invasion," Cha-Rod said resiliently, "but we can make it too costly to keep."

"A resistance movement?"

"We still have time," Cha-Rod said, nodding. "They are a good distance away, and on foot, but we must act quickly."

Oro' Korra scoffed and sat back in his chair. "We are old. Our glory days are well behind us. The current population has grown soft and weak under this new queen. Perhaps it's best to let the city fall."

"That my friend," Cha-Rod replied, eyes boring into his former commander, "is an idea proposed by someone who never experienced Tiikeri rule. I have no doubt that our people, as weak and diluted as they might be, will sooner or later rise up against them. We just need to make sure they have some training and leadership, or they will be destined to be a Tiikeri vassal state."

"Where would we even begin such an endeavor?" the old general asked with a frustrated sigh.

Cha-Rod leaned forward with his elbows on the table. "We start by pulling together as many of our former army comrades as possible."

Demetrius passed through the wide hangar opening entering Air Station East and followed the Bailian Air Boss' hand signals. He slowly banked the *Attila* to the left into the military hangar. All around him, airships of various sizes were being locked down for the notoriously inclement weather of the coming moonless.

"I've still got to get used to this," the pilot said, noting the guards on either side of the opening. "The military part that is."

"Extra security is the cost of being able to play with the newest toys," Okawa replied.

"Yeah, none of the security folks on the military side look like they have any fun."

"They don't," Okawa said, smiling at the assessment. "In fact, we specifically choose people with no sense of humor. It's a job requirement."

"Major?" Sitsa interjected, peering back at the Valdurian confused. "I fail to see how a sentient's inability to grasp abstract concepts of humor serves as a factor in acquiring the job of a guard."

Demetrius chuckled. "She was just kidding, Sitsa."

The humanoid moth retained her perplexed look. "So, this was also humor? I'm not sure I understand."

"That's okay," Demetrius said, maneuvering the craft into the designated slip. "There are plenty of humans that don't either."

"We should check in with the commander and the Valdurian Ambassador." Okawa suggested, rising to her feet. "I'm sure they've got a bunch more questions about that Singa army."

"I have yet to meet them," Demetrius noted, following her out the side hatch.

"Sandal's okay. I mean, he's in charge with all that implies, but he's basically a good guy."

"And the ambassador?"

"Well, let's just say she doesn't share her cousin Joc's good nature."

"Is good nature the same thing as humor?" Sitsa asked.

"Kinda, but not really," Demetrius replied, scanning the busy hangar.

"Perhaps one day I will understand." The Tinian shook her head trying to grasp the notion.

"When you find out, let me know." Demetrius said jovially.

Sitsa threw a panicked, questioning look at Okawa who smiled. "Humor again?"

The Valdurian agent nodded and the Tinian remained deep in thought.

"Hey, there's a guy I recognize!" Demetrius said, pointing to a group of two men and two women standing beside the hangar door actively engaged in a conversation.

A young man with red hair and piercing blue eyes pointed to a row of small attack craft that Demetrius hadn't seen before. They measured only ten feet long, tapered at both ends, with a glass bubble two-person cockpit set atop the front of the craft. The dual Trinilic rods and ballista tubes on either side spoke to the lethality of this miniature airship.

"That's Sandal," Okawa said, indicating the man with the close-cropped grey beard and beret. "The woman in the yellow robes is Valindra Valdur."

"She looks like she just smelled something bad," Demetrius noted warily.

This caused Okawa to give a brief, subdued chuckle. "She always looks like that. I don't recognize the other woman."

"The patch on her jumpsuit says she's an Air Scout."

The red-haired young man spotted them first and broke away from the conversation.

"Hey Demetrius, good to see you!"

"Quadar!" Demetrius greeted, clasping forearms. "Looks like you got a new line of ships."

The maintenance chief beamed with pride. "Fighter class. These babies are bad ass!"

Okawa saluted the man in the beret and he returned it. "Okawa, glad to have you back. Congratulations on the promotion."

"Thank you, sir."

The young woman in the jump suit and beret adorned with an eagle feather became excited upon hearing Demetrius' name. Her petite, pouty features and intense expression intrigued the pilot.

"You're Demetrius de Vana!"

"I am," Demetrius replied, pleasantly surprised at being recognized by a stranger.

"My name's Ausarta, everyone calls me Awsi," she said enthusiastically, vigorously shaking his hand. "You're the one that invented that wild technique, aren't you?! Man, you're a legend around here. You have got to teach me that, what do you call it?"

"Skirting the upwinds."

"Yeah, that's it!"

Valindra Valdur loudly cleared her throat. All attention settled on the tall, thin woman with golden brown skin and dark hair worn up in a bun. She greatly resembled her cousin Joc', in Zor, however her pleasant features were marred by a constant dour expression.

"Madam Ambassador," Okawa greeted formally, with a nod of her head.

"Major," she said coldly. "I trust you are here to assist us at this calamitous moment in history?"

"Yes ma'am, we've just deposited an intelligence asset into the city. He's meeting with the former general in the old Bailian army. Together, they're going to try to raise a resistance force in case the army marching this way makes it to Immor-Onn. They'll need access to this facility."

"I'll see to it," Sandal said seriously.

"So, what about those new ships over there?" Demetrius asked ardently.

"We just got them!" Quadar said, unable to mask his pride. "We're putting them through their paces in case that Singa army gets too close. They come equipped with new stabilizers using Cevot silk. It seems to be working well, so I've got my team installing them in the whole fleet. Now that you're here, maybe we can find out how they operate at a really high altitude."

"I was hoping you'd offer," Demetrius said, eyeing the line of six, small, two-seater crafts. "The moonless is almost here. I'll take one up next luna."

"I'd like to tag along," Awsi eagerly asked, watching both Demetrius and Sandal.

"I don't see why not," Demetrius said, gazing over at Sandal for approval.

"Yes," the commander firmly said. "In fact, I want as many pilots trained in skirting the upwinds as soon as possible, starting with the Air Scouts."

"Yes!" Awsi cheered, pumping her fist.

Sandal smiled at her exuberance. "With the combination of those fighters and that little trick of yours, we'll be able to drop a world of hurt anywhere in the Annigan."

As with every meeting, Supreme General Jal-Pi dominantly sprayed the base of the table before examining the battle map of the Twilight Lands before him. Peering around for any challengers, he moved one of the unit markers. The white Tiikeri general then peered up at his four advisors with a confident deportment. All four advisors swished their tails apprehensively watching the general, their claws involuntarily extracting and retracting.

"By now, Commander Ansi's Sikari raiders should have taken the first hamlet in the Os'Tor forest and General Baag-Tar's southern army should be approaching the first oasis in the Dark Waste. It is now time to begin considering phase two of this operation."

"Supreme General," an orange Tiikeri advisor across the table asked, bowing his head respectfully, "without Worrg confirmation or Ash-Ta report is it wise to anticipate phase two?"

Jal-Pi's ears pinned back and he shot the advisor an irritated glance. "All field commanders have been ordered to not deviate from the plan. For logistical purposes, we must assume these positions."

This triggered a round of heated discussion with the three other orange Tiikeri advisors until a mongrel aide rushed into the room and handed Jal-Pi a piece of paper. The general accepted it with a nod and the messenger hurried off. The aides silently watched their leader read the note and a look of relief crossed their faces when Jal-Pi smiled.

"Comrades, the moment we have been waiting for has finally arrived. I am pleased and proud to announce the birth of the Cub Prince."

A wave of excited chatter passed around the table and Jal-Pi seemed relieved the orderly transition had finally returned.

"Comrades," he proclaimed. "May the gods bless the cub prince and death to the enemies of the empire!

"BLESS THE CUB PRINCE AND DEATH TO THE ENEMIES OF THE EMPIRE!" they chanted.

Taa-Je, the orange Tiikeri daughter of Taa-Ze, felt both excited and nervous. After all, fortune favored her, having been bred by the king, and she hoped, beyond anything, the gods would smile upon her and she would give birth to the next Cub Prince. This would bestow honor on her whole family. She would be the royal consort and they all could move into the palace to live a life of ease and luxury.

The other alternative was too terrible to envision.

Of all the eligible daughters offered up to the sovereign for mating, only one would give birth to the black Tiikeri, known as the Cub Prince, who would eventually rule. All of his other babies would be put to death.

Her baby was due any luna now and Taa-Je was more than ready. Moving around her family's modest, but appointed, Hai-Darr den had long grown uncomfortable. The mobility she recently took for granted was gone with the baby kicking up a storm inside her extended belly.

She suddenly felt hungry again, which wasn't unusual. Her appetite had grown voracious ever since she started to show. She stepped out to a small corral beside the den. After licking her hands to wet them, she rubbed them around her mouth, cleaning it.

She then reached into the corral and grabbed one of the several small rodents scurrying about. It squawked loudly and squirmed in her hands, until she brought it up to her mouth and bit out its entire midsection in one bite.

She was returning to the den, devouring the rest of her kill, when she heard someone call her name. Rujo, a local mongrel domestic slave, ran down the street towards her, waving her arms and thrashing her tail excitedly.

"Taa-Je! Taa-Je!" she cried. "I just heard the news! The Cub Prince was just born! The Cub Prince has been born!"

The excited slave paused briefly to make sure she heard, before darting away broadcasting the joyous news. Taa-Je's heart sank and the meal she just consumed grumbled angrily in her stomach.

She *did not* carry the empire's new ruler and while this brought no disgrace to her and her family, the thought of having to kill her newborn sent a rush of profound sadness through her. Watching the mongrel messenger running down the street, her eyes welled up and tears started flowing down her cheeks.

This could not be. Surely, she couldn't have carried this child, *her child*, to full term only to have its young life snuffed out at birth. She would not allow it. In that moment she made a fateful decision.

With a determined stride, she went back into the den, packed some personal items and grabbed a handful of gems, while fighting down waves of panic. She had to be gone before her parents, especially her father, returned. It would be his duty to kill the baby. She also knew that he would hold her to blame.

Taa-Je would escape to the Unaligned City of Shun-Dra, the only safe place for her and her baby in the Land of Mists.

54

Demetrius found himself up before the moon rose and on his way to the air station. Okawa wasn't even out of bed yet and he wanted to get a closer look at those new fighters before taking one up on a test flight. Okawa had a breakfast meeting with Kai later that morning and would no doubt be discussing sensitive matters not suited for his ears.

The hangar bustled with activity by the time he arrived. Koren, the air boss, nodded at him, just before waving in a medium sized transport ship. A Valdurian marine, standing guard at the entrance of the military hangar, snapped to attention upon his approach.

"Morning Giles," Demetrius greeted. "Your shift should be just about over."

The young Human marine, with close cropped blonde hair and a baby face, smiled at being addressed by name.

"Yes, sir, that bed's going to feel good," he answered as Demetrius passed. "Uh... sir?"

The pilot abruptly halted. "Yes Giles?"

"Please express my apologies to Master Cha-Rod and General Oro' Korra," he requested, "we were unable to locate their missing dagger."

"That's odd," Demetrius commented, a puzzled look crossing his face. "Cha-Rod doesn't carry a blade."

"Master Cha-Rod said it was a gift for the general. He thought he might have left it on your ship. They had clearance. I didn't see the harm, but we couldn't find it. We even kept looking around the area after they left."

"I'll make sure I tell them. Thank you, Giles."

"Yes, sir, sorry sir."

Demetrius gave an assuring wave of his hand and crossed over into the military hangar. It didn't surprise him to see Awsi already there, excitedly fidgeting while inspecting one of the fighters.

"Everything look okay?" Demetrius asked, approaching the exuberant young woman.

"Yeah," she said, patting the ship. "So far, these fighters have been the most fun to fly. Really responsive."

"Had a lot of experience, huh?"

"I've flown every class of ship in the Valdurian fleet."

"What are you, all of seventeen?"

"I'm nineteen! My dad taught me to fly when I was ten."

"So, your dad was a pilot?" Demetrius probed, while settling into the cockpit.

Awsi nodded, slipping into the only other seat in the craft beside him. "My dad was the very *first* pilot."

The revelation took Demetrius completely by surprise.

"Really?!" He said, closing the glass dome over them.

"Yep, Marassa Serth may have been the one to build the first airship, but it was my old man who had the balls to take it up for the first time."

"Wow, well, I guess you get it honest," Demetrius said, turning on the Etheria engine and lifting the ship three feet off the deck.

"Yeah, who would have thought test pilot could be a family business."

Demetrius looked to the air boss for the signal to launch, when he noticed Awsi remove the feather from her beret and kiss it, before placing it back in its original location.

"For luck," she said, noticing him watching her.

"Yeah, I know a bunch of pilots with their own little preflight rituals," he acknowledged. "I don't know why, but I just never picked one up."

Suddenly, the air boss pointed at him and waved them on to the open hangar door, now clear of traffic.

"Okay, here we go," Demetrius announced, hitting the accelerator.

The unnamed fighter craft shot out of Air Station East and into the turbulent skies over the Twilight Lands.

"Wow, this thing really *is* responsive!" Demetrius yelled, after completing several rolls and a loop. "The new stabilizer makes it much more resistant to that relentless wind."

"I can't wait to see how it performs at a really high altitude," Awsi said, animatedly looking around.

"Let's take her upstairs and see."

"I really appreciate you taking the time to teach me."

"No need to thank me," Demetrius said, pulling up on the flaps." I'm under orders, remember."

"Still, to learn from the inventor… By the way where are we going?"

Demetrius glanced over with a confident grin. "I thought I'd pop us over to Zor, and you can bring us back."

"That's halfway around the world!"

"That's the point. Watch and learn."

The craft rocketed westward at a steep upward angle until Awsi mentioned she felt a little lightheaded.

"That's when you know you're at your apex," Demetrius said, leveling off and slowing the ship.

Awsi gasped at the view. She could actually see the curvature of the world and the continents below, set against the blue expanse of ocean.

"Okay, the trick here is being able to make out where you want to go," he explained, pointing to a large land mass cattycorner to their right. "That's Amarenia over there."

Directly ahead, in the distance, the Goyan Islands rapidly drew nearer.

"They're coming up so fast, and you slowed the ship!" Awsi noted in wonder.

"That's because of our altitude," Demetrius explained. "The trick is, knowing when to start your descent. If you figure it wrong, you could end up miles from where you intended to be… and… now."

From a level westward track, the craft's nose gently dipped and the Goyan Islands rotated beneath them.

"I took that slow to show you," Demetrius said, increasing their downward speed, "but soon you'll be able to do it in one fluid motion."

57

Demetrius pulled the ship out of its rapid descent and conducted a gentle bank around the sprawling metropolis of the high holy city, before heading eastward out over the Goyan countryside.

"Okay, think you can get us back?"

Awsi smiled broadly and nodded. Demetrius indicated the controls in front of her. Even with the less experienced pilot at the helm, the return trip went much the same. Her ability and seemingly natural skill impressed Demetrius. Just before he could compliment her in mid descent, a strong gust of wind caught the tail fins and rocked the craft.

"That wasn't supposed to happen!" Awsi said with a touch of concern.

"Yeah, I thought the new stabilizers were supposed to address that," Demetrius said, glancing to the ship's stern.

"This is the first time it's happened," Awsi assured. "I've been testing these since we got them five cycles ago."

"Yes, but this is the first time they've been this high up.

"I don't see what that has…"

Another large gust of wind rattled the back flaps sending them waving violently and cut short Awsi's challenge. She cried out when the craft began heedlessly spinning. The flap controls lurched out of her hand and began feverishly undulating in time with the out-of-control flaps.

The spinning airship now forcefully shook, all the while plummeting towards the ground below. In an attempt to gain control, Awsi lunged for the rapidly lurching lever. She misjudged its trajectory and the control arm smacked her wrist with a resounding crack. The young pilot screamed in pain and her arm went limp in her lap.

Now, merely hundreds of feet above the Os'Tor Forest, the treetops rushed at them with breakneck speed.

"You keep on the wheel!" Demetrius ordered, grabbing the two heaving levers. "Concentrate on steering!"

It took all of his strength to steady the out-of-control craft. He stopped its perilous plunge and they just brushed the tops of the trees. Leaves and branches showered the clear glass canopy above them, until the stiff, surface winds blew them off while the ship peacefully hovered.

Both pilots paused for a moment to catch their breath. Each looked at the other, both realizing how close they had come to perishing. Awsi winced in pain while gingerly supporting her wrist.

"I'll bring us in," Demetrius said, peering around to get his bearings. "We'll get that arm looked at. However, there is a piece of good news though. Even going through all that, you weren't very far off the mark. Good job!"

Awsi appeared unamused. "I just want to know what happened to that damn stabilizer."

When they removed the bag from the man's head, he blinked several times while his eyes adjusted to the light, and then looked around in a panic. He sat in a small featureless room, bound securely to a low stool.

His arms were extended out in front of him, suspended over a large glass tank filled with water, with each wrist attached to a wooden lever. A white ball, about six inches in diameter, undulated in the middle of the liquid. An attractive, petite, Human female with short brown hair, stood by the levers on the other side of the tank.

"Where am I?" he stammered, his clean shaven light brown features displaying unnerved confusion. "What the fuck's going on?!"

"Lopov de Mak," Kem said coyly, ignoring his questions. "Your name crosses my desk so often I'm thinking about having it engraved. In this case, however, you and your friends have been badly misbehaving."

Lopov's face soured. "I didn't do nothin!"

"Oh, I seriously doubt that," the spymaster said, chuckling, "but I'm just curious why it took four of you to kill an old man and a kid?"

"I don't know what the fuck you're talkin about," he answered with an obstinate sneer.

Kem rubbed her temple and glanced down. "Echoes from the street say different."

When she peered back up, her disposition turned grim. "So, I've got a few questions for you. And just in case you're going to pull the strong silent type on me, I brought along a little incentive."

She nodded towards the white ball freely floating in the tank.

"Now, I want to know who your playmates were two Kan's ago, when you hit the armory? Who hired you? Why did you steal those particular weapons and what did you do with them?"

"What weapons? I got no idea what yer talkin about ya crazy quim!"

Kem gave a resolved sigh. "It looks like you need a little incentive."

The mobster's eyes widened when Kem grinned at him sadistically. She gestured towards the floating ball.

"Do you know what that is?" she calmly asked, before continuing without waiting for his response. "They're called Perrikin, very tiny carnivorous fish which hibernate in the cold waters of the Ocean Deep in balls just like that. Their schools can number twenty thousand or more.

"Every now and then, their hibernating balls drift into a warm Goyan current, waking the little fellas up. Then, they hatch, swarming the shallow sea, and any other bodies of water they can swim into, in what's known as a Parrikin Run. They mindlessly devour anything in their path, until exiting back out into ocean deep, where they go back into hibernation. A school can strip a Sunal EEtah down to the bone in a few centi, but that's thousands of them and I've only got about fifty here."

Lopov stared ominously at the undulating sphere, before giving Kem a quick frightened look, but said nothing.

"Let's start with who hired you?" Kem asked.

The obstinate mobster sat silently, scowling.

"Suit yourself," Kem said shrugging.

She reached up to one of the levers and pulled it straight down. The gear mechanism creaked when his left hand dropped into the water with a splash.

"Wakey, wakey…" Kem said in a singsong to the tank.

Once disturbed, the ball broke apart into dozens of tiny blue and gray fish, no more than two inches long, with huge mouths full of serrated teeth. The water boiled and frothed at a frantic rate, while turning a sickening shade of red. Lopov's high pitched screams immediately followed.

Kem pushed up on the lever and Lopov's partially eaten hand rose out of the water. The Perrikin stripped most of his fingers to the bone and blood dripped into the water, causing it to continue rippling violently. Several of the voracious fish launched themselves into the air, snapping at the bleeding appendage just out of reach.

"Now, to the question at hand. Who hired you to rob the armory?"

Lopov's screams could be heard all the way down the hall but they stopped just before someone rapped twice on the door to the interrogation room.

Not waiting for a response, Colonel Velitel poked his head in.

"Kem," he said, motioning for her to join him in the hall.

The spymaster glanced back at the bleeding man who began to whimper. "You stay put now. We've got a lot more catching up to do."

Once the door closed behind them, Kem gave a satisfied smile and jerked her head back indicating the room. "I got one of the guys that hit the armory a few Kans ago."

"That was fast!" Velitel said, pleasantly surprised. "How did you nab him so quickly?"

"One of my echoes overheard him bragging after a few drinks in a tavern."

"Impressive!"

"Yeah, thanks, and get this. Our boy in there just told me, he and his pals were hired by a man-tiger who spoke fluent Common."

The commander of the city guards stood staring in astonishment. "Really?!"

"That's what he says."

Velitel waved a piece of paper in his hand. "Well, that certainly coincides with this dispatch I just got."

Kem's eyes narrowed at the paper.

"It would seem there's a mawl army on the move," he continued, "raiding in the Twilight Lands."

ACT TWO

Conflagration

B aal-Suzor liked calling the Lor-Danta Oasis home for a number of reasons. First and foremost, because of its remote location at the eastern most reaches of the Dark Waste Desert. The six, giant, Tanem Charts, carved into the obsidian field beside the oasis proper, served as a constant reference to the starry skies of Nocturn.

If for some reason he had trouble deciphering the enigmatic oracle, the Arron-Nin Astrologers, who also called the oasis home, were there to help. The refining and combining of Etheria took up most of his time and he only dabbled in astrology. The Bailian master lapidary spent his lunas plying his gem fashioning skills to the constant supply of raw Etheria Crystals from the Barrens to the north.

Business continued to be good for the old Bailian. Sentients from across the Annigan kept him and his small staff of Gilas busy, despite the perilous journey across the sands to enlist his services.

His latest project, almost completed, needed just a few finishing touches. Peering through a large magnifying glass mounted to his worktable, he watched his slender blue fingers thread a needle thin shard of milky white Amonite into the brown Carnelian sleeve, which appeared slightly wider. This particular little bauble would bestow calm and inner strength to his anxious patron.

"There!" he said, stepping back and examining his work. "If that doesn't do the trick, I don't know what will."

"It should, sir," said a young Gila standing beside him.

"What in the name of the gods is that?" the Zadim asked, when high-pitched squeals filled the air outside.

His assistant turned to answer, when the front door flew open and two large bipedal figures outfitted for desert travel stepped into the room.

Behind them, Baal-Suzor could see quite a few more of the robed figures rushing around outside. Humanoid bats filled the sky, erratically swooping and diving. Several perched on one of his giant cyclopes lying motionless on the ground. The young Gila glanced around in a panic when one of the figures closed the door, cutting off his view of the horrific spectacle.

Furry hands reached up and pulled back the hood and face covering revealing an orange Tiikeri and Singa.

The two desert sentients had never seen mawls before and they watched them approach in stunned silence.

"I am General Baag-Tar," the Tiikeri said commandingly. "And I claim this oasis in the name of the Tiikeri Empire."

Demetrius yawned and rubbed his eyes. "Why do I let you keep me up so late?"

Okawa shot him a look of mock indignation. "Me?!"

"Uh huh," he confirmed, before yawning again.

They both paused at the double doors leading to the flight control room of Air Station East.

"As I recall, I didn't hear you complaining," Okawa said, playfully tweaking his nose.

"That's because you were naked. I rarely complain when you're naked."

"So, I've noticed."

Okawa pushed open the doors and led the way into a room fifty feet square, with massive picture windows on two of the walls. One of the windows looked down on the commercial and military flight decks of both hangars. The other window faced the turbulent skies above Deep Ocean, just off the cliffs running along the coast of the Twilight Lands.

A narrow table, with pads of paper and spy glasses evenly interspersed, sat just under the windows. Each table's spy glass station included a mounted, circular Larimar and Calcite Etheria disk for communication and navigation.

Quadar, and three Bailians wearing green jumpsuits, peered intensely out the window overlooking the sea. The red headed maintenance chief looked up at the pair when they entered.

"Hey there, sleepyheads, good of you to join us," he teased. "You know, I'm not exactly sure what you special operations folks actually do. I mean, you get to sleep in, drink at all hours and play with some pretty cool toys."

"Well, I could tell you, but then I'd have to kill you," Okawa jabbed back, stepping up to the group.

Quadar sighed deeply and resumed his vigil. "Well, it's like my grandmother used to say, 'Let the mystery be.'"

"So, what's with the skeleton staff?" Demetrius asked, grinning from the lighthearted exchange.

"The moonless' winds still haven't died down. Bad for business but great for testing out those stabilizers."

"Is that wise, given what happened last luna?"

Quadar picked up a spyglass and peered through it for a better look. "Inconclusive. We don't know if that happened because you skirted the upwinds or any number of other factors. I've got a team looking at it."

He lowered the glass and nodded his head in the direction of the window. "Right now, Awsi is putting the *Easif* through its paces."

Demetrius nodded approvingly at the Resistance Class cruiser gliding effortlessly through the heavy gusts and rain laden clouds.

"We fitted it with the stabilizer a few lunas ago," Quadar said. "It looks like she's doing okay. One way to find out."

He reached down to the table and touched the Larimar disk. The white crystal with blue striations glowed slightly.

"*Easif,* this is Big E Control," he said. "Do you copy?"

"Big E this is *Easif,* I copy." The young pilot's voice filled Demetrius', Okawa's and Quadar's head.

"How's she handling, Awsi?"

"It's blowing a hundred out here, Quay," she answered. "So far, so good. I could put on my makeup out here... if I wore makeup."

"Okay, *Easif,*" Quadar replied with an entertained grin, "I'm convinced. Head for the barn."

"Copy that."

Quadar took his hand off the Etheria talking stone and faced Demetrius and Okawa. "When she gets in, we can do a side-by-side comparison with that fighter."

"Mayday, mayday, mayday!" Awsi's fear laden voice exploded in their ears.

"This is the *Easif*!" she cried. "We have a catastrophic failure! Repeat, we have a catastrophic failure!"

All spun and looked on in horror at the *Easif* violently fishtailing and spinning in the swirling turbulence.

"Red Cord it!" Quadar snapped.

One of the Bailians rushed over to five chords hanging in a ceiling corner, each cord's color corresponded to a different toned bell over the flight deck. He pulled the red chord multiple times. A loud clanging report echoed through the hangar complex and everyone on the flight deck below began scrambling about.

"Awsi," Quadar said, touching the Etheria once more. "Can you get it up here? We've got the area cleared and a crash team ready. Can you get it in the hole?"

"I'll try Quay, but I've got almost no controls," came the apprehensive reply.

"You've gotta try!"

"Copy that!" she yelled. "Cross your fingers!"

The *Easif* flew within a hundred yards of the cliff face entrance, fighting for each foot traveled. They anxiously watched the wounded ship stabilize and travel a few feet closer, before being rocked and spun like a top.

Demetrius felt a guarded sense of optimism, when after several spins the craft steadied, aligned itself with the hangar opening directly below them and closed half the distance.

"Come on… come on," Quadar quietly encouraged under his breath.

"Come on kid," Demetrius found himself pleading. "You can do it."

As Awsi navigated the final few yards, the airship began fishtailing again. It seemed like she got the swaying under control when it entered a full spin.

"Just a little bit further," Quadar mumbled, watching the nose of the *Easif* pass out of sight into the hangar opening.

A sudden gale force gust caught the rear fin of the partially secured ship and smashed the hull against the portal's entryway with a loud crash. The Ukko Wood hull bounced off the impact, as intended, but this allowed the wind to catch the exposed fin. The ship spun out into the tempest once more.

"Awsi looks unconscious!" Okawa yelled, pointing.

They could see the pilot's slumped figure through the cockpit, proving the Valdurian agent's dire observation correct. The pilotless ship flipped over onto its back, before plunging nose first in a tailspin onto the jagged rocks below.

The *Easif* crashed onto the narrow rocky beach between the twin ship's harbors with a thunderous roar. It stood upright against the storm's fury, impaled through the windshield by a thin, ragged stone column.

A grief-stricken hush enveloped the control room. The trio stared at the wreckage below in tormented disbelief.

"Awsi might still be alive," Okawa said resolutely, first to break the silence. "We can't leave her out there! She might only be hurt."

Okawa spun and bolted towards the doors. "I can get to her from one of the harbor's mouths."

The Kan fog rolling in did little to dampen the spirit of the party going on at the estate of Lord Hanara, on the outskirts of Makatooa. Light blazed from virtually every window in the three-story mansion. Music, laughter and conversation streamed out, along with the light, over the perfectly manicured grounds.

The city's elite had come out to play at the coveted, personal invitation of the lord of the manor himself, Lord Hanara. He didn't hold this moment of gaiety on a whim to flaunt the wealth of the richest sentient in the Spice Islands, but rather as a coming out affair for the city's newest, prominent, and most controversial citizen, the Cul-Ta known as Chu-Chu.

A small crowd gathered seeking refuge for conversation away from the noisy festivities, on a large, second-story balcony overlooking the northern gardens. Kem stood beside Mz. Lau, who sipped on her glass of wine, while Blyth Calden and Lord Hanara sang the praises of their guest of honor to a small crowd of the city's most elite.

"Why Si. Chu-Chu, how fortunate you were able to rally your people," praised an attractive, middle-aged woman in a glittery, flowing purple gown. "I know that I, and the others of our fair city, are in your debt. To get the town and, most importantly, the docks rebuilt so beautifully and in record time is *such* a blessing,"

She raised her wine glass, saluting the man-rat, and her chocolate brown skin crinkled along the edges of her full lips. She elevated the glass, at arm's length, above her greying hair piled high on her head.

"Here, here," the small crowd chanted enthusiastically.

Kem smiled inwardly at the woman making the toast. Dhani Cole was no doubt glad to see the Makatooa wharf back and better than ever. She came from Makatooa old money, widow to a vast Otick pearl exporting empire. The return of the docks, and her warehouse, meant getting her operation back on a paying basis.

"I'm petitioning the governor for a lordship for Si. Chu-Chu," Blyth said, also raising his glass.

This announcement set off an approving round of chatter.

"I can think of no one who deserves it more,' Hanara cheerfully concurred.

Everyone froze when two of the female guests screamed. A dozen grimy Cul-Ta, armed with very new blades, vaulted up onto the balcony's railing. Kem immediately recognized the stolen weapons from the armory heist. Most brandished double-edged daggers but several held short swords, which resembled great swords in their tiny hands. The brand-new blades twinkled in the lights, illuminating the celebration.

While the partygoers panicked, Kem quickly drew her Mark Four pistol crossbow and pulled the side lever, chambering a bolt. She waved the pistol from side to side at the row of perched vermin hissing menacingly.

Haa-Chu stood on the railing behind Dhani Cole. He grabbed her piled up hair and pulled her head violently back, exposing her throat.

"Shut up, stupid humans!" he hissed, holding the dagger to the weeping socialite's neck. "No move or rich lady dies."

Everyone quieted nervously. Kem, Lau and Hanara, the only partygoers not to appear frightened, stood coldly assessing the situation.

Well, at least we now know what happened to the stolen weapons and the reason for the thieves' choices, Kem silently thought, not lowering her weapon. *Why, in the name of the empire, would the Tiikeri arm the Cul-Ta?*

"I see you, and the rest of your sell-outs," Haa-Chu said, directing his attention to the guest of honor, "are enjoying the finer things in life, cousin,"

Chu-Chu pulled the monocle from his eye and pointed it at Haa-Chu. "You were given the opportunity cousin. All of you were. You chose the ways of sloth and envy instead of earning a place in society. This is your doing!"

The retort had no effect on the enraged rat-man. He pressed the blade tighter to Dhani's throat, causing the terrified woman to launch into a new torrent of sobs.

"Quiet!" Haa-Chu scolded, and then addressed everyone. "You will all be sorry for what you did to us! Cul-Ta have new friends, powerful friends. You'll see!"

His threat complete, the Cul-Ta leader jumped backwards off the railing, simultaneously cutting the woman's throat. Dhani's eyes went wide in shock and she brought her hands up to her neck, attempting to halt the river of blood flowing from the gaping wound onto the front of the expensive gown.

The other Cul-Ta followed their leader's retreat, leaping off the balcony, but not before Kem managed to shoot a rat-man brandishing a short sword. The Na-Kab Carbon projectile, traveling just short of the speed of sound, impacted with a muted explosion, blowing the Cul-Ta's head and torso into a fine red mist over the garden below. Its sword clattered noisily off the railing, while its legs teetered and then followed.

People screamed and fumbled around the relatively small balcony, reducing it to a scene of chaos. Kem futilely attempted to treat Dhani's mortal wound, while Hanara and Lau stood motionless, faces contorted in rage.

"It's obvious Gavin isn't coming back," the Hammerhead EEtah said. "We've gone too long without a fixer and I don't trust the city guards to get this under control. At the lifting of the Kan, make sail for Soonokai, there's a man there I need to talk to. Bring him back here."

Mz. Lau silently nodded, the determined expression not leaving her face.

Okawa was finally able to get a close up look at the wrecked airship from the cave opening of Rilli-On Harbor and her heart sank. The large, jagged rock impaled the ship and punched through the windshield, completely consuming the cockpit.

No one could have survived that. Especially if they were already unconscious, she thought, heaving a deep sigh and sadly shaking her head.

"Looks like we got a recovery," she addressed Quadar and the three mechanics standing next to him. "Have them drop a line from the hangar. We'll attach it to the tail and winch her up.

"What a darn shame," Demetrius said woefully. "She was a good kid and a very gifted pilot."

"You think it was the stabilizer?"

"It's a good bet," Demetrius replied. "It acted the exact same way last luna."

"Only one way to find out," Okawa added, watching the thick strand of rope tumble down from the hangar above.

Two Outer Clan EEtahs winched the broken hull of the *Easif* into the hangar and out of the howling wind. Without the gusts to carry it away, the overpowering smell of the shoreline made Demetrius' nostrils flare. Through the missing windshield, he could see the mangled interior painted in a ghastly shade of red. Okawa and Quadar stood beside him in horrified silence.

Once they set the craft down on the flight deck, Okawa headed for the side hatch, while Quadar made his way over to the tail assemblage. Demetrius held back, closing his eyes and sighing deeply. Okawa appeared in the doorway moments later. With sad eyes and taut lips, she shook her head and hopped out.

"The entire cabin is pretty chewed up," she said coldly. "All that's left of Awsi are her feet and ankles."

Demetrius lowered his head sorrowfully. "She was a good kid."

"You might want to have a look at this," Quadar said, gazing up at an open panel housing the steering mechanism.

"What am I looking at?" Okawa asked, staring at the network of interconnected control rods.

"It's what you're *not* looking at," Quadar replied pointing to the newly installed stabilizer unit.

"Where are the silk connector chords?" Demetrius asked puzzled.

"Exactly!" Quadar said suspiciously. "No wonder this bird went down. That broken stabilizer compromised the entire control and steering mechanism."

A befuddled Demetrius shook his head, at a total loss for an explanation. "That was Cevot spider silk. What in the name of the gods could have done that?"

Quadar ran his finger through a layer of fine white powder directly below the crippled equipment. "I'm not exactly sure but I'm willing to bet this has something to do with it."

"Is that what's left of the silk?" Okawa asked, straining to get a good look at the substance.

Quadar ran the powder between his thumb and forefinger.

"It doesn't feel like it," he answered. "We need to get a closer look."

The Valdurian Maintenance Chief led them to a long workbench against the wall. He brushed the powder off his fingers and onto the table, pulling over a large round magnifying glass attached to a mechanical arm.

Quadar peered through the lens and whistled softly.

"Well, I'll be…" His voice trailed off and he looked over at Demetrius and Okawa with a concerned, confused expression.

"Have a look," he said moving back.

Okawa stepped up first and took a peek.

"They look like tiny cocoons," she said, her furrowed brow betraying a clearly puzzled agent.

It was now Demetrius' turn to appear baffled. He peered through the lens and an unknown voice spoke up behind him.

"Hey, that looks like what we found in the fighter from last luna. Only the damage wasn't that extensive."

All spun to see a maintenance worker in a green jumpsuit.

"They looked like this?" Quadar asked, pointing at the substance.

"Yeah boss," he answered, "right up to the time they started hatching and flying around. There must be millions of them. They're so small the swarm looked like whisps of smoke."

"That can't be a coincidence," Okawa said, peering back through the glass.

"Some kind of freak infestation?" Demetrius offered.

"I've never seen them before," Quadar said, rubbing the back of his neck. "Of course, that doesn't mean much. They're small and I'm no expert on bugs."

"Well, we need someone who is," Okawa said resolutely. "You've got a brand-new university here that the queen paid a lot of money for. I say it's time to put them to the test. In the meantime, we need to ground any ship that has one of those new stabilizers installed in it."

"By now that's almost all of them," Quadar said, sounding more than a little defeated.

"They all have to be checked," Okawa said sternly. "I don't like the timing on this. We've got an army marching on the city and if our fleet's grounded, this air station is just about worthless."

Taa-Je, tail hanging low, felt as if she couldn't take another step. Not only did her feet and back ache, but she also felt like the baby was performing acrobatics inside her.

It had been a little more than a luna since she left Hai-Darr. She knew they would probably be looking for her by now, first her parents, then the authorities. Once the king's forces became involved, her head start would be short lived.

They would no doubt dispatch a Sikari team the size of which would depend on how desperate they were. The lioness hunter/killer teams were known for their efficiency and lethality, so she must not be spotted. Inwardly, she couldn't help but feel self-conscious and sure her orange fur would be easy to spot.

Unfortunately, Taa-Je's condition restricted her progress. She couldn't move fast or navigate rough terrain, so she was forced to take one of the main roads north. Several times, she had to hide in the thick jungle flanking the wide path when traffic approached.

Deep down she wondered how long she could keep this up. Shun-Dra, still a hundred miles away, remained the only place in the Annigan where she and her child would be truly safe. No killing or violence would be permitted there. An inflexible law, enforced by a mysterious deadly mist whose judgment was absolute and final.

Finally, fatigue overcame her and she simply could not go on. She assessed a large tree just off the road to be suitable cover. Slowly lowering herself at the base of the tree, she faced away from the road and heaved a sigh of relief.

Once settled, she reached into her bag and pulled out a strip of dried meat. She bit off a chunk. At this rate, her provisions would only last her for three lunas, but at her current pace, Shun-Dra was at least five away.

The pregnant Tiikeri had time to contemplate her plight. A wave of self-doubt and second thoughts swept over her. Who was she to defy thousands of grands worth of tradition? There could be *only one* son of the king, the cub prince. They were well within their rights to kill her baby. Their fears of him rising up and challenging the cub prince for the throne one day were valid concerns. Then, there remained the fact they would never be able to leave Shun-Dra if they made it. So, it would turn out that their ultimate safe haven would also be their prison.

Taa-Je's heavy eyelids eventually disrupted her sullen ponderings and she fell into an exhausted, dreamless sleep.

Rasul de Rophan was not a well man. His back tended to give out with the slightest wrong move, and his bowels were delicate, slipping into open revolt at the hint of sudden movements or unpleasant odors.

He had also been spared the curse of good looks. His ruddy complexion, and badly receding head of red hair, all but guaranteed any affectionate attention he might stumble upon would have to be bought and paid for.

What the thirty-eight-grand-old Eldorian royal crier did possess was a booming baritone voice and a gift for passionate oration. The former patriarch, Warbel Eldor often used him as a bard at court, even though he played no instrument. There had been many a state dinner where they called on him to sing and tell stories.

Right now, Rasul wished he was back in the palace in Rophan, because the last four cycles had been torturous. He spent the entire boat ride to Otomoria with his head over the railing puking his guts out. Now, he found himself being jostled about on horseback, having to endure the pungent stench of livestock.

Thankfully, he rode at the head of the double column of the fifty lancers sent to greet him when they docked. He was glad they were with him, too. The message he delivered to the plantations and keeps along the Otoman River proved wildly unpopular and contentious.

When Rasul finally saw the Pyramid of Hasteen rise above the fields of waving wheat, he felt a small sense of relief knowing he neared the end of his mission.

"Ever seen a Dreeat before?" the patrol sergeant riding next to him asked.

Rasul gazed over at the young clean-shaven lancer and shook his head.

"The crocs take some getting used to," the sergeant added, "but they're generally glad to see us. They're really gonna be glad to see you when you read that piece of paper you're carrying."

"That will be a welcome change," Rasul said, fighting back a wave of nausea.

"Believe me, as pissed off as the river lords were, those crocs are gonna be happy in equal amounts."

Rasul didn't respond and rode silently the rest of the trip. Eventually, the fields of grain gave way to sugar cane fields and the berm bordered ponds of the Dreeat city. The main body of horsemen hung back when they reached the moat surrounding the giant step pyramid.

Rasul and the sergeant approached single file towards a growing crowd of curious humanoid crocodiles. They halted just before the sea of attentive, inhuman faces.

Rasul reached into his messenger bag and retrieved the only remaining scroll. He had heard and told stories about these large sentient reptiles, but this constituted his first time in their presence.

Fully knowing how to build anticipation and suspense, the veteran orator paused and allowed the crowd to grow. A large female with attendees made her way to the front of the group. By her bearing, Rasul assumed her to be the queen.

Once the queen stood before him, and he judged the audience to be of sufficient size, he unrolled the scroll with a dramatic flourish. As always, when he began his performance his nausea and discomfort disappeared.

His loud, pleasing voice resonated over the fields and reverberated off the pyramid walls. With the Larimar Diplomat Stone in his pocket, he was certain all would understand him.

"To all the Lords of the Western Fork of the Otoman River," he read, *"their subjects and charges, give your attention to and heed this royal decree.*

"For the crimes of open aggression, restriction of trade, theft and general criminal mischief; I, Shom Eldor, Sovereign of House Eldor and protector of the Realm, hereby revoke the charters of the following houses: Kenyev,

Sorbornef, Volga, Targoff, Annov, Vladof, Donvob, and Booska.

"Said revoking of the afore-mentioned charters is to take effect immediately. Furthermore, all lands and holdings of said former houses shall be returned to the Dreeat Empire. The land is to be vacated no later than the fiftieth cycle of the quinte Teine of this grand cycle.

"So ordered by royal decree, this tenth cycle of the quinte, Awal in this second grand cycle of the Na-Kab."

Rasul lowered the paper and stared out over a sea of silent, stunned faces. With an equally flamboyant flourish, he rolled the scroll back up and presented it to the queen.

It took a moment for the news to sink in that the Dreeat ancestral lands, annexed long ago by the vassals of House Eldor, were being returned. Then, all at once, a massive croaking cheer erupted from the throng of Dreeat and tears of joy streamed down the queen's face.

"Please express my eternal gratitude and friendship of the Dreeat people to King Shom," she said, her voice cracking with emotion.

Rasul smiled and nodded, before turning his mount. They rode back to the main body of lancers, followed by exuberant chanting.

"All hail the far-away king!"

"This is quite exciting!" the Bailian Pisar said, beside himself with enthusiastic abandon.

He looked up from the magnifying glass at Okawa and brushed aside several errant strands of long gray hair.

"Where did you say you got these?"

"I didn't say," Okawa replied guardedly. "What are they?"

"These little fellas are Zeta Moth cocoons, and by the looks of them, they're about ready to hatch. I only asked because they can only be found exclusively in the Cevot Caves in the Os-Ani Mountains. To see them anywhere else is unheard of."

"Are they dangerous?"

The old scholar chuckled and adjusted the sleeves of his blue robes. "Goodness no, their larva feed on Cevot spider silk. Then when they're full they spin a cocoon and become a moth. They then fly off in search of more silk. They're an important part of the eco system. Otherwise, the caves would be overrun with webbing."

"Could they have gotten here by themselves?"

"I don't see how. Their life span is only a few lunas. They couldn't have made the flight."

Okawa scowled, lost in thought at the news.

"Might I keep these?" the Picar asked with an enthused smile. "I would like to do some in depth observation. As I said, this is very exciting!"

"Huh?" she responded, deep in thought. "Oh, yeah, sure. Thank you for your time and expertise Picar."

"Happy to help," he said, peering back into his magnifier.

Okawa left the lab with her mind a jumble of assorted potential plots. Of one thing she was certain, *they had a saboteur in their midst.*

Okawa caught up with Demetrius just as he came out of Air Station East. She grabbed him by the shoulders, pulled him into a vacant doorway and held him close.

"Hey, I like this," he said, snuggling against her voluptuous body.

"Demetrius, not now," the Valdurian agent snapped, her expression serious and scowling. "This is serious!"

"Okay," he said, taking a small step back.

"I just left Picar Emira-Ton. Those bugs are called Zeta Moths and they're only found in the Cevot caves up in the mountains. They eat Cevot silk. And get this, their life span is so short they couldn't have got here on their own. They were planted."

Demetrius' face now mirrored Okawa's stern expression. "That means…"

Okawa nodded. "Sabotage."

"Unbelievable," Demetrius said, shaking his head in amazement, "someone actually weaponized insects!"

"Believe it," Okawa said grimacing. "As of right now, you're the only one I trust around here."

Demetrius gave a weak smile.

"Gee thanks, I know trust isn't your strong suit." The pilot paused awkwardly. "I, um, suppose this would be a bad time to tell you that I really do love you?"

Okawa blinked and tilted her head. "A bit of a bad time, but the sentiment is appreciated and returned."

"Really! You do, I mean, that's great!"

"I'm moving in with you, you idiot. *Of course, I love you.* Now, can we focus on the problem at hand?"

"Uh huh."

"Good, let's concentrate on what we've got."

"Uh huh."

"So, these moths…" Okawa came back to the subject, her patience tested. "I dare say they're a specialty item. To find someone who can get them for you will require intimate knowledge of the city. The fact that they had access to the hangar, means they're close... Demetrius! Are you listening to me?"

"Uh huh."

"Cuz you're staring at me with those puppy dog eyes."

Demetrius briefly looked away. "It's just..."

"What?!"

"It's just... this is the first time either of us has... you know... actually said those words," he stammered. "It's a pretty big deal for me."

Okawa paused and smiled appreciatively.

"Me too."

Demetrius leaned in and gave her a lingering kiss. As quickly as it started, Demetrius backed away and adopted a business-like tone.

"Believe it or not," he assured, "I really do realize the gravity of the situation. So, what's the plan?"

Alto loved Taleeka's serious attitude and facial expressions during her lessons. She had worked studiously for the last deci under his and Zaad's watchful eye and was finally starting to tire.

"Avoid attacking if you can." Alto said, sensing her weariness. "Let your opponent make the first mistake. Just make sure you are in the proper position to take advantage of that mistake."

Detecting the session winding down, Taleeka lowered her blade, listening intently.

"This is why footwork and balance are important," the swordmaster continued. "If you must strike, there are three things to consider; When you strike, where you strike and most importantly, why you strike. To strike out of fear or anger is to attack from a position of weakness."

"The three enemies you talked about before!" Taleeka recalled enthusiastically.

"Correct,"

Taleeka nodded she understood and then bashfully lowered her head. "Alto, can I ask you something?"

"Of course."

"Zau and Zaad have been calling you, my dad, and Mal, my mom… Are you?"

"Only if you want us to be, little one," Alto answered, smiling at the innocence of the question. "You've already taken the name Kameron. So, it would seem so, but ultimately that question rests with you."

"So, I can call you dad?"

"If you wish," he granted, "but there's only *one thing* you may not call me."

Taleeka's face turned serious, "What's that?"

Alto smiled playfully. "Late for dinner."

Zaad groaned and Taleeka flashed a grin at the swordmaster's well-worn joke before growing timid again.

"What about Mal?"

"Well, you'll have to ask her, but something tells me she would like that."

"Okay!" she said, bounding up to the cabin.

Taleeka stopped between the command chairs and stared at Mal. The Spice Rat had just finished conferring with Zau about their current course to The Land of Mists and brightened at the child's arrival.

"And what can I do for you, Mz. Tally?"

The ten-grand-old took a deep breath.

"I was wondering if you and Alto were my new mom and dad Zau and Zaad say so and Alto said you were and that I can call him dad and he said I had to ask you if it was okay if I call you mom." Taleeka finally took another breath. "Is it?"

Zau put a hand over her mouth, suppressing a snicker and a knowing grin. Mal looked back at Alto with a helpless expression and the swordmaster gave a resigned shrug.

"We share the same last name," Mal said with a nod. "So, yeah, that would be nice."

Taleeka broke into a wide grin and threw her arms around Mal. "I love you mom."

Mal put her arms around her daughter and kissed the top of her head. "I love you too Mz. Tally."

Taleeka, curiosity now satisfied, skipped back to her seat and picked up the book she had left there.

"I thought you didn't do well with children," Zau said wryly.

"Shut up," Mal snipped watching Taleeka contentedly open the book and begin reading.

"Captain," Kumo said in a soft voice, "we are nearing an entrance to the Do-Tarr's southern hive."

Mal stared out at the approaching mountain while the *Haraka* descended from the safety zone just above Ash-Ta airspace.

"Captain," Zaad said, sitting forward. "I know we're getting paid a bunch to deliver the barrel back there to the bugs, but I don't trust the Do-Tarr. They don't think like us. What could be important enough to send us back to their hive with... what did you call it?"

"It's called a pheromone blocker," Mal said. "It's a gift from the Valdurians to the Do-Tarr. They hope it will put them on our side and give them a fighting chance against the Tiikeri in case those devious fuckers try something aggressive. Basically, it blocks the pheromone which renders the Tiikeri invisible to the bugs."

"I thought the Do-Tarr remained neutral," Zaad said.

Mal chuckled. "Not when it comes to the Tiikeri. The bugs fucking despise them."

"If nothing else it gives our enemy's enemy a new weapon," Alto added optimistically.

The *Haraka* slowly approached a perfectly rectangular opening carved out of a sheer cliff face. The moon's rays highlighted the exterior of the forty-by-twenty-foot tunnel but didn't reach very far within its recesses.

"And here we are," Mal noted with a sigh. "Okay, Kumo, drop the side hatch *gently*, then hover and wait. Alto and I have got this from here. Everyone else stay put. This shouldn't take long."

Mal was getting to her feet when Taleeka came bounding over to her. "I want to go mom!"

It took a moment for Mal to register the new title and realize it meant her.

"Absolutely not!" Mal immediately responded.

Taleeka pouted, crossed her arms and huffed. "You never let me have any fun!"

Mal closed her eyes and gave a frustrated sigh, wondering if the whole "mom" title might be a bit premature. Deciding to take a softer approach, she sat back down at eye level with Taleeka and drew her close.

"The Do-Tarr are not like other creatures" she explained. "They're more like insects and their hive means everything to them."

"But I wouldn't hurt their hive. I promise!"

"Tally, they don't have a word for accident. You could be innocently running your hand along a wall, and if a grain of sand falls off, they might kill and eat you. Probably us too, for bringing you into their home. I can't take that chance."

"Oh, okay," she whined, her pout remained but her facial features relaxed and she unfolded her arms.

"That's a good girl," Mal said. "Now give me a hug."

By the time they finished the embrace, Taleeka's mood had completely reversed. She then spun to face the Singa.

"Zau, can I have something to eat?"

"Sure kid."

Alto hefted the small keg and the pair stepped out of the craft and into the southern hive of the Do-Tarr nation.

"I hope to fuck she doesn't do that every time she can't come along," Mal said softly once they entered the tunnel.

They traveled only twenty yards down perfectly squared passages, when they heard the clicking of mandibles and exoskeleton feet on the stone up ahead. Soon after, the swordmaster made out figures emerging from the darkness. Five of the four-foot-tall humanoid mantises approached. Three scurried along the floor, while the other two deftly glided along the wall and ceiling.

Of all the strange attributes these creatures afforded, their eyes disturbed Alto the most. While fierce and unreadable, the unchanging expression in those black, lifeless eyes spoke to their completely alien nature.

"Greetings, Alto and Maluria." The lead Do-Tarr's dispassionate voice resonated in their heads. "We welcome your return,"

"Thank you for receiving us," Alto replied formally with a nod of his head. "We have a gift for your queen."

"She will be pleased to see you. This way."

The Do-Tarr led the humans deep into the southern hive. Just as they remembered, the warm, humid air held the cloying, peppery odor of the queen's nectar. They passed many tunnels on their downward trek and could hear the scraping and hammering of Do-Tarr miners just out of sight of each level they descended. Every so often, a mantis head appeared from the gloom to get a better look at the strange visitors in their home.

"It would appear as if we are still a bit of a novelty," Alto whispered as several ran their hands across them when they passed.

"Good thing we've been marked as friends," Mal replied softly.

By the time they made it to the boundaries of the queen's chamber, both humans were sweating profusely, soaking their clothes.

A thick, viscous membrane, with an oozing slit running vertically down the middle, covered the wide, perfect, rectangular entrance to the queen's abode. The lead Do-Tarr parted the gelatinous barrier and stepped through.

Mal inwardly winced, totally repulsed by the doorway's covering but made sure she showed no signs of revulsion or discomfort. Insulting the Do-Tarr in their own hive, meant certain death.

By the time they entered the queen's chamber, they were a sweaty, slimy mess. A thick glob of goo dripped off Mal's hand when she swept away the hair plastered to her forehead and her boots squished with every step.

The Do-Tarr queen stood almost twice as tall as her subjects. Initially, she ignored Mal and Alto and appeared distracted with the hive mind rattling in her head, always watching and listening to the goings on in her realm.

Attendants milked the black nipples of the six breasts adorning her chest. When one of their teardrop shaped sacks filled with her nectar, they immediately took it away.

At her side stood the new king, a young male with a regal bearing. *That must be the one whose birth we witnessed*, Mal noted to herself.

"Alto, Maluria, welcome once again to our home," the king said pleasantly. "The last time you merely passed through and now you return bearing a gift. We are indeed flattered, aren't we dear?"

The queen broke away from her remote viewing with an irritated glance at being interrupted from running her hive.

Mal briefly wondered how they knew about the gift. She then recalled the Do-Tarr's hive mind. The queen's vision extended through all her subjects except the king, who maintained the ability to join or leave the hive mind at will.

"Yes, yes of course," the queen curtly replied, before returning to her watch over the realm.

"So, a gift?" the king asked nervously, after a tense moment of silence.

"Yes," Mal replied, taking the keg from Alto and setting it at the queen's feet.

"Oh, you've brought me a gift," the queen acknowledged dispassionately, glancing down at the small barrel. "Tell me why you did not return Kyopp to the hive?"

"Kyopp is dead," Mal said in a definitive, yet courteous tone. "He died in battle, saving my life."

"Dead!?" the queen's head snapped in Mal's direction and her outraged voice thundered in their heads. "The fact he died saving you does not console me from the hive's loss! Why did you not return his body to be rejoined with us?

Hearing the monarch's annoyed timber, Mal felt a twinge of uneasiness creeping up her spine. No one, especially humans, wanted to deal with an angry Do-Tarr queen.

Thankfully, Alto, with his courteous, diplomatic deportment took over the conversation. "Your majesty we apologize but the body was lost in combat."

The swordmaster then pointed to the cask at her feet.

"When it was later recovered," he continued, "our alchemists were able to extract this from his body. It's a liquid that will enable you to detect your Tiikeri enemies."

The queen paused at the news. "The accursed tiger people from above will no longer be invisible to us?"

"That is correct, Your Majesty."

"This is of course, a great gift," the queen reluctantly admitted, her tone immediately losing its aggravated edge.

"It also means that Kyopp has returned to us," the king added positively.

The queen ignored the placation and returned her focus to the constant barrage of information her encompassing extra perception provided her.

"The Do-Tarr indeed thank you," the king warmly said, stepping over to the relieved pair of humans. "Is there any other business to be conducted?"

"Yes, Your Majesty," Alto said, tactfully smiling. "We would only ask that one of your people go to the penal colony called Rapscalia, located on the far border of your hive, and bring us the Singa called Lazio."

"An enemy you wish to bring to justice?" asked the king.

"Hardly, Your Majesty," Alto replied. "He is a great ally, whom I fear we will probably need very soon."

Bosco Savador had always been known as a skilled economist and lecturer at the University of Marassa. He had been asked to join the Zorian Monetary Council in his early thirties after publishing his groundbreaking paper on international currency exchanges. Now, at age fifty, the direction the council headed concerned him. The death of Gyara four cycles ago, and the recent ouster of Cedar Aramos, left the esteemed economic body with gaping holes in its leadership... *and him.*

Bosco glared at Banavor, standing at the far head of the long, polished table sporting a smug, confident expression. He dressed in his usual whorish attire with sheer white stockings that came to his upper thighs. A white bare midriff blouse showed off his smooth stomach. Instead of pants, he wore a matching white cock ring tightly cinching in his hairless genitalia.

He reluctantly had to admit, the kid knew how to work the markets. The comely young man couldn't be more than seventeen but possessed an uncanny knack for making money. In the short span of the last deci, he managed to amass more wealth than even veteran traders like himself. A new trader calling a meeting of the Zorian Monetary council would have also been unthinkable a deci ago.

"Esteemed council members," Banavor said, addressing the three men and two women staring at him. "The Goyan Islands are replete with a bounty of agriculture, minerals and livestock as well as a wide variety of Human resources. Many of these assets are grossly underdeveloped due to our current economic model which I have been studying."

Banavor paused to gauge everyone's attentiveness.

"The good news," he continued, "is I have discovered a single, simple fix to this problem. My solution will effectively unleash the economic potential of this vibrant yet underdeveloped part of the Annigan."

Bosco sat back in his chair and smirked, clearly skeptical.

"I'm eager to hear this simple *fix,*" the economist interjected, "to a problem I had no idea existed."

"So often," Banavor replied, giving the economist a lingering, superior smile, "we are too close to the situation to see the inherent flaws in it, blinded by complacency and anxiety at the notion of rocking the boat, so to speak."

"We're talking about the economies of multiple world governments here," Bosco countered. "I believe caution should be the watch word."

"In most cases I would agree," Banavor answered, "We, however, stand at a new economic crossroads. Recent events, one being the Na-Kab and their carbon, have added a vibrancy and potential to virtually unlimited growth.

"There is capital out there just waiting for the opportunity to be put to use. It is the Zorian Monitory Fund's duty to enable these potential individual stockholders to feel confident their investments will yield the maximum profit. This can be accomplished by repealing the Commodities Standard Act."

A nervous murmur swept around the table.

"Let me get this straight," a thin woman with grey hair and a dour expression said. "You don't think the issuers of Commodity Notes need to have the appropriate amount of commodities to back those notes up?"

"Precisely," Banavor replied assertively. "The current system stifles the free flow of capital and restricts investment."

"If a physical commodity is no longer necessary, what will determine the value?" another member asked cynically.

"The free market," Banavor answered rapturously.

Bosco now sat forward, listening to the brash young man, and scowled in disbelief. The other council members now stared at him for his reaction.

"Young man," he said dismissively. "One can hardly call something a *Commodity Note* if there is no *commodity* to back it up and give it legitimacy. What you are proposing is little better than selling air."

Banavor leveled a malevolent stare at Bosco when the council unanimously mumbled agreement at his assessment.

Bosco ignored him. "I'm afraid we must reject this idea of folly you propose."

"*Afraid* is the correct word sir," Banavor said coldly. "Your fear leaves you vulnerable and impedes prosperity. We'll just have to see how you feel about your commodities on hand tomorrow."

"Is that some sort of threat!?"

Banavor didn't respond and just swept his indignant gaze around the table, causing all to fidget nervously.

"We'll talk soon," he said, before abruptly turning and leaving.

When the door closed behind him, an eerie silence descended on the room. The council members anxiously searched each other's faces, unsure how to deal with the lingering dread now shrouding the proceedings.

The *Haraka* streaked westward in the skies over the Land of Mists, heading for the Twilight Lands with their newest passenger. Lazio peered nervously over Zau's shoulder at the moonlit ground below.

"First time in an airship, general?" Mal asked.

"A new and somewhat humbling experience, I must say," the Singa said, not taking his eyes off the passing ground.

"You get used to it," Zau said, just before the Larimar disk glowed in the overhead panel. "Looks like someone wants to talk."

Mal reached up and touched the pale white Etheria crystal with blue striations.

The Singas watched Mal's expression go from curious to concerned, while listening to a brief, one-sided discussion with Okawa in her head.

"Got it," Mal grimly signed off.

The Spice Rat sat back and stared silently into space.

"What is it, Captain?" Zau asked, seeing her disturbed look.

"The Etheria," Mal muttered. "They're making a play for the Etheria."

"What are you talking about?"

Mal abruptly sat up. "I should have *fucking known* with the whole Trinilic affair we just went through!"

"You want to enlighten us?" Zau asked testily.

"That was Okawa," she answered. "A large Singa army massed off Gar-Yesh Point and the Hamlets in the Os'Tor Forest are under attack."

"Who is attacking the hamlets?" Lazio asked.

"Female hunter-killer squads," Mal replied, curious at the question.

"It's a diversion," Lazio proclaimed. "If they were serious about attacking, they would have used the male shock troops approaching from the other side of the continent."

"Good money says those fuckers are making a play for the Etheria fields."

"It's fortuitus you're here," Mal said, addressing her Singa companions. "We're gonna need you. The Onay don't know what's coming. They're too busy squabbling amongst themselves to be any real deterrent. We gotta get there fast."

She strapped on her seatbelt and turned to the crew.

"Zau, find me a portal" she ordered. "Alto, grab a barf bag. We're headed for the Barrens!"

Lau de Mak stood by the railing of the morning dispatch shuttle watching the docks of Soonokai, Makatooa's sister city, come into view. She closed her eyes and allowed the refreshing, post-Kan sea breeze mist her face. When she lazily opened them back up, she felt comforted by the familiar surroundings.

The same architect who built Makatooa designed the bustling seaport of Soonokai on nearby Gom Island. The sibling metropolis was practically an inverse mirror image of the other, the difference being, Soonokai was smaller due to geography and, as of late, circumstance.

The petite human female, with straight black hair, upswept eyes and a pervasively frumpy demeanor, stood absolutely still, observing the approaching boat dock. She didn't wait for them to complete mooring and extend the gangplank to disembark. Busy, aggressive couriers—eager to convey their master's messages—reluctantly stepped aside for this small unassuming human. Everyone knew who she worked for, and no one wanted to be considered someone who obstructed her. This was one of the many perks Lau enjoyed while being in the service of Lord Hanara.

A cautious sentient, Hanara could sometimes be exacting in nature, but his generosity to the faithful—as well as the respect afforded by the community—made dealing with his obsessive fixation on the details more than worth it. Her lord saw the big picture component of the Nallor Cabal and Lau concentrated on the details of getting things done.

Like now.

Lau knew exactly who she was looking for, even though Lord Hanara never invoked his name.

She had called on him and his services several times before, all with exemplary results.

Her lord was fair. He had extended ample opportunities to the local talent to serve him as his "fixers."

All had failed.

The time had come to call upon independent professionals like Silovik de Zolene.

Lau stepped off the gangplank onto the busy wharf and turned in the opposite direction of the morning chaos. She travelled through the thinning crowds, focused on a ruckus group of a half dozen men engaged in a dice game just ahead. An enthusiastic crowd surrounded the contestants, cheering them on.

The formally dressed woman drew stares when she approached the group but ignored the salacious comments. She concentrated on one of the men kneeling in the center of the circle, shaking dice in his hand, preparing to throw.

Silovik de Zolene wasn't an especially large man, coming in at just under six feet tall. The burn scar covering the entire left side of his face set him apart. The ominous looking disfigurement gave the appearance of a permanent scowl. The old wound identified him as a follower of the fire goddess, Jalaana, whose temple dominated Zolene, the small town of his birth.

Lord Hanara hired him from time to time for the special abilities afforded him by his fire goddess.

She stood amongst the game's rowdy onlookers, waiting patiently while Silovik tossed the dice against the side of a small crate. The twin cubes bounced off the structure and rattled to a stop before a small pile of silver coins. Silovik and half of the crowd erupted in cheers at the outcome of the throw, while the others groaned in disappointment.

"Nice doing business with you!" Silovik said enthusiastically, scooping up the coins.

While pocketing his winnings, he looked up and saw Lau standing there with a weak smile of recognition. Their eyes locked and he nodded at her.

"Alright boys, time for a new shooter," he announced, rising to his feet. "I'm out."

"What the fuck are you talking about?!" a large dockworker, with thick muscled arms and short brown hair, protested above his fellow gamblers' exasperated grumbles. "You got to give me a chance to win my money back!"

Silovik ignored the protest and stepped over to Lau who led him beyond the gambling crowd.

"Well, if it isn't the unflappable Mz. Lau," he cheerfully greeted. "I'm guessing our mutual friend wants to see me?'

"Well, I certainly didn't come here to play dice," Lau said with a smirk. "It looks like you're on a roll."

"Eh, I needed some pocket change for the cycle and these folks were happy to oblige."

"Apparently all but one," she noted watching the upset gambler approaching.

"Hey!" the angry loser interrupted, stepping up behind Silovik. "I said you weren't going anywhere until I get the chance to win back my money!"

He then violently grabbed Silovik by the shoulder and attempted to spin him. Screaming in pain, the irate gambler recoiled his hand the instant he latched on.

He stepped back and continued shrieking while examining his badly burnt palm. His normally coffee brown skin turned bright red and already started blistering badly.

"What the fuck did you do to my hand?!" he thundered, clutching his wrist.

With the game now dispersed, the onlookers apprehensively backed away.

"Shh," Silovik said, putting a forefinger over his lips while stepping up to the wounded man. "You're upsetting my friend."

The man whimpered through his tightly clenched lips when Silovik reached out and touched the same forefinger to the man's lips just below the nose. The touch had the same effect as on his hands. An angry red mark now ran vertically across the center of his mouth. The man's eyes bulged in pain and he attempted to scream through fused lips. Horse, guttural, rasping sounds accompanied the cries of agony escaping the sides of his mouth.

"I told you to be quiet," Silovik calmly ordered, poking his forefinger at the man's forehead.

The force of the super-heated digit plunged through his skull down to the second knuckle. Silovik snapped his hand back, finger still extended, watching the gambler's face go blank and stop screaming. Steam from his boiling brain now escaped from his nose and mouth. The pressure ruptured the skull with a loud cracking sound and a foul-smelling burst of vapor from the top of his head.

The now dead protester teetered for a brief moment before toppling onto his back, staring blankly upward with a smoking, cauterized hole in the center of his forehead. The crowd panicked and scattered past Lau, who dispassionately examined the corpse on the deck before them.

"Now, as I was saying," she continued unfazed by the incident. "Our mutual friend is in need of your services. Which, I can see, are in good form."

"Always happy to help out our mutual friend," he responded, nodding at the body. "I guess we better trundle along. I appear to have worn out my welcome."

"Then there's the city guards, which should be along shortly," Lau said, turning to leave.

"That too," Silovik replied, moving off beside her.

It had been a mere nine cycles since Dolan Aramos seized the throne and declared himself sovereign. Since that time, House Aramos instituted sweeping changes throughout the cities and territories it governed. The militarization of the noble house being the single most noticeable change. They imposed an often-repressive military style of regimentation and discipline on the citizenry.

With military service now compulsory, soldiers became a constant presence everywhere. When children reached the age of fifteen, regardless of gender, they drafted them into a required minimum of two grands of service. This proved wildly unpopular amongst farmers and tradesmen relying on their children for labor and apprentices. These things, along with a bevy of new taxes and a mandatory census, did not make the new sovereign any friends.

And he didn't care.

All around the palace, and especially in the throne room, they carried out the business of the empire with systematic precision. Bespoke lords entered, saluted, gave their daily report, saluted again and rapidly exited. The next immediately came before their king and repeated the same procedure. The lords especially dreaded when the king asked questions. This usually meant something in the report displeased him or he sensed something amiss.

Hangings became the frequent and preferred method of disposing of anyone who dared upset the brutal new sovereign, especially the bespoke lords.

The Lord of Works was in the middle of his report and the Lord of Harbors waited to give his, when the doors flew open and Mundra, Lord of Currency and Shido, Lord of Seed rushed into the room. Dolan, who sat on his throne flanked by his Lord of Riddles and Lord of Words, angrily glared at the intrusion and break in protocol.

"What is the meaning of this?!" Dolan angrily bellowed.

The two bespoke lords hurried beside the Lord of Works and nervously saluted.

"Sire, we apologize for interrupting," Mundra said, his clean-shaven jaw trembling, "but there is a dire situation!"

The king's eyes narrowed. "Speak."

"Sire, it's the treasury. It's been changed."

"Changed? What do you mean changed?!"

"Sire, the gold has turned to lead," Mundra said. "The silver is now iron! They've been rendered worthless!"

Angry confusion washed over the ruler of House Aramos.

"My Sovereign," Shido added, her voice cracking in fear. "All the grain in storage has rotted."

Dolan now looked around wildly and sputtered, "What kind of alchemical treachery is this?!"

Naza, the Lord of Riddles, listened to the frightened Lord of Seed. His thin, clean-cut face, and sleepy yet sinister eyes, peered out thoughtfully from under his red fez.

'What about the grain in the fields?" he asked calmly.

"They are unharmed, Lord Naza."

Naza nodded, deep in thought.

"What is it Naza?!" the king demanded in a roar.

The Lord of Riddles raised a finger and stared into space. "A moment Your Majesty."

"Stored." He said in a low voice before addressing the room. "Everyone with a coin purse on them should check it now!"

97

Several in the room fumbled open their purses only to find their coins also converted.

"Your majesty, I believe whatever sorcery that is upon us only effects accumulated wealth. In whatever form it may be," Naza said with a confident nod.

"I want to know who did this and how! Most importantly' HOW DO WE FIX THIS!"

"We also need to know how far reaching this is," Naza said, keeping his composed demeanor. "With your permission Sire?"

Dolan waved him on, face creased in worry.

"Send gulls to the other houses," Naza ordered one of the two of the runners by the door. "See if they too are affected."

"I shall draft the request immediately," the Lord of Words said, getting up and saluting, before leaving with the runner.

"You, get over to the Imperial Bank," Naza ordered the other runner. "Bosco Savador is the most senior member of the Monetary Council. Marassa Hauts is the head of the School of Alchemic Studies at the university. Bring them both here."

Dolan Aramos called upon every ounce of martial discipline to fight back waves of panic.

He spoke in a low growl, "Whoever did this will…"

"If it indeed is a who, Sire," Naza interrupted. "This is powerful magic. If the other houses are also affected, we may be dealing with a *what*, not a who."

For the fifth time this moonless, the baby's kicking, and an overwhelming urge to urinate, awakened Taa-Je. She clumsily rolled onto her side, worked herself up on all fours and then pulled herself erect. With an exerted sigh at the now laborious act of standing, she rubbed her lower back and headed for a nearby tree.

Making sure the ground sloped away from her, Taa-Je put her back against the tree trunk, flicked her tail up to keep the spray from splashing back on her and slid down into a squat. She sighed with relief when the pressure on her bladder released but knew it would be short lived. She was well aware there would be several more calls of nature before the moon rose.

She listened to the liquid raining onto the ground and felt both relieved and concerned at the urine's scent. The pheromones she smelled indicated the baby was healthy, but the odor would leave an unmistakable trail for any pursuers.

Taa-Je had just finished and was sliding back up the trunk to her feet when she heard the rustling of the bushes and three dull thuds from where she had been sleeping. She froze and pressed herself against the tree, her heart pounding.

"She was right here! Where did she go?" a surprised female voice called out in Singa.

"She couldn't have gotten far," a second female replied. "Her pack is still here."

The Sikari had found her. She took a small bit of comfort that the simple act of peeing had saved her from being ambushed. Now it would be up to her to survive.

She quietly slid back down the trunk, retrieved a footlong stick from the tree's exposed roots and came back to her feet. Careful not to extend her arm out from behind her cover, she tossed the switch into the undergrowth to her right. As expected, the broken branch crashed through the foliage.

The Singa's went immediately silent and Taa-Je heard the two of them softly padding in the sound's direction. Listening intently, her Tiikeri senses determined they would pass right by her location.

Taa-Je would have much preferred just slipping away, but she knew she couldn't outrun them in her condition. She had to engage them and the only way which stood any chance of success would be if she could reverse the ambush on them.

Keeping as close to the tree as possible, she waited. A brief moment passed as she listened to the sounds of their footfalls drawing near. She heard them split up in different directions as they went around the tree.

The one on the right appeared first.

Without waiting Taa-Je lashed out, raking her claws downward with all her strength and using gravity to her advantage. Her much more powerful Tiikeri claws opened up five jagged wounds down the entire front of the startled Singa. It roared and yelped in agony before dropping to the forest floor.

Before Taa-Je could turn to get her back to the tree she felt a sharp pain in her upper back and realized one of the other's throwing knives struck her. She extended her left arm, claws out, and slashed across the torso of the second Singa, just as it prepared to launch another blade at her.

The momentum of the spin, and the force of the blow, opened up the Sikari's chest, propelling her six feet away into a thick patch of thorn bushes.

Taa-Je slumped down and unsuccessfully tried to reach the small blade in the middle of her upper back. Her chest heaved and she felt drained of energy. When the adrenaline finally subsided, and her breath returned to normal, she picked up her pack. Summoning her strength, she set off with the blade still lodged in her.

There was no sleeping now. She needed to keep moving.

Long Snout paused, began panting and raised his furry hand. He then crouched down and sniffed the ground furiously. The man-wolf's humanoid features subtly blended with his mostly canine appearance. Long whiskers, flanking his primarily hairless face and extended muzzle, twitched as he inspected the area for any olfactory anomalies.

The other four Onay in the scouting party felt fortunate that Long Snout led them. True to his name, this master tracker's snout was longer than most, giving him a distinct improvement over their race's already keen sense of smell.

The patrol then followed suit, dropping down on all fours, with tails lowered and the hair on their backs bristling, nervously peering around the crystalline forest for any signs of movement.

Refracted moonlight danced about the white surface of the ankle-deep, fresh powdered snow. They looked past the light show and saw no tracks. Long Snout sniffed the air and, sensing nothing, gave the signal and the pack resumed its wary trek.

Long Snout of the Bari Horde felt justified in his caution. They were patrolling in the thin strip of neutral territory separating their horde from the neighboring, and much larger, Kaler Horde.

They made it another thirty yards when they all heard a slow rhythmic crunch of snow and a low chant ahead on their right. Flattening themselves out against the trees, they spotted three Bailians in black robes slowly plodding through the snow.

Two undead Onay ambled along, with vacant stares, on either side of the Bailians. One of the revenant's chests was cleaved completely open, revealing dried up internal organs.

Long Snout recognized them immediately as Ghorn necromancers traveling between Darwain villages. The Ghorn served as shamans to the simple sentients, especially for their death rituals. The unidentifiable, reanimated Onay had obviously died in combat and the Ghorn needed some unthinking muscle.

Long Snout sensed the eagerness of his pack to ambush the unsuspecting procession but knew they didn't dare. Secrecy and stealth were this patrol's mandate. The three skulls suspended from the lead Ghorn's belt also told Long Snout that this was a high priest, capable of some pretty potent death magic. If they did attack, it was doubtful they would emerge from the conflict unscathed.

No, they would let them pass.

When the Ghorn were directly parallel to them, the air became electric, causing the Onay's fur to stand and skin tingle. The Ghorn felt it too because they stopped and looked around uncertainly.

Up ahead, two tall, purple crystal trees flared into a brilliant blue light, which quickly began strobing. Follqwed by streamers of blue lightning easily spanning and filling the thirty-foot distance between trunks.

Both Onay and Ghorn shielded their eyes from the crackling curtain of energy. Long Snout considered running, when the *Haraka* burst from the portal, crashing through the Etheria trees. The collision sprayed shards of semiprecious stones over the entire area. The projectiles made swooshing sounds when they plunged into the snow and several shattered on the crystal trees with a sharp ringing.

Both parties watched in wonder as the strange object sped past them and halted in a small clearing. The *Haraka* then turned so it faced them and settled to the ground.

Long Snout was torn as whether to run for their horde's territory or stay and observe this genuine curiosity. He decided to stay when the side hatch dropped and several strange creatures, the likes of which they had never seen before, stepped out.

The leaders looked like Bailians enough to form a frame of reference. The main difference was their skin was a golden brown. Having never seen an EEtah or Singa before, he had nothing to compare them to.

So, the camp tales of the strange creatures in the flying den were true, he mused in wonder.

One of the leaders, a female, placed her hands on her hips and gazed over at both the Onay and the Ghorn groups.

"Don't be shy, boys," she said. "Come on out, we need to talk."

Both Ghorn and Onay were completely taken aback that they both heard her in their own languages.

"You really need to quit fucking around," she said, a touch irritated when neither party complied. "We are all running out of time!"

Slowly, both sides approached the airship, eyeing the other suspiciously. When they got within thirty feet, the Onay began growling and the Ghorn hissed back their menacing reply. Mal shook her head and loudly exhaled.

"Why does it always come down to dick measuring?" she asked Zau, standing beside her.

Mal didn't wait for a response and stepped in between the two combative groups.

"Alright!" Mal said in a commanding voice. "I know in the past your peoples haven't gotten along…"

Immediately both sides launched into a litany of grievances. The tension grew with each complaint.

"HEY! LOOK. I DON'T GIVE A FUCK ABOUT YOUR PROBLEMS!" The Spice Rat's outburst quieted the groups, and they began grumbling under their breath.

"The fact is there's a shitstorm at your doorstep. If you don't work together, and I mean fast, you're all going to be subjects of the Tiikeri Empire!"

"The Bari Horde is subject to no one!" Long Snout bloviated.

Mal gave another annoyed sigh and eyed the defiant man-wolf. With a frustrated grimace she pointed over her shoulder to Lazio's seven-foot frame.

"See him?" she asked. "Imagine an army of them!"

On cue, the male Singa let out a deafening roar, which echoed through the crystal trees, causing both sides to cringe.

"They're coming to take this land," Mal said, pointing at both groups. "*Your* land. So, let's beat them together. Then, you can go back to killing each other all you want."

"If what you say is true," the Ghorn high priest asked skeptically, pointing at Lazio, "how do we defeat an army of those?"

"By fighting smart," Mal answered, grinning deviously. "That's where we come in."

In his twenty-five grands of service to House Whitmar, Merin Wolff witnessed and committed too many atrocities to count. As a boy of thirteen, he survived a slave revolt on his family's plantation, which left his parents dead and the left side of his face hideously scarred. At sixteen, he began working in the slave markets of Nier, eventually becoming a runaway slave hunter and finally a fixer for the noble house.

With all the awfulness he had experienced, Merin thought he had seen it all. He was wrong.

Merin heard cries of pain and anguish the moment he exited the carriage and stood at the guarded doorway to Addoon Prison. Two sentries nodded their greeting and one opened the door. Merin entered into a scene of chaos, with prison staff rushing around the central courtyard in a panic.

They divided the prison into two distinct areas. The west wing housed the Indentures in the minimum-security area, with its relaxed, almost comfortable furnishings and minimal guards. The east wing held the punishment slaves in the maximum-security area, heavily fortified with bars and guards. The temporary residents of both areas were all bound for the auction block.

"Where's the boss?" Merin asked a clerical worker with a frightened expression.

"Lord and Lady Whitmar are over in the max side! This is terrible, just terrible!" she exclaimed before hurrying off.

The Whitmar agent took a deep breath and passed the guards through the heavy iron door. He couldn't help but notice the unnerved look on their faces. Once inside, the wailing and crying grew almost deafening.

The normally unflappable Merin Wolff looked on in horror and disgust while he passed the cells. Something had reduced every prisoner into boneless piles of flesh, still alive but in great torment.

His boss and spymaster, Kacha Whitmar, stood staring into one of the cells flanking the wide hall up ahead. Her thin body coiled with tenseness and her normally beautiful features formed a scowl, accentuated by her bald head.

She spoke to her brother, the warden of Addoon, and family slave master, Clayton Whitmar. He brushed back strands of his shoulder length black hair and Merin could make out a distinct frown beneath his thick beard. Both Whitmar siblings broke off their conversation at his approach and looked up with grim expressions.

"What in the name of the gods happened here?" Merin asked, staring through the bars at the limp piles of skin looking back helplessly and moaning in agony.

"It happened during the Kan," Kacha said, her face tightened with anger. "Their bones just dissolved, leaving them like this."

"This is going to cost us millions," Clayton lamented.

"You need to find who did this and terminate them with extreme prejudice," Kacha ordered tersely.

Merin nodded his acceptance of the mission unable to take his eyes off the formless bodies.

"I've got a pretty good idea where to start," Wolff announced confidently. "I'm headed back to Zor. There's a certain economist cleric I need to pay a call on."

Supreme General Jal-Pi got a bad feeling when he entered King Kar-Gor's chambers and saw him conferring with Raa-Ja in hushed tones, while absentmindedly batting around a dazed, fawn-colored, mongrel slave. The king's playful assaults had already cut the unfortunate prisoner in multiple places and blood now matted its fur.

Jal-Pi couldn't care less about the condemned mongrel. They set aside a certain portion of the criminals captured for the king's amusement. What troubled him was the priest's close proximity to the monarch. It seemed the High Priest of Pa-Waga sank his claws of control deeper into the Tiikeri ruler every luna. They both halted their private conversation and silently watched Jal-Pi cross the throne room.

"Your majesty, I have good news," the general said, after shooting Raa-Ja a contemptuous glance. "We just received word by Ash-Ta messenger. They've taken the first oasis and General Baag-Tarr advances on the second."

"That is indeed good news," King Kar-Gor replied, backhanding the mongrel in the face and breaking its nose.

"A fitting accompaniment to the birth of your son, Your Majesty," the general congratulated.

"I, too, have good news!" the king exuberantly said, taking another swipe at the teetering victim. "And our most recent victory tells me that my decision is a righteous one."

The general bristled at the king's religious terminology but remained silent.

"I have decided to have the Cub Prince baptized into the service of Pa-Waga. Furthermore, I will decree Pa-Waga to be the only form of worship allowed within the empire. All must convert or face expulsion."

The general stood in stunned silence, flabbergasted by the news. "Sire, are you sure that is a wise decision? The people, especially the nobles, will not like being told how to worship. How can it even be enforced?"

"His majesty will direct a portion of the military under my command as Piety Watch," Raa-Ja proclaimed triumphantly.

"Your majesty!" Jal-Pi gasped. "I would respectfully disagree with such an action! Our forces are engaged at this time. Any change in plans could be catastrophic!"

"Come now, Jal-Pi," the king replied flippantly, playfully smacking the mongrel on its back sending it lurching forward, "don't be so dramatic. The Piety Watch won't be mobilized until after we conclude our current operation."

"Sire, it shouldn't be mobilized at all," the general pleaded. "Militarizing zealotry is never a good idea."

The king's expression turned angry hearing the general's protest. He seized his wounded, living toy by the throat with one hand, grabbed the top of its head with his other and twisted, snapping its neck with a crack. With a sneer back at Jal-Pi, he casually tossed the dead mongrel aside.

"Be careful with your words and tone Jal-Pi," the king's tone went icy. "We go back a long way. You were one of those that put me on the throne, but I won't stand for insubordination."

"My apologies, Sire."

"Think of the possibilities," the king said, turning conciliatory. "With Pa-Waga as our guide, success in this operation will continue, and with control of the Etheria, our dominance of the Annigan is assured. This will be the legacy for my son. Under His rule, the Tiikeri banner will fly over every part of the Annigan and Pa-Waga will ensure its prosperity. We serve a mighty god!"

"We serve a mighty god!" Raa-Ja enthusiastically repeated.

"Don't look so glum, Jal-Pi," The king said. "A great triumph will soon be ours. Go and make it happen. Report back when we have achieved our next victory."

"Yes, Your Majesty," Jal-Pi said, all the while seething inside at Raa-Ja's gloating smile.

The Grand Turine in the Zorian harbor rang nineteen times and the two Farak Sunal EEtahs standing outside the Capital Pub watched the stragglers of the late breakfast crowd meander out into the busy street. The morning bustle of activity clattered and hummed all around them. Wagons full of merchandise and produce passed in both directions to and from the docks.

Luft's nostrils twitched when he sniffed the air and caught the smell from the nearby fish market.

"Hey Naggy," the ten-foot-tall man-shark said, stomach growling, "after the job let's get a bite before we report back."

Nagrada huffed, and continued searching the passing crowds, refusing to look at his partner.

"Come on, Naggy, you're not still mad are ya?"

"You cost us our bonus on that last job! What do you think?!"

"The bounty said dead or alive, and I was hungry!"

"Yeah, well that was one expensive meal."

"And he didn't even taste all that good," Luft admitted, pouting.

"Look, we gotta keep our head in the game if we ever hope to go independent," Nagrada admonished, finally looking at his repentant man-shark partner.

The chastised EEtah gazed meekly downward.

"I know," Luft said, sounding defeated. "I'm sorry, Naggy."

"Remember, concentrate on the mission. No adlibbing!"

"I will, Naggy."

Nagrada shook his head in frustration, then straightened up when he saw Merin Wolff moving through the crowd in their direction.

"Alright, here he comes. Remember what I told you."

"I will, Naggy."

Wolff walked briskly, his eyes narrow slits. He stopped and glared upwards at the much taller humanoid sharks.

"Is he still in there?"

"Uh... yes, sir," Nagrada replied. "There're only a few other patrons at the bar. He's the only one left in the dining room."

"Yeah, we made sure," Luft said with a weak grin.

Merin critically assessed the man-shark with a sneer.

"What are you, some kind of idiot?"

Luft's innocent smile transformed back into a pout. "No."

Merin sighed deeply and shook his head.

"Alright, let's get this done," he ordered. "If you don't screw up, you can eat the body afterward."

Luft immediately perked up. "Oh goody, I was just telling Naggy here that I was kinda hungry."

Wolff shot Nagrada an irritated, questioning look before reaching for the door handle.

"Everything on my command only," the Whitmar agent ordered, stepping inside the pub.

The trio paused for their eyes to adjust to the considerably dimmer light within. The dining area contained a dozen tables and Wolff noticed a bar serving an adjoining room.

Luft's stomach grumbled again at the smell of the food being prepared in the kitchen, but, remembering his partner's warning, he managed to stay focused.

Wolff's eyes locked on the only other patron. A young man casually dining at a table in the corner. Merin drew his pistol crossbow and held it behind him, leading the two EEtah's across the room to the only occupied table.

"You're the one called Banavor?" he gruffly asked.

The young man, who didn't acknowledge their approach, finally stopped eating.

"I don't know how they do it," he replied staring at the plate of partially eaten food. "The venison has absolutely no gamy taste." He then gestured at the plate with his knife. "And that garlic sauce they used is to absolutely die for!"

Wolff raised the pistol and pointed it at Banavor who had calmly resumed eating.

"Speaking of dying," Wolff said, pulling back the bolt. "Are you Banavor?"

The young man stopped and demurely dabbed his mouth with a napkin, before slowly facing the menacing threesome.

"Well, seeing how you're pointing a weapon at me, the sensible thing to say would be, no," the young man said thoughtfully, while sucking on a tooth. "However…

His face brightened seeing the EEtah. "Oh my! You know, this is the first time I've been in close proximity to an EEtah. And I must say, you two are very impressive!"

"Aww, thanks," Luft said, blushing.

Nagrada threw Luft a dirty look and Wolff scowled at the interruption. "I asked you a fucking question!"

Banavor's attention snapped back to Wolff. "Well, there's no reason to be rude. Yes, I *am* Banavor. I imagine you're here because of some perceived infraction on my part?"

"You destroyed House Whitmar's slaves that were headed to market!" Wolff growled. "That little stunt cost my house millions."

Banavor cast a surprised look at the Whitmar agent before returning to his meal. "Don't be absurd, why would I destroy a commodity worth so much. Mine is a god of prosperity and profit, not destruction. They're merely in an inoperative state until the Zorian Monetary Council comes to their senses. Rest assured they'll be restored."

"You expect me to believe that?!"

"I *do* serve a mighty god," Banavor casually said, before taking another bite.

"Well, get ready to meet him."

Banavor sighed, dabbed his mouth again, and addressed the EEtahs. "Whatever he's paying you, I'll double it."

Wolff began to laugh at the offer.

"That's not the way it works, moron," he gloated. "They're under contract to me and…"

Luft suddenly leaned over and bit Wolff's head off, cutting short his self-confident monologue. He ripped it away from the body with a wet tearing sound.

Nagrada spun, his eyes bulging in wide-eyed horror. The EEtah bounty hunter's mouth dropped open, unable to utter a word. Luft spit the head of the Whitmar agent at the feet of a grinning Banavor. It bounced, rolling several times, before coming to rest staring vacantly at the ceiling.

"Pay up," Luft said expectantly.

"WHAT IN THE NAME OF THE GODS!" Nagrada thundered when he finally found his voice.

Luft gave an awkward grin and shrugged. "You said you wanted to go independent. Just think Naggy, he could be our first client."

Wolff's body miraculously still stood upright, erupting fountains of blood over the EEtahs, as well as the surrounding floor and tables. Nagrada could only stand and stare, silently in shock, while being showered in a veritable monsoon of blood.

"You're welcome," Luft said innocently.

When Wolff's headless body finally toppled over, Banavor dispassionately watched it fall and then glanced back up at the EEtahs with a pleasantly surprised smile.

"You're hired."

The cloying stench of desperation hung over the dining hall of Castle Volga. Rahil Booshka saw it etched in the sour expressions of the seven other fallen river lords seated around the table debating their next course of action. They needed to come up with a viable plan or the Lords of the Western Fork would be no more.

Rahil's daughter, Mérges, held an animated discussion with Sani Volga across the wide table. The former Sorbornef listened intently while her hot-headed offspring gesticulated wildly. Sani's husband, the always quiet Arn Volga, sat beside them. His clean-shaven, youthful features highlighted the intensity radiating in his eyes, as they darted back and forth following the two young women's conversation.

Midas Kenyev and Gregor Vladof sat across from each other at the heads of the table, engaged in equally boisterous dialogue. Rahil marveled at the similarities in their appearances. Both shared olive skin, dark hair and unkept beards, with Gregor's wild bulging eyes and curly hair the main distinction between the two.

The hulking, six-foot-four Max Donyeb silently took note of their conversation. His fair complexion complimented his short blonde hair and beard.

The Volga patriarch, Pablov took in the verbal maelstrom while stroking his grey goatee. Rahil respected Pablov Volga, as they were two of the most senior river lords, evidenced by their heads full of silver hair.

Pablov rapped loudly on the head of the table with the pummel of his dagger attempting to get the meeting in order.

"Noble lords," he said, firmly but calmly. "Now is not the time for bickering. Unless we band together and agree on what is to be done, we're…"

"Haven't you heard?" Gregor interrupted. "We're no longer noble lords! That puff boy of a king saw to that!"

The wild-eyed river lord stood, drew his dagger and sneered. "I'd like to carve on that pretty face of his, then cut off his balls!"

Pablov threw a disappointed look in his direction. "And there may come a day when you get to do just that, but for now, we need a more workable plan."

The enraged Gregor Vladof huffed frustratedly, plunging his blade into the table before sitting down.

"Perhaps if we sent an envoy to the king," Rahil coolly offered. "Express remorse for our actions and give assurances that…"

"That's just like you, Rahil!" Midas Kenyev said, suddenly cutting her off. "Attempting to negotiate from a place of weakness. It's no wonder your wharfs are barely on the western fork. You're hardly one of us!"

Mérges Booshka bolted to her feet and angrily pointed a finger at the Kenyev patriarch. The fiery red bandana she always wore perfectly framed the indignant look on her face.

"You don't talk to my mother like that!" she yelled. "She's every bit a Lord of the Western Fork as you, you smug bastard!"

"Noble lords," Pablov pleaded. "It is this kind of in-fighting that is getting us nowhere. Now, we have to the end of the next quinte to think of something. I suggest we get this council moving in a more productive direction. We now have a proposal on the table from House Booshka. Is there any constructive discussion?"

"After the Dreeat incident last quinte, the crown will never go for it," Sani Volga said, shaking her head.

"An incident started by *your* father and older brother," Midas Kenyev snipped.

"An incident that *you* enthusiastically joined!" Sani coldly countered. "My family paid for their actions with their lives. *You* however, seemed to have come through it rather, *unscathed.*"

"Are you calling me a coward?!"

Sani remained unflustered. "You may take it any way you wish, Lord Kenyev."

Max Donyeb's massive frame rising to his feet interrupted the looming conflict between the two. "Mmmy ffamily hhhas bbben hhere for tthousands of of of gggrands. Iii'm nnot ggoing aany wwwhere!"

"As have all of our families," the elder Volga replied. "The question is, what do we do?"

Gregor Vladof defiantly rose once again, pulled his dagger from the table and waved it in front of him. "Fuck the empire. I say we stand and fight for our lands!"

"Yeah, fuck the empire!" both Mérges Booshka and Midas Kenyev said in unison.

The statement and subsequent cries of approval caused Pablov and Rahil to trade concerned stares from the opposite ends of the table.

"Together?" Arn Volga warily asked, finally speaking up.

"Iii aand mmy people wwwill wwill will ffffight with yyou!"

"And then what?" Pablov asked, looking around the table.

"There is no reason the Lords of the Western Fork cannot rule themselves!" Sani Volga replied.

"You do realize what we're talking about here?" Pablov warned. "Taking on House Eldor and their allies is what some would call suicidal."

"What choice do we have?!" Gregor asked, spittle spraying from his mouth, accentuating his wild-eyed appearance. "They are taking everything from us!"

"What about the Dreeat?" Rahil pensively asked.

"Fuck them, too!" Sani spat.

"So, you're proposing we take on both House Eldor and the Dreeats?" Pablov asked skeptically. "As I recall, that didn't end well last time."

"This time we will all be united, not just a few houses!" Sani boldly said, sweeping her outstretched arm around the table. "And, as for allies, I know where hundreds perhaps thousands may be found. Powerful allies."

Rahil gave a questioning look. "Exactly what allies might you be referring to?"

A sinister smile played at the corners of Sani's lips. "The new lord of Staghorn wants to be a river lord. Let him prove his worth. We cannot fail with an army of cat creatures fighting by our sides!"

This proposal set off a chain of nervous chattering around the table.

"You've certainly changed your tune about the Tiikeri," Pablov said, with a touch of irony.

"That was all before the royal decree revoked our charters. Desperate times call for desperate measures!"

"Hhhhow dddo wwwe eeeven kknow if the the the Tttiikeri wwwill hhhelp us?"

"In this case," Rahil explained, "the Tiikeri have just as much to lose as the rest of us."

"So, it's agreed then," Pablov confirmed. "We break with house Eldor and throw our lot in with the Tiikeri Empire."

Taa-Je awoke with a start to screams of pain, the likes of which she had never heard before. The short, anguished squeal set off a torrent of panicked squeaks and grunts.

She determined that the moon had risen a short time ago by its position in the sky. She was sleeping on a makeshift bed of straw, just outside of a round, open sided, Singa style, communal hut.

Peeking outside the hut, she saw the commotion came from a pen full of adult pigs, scrambling about their confines in absolute terror. The reason for the swine's trepidation hung lifelessly from the low branch of a nearby tree. A mongrel family of three had slaughtered one of the swine's numbers and now rent open the carcass and ravenously feasted on its flesh.

The pig farm! She recalled staggering upon it in the middle of the moonless just before passing out.

She slowly sat up and took in her surroundings. Several pens encircled the hut. The pen next to the one nearest her contained three nursing mothers and a dozen piglets suckling away voraciously. The other held several females ready for mating. Even though Taa-Je considered this beneath her, she understood the numerous small farms like this across the countryside supplied valuable meat for the Tiikeri society.

She had fled beyond the rainforests of the Dasos region and made it to the border of the rolling foothills of the Kel-Raku Mountains. Her destination, the Unaligned City of Shun-Dra, lies just to the north. She may be closer, but now she no longer had the forest to hide her escape.

The mother mongrel, a fawn colored with white spotted fur, seeing that Taa-Je was awake, tore off one of the slaughtered pig's front legs. The mawl approached slowly and knelt down beside the seated Tiikeri.

"You must be hungry," she said, offering her the morsel with a bloody smile.

"Yes, thank you," Taa-Je answered, accepting the severed leg.

"I am called Permeri," she said, watching Taa-Je tear into the flesh. "That is my mate, Boer, and our son, Nwoke. You were in quite the state when you arrived last moonless."

Boer left his feast and made his way over to them. Larger than the average mongrel at just under six feet tall, his broad muscular shoulders and dark grey fur appeared menacing, as did the scowl on his face. He gruffly jerked his head back towards the meal. Permeri looked down meekly, stood and promptly moved away.

Taa-Je stopped eating and stared up at the glowering mongrel father. She took an immediate dislike of him and fought to contain any snide comments to the lesser creature looming over her.

"My mate took you in because she has a kind heart," he said coldly.

He then tossed a small object beside the Tiikeri. Taa-Je looked down to see the sickle shaped throwing blade.

"I pulled this out of your back shortly after your arrival," he added accusatorily. "Why do the Sikari hunt you?"

Taa-Je remained silent and met his critical stare with one of condescension.

"You don't have to answer," he said, glancing at her belly. "The new Cub Prince was just born. And now, a pregnant Tiikeri shows up with a Sikari blade in her. I'm not stupid! Did you think you were the only king's consort who wanted to keep their child?"

Taa-Je stayed defiantly quiet.

"You will bring nothing but trouble to my home," Boer growled, sneering. "As soon as you are able to travel, I want you gone!"

The moon would soon set over the Tiikeri capital of Hai-Darr and Raa-Ja still had much to do. The Yagur High Priest of Pa-Waga exited the throne room with a purposeful stride and a firm confidence that soon the entire empire would dwell within the bountiful bosom of the lord. There were still obstacles, like the generals, but the king pledged his son and his people to the holy cause. What could a few, admittedly high ranking, mawls possibly do to stand in his way?

The answer to his internal question came when he turned the next corner and found his path blocked by two large male Singas in military tunics. He abruptly halted and eyed the imposing mawls suspiciously and his tail twitched in annoyance.

"What's this?" he impatiently asked. "Stand aside!"

The two lion-men said nothing but continued to stare menacingly. Raa-Ja felt the fur rise on his back and was about to make a second demand when he sensed a presence behind him. He spun and came face to face with two more Singas, identical to the ones in front of him.

Now trapped, the dark cleric felt a touch of panic rise and his throat went dry.

"I thought we might have a word away from his majesty's presence," came Jal-Pi's voice out of one of the many doorways on his left. The Tiikeri general stepped confidently into view, a condescending scowl on his face.

"I have nothing to say to you," Raa-Ja spat.

"That's alright, I'll do the talking," Jal-Pi said, stepping up to the high cleric. "You may have the king's ear right now but make no mistake. I risked my life to save the empire and put him on the throne. I have no intention of allowing it to fall into the hands of you and your dark god."

"Dark god," the Yagur repeated mockingly. "His majesty was right. You do have a flair for drama."

Jal-Pi gave an evil chuckle.

"I'm warning you, *priest*," the general said in a low threatening growl. "Back off from the king and his family."

"Or what?!"

The Tiikeri Supreme General locked eyes with Raa-Ja and just gave an ominous smile. Winking, he stepped around the Yagur and walked away with his men following.

Taleeka found herself bored.

She had spent a good portion of the morning practicing her knife drills and missed her mom and dad's presence.

The crew had split up their duties in preparing the Barrens for invasion.

Alto and Mal conferred with the Ghorn. The youngster knew her dad hated the Onay for what they did to his dog, Defari. Her mom, knowing full well Alto's vengeful side, had wisely assigned him to deal with the foul smelling Bailian death priests. Taleeka scrunched her face and wiggled her nose at the thought of the necromancer's odor.

Zaad and Lazio taught the wolf people how to fight sneaky. She knew this contained its own difficulties because she saw that the Onay tended to growl before an attack.

Zau and Kumo stayed with the ship, as usual, protecting and maintaining it.

Now, before bugging Zau into giving her her daily lesson in the mawl language, the precocious ten-grand-old decided to stretch her legs. After stern warnings from the lioness against straying beyond Kumo's web perimeter, she slipped past the sleeping spider-woman and out the side hatch.

The air felt cold and snow crunched under her feet. The white flakes glistened across Kumo's web suspended between the crystal trees ten yards away from the ship. She wandered around the *Haraka's* security perimeter, taking in the strange landscape devoid of any vegetation.

Taleeka made it to the far side of the ship when an unusual sound from the forest beyond got her attention. It appeared to come from just inside the tree line and consisted of quite a few angry squeaks, punctuated by growls and yelps of pain.

She listened for a brief moment before her curiosity got the best of her. Cutting a small slit in the webbing near the ground, she crawled out and made her way over to the source of the noise. Approaching the trees, she heard what sounded like a conflict of some sort, so she slowed her gate to a more cautious pace and drew her weapon.

Just inside the border of trees in a clearing, a pack of a dozen mice, no more than two inches long, were attacking a small furry creature. It looked young and measured about two feet in length. Long, honey brown hair covered its entire body with the exception of its slightly humanoid face. Large round eyes, that Taleeka could easily find endearing, squinted in rage. Two-pointed ears, resembling horns, poked out from the fur on the top of its head. A mouth filled with long sharp teeth gnashed at its miniature attackers.

Several dead mice lay around her bleeding in the snow and staining the formidable claws on her feet red. It surprised Taleeka she could actually feel the waves of fear, pain and anger radiating from the creature as tactile sensations.

Its several bleeding wounds filled her with concern. An overwhelming feeling of empathy for the outnumbered animal washed over her and she decided to act.

She stepped up to the embattled creature and brought her knife down quickly two times, severing in half as many mice. Then, using the flat of the blade, she roughly swept at the other four, sending them flying.

When Taleeka killed two more, the remaining attackers quickly scattered. She then felt the small beast's aura shift and anger gave way to a guarded curiosity at the human who had come to her aid.

Taleeka sheathed her knife, knelt and began to speak in a soothing tone. She still could feel the animal's pain and knew it would be unwise to approach.

"Hi there," she said, extending her hand. "That sure was scary."

She felt the animal's anxiety slowly recede, while its nose twitched furiously. "It's okay. You're safe now."

When it started inching closer, Taleeka made sure to stay still and calm. By the time it finally reached her outstretched hand, she felt its wet nose on her fingertips and smiled.

"See, everything's going to be okay," she soothed, feeling the last traces of fear depart the creature.

A smooth tongue slipped out from between its thin lips and licked Taleeka's hand. It then leaned forward and nuzzled its neck on her fingertips. Using small gentle strokes, the young girl scratched the side of its neck each time the creature nuzzled against her.

Finally, it moved closer, and leaning against her, it began to whimper in pain. Taleeka reached down and picked the animal up, making sure not to touch any of its wounds.

'Come on," she said, rising to her feet. "Let's get you looked at."

The wounded creature buried its head in the folds of Taleeka's arms and continued moaning during the short walk back to the ship. When she entered the *Haraka,* the animal poked its head out and looked around at the different surroundings but remained calm.

"What ya got there, kid?" Zau said, getting up from her navigator's chair.

"I heard a noise on my walk and when I went to check it out, I found her... I think it's a her... being attacked by all these mean mice, and I made them leave her alone, but she's hurt and I thought we could help." Taleeka finally took a breath and peered up at the Singa with a pleading look.

Zau smiled understandingly and leaned in for a closer inspection. "Let's see what we've got here."

When the lioness' head got within two feet, the creature suddenly came to life in Taleeka's arms. It violently lunged at Zau, growling and snapping its jaws.

"Woah!" The startled Singa jumped back, raising her hands defensively.

"Shh, it's okay," Taleeka comforted, stroking its neck.

The animal calmed immediately and resumed its soft whining.

"I've got an idea," Zau said.

She walked back up to the command chairs, reached under Mal's seat and removed a single brown ball from a bag of Dreeat confections.

"Here," she said, placing it in the seat next to Taleeka. "She probably doesn't need to eat a whole one. Rub your fingers on it and let her lick it off."

Taleeka did as suggested, and when offered, it sniffed her fingers, before slowly licking the film off them. With each pass of its tongue, the whining gradually diminished until its eyelids grew heavy and it fell asleep, snoring in her arms.

Taleeka looked back up at Zau with an accomplished smile. "I'm going to call her Maddy!"

Oh, the Captain is just going to love this, the Singa thought, returning the smile.

Taa-Je could hear them arguing about her. From the snippets she caught, Boer seemed adamant, she was awake and able to take in nourishment. He wanted her gone, *now*. Permeri staunchly favored letting her stay, at least until the next luna.

The argument rapidly heated up, with hisses and high-pitched growls. Taa-Je feared something amiss when she heard Boer summon his son. She then watched Nwoke sprint away on all fours from the farm.

Taa-Je heard Boer grumbling, "I've got work to do!"

The mongrel pig farmer stormed past the pregnant Tiikeri, leering at her the entire time. He entered the pen beside her and led a pig away to the other side of the compound. A few moments later she heard it squeal and then go silent. She knew its fate.

Just then she heard the rumble of wagon wheels and saw Permeri driving a small lizard drawn wagon. It abruptly stopped beside her and Permeri leapt out.

"My single-minded mate has sent Nwoke to get the Sikari," she said in a rushed whisper. "Boer will be busy for a while butchering and smoking that pig. We've little time to lose."

The mongrel took Taa-Je's arm and helped her into the back of the wagon.

"You'll never make it to Shun-Dra on foot," she said, covering Taa-Je in hay. "Lay still and I'll have you there by moonfall."

Rahil Booshka caught the pungent smell of ammonia the moment the peaked roofline of Staghorn plantation came into view. Her lizard mount smelt it too and recoiled. It took a concerted effort to steady her mount and keep it moving forward towards the stench. Riding beside her, Merges had similar troubles steadying the beast beneath her.

"Mother, what is that awful smell?"

"Cat spray," Rahil replied, disgustedly.

Merges huffed loudly and shook her head. "And I thought the crocks were nasty."

"Looks like the new lord of Staghorn is making some changes," Pablov Volga said, riding just behind them.

A group of twenty long neck herd animals grazed in the adjoining cornfields. The strange looking creatures, with long brown fur and wide mouths full of thick blunt teeth, easily pulverized the fibrous stalks.

"What in the name of the gods are those?" Merges asked, staring in wonder.

"I don't know," Pablov answered.

They watched a bull sniff the hindquarters of a grazing female. He raised up on his back legs with a loud bellow and mounted the female. The bored object of his affections continued her chewing, totally ignoring the male pumping away behind her.

Approaching the stable, they saw movement inside through the wide-open doors. Instead of horses, several more herd animals milled about in the corral.

When they got within ten feet of the open doors Bo-Lah stepped out to greet them. Blood stained the orange Tiikeri's snout, hands and the front of his white blouse red. Inside the barn they could see the female Singas tearing into the carcass of one of the long-necked herbivores.

"Well, if it isn't the noble Lords of the Western Fork. What brings you to my humble plot of land?"

"It's not going to be your land for long," Pablov said firmly. "I trust you received the decree?"

"Oh yes, a royal herald came by a while ago, yammering on about revoking charters and the like. I don't see how it concerns me."

Pablov stared in disbelief. "The Sorbornef charter has been revoked. This land is going to be taken, by force if necessary, and given to the Dreeat."

Bo-Lah smiled confidently. "I am not a Sorbornef."

"You can use all the fancy word play you want," Rahil said, leaning forward in the saddle, "but the charter wasn't just for the Sorbornef name. It included the land granted by the king. If you think they're gonna let you stay, you're fooling yourself."

"Ah," Bo-Lah said, still showing little sign of interest. "What makes you think I haven't already made my own deal with the crown?"

"Because they're giving the land to the Dreeat," Pablov replied assertively. "They're not going to leave an area smack dab in the middle of croc country."

"I see," Bo-Lah said smugly. "It sounds like you're in quite the predicament."

"You're in it with us," Rahil said grimly, locking eyes with the Tiikeri.

Bo-Lah remained apparently unphased. "You have some thoughts on the matter I imagine, that *is* why you are here, is it not?"

"We're going to stay and fight for our lands!" Merges defiantly stated, shaking her fist.

The statement caused a knowing grin to spread across the Tiikeri's face. "Ah the brashness of youth."

"We all voted on it," Pablov confirmed.

"You really think you can stand up to your overlords and win?"

"With your help, yes," Rahil said, obviously beginning to tire of the banter.

"Finally, the answer to my original question," Bo-Lah said, sweeping his attention over the group. "I can appreciate your situation, but there is only myself, two Singas and the slaves that came along with the plantation. Hardly a force to be reckoned with."

"Don't play games with us!" Merges said, sneering. "We're talking about the armies of your homeland!"

Rahil reached out and gently touched her daughter's arm to calm her. The Tiikeri ignored the outburst and stared directly at Pablov.

"You are proposing an alliance with the Tiikeri Empire?"

"*Our* situation," Pablov corrected. "An alliance is possible, *if* they will help us keep our lands."

Bo-Lah's calm demeanor covered a growing excitement within. Securing a full enclave of the Tiikeri Empire in the heart of Lumina would ensure great honor upon him.

Bo-Lah contemplatively nodded his head. "At the risk of sounding mercenary, what's in it for me?"

"You would hold full status as an Otoman River Lord," Pablov replied officially.

The conversation paused, while both parties weighed the offer. Only the sound of growls and tearing flesh could be heard from inside the barn.

"A few cycles ago, your daughter-in-law seemed quite adamant that was never going to happen," Bo-Lah said to Rahil, sounding unconvinced.

"She had a change of heart," Pablov declared firmly.

Inside, Bo-Lah was already celebrating. This mission had now exceeded his wildest ambitions. Outside, the Tiikeri appeared calm and cautious.

"I want to hear that from her own lips, Lord Volga," he requested. "If she recants to me personally, we have a deal."

The moon slowly set over the Barrens until only the vast array of stars overhead illuminated the crystalline forest. Ten Gila Dolins, their bulging eyes independently rotating, darted between the shadowy trees in a crouch. They stealthily approached a lone stand of roughhewed, multi-colored towers of Etheria jutting from the snow. The seasoned Etheria hunters left the wagons away back so as not to alert the inhabitants.

Their leader, a six-foot tall Bailian-Gila hybrid named Hankap'Vor, motioned for the archers to take up positions. Four of the group nocked arrows and aimed them at the lone inhabitant of the stand, a seven-foot-tall bipedal creature slowly lumbering from one tower to the other, stopping and licking off the condensation.

An older one, Hankap'Vor thought. *This probably won't be easy.*

The Dolin leader felt justified in his caution. The E'Notts who called these Etheria towers home were some of the most magical creatures in the Twilight Lands. The hairless, blue skinned beings may be slow moving, docile and spend their lunas licking the condensation off large outcroppings of Etheria crystals, but this solitary diet allowed them to wield powerful defensive magic if threatened.

When the E'Nott made its way around a bronze-colored crystal tower, and turned its back to them, Hankap'Vor dropped his arm giving the signal to fire. Four projectiles sliced through the cold air. Two struck its upper back. The creature lifted its face skyward and bellowed in pain.

It spun towards the attackers, extended its arms palms facing outward and roared again, this time in anger. A wave of repulsing force immediately shot out from its palms. The blast knocked two of the archers violently to the ground, leaving them unconscious.

It propelled the third back against a tree, impaling him on a crystal branch. The pale blue Etheria shard jutted from his chest, contrasting starkly against the red blood gushing from the wound.

The fourth wisely ducked back behind a tree after his shot, dodging the force. During the magic strike, he had nocked another arrow, and when the shock wave passed, he quickly stepped from behind the tree and fired. The arrow struck the E'Nott in the head with a dull thump. It grunted and grabbed at the securely implanted projectile but couldn't dislodge it. It dropped to its knees, grunted again, and fell onto its back.

Hankap'Vor stood, sheathed his blade and looked around at their ill-gotten prize.

This is a good sized Etheria field, especially so close to the western shore, he pondered. *It could have easily supported a family of those creatures. No matter, it's a good haul. It'll easily support us.*

He watched the two archers get to their feet and his remaining crew of Gila's bring up the wagons.

They had just begun unpacking the two-person gem saws, when a loud guttural cry resounded from the surrounding trees. The strange call echoed off the hard surfaces and resonated through the forest.

The Gila Dolin grew suspicious and his team stopped working. Their omnidirectional, independent eyes peered around in confusion. Hankap'Vor had been an Etheria harvester for a long time and had run into just about every creature that called the Barrens home. This cry definitely belonged to some sort of unfamiliar beast.

When he saw rapid movement through the trees, he gave out a hiss of alarm and drew his sword. With the warning given, his men dropped their tools and brandished weapons.

Growling cries now surrounded them and the lizard steeds hitched to the wagons shifted about nervously. Their long tongues flicked furiously at strange smells.

"Secure those wagons and find cover," Hankap'Vor barked. "Archers at the ready!"

Before any could get to the wagons, one lizard panicked and broke for the trees with the empty wagon bouncing wildly behind it. The harnessed wagon smashed against the crystal trunks and shattered. The rapidly moving lizard disappeared into the forest. No sooner had the beast of burden vanished when its cries of pain echoed above the growling, then abruptly ceased.

The other two lizard steeds, spooked by the pandemonium, bucked wildly as their handlers attempted to control them. Several sickle-shaped, throwing blades shot out from the tree and embedded in the beasts. They briefly bucked about in agony, screeching wildly, before falling dead to the ground.

Concern, bordering on panic, painted the faces of Dolin's team. They looked about nervously, raising their weapons.

"Over there," one called out, spotting the first female Singa. "By the gods, they're cat people!"

The words had no sooner escaped his mouth than a sickle blade struck him squarely between the eyes. It rocked the stunned lizard man backwards into a spin and he toppled into the snow.

They didn't have time to assess a strategy, so the Gila archers just formed a quick defensive circle when they heard rumbling to the west. It grew louder, building to a thundering crescendo, until the forest filled with thousands of male Singa shock troops. The lion men ran on all fours, their mane's fluttering behind them.

The archers which managed to get off shots at the advancing army were shocked when, with the exception of headshots, their arrows only slowed and angered the wounded Singas. The frontline of shock troops leapt into a twenty-foot flying attack. Inch-long talons extended from their paws mid-air and they landed claws first on the archers. The shear impact rent heads and limbs from bodies.

The ones wielding swords cowered when the Singa's reared up on two legs to their full seven-foot height. They quaked, watching several hundred Singas surround them while the main body of the mawl army swept past them onto their next target.

With the archers now dead, the remaining six Etheria hunters faced off against the vastly superior force of humanoid lions.

Hankap'Vor wondered why they weren't attacking, when the lines parted and a lone Singa and white Tiikeri stepped forward, followed closely by a robed Yagur.

The Tiikeri paused and unemotionally scanned the frightened faces of the Gilas.

"I am General Ja-Wee," he announced with a commanding presence, "and I claim this land in the name of the Tiikeri empire!"

The confused Gila's gazed around at each other wondering what to do.

"Who is in charge here?" Ja-Wee asked forcefully.

All eyes went to Hankap'Vor, who lowered his weapon and stepped forward. "I am."

The Tiikeri's eyes swept over the bald humanoid with scaly blue green skin. "Because the Tiikeri Empire is merciful, I offer you and your people a choice. Become vassals in the service of the Tiikeri Empire, and continue your labors for us, or perish. Decide now!"

Banavor casually strolled through the tumultuous streets of Zor on his way to the imperial bank, impeccably dressed in a see-through purple mesh silk shirt, leather riding pants and boots. His two new EEtah bodyguards, Luft and Nagrada, followed just behind him.

Three cycles after Pa-Waga rendered all stored wealth useless throughout the Goyan Islands, the situation grew desperate. Food had become scarce because all the stored grain spoiled and prepared foods were quickly depleted.

Without precious metals in treasuries, commerce ground to a halt. Fishermen refused to bring in their catches because of the hungry, riotous crowds awaiting them at the docks.

Up ahead, the young acolyte of Pa-Waga saw a small crowd involved in a violent fist fight outside a butcher shop.

"I'd be willing to bet that a hunting party just delivered some sort of fresh meat," he said glibly over his shoulder to the EEtahs.

Drawing nearer to the altercation, Luft and Nagrada took the lead to clear a path through the turmoil. Angry men fighting over scraps of food proved no match for the towering man-sharks who pushed their way through, casually tossing the brawling citizens aside. Banavor moved through the scene, keeping a serene, regal bearing, while his guards eagerly dealt out brutality to any who got in his way.

Once away from the unrest, they turned a corner at an intersection of main thoroughfares. The financial institution lay just ahead. Banavor looked over his shoulder when he heard a desperate voice from behind.

"Good sir!"

All three turned to see a man in his mid-twenties, shabbily dressed holding the hand of a grimy, naked young girl.

Banavor gave him a condescending glare.

"Good sir, my family is starving. We had little before the recent horror, now we have nothing. If you could see fit to help me, some bread perhaps, anything. I... I can offer my daughter if you like."

Banavor glanced down at the girl with greasy matted hair and sad eyes, then back to her father. "The Proffitt says that productivity is the only true path to prosperity. In some places, beggars are beaten. You, however, have offered me something in exchange. This is good. It shows me there is hope for you. I offer you a job starting immediately."

The man's face changed from pleading to relieved and he let go of his little girl's hand.

"Oh, thank you, good sir, thank you!"

"Do you accept?"

The man quivered in excitement. "Oh, yes sir, yes sir!"

"Very well, we have a verbal contract," Banavor said, knowing by his blank expression, the man didn't comprehend the concept. "I am Lord Banavor, retainer of Pa-Waga. What do they call you?"

"Stovle, sir."

"Very well, Stovle, you are my new boot boy."

Stovle's face registered a mixture of confusion and disappointment. "Boot boy, sir?"

"Yes, you will be in charge of my boots. You will organize them. Put them on me. Take them off me and clean them."

A long moment passed under the young father's demanding gaze. When he finally registered the expected immediacy, he glanced quickly around and then dropped to his knees in utter humiliation. He began removing the dirt, mud and street debris from the fine leather footwear with quick brushing strokes.

Ah, ah, ah," Banavor admonished with a wag of his forefinger. "Mouth and tongue only."

The man looked up mortified and Banavor lightly tapped his lips for clarification. He quickly glanced over at his daughter.

"Run along home, Mazie," he said, in a last-minute attempt to avoid the degradation in front of his daughter.

"Oh no, no, she was part of the offer. I'll put her to work back in my kitchen."

Stovle gave Banavor a defeated stare and timidly licked the top of the boot.

"Oh, I'm afraid you'll have to do better than that."

With the rebuke, the man began enthusiastically licking his way down.

"That's more like it! Alright, get up and come with me. I've got an appointment to keep."

Banavor took off again at a somewhat brisker pace, with his growing entourage following. He paused in front of the Imperial Bank and peered up the steps leading to the wide portico and ornate double doors guarded by two EEtahs.

"This should be amusing," he said, before starting up.

Once on the porch, he eyed his two newest staff.

"You two stay out here," he ordered. "Neither of you are appropriately attired to enter such a holy place."

He then looked down at his boots.

"And neither are my boots."

A demanding glance at the Boot Boy sent him back to his knees. Banavor nonchalantly inspected his nails, while the four EEtahs watched the man lick his boots clean, removing clumps of mud with his teeth.

"Do hurry, will you? I have an appointment that I feel is going to be very satisfying."

The boot boy quickly complied, and looked up at Banavor, a pleading smile on his now filthy face.

Banavor dispassionately examined his work then nodded his approval. "Clean your face before I get back."

He then turned his attention to the two EEtah guards with an amused, superior expression. "I believe I'm expected."

Both EEtahs scowled and opened the doors.

The same five faces which radiated arrogance three cycles ago, now appeared frightened and humbled. Bosco Savador rose when Banavor entered and stepped up to the head of the table. They couldn't help but note Luft and Nagrada standing back by the door.

"We have been conferring," Bosco timidly began. "and given the light of recent events, we have decided to rescind the Commodities Standard Act, as per your suggestion."

"Splendid!" Banavor said exuberantly. "I'm delighted the council reversed its previous decision."

"What choice did we have?" a women said, her voice laced with contempt. "You extorted us!"

Banavor appeared genuinely shocked. "Madam, I did no such thing! Any misfortune which has befallen you is no doubt the result of the Lord's displeasure with your short-sighted restrictions."

"We've done what you asked," another member said angrily. "What more could you possibly want from us?

Banavor grinned and shook his head. "Nothing at this time. The lord will bless this decision with prosperity. You'll see. And I'll see you all tomorrow on the trading floor."

Permeri flicked the reins, spurring the lizard steed pulling the wagon down the hard-packed road, which gently caressed the rolling foothills of the Kel-Raku Mountains. It rose out of the pervasive mist at the crest of every peak, vanishing again in the fog running down the slope, only to reappear at the next crest.

She had traveled with Taa-Je hidden in the wagon bed for the better part of the luna and the moon would set soon. The mawl mongrel knew better than to push the steed too hard. The peaceful looking road could be treacherous when it dipped into the foggy clefts between hills. Even the slightest unseen obstruction could spell disaster to a fast-moving carriage.

Permeri caught sight of movement off to her right on the crest of a low foothill. She had encountered a host of antelope type creatures who made the lush grasslands their home on her mostly uneventful trek. This, however, was different. Something out there started running parallel with the wagon, easily keeping pace.

Every so often, she caught glimpse of a muscular, tan, fur covered back rising above the tips of the mist shrouded grass. The sight of the skyline of Shun-Dra in the distance comforted the mongrel briefly but a touch of panic rose from the pit of her stomach when a second shape joined the first, moving quickly through the grass.

Even though she knew it to be dangerous, Permeri pulled the buggy whip from beside her and flicked it against the steed's hindquarters. The large reptile bolted forward, rocking both wagon and rider. For the briefest of moments, the wagon lurched ahead of the mysterious pursuers. The advantage, however, proved short lived and the figures now angled inwards towards the escaping wagon.

Permeri helplessly watched the pursuing pair grow steadily closer. Suddenly, the vegetation beside them exploded when a female Singa leapt onto the back of the lizard. The beast of burden screeched in pain when the Sikari dug its claws in and increased its speed to a perilous level.

Using the only weapon at hand, her whip, Permeri gave several stinging strikes at the Singa's head. The first landed on the back of the neck, which did little damage, but distracted the humanoid lioness from biting down on the lizard's neck. The next two connected with the Singa's ear. The assaulting creature roared in pain, before dropping off the lizard's back and disappearing into the misty grass.

The second Singa leapt at them when they descended into a gully. Permeri was ready and caught the lioness square on the snout in midleap. The whip cracked and connected to the creature's sensitive nose. It howled at the painful sting and fell short of its mark.

In a darkly ironic twist, it wasn't the attackers that finally stopped the wagon's progress, but rather a large rock at the base of the gully. The wagon's left rear wheel clipped the hidden granite obstruction, breaking several spokes and nearly separating from the axel.

The damaged carriage managed to hobble to the peak of the next hill before the rear wheel section tore off completely. The rear corner of the cart dropped onto the road with a loud crash, flinging hay. Taa-Je sat up, clinging to the wagon bed and desperately looking around. The rear corner of the wagon ground against the hard packed road, spitting out straw behind it.

Permeri could see the twin obelisks marking the entrance to Shun-Dra less than twenty yards away, when the overworked lizard finally dropped from exhaustion with a grunt and the wagon rocked to a halt. Behind her, she saw the grass parting as the Sikari ran down the hill after them.

"Get to those obelisks!" Permeri shouted, jumping down from the buckboard. "I'll hold them off."

The pregnant Tiikeri hardly needed to be told twice. With a labored gait, Taa-Je hopped out and trundled towards the safety of the Unaligned City of Shun-Dra. Permeri stood in the center of the road and snapped her whip at the advancing Singas. Having already been painfully subjected to its stinging tip, the Sikari warily approached, snarling and baring teeth.

When they saw the hobbling figure of Taa-Je almost at the city entrance, they pulled and threw several knives from their crossed bandoliers. One sickle shaped blade struck Permeri in the heart, killing her instantly. She dropped her whip and tumbled onto the road. The look of defiance remained etched upon her face.

The other Singa's blade just missed Taa-Je as she passed by the two square pillars. The Tiikeri stopped in the dense, ankle high mist and sighed in relief after the blade whistled by her head. As soon as the throwing knife passed between the pillars, two large tendrils of mist shot out from the city's boundaries and grabbed each leg of the offending lioness.

The other Sikari, Permeri's killer, ground its groin against the dead mongrel, spraying it and howling. It halted its victory marking, and looked on in shock, while the fog seized her partner's legs and, in a single motion, violently rent her in two, showering the road in gore. The mysterious vapors then closed around its victim and gently carried her into the city.

Taa-Je watched on in awe as the bloody halves of the Singa huntress floated serenely past her, but the sensation of liquid rushing down the inside of her thighs quickly overshadowed her astonishment. Her water had broken.

The baby was coming.

Silovik heard the sewer grate rattle at the end of the alley and knew he had made the right choice in locations. The sound of Cul-Ta chattering through the Kan fog soon followed and he guessed there were about twelve of the rogue rat-men. He stood in the recess of a doorway by the alley entrance when he finally caught sight of them marching his way through the dense mist.

He could tell they meant trouble when they crossed the wide main thoroughfare towards the new Cul-Ta neighborhood of Makatooa. By the weapons they carried, he knew it would be deadly.

Silovik uncorked a small barrel he placed by the doorway earlier, kicked it over, and stepped out from the shadows. The Cul-Ta jumped at the sound but failed to notice the oil pouring out onto the alley floor. They hissed angrily and readied their weapons when they saw Silovik.

"Wonderful weather for a stroll, wouldn't you agree?" he asked cheerfully. "Seeing how you're so well armed, I was wondering if you might accompany me? I've heard this part of town isn't safe."

The lead Cul-Ta sneered and raised the short sword with both hands.

"Not safe for you maybe," it said, menacingly.

Holding the sword above his head he gave out a squeal and the group charged.

Silovik stood calmly and pulled out a small piece of paper from the pocket of his pants. He casually held it up with two fingers when the Cul-Ta encountered the oil.

With cries of alarm, the rat creatures slipped on the slick surface, toppling to the hard cobblestones. Their weapons clattered noisily around them.

Still maintaining a calm bearing, Silovik smiled and peered at the piece of paper he held. Furrowing his brow in concentration, his two fingers holding the paper glowed red and the paper ignited. Silovik tossed the burning article onto the oily floor in a single motion. The combustible liquid burst into flames and the wall of fire rapidly traveled across the alley.

The Cul-Ta screamed in panic and tried to run but even getting to their feet on the slick surface proved all but impossible. When the advancing field of fire finally overtook them, the alley filled with screams of agony and the smell of burning fur.

Silovik stood amongst the flames, watching the rat-men burn, basking in the warmth of the Goddess' embrace. The smell of burning flesh was an intoxicant, reminding him of home and the temple of the Goddess Jalaana.

He caught sight of a lone Cul-Ta crawling away just outside of the inferno. The fire had slightly singed its fur, but otherwise it appeared to have escaped the inferno.

Giving a resigned sigh, Silovik made his way across the burning alley. He reached down, grabbed the humanoid rodent by the neck and lifted him up just above his face. The creature wiggled slightly and weakly squeaked in protest but was in too much shock to put up much of a fight.

"You there, hold!" came a sudden commanding voice from behind.

Still holding the Cul-Ta aloft, Silovik peered around to see two city guards with swords drawn at the alley entrance.

"Hello," he greeted happily, "be with you momentarily."

Not taking his eyes off the guards, he furrowed his brow once more. The hand holding the Cul-Ta glowed and the dazed creature began smoldering, and then burst into flames.

The creature shrieked and squealed with notes so high it actually hurt the city guard's ears just before the internal combustion caused the rat-man's eyes to pop from their sockets. After reeling from the shrieks, the two city guards stood in stunned amazement. Standing unaffected in the middle of a burning patch of fire, a human male had set a living creature ablaze with just his hand.

Still smiling, he tossed the engulfed Cul-Ta onto the pile of his burning comrades.

"Now then," he said stepping towards the patrol. "How can I assist the City Guards this Kan?"

Both guards were wary, however the man was unarmed, made no hostile actions towards them and appeared friendly.

"You just hold it right there," one of the guards ordered suspiciously.

"I can assure you that I mean you no harm," Silovik said extending his hands palms up.

"All the same, hold it right there," the guard warned before glancing over at his junior partner. "Better go get Colonel Velitel."

"I see another actor has entered the stage!" Velitel commented upon entering the alley.

The flames finally died out leaving twelve smoldering Cul-Ta bodies scattered about. One of his guards, sword lowered, chatting with a badly scarred man.

"Looks like we missed the first act," the colonel said, stepping over to them. "I'm Colonel Velitel, Commander of the city guards. I would offer you my hand, but my men have advised me against it."

Silovik smiled knowingly. "You have nothing to fear colonel. The Goddess only smites the unworthy."

"As you say," Velitel acquiesced. "Now, let's start with your name and the reason you're starting fires in my city?"

"My name is unimportant. A client hired me to attend to their rodent problem."

"I would disagree sir. An actor's name is always needed for the program booklet, and the name of your patron would also be nice to know."

Silovik paused, assessing the request. "Very well, my name is Silovik de Zolene. As for my client, revealing them would be unprofessional in the extreme and detrimental to acquiring any future clients who may wish my services."

"Yes, I've been told about your services. That's some trick you've got there."

"I have no tricks colonel," Silovik said slightly defensively. "I am merely a keeper of the flame, a vessel for the Goddess' use."

"I see," Velitel said, knowing full well who his client was. "Lord Hanara doesn't have a rodent problem, this city does, and that falls under my direction."

"Colonel, I have great respect for city guards. Yours is a dangerous and thankless job, but even the most efficient of operations must still deal with levels of bureaucracy which I do not. It's not against the law to kill Cul-Ta, is it?"

"Not unless they're citizens."

"Once again, the righteous have nothing to fear from the Goddess."

"Then there's the matter of starting fires in a crowded city."

"Colonel, am I under arrest?"

"Not yet."

"Then in that case I promise to be more careful, and I wish you a pleasant rest of the Kan."

The city guards watched Silovik leisurely stroll out of the alley and disappear into the Kan fog.

"Why didn't you order him held, sir?" a guard asked. "He seemed potentially dangerous."

Velitel shook his head, deep in thought.

"I'll have some of Kem's people keep an eye on him and see if we can find out anything on our little firebug. Something else is going on here. I want to see how this plays out."

Hankap'Vor watched the moonfall over the Barrens and considered himself lucky to be alive. Their captors held him and his remaining Dolins together in a small, shallow ravine adjacent to the Etheria outcropping. Several female Singa guards ensured no one wandered off.

From the best he could tell, catching snippets of conversations, the general planned to take the bulk of the troops off with the main army and leave a small force of about a hundred to hold the Etheria field.

Hankap'Vor watched one the mawls wearing robes and hoods slowly approach the dead E'Nott, sniffing furiously.

He dropped down on all fours to conduct an even closer inspection. Then, with a satisfied smile, he knelt down and removed his robes and extended a single claw from his forefinger. The mawl sliced deeply down the center of the dead creature's torso, peeled back the skin, reached in and violently pulled apart the ribcage. Sniffing the open wound, he nodded in satisfaction before feasting on the esophagus and surrounding internal organs.

"It seems like a pretty well-regulated group," the Dolin leader whispered, leaning in close to his second in command, I-Kinci. "The striped ones are in charge. The ones with all the fur around their heads and neck are the muscle and that one with the spots over there gorging himself, that's their shaman."

"How do you know that?" I-Kinci whispered back.

"Look at what he's eating. E'Nott's just drink the Etheria condensation. They're gullet filters the water into their body. He's eating the organs that accumulated the most PSI."

"What's that mean to us?"

"Right now, probably nothing, but we need to keep our eyes and ears open for any small detail that can give us an advantage in the future."

I-Kinci scoffed. "You actually think we've got a future?"

"I do," Hankap'Vor replied confidently, continuing to watch the Yagur feed. "They need us. They don't know how to harvest or process Etheria. So, we bide our time and do what we're told."

"ALRIGHT," the Tiikeri general roared. "THOSE REJOINING THE MAIN FORCE ARE WITH ME. LET'S MOVE OUT!"

The Dolin prisoners watched the majority of the conquering force bound off behind their leader on all fours. Just as Hankap'Vor had overheard, a force of a hundred Singas stayed behind.

A lone Singa broke from the remaining guards and stood over the gully, staring down at his prisoners.

"I wish to welcome you as the newest members of the Tiikeri Empire," he said in a friendly voice. "I am Captain Tralor and I have been given command of this part of the operation. Get some rest. Tomorrow, you get to work harvesting this field."

The size difference between Lazio and the crowd of Onay surrounding him seemed stark. The humanoid lion stood seven feet tall, almost double their height. With his mane fluttering in the wind, he made a commanding figure.

The former Singa general found himself growing frustrated with the stubborn, hostile and clannish wolf-men of the Barrens. Over the past few lunas, they had challenged almost every teaching point he tried to get across and he grew impatient. The Singa could only imagine Zaad had the same problems with the horde they assigned to him.

Lazio also found it darkly ironic that he now trained forces to go up against his own people, under orders from a human king he helped put on the throne.

"This sneaking around you propose is the way of cowards," a brash Onay, with bristling grey and black fur, protested with a sneer. "We are stronger together. I want to fight amongst my brothers!"

Lazio sighed and tried not to lose his temper. "And you will, but your strategy must change, or you and your brothers will die together!"

He paused for emphasis and pointed out at the crowd. "You can't overcome these enemies as a pack, like you're used to. Your enemy is too strong, too disciplined and too numerous. You must break up into smaller fighting units.

Strike where they are weakest, then disappear back into the forest. It is the only way you can hope to win."

A grumble of acceptance, accompanied by frustrated yips, passed through the throng of humanoid wolves and Lazio turned to Swift Foot, the pack's alpha.

"You know who works best together'" he said. "Break them up into groups of twenty. Position them so that they can operate independently or band together if the situation calls for it. We don't have much time."

From off in the distance, they heard a lone Onay's howl carried on the wind, echoing off the trees. Others picked up the call and relayed it across the Barrens.

The message was as simple as it was ominous, *invaders*!

The Singa's face turned grim. "I stand corrected. We're out of time."

"I don't give a fuck if we are on the same side this time, Ghorn give me the creeps," Mal said, stepping up to the *Haraka's* side hatch.

"They deal with the dead and undead," Alto replied. "It is only to be expected."

Once inside, she slid off her pack and hung it on the back of her seat.

"How'd it go, Captain?" Zau asked with a sly grin.

"About as well as can be expected," Mal said, noting her amused look. "What?"

With a nod of her head, she directed Mal's attention to Taleeka sitting with an adorable ball of fur asleep and snoring in her lap. Her daughter gently stroked its long fur, speaking softly to it.

"What the fuck?!" Mal asked incredulously. "I leave you all alone for a few cycles and you turn my ship into a fucking zoo!"

"She brought it in shortly after you left." Zau said, obviously enjoying her predicament. "It was wounded and she rescued it. She's been nursing it back. She's hardly left its side the entire time. It won't let anyone but her near it."

Mal gave a frustrated sigh and rubbed her forehead.

The Singa seemed almost giddy. "She's already named it."

Zau's statement brought back the Spice Rat's attention.

"It appears to be very young," Alto said, appraising the sleeping animal. "We saw several on our return to the ship. They get much larger."

"And they're vicious as fuck!"

Zau chuckled. "It appears our little Tally has a way with animals."

"You are enjoying my torment way too fucking much!"

Zau kept her entertained demeanor. "What can I say, cruelty is the basis for all humor. Come on captain, she's nurturing. She's never had anyone nurture her before you two. She's passing it on."

"Well, she's going to have to nurture something else. We can't have a fucking ferocious wild animal that nobody but her can get close to, running around the ship."

Mal suddenly felt tiny arms wrapping her waist in a warm hug. Glancing down, she gently put her hand on Taleeka's head. "I missed you too Mz. Tally."

As suddenly as it began, Taleeka broke the embrace and beamed up at Mal with an excited look. "Mom, mom, come and see my new friend!"

"Yeah, I've heard all about your new *friend*," Mal said skeptically.

"Come on, I'll show you!" she said, taking Mal's hand and leading her back to the seating area.

The animal, now awake, stood in the chair, baring its teeth. The growl from its throat grew louder the closer Mal got to it.

"Okay, I'm stopping right here," Mal said, from a safe distance with a look which read, *are you kidding me?*

Taleeka's face remained a mask of innocence. "What?"

"Let's go back up front before it tears our throats out." Mal led her daughter up to the ship's bridge and sat down so they were at eye level. "Alright, Mz. Tally, you know you can't keep it."

"But… but she's my friend," she protested. "I rescued her. Her name is Maddy!"

"Tally, she's not your friend," Mal explained, shaking her head. "She's a wild animal. She's going to get bigger and meaner. She's not doing it on purpose, it's her nature."

Taleeka pouted, searching the faces of both Zau and Alto looking for an ally.

"Sorry kid, I'm with your mom on this one," Zau said firmly.

"As am I, little one," Alto sympathetically agreed.

Taleeka's tucked her chin into her chest and drew her mouth tight.

The sudden echoing howl of an Onay sliced through the cabin, ending the argument. All but Taleeka shot an alarmed glance out the windshield. Others picked up the cry and repeated it, traveling across the crystal forest.

"Okay folks, it's show time!" Mal announced, before returning attention to her pouting daughter.

"Alright, sweety, we gotta go, and I mean now!" she said in a patient but firm tone. "So, take your little friend outside and say good-by, but do it quickly."

Taleeka nodded, her mouth pulled downward in a resigned frown. She then silently moped back to her seat and her transitory pet they now forced her to part ways with.

Mal spun around in her chair and heaved a sigh, before checking the dashboard controls. "Hold on to your hats, kids. We've got a date with some spiders."

"Your Majesty, we must get you out of the city and to safety!" Kai insisted.

Queen Shula winced under her spymaster's penetrating gaze. "I can't leave my people! What kind of a ruler would I be if I ran at the first sign of danger?!"

"A living one," Kai replied matter-of-factly. "Your Majesty, with all due respect, I didn't rescue you from the clutches of the Tiikeri Empire only so you could hand yourself right back over to them."

The Bailian queen peered down at the pet Cheepa in her lap and sighed. "I know my little savior, but how do we know they are headed here?"

"I've been getting steady reports ever since they were spotted moving up Gar-Yesh Point. The main force split to implement a two-prong attack. One army moves through the Dark Waste and has already taken the Lor-Danta Oasis. The other marches through the Barrens securing Etheria fields. They both head for Immor-Onn."

"What about the inhabitants of those lands?"

"Demetrius and Okawa just got back from warning the On'Dara."

"Were they receptive?"

"Only after Okawa warned them the invaders would use their herds of horses to feed their armies. At last report, Mal and her group are in the Barrens."

The queen shook her head in disbelief.

"The Valdurian reinforcements have already set themselves in position and are well armed," Kai continued. "They also placed secret assets on the streets to rally a resistance. Should Immor-Onn be occupied, they will disappear into the city and harass."

"With all that," the queen asked, "and you still want me to leave?"

"Not just you, Your Majesty, but the Avatar and its entourage, and the Do-Tarr work detail have to go as well. We can't risk any of you falling into Tiikeri hands. The Valdurian transport which brought the reinforcements is ready and waiting. I've also arranged for them to load the treasury as well as any sensitive papers."

"What about you?"

"I'm staying to assist the Valdurians, as is Commander Sandal and Air Boss Koren."

"No, my little savior, I can't risk losing you!"

"Your Majesty, I would be of no use travelling with you. I need to be here."

"I guess you're right." the queen agreed with a forlorn sigh and continued petting Manar.

"Thank you, Your Majesty. Collect your personal things. You need to go now. Time is of the essence."

"I still don't like abandoning my people."

"It's the only sane strategy. Don't worry, Your Majesty, the Tiikeri will quickly discover this will be a costly piece of land for them to hold on to."

Ushtar longed for the misty grasslands of home. He missed his mate and cub, but mostly he missed his freedom.

He saw no point in lamenting about it, he still had three more grands of service to the empire. He didn't especially *like* the Tiikeri, but the end of his contract guaranteed the promise of full citizenship and all the benefits of that title.

The Singa foot soldier sighed, leaned on his spear and rubbed the side of his head on the shaft, scenting it. He had never seen snow before and now he had seen enough of it to last a lifetime. He felt it represented the bleakly perfect accompaniment to the forest of crystal trees before him.

He could hear fellow guards trudging through the ankle deep cold. Behind him, he heard the sounds of the rest of the detachment sleeping away the moonless.

They camped under a massive outcropping of jagged crystal towers, some as many as twenty feet high. Ushtar had no idea what the Tiikeri wanted with those oversized gems, or even why they were invading this land. That was not for him to ponder. Right now, he just wanted to get through his watch and get some rest.

A movement in the snow just in front of him interrupted the Singa's wistful reflections, then a growl behind him and a commotion on his right. He straightened up and readied his polearm, straining to see in the dim light. The movement in the snow seemed headed his way.

Before he could react, he felt a searing pain behind his left knee, followed by a muted growl. Ushtar cried out, feeling muscle and tendon ripped away from the bone. The attack came from an Onay who completely bit out the back of his knee and lower thigh. With nothing left to support his weight, his leg buckled out from under him.

On his way to the ground, the snow in front of him erupted in a spray of white powder and another wolfman lunged. Despite the pain and confusion, Ushtar's martial skills kicked in and he drove the spear into the charging Onay. The impaled attacker yelped in anguish and grabbed at the spear's shaft.

With his weapon now lodged, it left the wounded Singa all but helpless against the three other Onay who appeared out of the darkness.

Hankap'Vor didn't mind sleeping on the cold, hard ground of the Barrens. However, this felt different. He and his team were prisoners. With the rising of the moon, they would be all but slave labor and he found his sleep restless.

He suddenly opened his eyes, snatched out of his agitated slumber by growling and the sounds of a struggle. Bolting up, he reached over and shook I-Kinci's shoulder. The Gila groggily came to, while the head Dolin scanned the ridge line of the gully above them.

The two Singa guards couldn't be seen. Cries of pain rang out into the moonless, along with the sound of flesh tearing and bones being crushed. All of the prisoners, now awake, looked around in a dazed panic.

Hankap'Vor just got to his feet, when the first two Onay leapt over the side of the gully and into their midst. Several prisoners cried out in alarm when two more of their pack joined the wolf-men. The four Onay wildly bit and clawed at the unarmed Gila's. Those not immediately subjected to the indiscriminate slaughter desperately attempted to escape by scrambling up over the gully's side.

Hankap'Vor's heart pounded wildly in his chest, as he frantically groped about the snowy ground for anything to assist his escape. He realized all was lost when he popped his head up over the side and witnessed the carnage of the entire Onay pack ripping and rending the motionless Singas.

The Dolin leader barely had time to reel in shock when powerful jaws clamped down on his ankle. He heard his bones snap and his own agonized cries before they savagely yanked him back into the ravine.

By the time Captain Tralor woke from his restless slumber and rallied his garrison, the assault had ended, and an eerie stillness hung over the crystal forest. He ordered his men to fan out, but the attackers had vanished into the trees and the darkness.

The Singa commander's ears pinned and whiskers twitched furiously each time he swore out loud gruffly assessing the devastation. He had lost all three guards around the Etheria field and the two guarding the prisoners. He found them savagely mauled, with limbs torn completely off and large chunks of flesh ripped away.

Tralor discovered the attackers' only casualty lying beside one of the dead guards. He had never seen an Onay before and found himself staring at the impaled wolfman.

"Captain," one of the men called out, breaking him from his trance.

The Singa soldier stood peering into the gully with an expression of disgust. Tralor joined him and groaned in frustration. Mangled corpses and body parts strewn along the entire length of the ditch painted the snow completely red.

"Looks like they killed all of them, sir."

"How in the name of the empire could they do all this in such a short amount of time?" the Singa captain asked, beyond astounded.

"Captain, if the harvesters are dead who's going to tend to all those crystals?"

"Private, if this is what we can expect every moonless, those crystals are the least of our worries."

Banavor stood on the second story balcony watching the lady of the house sob openly into a dainty white handkerchief and quietly board the coach in front of the mansion he just had acquired. The previous occupants had agreed to vacate by the close of business.

The former master of the estate, a rival trader, kept his head lowered in shame and degradation. He had made several risky purchases over the past few cycles on credit Banavor extended him. When their value plunged, it devastated his tenuous fortune and forced him to liquidate everything at a bargain price.

Banavor was there, of course, ready to accept his home as payment. The spoils of this particular victory were especially sweet; a fully furnished, luxurious thirty room mansion and grounds. The purchase also included the staff of twenty indentures and the Pa-Waga acolyte had plans for them.

He watched the carriage rumble out of sight. In the distance, the Grand Turine in the Zorian Harbor rang five times, indicating the Kan would start soon.

I serve a mighty god, he silently proclaimed, feeling the cool damp breeze on his face.

"Master?" a voice approached from his right.

"Yes, Stovle?" he replied, keeping his gaze fixed out on the well-manicured lawn.

"The EEtahs are gathering the staff, as you ordered, but there was something..." The former beggar's voice trailed off and he dropped to his knees.

"What is it, Stovle?" Banavor finally faced the kneeling servant, who meekly bowed his long thin face.

"Master, I know I'm not smart like you, or brave... or anything like that..."

"Yes?"

"But these past few cycles, I've seen the power of the Lord. I know I'm not worthy, but I'm ready to give my life over to Him. That's if He'll have me. I'm willing to pledge my daughter's life too."

Banavor smiled and placed his hand on the top of Stovle's head. "The Lord welcomes all who seek Him. Wisdom and prosperity come with acceptance of Him. However, I cannot accept your daughter's pledge. Children must be pledged before their first birthday. She must pledge herself."

"I understand, master."

"Good," Banavor said, walking around behind him. "Are you ready to receive the mark of the Lord?"

"Yes, master. Thank you, master!"

The young Pa-Waga acolyte ceremoniously raised his arm and extended a forefinger. His nail grew long and pointed, just like his predecessor.

"In the name of the God Most High," he declared, carving a small X on the back of Stovle's neck.

He carved another X to the left of Stovle's spine and a single I on the other side of the neck. "I consecrate your body and soul to his service."

Banavor stepped before his servant and placed a hand on the back of his head.

"You have now entered into a new life," Banavor said reassuringly, "and because you have shown industriousness, in the simple act of caring for my boots, you shall be rewarded. For the Lord says that 'he who cares for the smallest of things shall be granted greater things than can even be conceived.' You are no longer my boot boy. For reaching out to the Lord, I shall raise you up from that lowly position and make you, my assistant!"

"Thank you, master!"

"Your first task, as my assistant, is to show your master and lord how much you love him by rendering assistance."

Banavor reached down with his free hand and pulled aside his only garment, a long, black, bejeweled loincloth. His flaccid penis tumbled out inches from Stovle's face.

Charmed by Banavor's Etheria jewelry, a charge of arousal shot through the newest convert to Pa-Waga. He felt his master's hand guide his head closer and, although repulsed by the act, found his mouth expectantly opening. Without hesitation, Stovle sucked in the soft organ and felt it immediately begin to stiffen.

Bo-Lah looked down at the sleeping infant, his son, and felt nothing but revulsion and disgust. *Abomination!* kept repeating over and over in the Tiikeri's mind.

By human standards the baby looked adorable. Its human characteristics were symmetrical and pleasing to the eye. Its pale white skin and muted grey tiger stripes set it apart from the normally dark-skinned people of the Goyan Islands.

He sneered in contempt hearing it coo in its sleep. When the baby opened his eyes and started fussing out of hunger, Bo-Lah felt like reaching down and crushing its head. The Tiikeri were the only mawls who forbade interracial breeding to preserve the purity of their bloodlines. He fought every instinct embraced by his people to not kill it and place it on the funeral pyre next to its dead mother.

Unfortunately, to achieve his plan, the child must live long enough to ensure Bo-Lah's place as an Otoman River lord. The assurances he received a few cycles ago put that plan well on its way to fruition, which meant the child's days were numbered.

"Oh, it sounds like someone's hungry," came a kindly female voice across the nursery.

Apolo, a short, dark-skinned woman with wild black hair, placed her knitting down on a nearby table and rose to her feet. Originally purchased by Matriarch Matka Sorbornef because of the place of her birth, they had retained Apolo on the Staghorn staff for many grands.

The females of her people from the island of Wou-Late were renown throughout the Goyan Islands as wetnurses. They were sturdy women, with large breasts which never seemed to run dry, as well as very tough nipples. She had nursed all of the Sorbornef children and the recent tragic events killing off the family greatly saddened her.

She found the new Lord of the Manor's ways strange and sometimes terrifying, but she, as well as the rest of the slaves, came with the estate and slaves had no say in the matter. She performed light cleaning and kitchen duties, but mostly she tended to the medical needs of the plantation in her current position as a wetnurse.

Wearing only a simple red skirt, her enormous breasts swayed when she walked over to the crib. Picking up the infant, she returned to her chair and offered the baby her nipple. The baby boy needed no prompting, grabbing on to the breast and enthusiastically suckling.

"He's such a happy baby," she proudly said smiling down at the child's adoring stare, "and smart too."

Bo-Lah remained silent, staring at the nursing pair.

"Have you thought of a name yet, Lord Bo-Lah?" she asked, not taking her gaze off the feeding child.

"No!" he replied curtly.

"Oh, you really should give him a name," she said, finally looking up. "It's bad luck if you wait too long."

Bo-Lah ignored the advice and tuned out her doting and baby-talking with the nursing child.

"After he's through feeding, you really should hold him," she said, continuing her motherly counsel. "You haven't held him since I put him in your arms right after he was born. A baby needs their parent's touch. It helps with the bonding process."

There will be no bonding you stupid cow! Swept across Bo-Lah's mind.

"It is not our way," he said dispassionately.

"Pity," she said with a touch of sadness. "A boy should feel his father's love."

The only thing that monstrosity will feel is my hands on its throat and the sweet release of death, he thought, stepping over to the door.

"I have things to attend to," he said, covering his eyes and stepping out into the bright Lumina sunlight.

As ordered, the twenty staff members were lined up naked in front of the mansion's large double doors. The twelve men and eight women fidgeted nervously, unaccustomed to being unclothed in public. At each end of the line the EEtahs Luft and Nagrada stood watch.

"Quit yer twitching," Nagrada admonished gruffly. "If I was you, I'd get used to running around without clothes. That's the way Lord Banavor likes it."

Almost on cue, the doors opened and Banavor stepped out onto the cobblestone driveway with Stovle following closely behind. The young priest of Pa-Waga smiled lecherously at the row of naked bodies. Without a word, he slowly sauntered down the line and gently ran his hands over his slaves exposed flesh.

He paused in front of a tall, muscular field hand with long brown hair. Reaching down he fondled the man's ample organ and dangling balls. Despite his obvious discomfort at the situation, Banavor's lust inducing bauble began to affect the slave's libido and his cock began to grow hard.

"Be cleaned and in my bedchamber at nine bells," Banavor ordered in a husky whisper.

The fieldhand scowled despite his crotch's response. "Sex was not a part of my contract."

Banavor raised an eyebrow and gave an amused smirk.

"Yes," he said, addressing the line, "if anyone is willing to receive my mark and serve me, I am prepared to buy out your contract."

The announcement caused the staff to forget their awkward situation. Excited murmurs swept down the line.

"That's just trading one form of slavery for another," the groped fieldhand said insolently. "I've only got one more grand left on my contract."

Banavor kept his pleasant demeanor. "My, my, aren't you the spirited one? You know what? I'm going to buy out your contract anyways."

Banavor gave a satisfied bob of his head and the man adopted a suspiciously confused look.

"You see, now you have no more contractual abstinence."

"Hey, wait a minute!" the fieldhand protested.

"Oh, not for me, mind you." Banavor said salaciously. "I've recently been placated. My men however…"

The man had no time to respond before Nagrada grabbed him by the arm. The fieldhand struggled against the man-shark's grip and let loose a torrent of obscenities. The rest of the staff looked on nervously as Nagrada gruffly shoved the man into Luft's arms.

"Aww Naggy." the EEtah objected, "I thought it was still my turn. I can't help it the last one died before I finished."

"Tough," Nagrada countered, unbuckling his belt.

"Aww," Luft whined in acceptance.

Luft gripped both of the man's thickly muscled upper arms by the back and lifted him into the air. The fieldhand's muscular physique proved no match for the seven-foot humanoid shark. Luft easily pinned him securely, with chest facing out and feet dangling.

The onlookers gasped in shock when Nagrada dropped his pants. The EEtah's organ grew rapidly hard before the gasping crowd and measured over a foot long and two inches in diameter when fully erect, with a tip tapering into a point.

Still screaming curses, the fieldhand flailed and kicked his legs when the aroused man-shark moved behind him. Nagrada easily caught his legs and wrenched them open.

"I like dirty talk," he said with an evil grin. "Don't stop on my account."

Without finesse or restraint, the EEtah violently plunged his massive flesh pole into the man's exposed orifice. Immediately, inhuman shrieks of agony replaced the stream of swearing and threats. Most of the staff looked away in disgust while the EEtah pounded away furiously.

"I can assure you, my bedchamber would have been significantly more pleasurable," Banavor said over the man's wails of pain. "Thankfully, EEtah's aren't known for their sexual stamina."

Within a short moment, Nagrada bellowed his release. The force, and amount of ejaculate expelled from his member, lifted the unfortunate slave out of Luft's arms and onto the ground, twitching in shock on his hands and knees. A torrent of semen and blood poured from his gaping anus while the obstinate slave whimpered in pain and humiliation.

"Take him to the cellar and put him in holy restraints," Banavor ordered. "I still have a use for him."

Before the command could be carried out, a small thin man at the end of the line, who wept throughout the rape, broke and ran. He had made it off the driveway and onto the lawn before Banavor nodded at Luft.

The Sunal EEtah deftly slid the Yudon harpoon off his back and hurled it at the escaping slave. The barbed projectile struck the fleeing man squarely in the back and sent him hurtling forward onto the lawn, dead long before he hit the ground. Several of those watching cried out in horror.

"You have your orders," Banavor said to Nagrada as he stuffed his now flaccid organ away and closed his pants.

He turned to Stovle. "Get that body off my lawn."

His new assistant nodded nervously, rushing to comply.

"As for the rest of you," Banavor continued, "I hope we understand each other now. I serve a mighty god, who is generous to his followers and merciless to his enemies. By serving me you serve the lord and through your good works you might one day become a true follower, like Stovle. Always remember the words of The Proffitt, 'The only path to prosperity is through productivity.'"

Slowly, the line of ten men and eight women dropped down on their knees. Banavor stepped up to the first person in line, a frail, older woman with a terrified look. He smiled and stroked her cheek.

"Fear not, you have chosen a better life and higher calling." The encouragement seemed to slightly ease the woman's worried deportment.

"Do you willingly receive my mark and swear to serve the lord and myself faithfully?"

The woman nervously nodded and Banavor carved a small X on her forehead between her eyes.

"I release you from your earthly contract and welcome you into the bosom of the lord!"

The *Haraka* banked gently to port, providing Taleeka an unobstructed view of the moon rising over the peaks of the Os-Ani Mountains. Brilliant shafts of moonlight shot through the swiftly moving clouds and glinted off the dew-laced webbing stretching between the fingers of stone pointing to the sky.

"That looks just like the spiders web in the corner of the balcony back at home," Taleeka said in wide eyed wonder.

"That's because it is," Mal answered, rocking the young girl in her lap, "but the spiders that made these are just a lot bigger and smarter."

"Is that where we're going?"

"It sure is." Mal leaned to the side and peered back to Kumo at the ship's wheel. "Speaking of webs, be careful, these canyons and valleys are laced with webbing."

"Indeed," Alto agreed with a nod. "As I recall, getting off that web was quite the ordeal."

"Yes, Captain," Kumo confirmed.

"So, what are we doing here captain?" Zau asked, nervously watching two Cevot spider people scurry across the web motioning up at them.

"We gotta find a way to get these Cevot folks on our side," Mal replied.

"Hey, they look like Kumo!" Taleeka noted excitedly.

"That's right," Mal replied. "Kumo, this is where you come in. We need someone to get them talking to us, instead of trying to eat us. For that we're gonna need a grand entrance. You say these people are descendants of yours?"

"Yes, Captain," the spider-woman replied softly. "My people seeded this race long ago."

By now, Cevots and their spider workers streamed from a cave in the cliff face onto the webbing. The sentient spider-people stared and pointed up at the airship.

"Alright Kumo, you're in charge of the introductions. Take us down to ten feet off the web."

The mesmerized spider people curiously watched the strange object slowly descend. The cargo bay doors opened underneath the rear of the ship and Kumo gracefully dropped onto the web.

"That should get their attention," Mal said, watching the Cevots cautiously approach her pilot.

"Be ready to pull her out just in case they decide to attack for some fucking reason," Mal said over her shoulder to Zau, who had taken the wheel.

"You got it captain."

Mal felt a moment of apprehension when the Cevots surrounded her, but relaxed when she witnessed them conversing and Kumo gesturing back at the *Haraka*. Then the Cevots led Kumo back to the cave they had exited from.

"All right, looks like we're in," Mal said. "Take her down to a little over head height and follow."

From what the Spice Rat could tell, the mood of the spider people actually seemed excited and even reverent of the Makara in their midst.

The ship settled down and hovered a few inches above the stone floor inside the cave mouth. Mal lifted Taleeka off her lap with a resigned sigh and rose to her feet.

"Okay, this is why we earn the big money. Drop the side hatch and let's see how convincing we can be."

"Are we all going, Captain?" Zau asked pensively.

"Someone's got to stay with the ship," Zaad said. "I've got things I could catch up on. Besides the space in there could get tight. I wouldn't be much good to you."

"Makes sense," Mal said, pulling the lever to lower the hatch. "No wild parties while we're gone."

The man-shark chuckled and Mal led the way down the ramp.

"My friends," Kumo said, introducing them to the Cevots she had spoken with.

Mal's and the crew's eyes adjusted and they took in their cavernous surroundings filled with humanoid spiders and their spider workers.

The Cevot stood five feet high, with a human torso and head sitting atop an arachnid's body. Like Kumo, they had four small, black eyes set across their forehead along with two humanoid eyes below them. Black, hairy, two-foot-long spiders served as their beasts of burden. Multiple layers of webbing covered the walls and ceiling. The sour, rotting aroma of numerous cocooned bodies stored within the webs filled the thick, humid air.

"Looks like the cargo hold of my ship," Mal noted nonchalantly to Alto, just before stepping up to Kumo and their hosts.

"You are friends of the Strasta?" a large female asked.

"What… you mean Kumo?" Mal answered. "Yes."

"The prophecy has come true!" the female announced to her people. "The Strasta has returned!"

An excited murmur went through the brood and the female returned her attention back to Kumo.

"The queen will want to see you immediately."

An exuberant Mal spun to face her crew. Taleeka peeked out from behind Alto, whose serene face concealed his body's stance poised to draw and strike.

"Relax everybody," she said, seeing the tension in their faces. "We're here to see the queen!"

By the time Banavor made it down into the basement with Stovle in tow, the EEtahs had already secured the rebellious man in 'holy restraints.' They suspended him by his feet from a beam in the middle of the large, empty room, bound his hands behind his back. On the floor below his head a small pail rested ominously.

Banavor wiggled his nose at the musty damp smell and casually walked over to the bound slave, while pulling off his loincloth. He stood naked before the hanging slave and ran his hand across the man's sizeable cock and balls dangling against his abdomen.

"What a pity for this to go to waste."

He then knelt down face to face with the fieldhand. The man's eyes contained an intoxicating mixture of fear and pain, causing Banavor to smile.

"Don't you worry, you're *still* useful to me. I might go so far as to say critical."

Maintaining the smile, Banavor placed his forefinger with the sharpened nail against the slave's neck and slowly pulled it across his exposed throat. The victim's eyes went wide with the realization of his throat's laceration. He attempted to cry out but only a frantic gurgle sputtered from his mouth.

The wound erupted and sprayed outward. Blood painted the light brown skin of Banavor's face and upper chest a macabrely complimentary shade of crimson.

"Shh," Banavor comforted the panicked dying man, placing his hand tenderly on his cheek. "Your death serves a much higher purpose than trimming my lawn... or even fucking me for that matter."

The man shuttered out his death rattle. Banavor stood back up to watch the blood cascade downward into the pail. When half-filled, he nodded at the pail and walked over to the back wall.

An *extremely* unnerved Stovle picked up the bucket and followed him. Banavor gave his assistant a comforting smile and indicated he should hold the container out in front of him with both hands.

"Don't be afraid, Stovle, we are on the cusp of a new day for this world and *you* get to be a part of its inception."

Stovle nodded nervously and remained silent.

Banavor dipped his finger into the bucket of blood and used it to paint an X and I on both their foreheads. Facing the wall, he began writing lines of the binary glyphs. When he had completed five distinct rows of runes, he took the pail from Stovle and poured the remainder in a line across the floor directly below his markings.

Stovle anxiously looked around when the room shuddered beneath him. The worried assistant followed Banavor and backed towards the middle of the room.

A serene expression descended over Banavor when the room rumbled once more and the distinct odor of ammonia laced the air.

"He's here."

A black amorphous shape oozed up from the cracks in the floor where Banavor drizzled the blood. The shape pooled just below the writing on the wall. Multiple fields of X and I runes glowed blue and strobed across the blob's surface.

Stovle visibly trembled when the gelatinous substance undulated into shape. Banavor noted the condition of his assistant silently and placed a calming hand on his shoulder.

The blob morphed into the form of a humanoid cat statue with few discernable features and the strobing runes faded away. Stovle dropped to his knees and Banavor reverently bowed his head when the statue opened its eyes.

"Let the age of prosperity begin!" its voice thundered in their minds.

Commander Zabit stood at the bow of the lead attack boat with the rising moon to his back. The south winds still blew hard and the Singa's mane fluttered wildly around his head and shoulders.

He watched the massive cave entrances of Immor-Onn's twin harbors grow ever closer. The morning airship traffic flying in and out of the commercial harbor of Rilli-On was as sparse as the merchant ships sailing below. A single, small ocean liner made for port through the other cave entrance leading to the passenger harbor of Fall-Arak.

Twenty ships of the invasion fleet, carrying a thousand Singa shock troops, followed him into Rilli-On. He decided to divide his force in two and his most trusted officer, Colonel Kalred, led the rest of the fleet into Fall-Arak. He would regroup forces at the opening connecting the two harbors near the rear of the caves and sweep the city.

Zabit felt confident he had identified critical locations throughout the city from the regular reports received from Cheepa spies before their Worrg network went dark. The palace, and the two eastern gates leading to the Os'Tor Forest beyond, stood foremost on the list.

They would also confiscate the contents of the few Etheria shops in the city and detain the Etheriats. Since the air station was the sovereign property of the human House Valdur, and they didn't want a fight with the humans at this point in time, they would sequester but not occupy it.

He received strict orders to keep damage and casualties to a minimum and only quell the resistance. The generals wanted a functional city to present to the king.

"This is exciting!" Te-Sor, the Pa-Waga cleric assigned to his force, joined Zabit on the bow. "Conquering new lands in the name of the Lord."

The Singa commander ignored the robed Yagur and continued surveying the harbor entrances.

"New acquisitions," the priest continued to babble, tail twitching excitedly. "The lord truly blesses this cause."

"I care nothing for *your* god, priest," Zabit hissed, not taking his eyes off the looming cave mouths. "The only reason you are here is because of orders. This is a military operation. Stay out of the way!"

A smug look crossed the Yagur's face. "It's fortunate King Kar-Gor cares about *my* god then, don't you think?"

Zabit sneered at the cleric, whiskers shuddering in frustration. "Stay out of the way!"

The wind died and water grew much calmer as they entered the harbor. The orange glow of crystals high overhead in the cave's ceiling replaced the rising moonlight from outside.

The mongrel Ves-Lari rowers slowed the crafts, making ready to dock, when a volley of crossbow bolts erupted from the wharf. Zabit and his men crouched while the Singa archers returned fire. Arrows rained down on them, making swishing sounds entering the water and sharp cracks when lodging in the boats.

The commander heard the telltale report of projectiles striking flesh to his right, as well as behind him, followed by anguished cries. Zabit glanced up to see the Pa-Waga cleric teetering with a bolt protruding from his chest and a shocked expression frozen across his face.

"I told you to stay out of the way!" Zabit said, giving him a shove. "Where is your god now?"

The lifeless Yagur toppled over into the water and the boat rapidly slid up to one of the unoccupied slips. The Singa's quickly unloaded under heavy fire and Zabit could see his troops streaming out of five other boats. Once empty, they pulled away, allowing more to take their place.

The few Valdurian marines stationed in the harbor, seeing how badly they were outnumbered, began falling back. Two fell to Singa arrows, while the rest retreated, blowing their shrill alarm whistles.

Mal and party entered the immense Os-Ani Mountain cavern, which easily ran a hundred yards in diameter beneath an equally high ceiling dotted with stalactites. Webbing covered the walls and draped lazily between the stone protuberances extending from the cavern's roof. Mummified carcasses of various regional creatures hung from the roof, enclosed in silk cocoons.

Sheets of webbing connected with the floor at forty-five-degree angles, bleacher style, lining a fifty-foot-wide path to a receiving area in the middle of the room. Word of their holy prophet's return must have spread quickly through the brood, because Cevots of every size packed these arachnid grandstands. The crowd pulsed in anticipation and an excited chattering moved through the throng of humanoid spiders. Hairy legs thumped the floor and the air sweetened with the pheromones given off by the enthusiastic multitudes.

Three lone female Cevots stood on the far side of the cavern at the top of the web risers. Mal assessed the largest one in the middle, with a regal bearing, to be the queen. Standing to her right, a stern-faced, older one with large, exposed fangs suspiciously watched their approach.

The queen's advisor I'll bet, Mal surmised.

A much smaller female Cevot stood to the queen's left, attending to an intricate small web she suspended between her two front legs. She took note of the party, reached back to her thorax and shot a small amount of silk onto her fingertip. She then added it to the delicate pattern already adorning the grid.

Scribe, the Spice Rat silently noted.

The party came to a halt in the receiving area and all but Kumo bowed. Taleeka, who kept a close eye on her mom and dad, awkwardly followed their lead at Mal's prompting.

The sight of the Cevots unnerved the ten-grand-old at first, but her parents' calm demeanor comforted her.

"This is a joyous day," the queen announced. "The Strasta has returned as prophesied in the ancient records."

"Oh, Queen," the adviser said cautiously. "The ancient records say nothing of the Strasta returning with *friends*. How can we be sure?"

"Oh, Queen," the scribe spoke up, "the ancient prophecies do not state who she shall be returning with, only the manner of her return."

The scribe then closed her eyes and began to recite from memory, "And it shall come to pass, in the moon cycle of Neeot, that the Strasta shall return from the sky in which she ascended. Coming forth from her sacred cocoon to guide her children with a message."

The adviser threw the scribe an angry glance, while the queen appeared to be weighing both sides of the argument.

"You say you are the Strasta?" the queen thoughtfully inquired of Kumo.

"I do not," Kumo answered truthfully.

By the Goddess, Mal groaned inwardly, *of all the times for honesty, she fucking chooses now!*

The scribe immediately intervened. "Oh, Queen, it is also recorded in the ancient texts that the way to tell false prophets is that they come proclaiming their holiness. By not professing herself, she has proved herself to be the Strasta."

The queen nodded in agreement, succumbing to the scribe's well-presented case.

The queen's gaze returned to Kumo. "Strasta, do you have a message to guide us?"

"Sell it!" Mal whispered frantically.

"Yes," Kumo whispered back.

Mal heaved a sigh of relief. *Thank the Goddess!*

"I bring a warning," Kumo continued softly.

The statement caused the queen and crowd to shift about nervously. Some raised their front arachnid legs in alarm while others tapped their thoraxes on the floor.

"There are forces from distant nations to the east, which have their greedy gaze set upon this land and the holy mountains you call home."

This set off a murmur in the crowd and the queen quickly searched the faces of both advisor and scribe. Kumo waited for the words to register before continuing.

"They want to enslave you and steal your precious silk."

"What kind of forces do you speak of?" the queen asked with a touch of doubt.

"Cat creatures, calling themselves mawls. They are already making war against the Bailians."

The queen's eyes narrowed and she grew animated. "If what you say is true, let them come. We will entrap them in our webs and feast on them."

"This enemy is clever, resourceful and patient," Kumo replied, never raising her voice. "They don't have to come to you. All they have to do is cut you off from your trading partners and wait you out."

This gave the queen pause and she quietly conferred with her adviser. When she looked back at Kumo her face carried a concerned demeanor.

"What can my brood do?"

Kumo smiled. "Fortunately, there is still time to prepare, and my friends have a plan."

Jo-Rakk couldn't help but hear the chorus of alarm whistles rising from the harbor. The Tiikeri ambassador peered out the window from the diplomatic compound and saw human and Bailian marines rush down the street towards the wharf, crossbows at the ready. The city's defenders had prepared for an army marching their way from the east and an attack by sea obviously caught them by surprise.

"Sir, what's going on?" Takki asked, looking concerned.

"I'm afraid king Kar-Gor has succumbed to the darker side of his nature," Jo-Rakk sadly replied.

This perplexed the fawn-colored mongrel. "Sir?"

The white man-tiger silently watched skirmishes break out in the streets. He sorrowfully shook his head and flexed his claws in and out.

"The size of the bloodshed now depends on who they put in charge," Jo-Rakk said to himself.

"What do we do, sir?" the seneschal asked, noticing the fighting.

"Right now, there's nothing that can be done. It's too dangerous to be out there. We'll wait until things settle down, then I'll find their commander."

The Tiikeri didn't have long to wait. The same marines who ran towards the wharf, retreated in a full-on rout back in the direction they came from.

Singa foot soldiers filled the street directly behind the fleeing marines. Two female Singa criers, caterwauling to get attention, led the throng calling for surrender in broken En-Sul. They marched confidently, promising assurances of safety with the populace's peaceful compliance.

Jo-Rakk spotted the Tiikeri commander's entourage in the middle of the pack and heaved a sigh of relief when he saw Commander Zabit in charge. He had a reputation for not being prone to extremes.

"Well, thank the gods for that," Jo-Rakk said, heading for the door. "I think it's safe enough now,"

He walked out of the compound with Takki right behind. Jo-Rakk stood in the middle of the street with his arms folded while the Singa army flowed around the scowling, obstinate ambassador. Commander Zabit, his colonel, and several junior officers, came to a halt right before Jo-Rakk.

"ZABIT, WHAT IS THIS MADNESS?!" Jo-Rakk demanded.

The Singa commander calmly approached with a confident smile. "We're securing a legacy for the king and the new Cub Prince, ambassador, and I would appreciate any assistance you might be able to offer."

Taleeka skipped exuberantly up the side ramp into the *Haraka*, her face alight with joy. She immediately bounded over to the Navigator's chair where Zau had just finished conferring with her map. The phantasmal blue globe retreated back into the Singa's eye just as the out of breath ten-grand-old came to a stop.

"Zau, look what I got," she said, holding out a square piece of what the navigator first thought to be lace.

"The Cevot queen gave it to me." Taleeka's diminutive frame vibrated with excitement. "It's my own personal friend pass! It says that I'm a forever friend of the Cevot spiders and that they won't try to eat me!"

"That's pretty good kid. Let me see it."

Zau examined the trinket. The hardened silk frame ran three inches square and contained a delicate but extremely asymmetrical web suspended between its boarders.

"Nice!" she commented, returning it to Taleeka.

Zau then noticed Mal, Alto and Kumo trailing behind the energetic child. When she caught Mal's eye, she pointed out the Larimar Etheria disk on the overhead console glowed white, alerting them to an incoming transmission.

"This should be a fucking riot," the Spice Rat said reaching up and touching the communications gem.

Immediately Rafel's voice filled her head. Mal rarely spoke during her conversation, answering only with a few "uh huhs," and other placating utterances.

When she finished, the Spice Rat silently faced an understandably inquisitive Alto, Zau and Kumo. Taleeka ignored them and sat in her usual spot, entranced with the Cevot's gift.

"Well?!" Zau queried anxiously.

"Looks like we're heading back to the Dark Waste."

"What's going on, Captain?"

"A large Singa force is taking the oasis," she answered. "The furry fuckers have already taken Lor-Danta. The Gila's successfully evacuated Qua-Raman and it's expected to be occupied as soon as the next luna. That leaves the Asaro-He Oasis directly in their path.

"The University of Marassa has a researcher there. We need to extract her and the lapidary she's working with, along with all the Etheria we can carry. And we need to get it done before they're overrun."

"We were just there!" Zau groaned.

"Yeah, and it's the same fucking Zadim we got the Trinilic from a little while ago."

"Don't you worry," Mal said, "the university is going to get a bill that'll knock their fucking boots off.

"Kumo, let's push off," she ordered, peering back at the ship's helm. "Zau, plot us a course to the Asaro-He Oasis."

"Yes, Captain."

The once unthinkable had happened. Immor-Onn, the Independent City State and Jewel of the East, was under attack.

Frantic rumors shot through the city, describing a small fleet of open-topped ships, filled with cat people, sailing into the city's twin harbors. They said that the Valdurian Marines, acting as city guards, put up a fight, but much larger and more powerful lion creatures hopelessly outnumbered them.

Now, the citizenry found itself in a panic. The mostly Bailian crowds rushed about aimlessly, their screams and cries drowning out the windchimes overhead. Tam-Eez and Jetim, two of Kai's orphans, rushed down the streets filled with terrorized sentients, swept along with the confusion.

"They say not to fight and we won't be harmed," Jetim said, her voice trembling with dread.

Tam-Eez looked down at the younger Bailian orphan and he brushed the sweat matted, long black hair out of her large, brown eyes widened with doubt.

"You saw them roughing up anyone who happened to be in their way," he reminded her. "They may not kill you, but they sure aren't friendly. We've got to get off the streets."

"Where?!"

"Back to the Zephyr!"

Suddenly the crowd they were being swept along with stopped and started running back in the opposite direction, escaping a detachment of ten growling lion-men headed their way. Panicked screams erupted from the fleeing mob.

"Quick, in here!" Tam-Eez said, grabbing her by the arm and pulling her into an alley. "We'll hide here till they pass."

Tam-Eez directed her behind a small stack of crates. Once certain she was secure, the half Bailian boy, with mahogany hair, sought refuge in the deep recesses of a doorway.

They hunkered down and listened to the passing uproar from the besieged avenue. Both shrunk as far as they could into the shadows and froze in horror when they heard three Singas enter the alley.

A Singa sergeant and two of his charges warily searched the narrow side street, while the rest of his men continued herding the locals.

"I know I saw at least one of those damn blue skins come in here," growled the sergeant in his native mawl.

"Are you sure, Sarge?" one of his soldiers asked, confused. "We didn't see nothing."

"That's why you two grass eaters are still privates. You got your heads up your asses instead of paying attention."

Jetim felt the tears begin and couldn't stop trembling listening to the Singas clattering down the alley. She didn't dare look to see what was going on for fear of being spotted.

"We know you're here," the sergeant called out in broken En-Sul. "Come out and we'll be easy on you."

When silence greeted the Singa sergeant's request, his next utterance grew antagonistic. "Have it your way, blue skin, but you're not going to like it when we find you."

Jetim felt certain they could hear her teeth chattering which thundered in her head. She quickly stuck a finger in her mouth and clamped down on it to silence them.

She cried out in surprise and alarm when they yanked one of the boxes in front of her away with a crash. With wide eyes and trembling lips, she found herself staring up at the irritated sergeant. His lower lip quivered in anger and the small Bailian girl found herself focusing on an odd-looking patch of grey fur adorning one side of his chin.

"There you are!" he snarled, reaching down and grabbing her by the arm.

Tam-Eez watched helplessly from the deep shadows of the doorway. The much larger man-lion savagely yanked the little Bailian out of hiding and held her up in front of his face.

Gunahkar growled threateningly as she dangled helplessly in his grip, punching and kicking at thin air.

Finally, tired of his captive's struggling, he gave out a single frustrated roar before biting out her throat.

The screaming and scuffling immediately ceased. The young girl went limp in his hands and her blood stained the sergeant's face and chest a gruesome shade of red. Thrashing his head side to side, he tore away most of the flesh off the neck. Jetim's long, blood drenched hair swayed while her head bobbed about, held on by only the spinal cord.

"Hey, Sarge, I thought we weren't supposed to kill any of them?" a private asked.

The sergeant swallowed his morsel and scowled back at his subordinates.

"They weren't supposed to fight," he answered defiantly. "She was fighting. Besides, I'm hungry."

He then grabbed Jetim's corpse by the legs and stripped off her tunic.

"You two look like you could use a quick bite," he said, casually rending her arms from their sockets with a disgusting crack of bone. He tossed the severed limbs to his comrades and held the body up to his blood-stained mouth to bite into the torso.

Tam-Eez remained petrified with terror, his mouth agape in a silent scream. Tears streamed down his face and he felt a warm wetness filling the front of his pants. Not daring to move, he could only stand and watch his friend be devoured before his eyes.

Quadin rose shortly after moonrise. A gentle breeze wafted across the Rovina plains, ruffling her short brown fur. Peeking above the pervasive layer of mist, she could see the tops of the lush grasslands gently swaying. The Singa officer yawned, stretched and licked her paws to wash her face.

She peered out from the communal, open-sided hut and could see the pride's females tearing into a kill from the last moonless. The male elders, appetites already sated, lounged against nearby trees with their bloody snouts facing into the cool gentle wind.

A full twenty lunas had passed since Tiikeri conscription officers took away those eligible for military service—including her mate, Bajec. With most male Singas of age away in the service of the empire, the pride performed their morning rituals absent the familiar clash of arms and strained growls of sparring males.

They also enlisted more females for Sikari hunter/killer squads than ever before, so whatever operation the empire was planning, it must be big.

Being an officer, it hardly surprised Quadin when they called Captain Bajec's name first from the ranks of the Jaona Pride. They expected him to rally the rest of the troops and march them south to waiting ships on the shore of the Land of Mists.

As usual, she had no idea where the fleet headed or how long they would be gone. Her term of service as an intelligence gatherer had been over for several grands. Now, she could only perform her duties within the pride, care for her two cubs and pray to the gods for his safe return.

Quadin had just finished relieving herself and started covering the scat when she heard the Ash-Ta's cry. She gazed up excitedly into the moonlit sky and could see its erratic flight pattern headed her way. Keeping her eye on the humanoid bat, she rushed out of the pride's compound into the open where it could easily spot her.

The tried-and-true technique worked, just as it had so many times before. The Ash-Ta screeched, dove within twenty feet of her head, and released a rolled-up object from its feet. She retracted her claws and caught the scroll, careful not to tear the lizard skin. It was the first correspondence from Bajec since the campaign began.

Eager for news, Quadin headed back to her hut, but not before attracting the attention of several females who headed her way. She often shared letters with her illiterate pride mates. It excited them to hear of events outside their corner of the Annigan, even if it didn't involve them.

She sat on the side of her hut, undid the band and opened the scroll. A crowd of ten Singas gathered around her, softly chattering, with eyes fixed on the open document in anticipation. Smiling nervously, she peered down at the open scroll and began to read.

"Dearest Quadin,

Please forgive the tardiness of this letter, but they strictly forbid any outside contact before the operation is well under way.

The boat ride to the Twilight Lands was thankfully short, you know of my distaste for large bodies of water. This is the largest military maneuver I have ever been part of. There must be ten thousand of us.

Upon landing, the force split, with half of our soldiers heading across the northern part of the land. I am a part of the army marching across the southern half under the command of General Baag-Tar.

My love, this is a strange land indeed. They call it a desert. There is nothing but sand as far as the eye can see. It is completely devoid of any vegetation, except around widely separated small lakes called oases. It is these oases, and the communities surrounding them, that the high command seem most interested in.

The first oasis fell quickly with virtually no resistance. We are now marching toward the second of three and I fear the ease of our task is rapidly vanishing.

The people of this land are lizard-like in nature. They are docile for the most part, save a select group which now opposes our every step. It is their method of combat which is most unsettling and has my comrades and I constantly on edge. You see, these people have the ability to travel under the sand. They can rise and strike at any moment with no warning. We've lost many good soldiers in the last few lunas. They drag them down under the sand, never to be seen again.

My dearest, I cannot conceive of a worse way to perish than being buried alive. I pray we reach this oasis soon, lest we all succumb to this horrific fate.

Please give my love to the cubs and my regards to the elders. I cannot wait to hold you in my arms, provided I make it back, which at this point seems quite uncertain.

I remain your faithful mate,

Bajec."

Quadin closed the scroll and peered out at the anxious faces staring at her.

"I'm sure they will be fine," she said attempting to sound positive. "Baag-Tar is one of our greatest generals."

Inside, however, her stomach fluttered with anxiety at the thought of never seeing him again.

Supreme General Jal-Pi lifted his tail and sprayed the base of the table he presided over, just as he began every meeting, other than those with the king. During his career, this simple and singular act of dominance prevented many a contentious meeting from descending into chaos.

Opening ritual now complete, he examined the unit markers placed on the surface map of the Twilight Lands. Each token represented the specific army's last reported position. He reached across the topography and moved a marker from the open waters on the north side of the continent to just offshore of the only city on its west coast.

"By now, Commander Zabit is taking Immor-Onn," he said to the four advisers intently watching his every move, "and unless he is meeting more resistance than expected, we should be getting a report within the next few lunas."

The general stepped back from the table and stroked his chin thoughtfully while his whiskers twitched. He hated relying on the Ash-Ta to deliver much delayed messages, but he had no choice. It would be quite some time before their Worrg network was functional again.

A mongrel army runner interrupted his militaristic contemplations with a message. He accepted the small, seemingly blank piece of paper with a nod, and then sniffed out the brief note.

Orders delivered.
Assets in place.
Need to meet.
Moonfall, by the pit.
- Q

"Where did you get this?" the general asked, brow furrowed in confusion.

"A female Singa in uniform," the runner replied, before saluting and leaving.

Jal-Pi didn't understand the meaning of the note, but if it had something to do with the current operation, he couldn't chance missing some potentially crucial intel. The pit was across town. He would have to hurry to get there before moonfall.

Fortunately, the city's pre-moonfall's congestion eagerly got out of the way of his pachyderm driven coach. He arrived near the outskirts of Hai-Darr just as the moon dipped below the horizon.

Jal-Pi took in the sparce surroundings. Architects designed the single-story buildings dedicated to dispensing the judgement of the empire more ornately than the rest of the city. The architectural flairs and historical reliefs on the exterior walls gave the space a bureaucratic feel. They built the execution pit, a twenty-foot diameter smooth walled arena with a single deadly purpose, central to it all.

Now, with the moonless upon them, plazas and streets normally bustling with mawls stood empty and virtually lifeless. *The perfect spot for a clandestine meeting*, he silently assessed listening to his carriage rumble off.

Jal-Pi stood there for a moment, allowing his eyes to adjust to the deep shadows between buildings when he saw movement to his right. "Hello?"

He followed the shadowy figure around the nearest building, and no sooner turned the corner, when the entire area became bathed in bright orange light. From the surrounding building's recesses, the street quickly filled with the clatter of a dozen armed Singas wearing the tunics of the royal guard.

The burley lion-men silently glared at the supreme military commander with weapons raised.

"What in the name of the empire is going on here?!" he sputtered incredulously, giving a hiss of protest.

"An excellent question Jal-Pi," said a familiar voice from the rear of the surrounding mob.

The Singa soldiers parted and King Kar-Gor stepped through sneering contemptuously. Jal-Pi immediately assumed the worst when he saw the robed figure of the Pa-Waga High Priest Raa-Ja standing next to him. The Yagur peered out from under his cowl with a superior smirk.

"Your majesty," he said nervously with a bow.

"I'll repeat the question," the Tiikeri sovereign said, reaching out his hand to Raa-Ja.

The Yagur cleric pulled a small bag from under his cloak and handed it to the king. Kar-Gor maintained his confrontational gaze while passing it to a baffled Jal-Pi.

"Explain these, if you can," the king demanded.

The Tiikeri general warily peered inside the bag at six multi-leaf booklets.

"My Piety Watch intercepted your Agent Q before he could deliver your treasonous orders." Raa-Ja accused.

Jal-Pi opened one of the pamphlets in wide eyed confusion and his tail swished anxiously. The pages were blank but he smelled the scent codes. Sure enough, each one was addressed to one of his high-ranking aides. The pamphlet detailed plots to assassinate King Kar-Gor and the Cub Prince, launching a total coup of the government.

"Your Majesty," Jal-Pi protested, "I can assure you I have no idea what you are referring to. I am a loyal subject of the Tiikeri Empire!"

"Those orders to your co-conspirators spell out your treachery!" Raa-Ja said, watching Jal-Pi sniff the pages.

"They are in your scent, are they not?" The king asked, his voice trembling with rage.

"Well, yes, Your Majesty, but…" Jal-Pi then turned an angry gaze upon the Pa-Waga cleric. "You!"

"Do not include me in your treachery," Raa-Ja replied. "I am a humble servant of the lord and of the empire he looks down on with benevolence."

"Your Majesty!" Jal-Pi pleaded. "I am a loyal member of your inner circle. I was one of those who helped you regain your throne!"

The king's gazed at him mercilessly. "Which makes your betrayal even more heinous. My Piety Watch is rounding up your fellow traitors as we speak. We'll deal with them the same way we dealt with your Agent Q. It was he that we used to flush you out."

"I don't know any Agent Q! I don't know what you're talking about! I thought I was meeting with someone who had information on the current operation."

An unconvinced king nodded his head and the Singa guards seized the white Tiikeri general.

Jal-Pi, seeing reason was failing, turned a contemptuous gaze toward Raa-Ja. "I demand a trial by combat with my accuser. It is my right."

"Traitors have no rights," the king said, breaking Jal-Pi's death stare at the dark cleric. "Into the pit."

The royal order given, the Singas muscled a struggling Jal-Pi towards the looming hole in the plaza.

"IF YOUR GOD IS SO GREAT, AND YOU SPEAK THE TRUTH, FIGHT ME!"

With a vicious shove they tossed the Tiikeri over the side.

"COWARD! FIGHT ME!" resonated up from the pit.

Everyone gathered around the edge. The Singas unslung their bows and nocked arrows.

"Jal-Pi," the king said coldly, "for treason against the Tiikeri Empire, I, Kar-Gor, sentence you to death."

Jal-Pi looked up at Raa-Ja's gloating smile while Kar-Gor pronounced the sentence.

"YOU WON'T FIGHT ME BECAUSE THE GODS KNOW YOU LIE AND WOULD GRANT *ME* VICTORY!"

"Death to the enemies of the empire," the king proclaimed.

"Death to the enemies of the empire," the Singas chanted in unison, before releasing their arrows.

Raa-Ja stared down at the bloody impaled corpse and grinned with satisfaction, one more obstacle removed. Now, there would be no more challenges to his council to the king.

"Death to the enemies of the Lord," he added softly, before turning to leave.

They brutally killed his friend Jetim before his very eyes and Tam-Eez was taking it hard. So many emotions to deal with; survivors' guilt, helplessness for not being able to prevent her death, a profound sense of loss at a life ended too soon, but mostly, a burning hatred for the mawl invaders.

Kai stared across the table at the grieving teenager and her heart sank. She, too, missed the vibrant young girl who always had a kind word for everyone.

She realized that even though she also suffered with grief—first with Drucilla's death, and now Jetim—she would have to be the strong one. For these had proven to be troubled times, in addition to the two recent deaths, her city had been occupied and her beloved queen, exiled.

"We were headed back here," he repeated again, before taking a big gulp of ale from the tankard in front of him.

Tam-Eez rarely drank, but in this instance, Kai completely understood.

"I couldn't do anything but watch them eat her," he lamented, returning the mug to the table.

"And you're sure you can identify them?" Kai asked gently.

Tam-Eez nodded and several of his mahogany locks tumbled down onto his forehead. "It was really only one. I'm pretty sure he was the leader. I mean, I couldn't really understand them, but the two others didn't seem to want to have anything to do with it."

"You said he spoke our language?"

Tam-Eez nodded again. "A little."

Kai sat back in her chair and looked around. Light from the newly risen moon streamed through the windows and glass doors, illuminating the empty dining room. Singa patrols on the vacant streets just outside the Whispering Zephyr passed by in the eerie quiet. She watched them move out of her sight.

The front doors opened, drawing her attention. A white Tiikeri in blue robes stepped into the room with a confident stride, followed closely by two Singa guards. Tamm-Eez's face went flush when he saw the Singas. His focus locked onto the one with the patch of white fur on his chin, now stained red.

"That's the one, Kai!" Tam-Eez said in a strained whisper. "That's the one!"

"Stay calm," Kai whispered back, not taking her eyes off the mawls. 'Remember your training and let me handle this."

Both silently watched the trio of cat-men approach and stop just before the table. The Tiikeri stepped forward.

"Kai?!" he said, clearly surprised.

"That's right," Kai curtly replied. "And you're bad for business, To-Nok."

The Tiikeri looked around the empty room and then back at Kai with an amused grin. "My apologies for the inconvenience. I heard you had set up shop here."

"Yeah, and until you folks showed up, I was doing pretty well."

"This is temporary, until we set up a regional governor. You'll be back on a paying basis in no time."

"You could just pull your forces out and it would happen a lot quicker."

"I'm afraid I can't do that." To-Nok pulled out a chair and sat down with a sly grin. "You see, this city is now a part of the Tiikeri Empire and I am temporarily in charge."

"Please, have a seat," Kai said sarcastically. "So, King Kar-Gor wasn't satisfied with just ruling the Land of Mists, huh?"

To-Nok glanced over at Tam-Eez sneaking hateful glances at the Singa sergeant. "Leave us!"

A panicked look crossed the teenager's face and he quickly looked over at Kai for confirmation.

"I'm sure you can find something to do in the stock room," she said with a calm smile.

The unnerved teenager quickly left and the two old acquaintances resumed their conversation.

"The new Cub Prince has been born," To-Nok continued. "And King Kar-Gor seeks to leave him a legacy."

Kai nodded appreciatively. "Expanding the empire, that's some legacy."

"Yes, the king has found, *religion*. This particular faith values the accumulation of wealth and power. So naturally he wishes to pass this on to his son."

Naturally," Kai said, playing along.

"Your queen has fled, has she not?"

"Yeah, she high tailed it out of here when she got word of your armies on the march to the east."

"You and the queen were close?"

"I was one of her *many* advisors,' Kai said, deliberately playing down her role.

"Would you say the people look up to you?"

Kai shrugged. "I run a clean place."

"And may I inquire about your relationship with the Bailians?"

"The Bailians are alright customers. That's about it."

"No particular deep-felt loyalties beyond their money?"

"Not especially," Kai lied.

To-Nok smiled. "That's good to hear. I trust you'll let me know if there are any discontents rumbling in the populace."

"What's in it for me?" Kai asked greedily.

"We let you stay in business."

"Right now, thanks to you, I don't have any business."

"It's temporary, as will be the moonfall curfew."

The word, curfew, gave Kai pause but she decided not to say anything. In the current climate, there wouldn't be any moonless customers anyways.

"I've got some incentive for you to get things back to normal," she offered.

"I'm intrigued."

Kai got up and went back into the stock room. She returned carrying a foot long wooden box, sat down, and slid the oblong container in front of the Tiikeri, who gave her a questioning stare.

"Open it," she said coyly.

The hinges creaked slightly when the top opened and the Tiikeri's face lit up when he saw the contents."

"Where did you get these?" he asked, pulling out a long blue stalk of Maudo Grass.

"A girl's gotta have some secrets. The thing is, I've got a line on this stuff. I can get you as much as you want as soon as things open up. For now, consider this a gift."

To-Nok smiled, brought the stalk up to his mouth and deftly stripped off the petals. A serene expression descended on his face when they dissolved on his tongue.

"As I said, it's temporary," To-Nok confirmed after gaining his composure.

"That's good because my supply here is limited. In the meantime, your men can drink for free as long as they don't abuse the privilege. The Maudo Grass is for you and whoever you want to share it with."

A sinister grin played at the Tiikeri's mouth. "You realize we could just take what we want?"

"Sure," Kai replied confidently, "but if this was a loot and pillage kind of operation, you would have already been doing it."

"True," To-Nok conceded standing. "We have a deal then?"

Kai nodded. "A deal."

"I will limit my men to two drinks each and impress upon them to be on their best behavior," he said, stepping away from the table.

"My profit margin thanks you."

To-Nok gave a pensive smile. "By the way, your young friend, he is pure Bailian?"

"Sure," Kai lied again.

"It's just his hair color is so... unusual. I would shudder to think of any race mixing."

"This is a very cosmopolitan city," Kai defended.

"Yes, well, nothing a little order and discipline can't fix. Oh, don't worry, your margin of profit will remain intact."

Kai watched as To-Nok and the two Singas left. Once gone, Tam-Eez immediately rejoined her.

"What did he want?" the young man asked. "And how do you know each other?"

"We were briefly allies when we helped overthrow the mutant king and put the Cub Prince on the Tiikeri throne. I've offered him what he thinks is a safe haven here."

"You're not still allies, are you?" Tam-Eez asked uncertainly.

Kai gave the young man a stunned look. "Are you kidding?! I didn't risk my life liberating this city so it could fall into the hands of tyrants! Have the children spread throughout the city. We need to keep an eye on our invaders. Have them report through you. They'll probably be watching me. In the meantime, we're gonna let them think they've got everything under control."

"What about the one who killed Jetim?"

A vengeful scowl crossed Kai's face. "He's all yours."

The Kan fog barely receded before Kasha left her dormitory room at the University of Marassa and rapidly made her way along the streets of Zor.

All around her, the high holy city came to life with its usual gusto. Shops opened, wagon loads of freshly offloaded goods made their way from the docks and laborers crowded around food stalls for their morning meal.

Much like the rest of the city, the Zorian Forum just convened for the day's bureaucratic undertakings.

Kasha, in keeping with the morning mood of the city, rushed along the already busy halls. The head of the University's Language Arts Department found herself more than aware of her racing pulse and parched mouth.

She found the door to Colonel Zekoff's office closed and she vigorously knocked. Rafel cracked it open and peered out with a guarded look. Upon seeing the visitor's identity, he smiled and swung the door fully open. Kasha gave a friendly nod and caught the aromatic whiffs of evergreen pipe tobacco.

"Marassa Kasha," the spymaster said, his tone friendly, yet business like. "What can we do for you this morning?"

"Captain Rafel, please excuse this interruption but I needed to talk with you and the Colonel. I knew you had your morning briefing and I could catch both of you at the same time."

"This sounds serious," Rafel said, noting her austere demeanor and welcoming her in.

Entering the spacious office, the evergreen aroma became even more pronounced. Zekoff sat behind his wide desk, puffing out a cloud of smoke gathering lazily about his head.

"Kasha, good to see you." Zekoff lowered his pipe and fanned away the surrounding cloud. "What can the Zorian Guards do for you this morning?"

"I wanted to let you all know that I felt its presence last Kan, more so than on the night of the earthquake. This time, Pa-Waga reached out to me."

"Are you alright?" Zekoff asked in concern.

Kasha nodded and held up her hand indicating the large ring she wore. "Yes, I had the Etheria Studies Department create this bauble for me. It's got two different Etheria Crystals mounted on it. One for inner strength and the other is a psychic shield. I'm safe as long as I'm wearing it."

"Well, that's good," Zekoff said, visibly relieved. "We wouldn't want a repeat of what happened last time."

"You say he reached out to you?" Rafel asked. "How?"

"He was calling my name, searching for me. The shield prevented him from finding me, but he's close. As in, on this plane and in this city, close."

"Do you think you could locate him?" Zekoff asked hopefully.

Kasha shook her head. "Not without lowering my shield. I can't take the chance of him finding me again."

Zekoff took another puff off his pipe. "I agree, far too dangerous. Well then, it's a waiting game. We'll have to see what the Vicar of Pa-Waga's next move will be."

The moon had just set and Rasul raced through the busy streets of the Tiikeri capital of Hai-Darr. The humanoid cheetah and trusted messenger of the crown had found himself extra busy of late since they destroyed the Worrg Pits. Messages now had to be delivered the old-fashioned way, by hand.

He moved past the close-packed, single-story wooden structures and caught the scent address of each building. This time, however, an address proved unnecessary, as his destination happened to be the royal palace.

He had just left the Ash-Ta landing, where they removed the scroll from the bat creature's leg, determined its destination and assigned a runner. Since they had composed the message in scent code, invisible to the eye, it immediately went into his hands.

Rasul loved his job and always took it seriously. It turned out to be much better than scraping out an existence on the Rovina plains, precariously navigating around Singa pride territories.

Approaching the sprawling palace complex, the young cheetah-man reflected on the way the city and king had changed since the rise of the new religion.

The entire concept of religion baffled Rasul and his kind, as well as the Pomaku leopard people. For that reason, the Tiikeri left them alone, but had exerted incredible pressure on the other 'higher' mawl races to convert from whatever beliefs they formally held.

Up ahead, on the opposite side of the street, a group of red caped mongrels from the Piety Watch beat a mongrel worker for not performing his job quickly enough, just one of the many changes brought on by this new religion. Public idleness, now strictly forbidden, earned you a beating. Poverty, while not technically against the law, carried with it an aura of shame and failure. Whether you believed in this new faith or not, you were still subject to its laws.

Passing the public flogging, he arrived at the wide entrance to the palace. He nodded at the two-spear wielding Pomaku guards flanking the opening. Rasul, well known around the palace and the leopard-men, nodded back.

The doorway opened into a large courtyard surrounded by various offices and meeting rooms. His destination this time happened to be the door of the throne room on the opposite side of the plaza. Unlike at the main entrance a guard blocked his path.

"The king is in consultation with the high priest and is not to be disturbed," the Pomaku declared formally.

"This message is labeled 'urgent' and 'king's eyes only,' his majesty is going to want to see it."

The guard paused for a moment while considering the explanation. Finally, nodding, he stepped aside.

What first struck Rasul upon entering the spacious, virtually barren room was the copious piles of valuable gems littering the floor. He then noticed the partially eaten antelope laying on a small portable serving table.

The king himself also stood out, as he didn't look well. The black Tiikeri sovereign lounged about on his covered throne, talking quietly with Ra-Jaa the black robed Yagur and high priest of Pa-Waga. He had gained considerable weight since Rasul had last seen him. His eyes, sunken into his head, maintained a disturbingly vacant stare.

The quantity of flamboyant jewelry with which the once austere leader now adorned himself also proved unsettling. He wore ostentatious rings on every pudgy finger, a thick, jewel encrusted gold necklace draped around his neck, and an extravagant crown atop his head.

Trying not to stare, Rasul lowered his head and made his way over to his king, who immediately ceased his conversation with Ra-Jaa and gave the messenger an annoyed look.

Rasul dropped down on one knee in front of the throne and kept his head bowed. "Your majesty, I'm sorry to disturb you, but this dispatch just arrived. It's marked 'urgent and for your eyes only.'"

The ruler's look softened and he silently motioned for Rasul to approach. Once in possession of the paper, the king broke the seal and sniffed the seemingly blank sheet. Rasul, head still bowed, backed away to a discreet distance and awaited further orders.

"This is from our operative in Otomoria, Bo-Lah. He has established a strong foothold amongst the humans. He's confident, with military support from us, he can command the entire southern half of the continent."

"This is exciting news!" Ra-Jaa said, unable to contain his enthusiasm.

"Actually, this couldn't have come at a worse time," the king replied wearily. "The bulk of our military is engaged in the Twilight Lands. Even if I could redeploy some of them, we have no Worrg network to effectively direct them."

"Take heart, Your Majesty. We serve a mighty god! The lord has given us this opportunity for a reason. Think of the wealth this will bring to the empire. It will be a testament to your greatness and the will of Pa-Waga!"

"And how do you propose we accomplish this Ra-Jaa?"

"Sire, surely we have some troops available?"

Kar-Gor sat for a moment pondering the request.

"Well, the Cadam and Berow Singa prides are held back in reserve," the king conceded, "but the two combined would only make up a few hundred fighters."

"Your majesty, one Singa warrior is worth ten humans."

"Do not underestimate the humans, Raa-Ja," Kar-Gor said cautiously. "They are clever and resourceful."

"What about the new mongrels the Kherry Institute has been breeding? I have heard they are bigger and stronger than the average mongrel slave and don't need eye protection in the bright Lumina sun."

The king stroked the fur on his chin, deep in thought. "There *are* several hundred of those, too," he conceded.

"And, Your Majesty, we have something the humans do not. We serve a mighty god, one that wants us to prosper. We cannot fail!"

Slowly the king began nodding his head while maintaining his pensive stare. "Yes, yes, a great victory is possible."

"That country has boundless resources. It will be a glorious addition to the empire, an even greater legacy for your son and a fitting testament to our god!"

"Very well," the king said, coming out of his contemplative trance. "Rasul!

"Yes, Your Majesty?"

"Find me that new Minister of War and send him here at once!"

"Yes, Your Majesty!"

"Oh, and Rasul."

"Yes, Your Majesty?"

"Before you go, break me off a hind quarter of that antelope. Conquering is hungry work."

A little over one lunar cycle after Commander Zabit's naval infantry took the Bailian capital of Immor-Onn, it became painfully obvious to the Singa commander that, while taking the city may have been relatively easy, successfully holding it would prove quite another matter. The twin wharfs of the city state, crucial to the operation's plans, now firmly rested under their control and that greatly pleased him. The outlying agricultural areas, however, still gave limited resistance, and the slums of the southeastern city called Viri-Tra proved the most troublesome.

His troops found themselves unaccustomed to fighting in an urban environment and the casualties continued to mount. The slums became a porous barrier from the city to the Os-Tor Forest where the resistance and their supplies flowed.

"I should burn that blight from the city and be done with it!" Zabit said in a frustrated growl.

Jo-Rakk held open the white lace curtains, staring out the second story window of the confiscated palace office which constituted Zabit's new command center. Down in the street. an eerie calm hung ominously in the air.

Singa sentries stood at every intersection closely monitoring the city's inhabitants while they attempted to navigate around their occupied home. The Tiikeri could easily make out the looks of fear and loathing directed at the invaders by the stunned populace.

"That, would prove to be the crowning act of folly in this already ill-conceived endeavor." Jo-Rakk said, allowing the curtains to fall back into place.

Zabit huffed and watched the distressed ambassador slowly spin to face him. "Ambassador, I know that living amongst these peoples for so long you've grown fond of them, but remember where your loyalties lie."

"Commander, I don't need to be reminded of anything. I was one of those responsible for putting Kar-Gor on the throne. My loyalties have always been with king and empire. Not with some dangerous religious cult on the rise."

"Your feelings about this new religion are immaterial, as are mine," Zabit said firmly. "Whether we like it or not, the king is now a believer, and he has agreed to raise the Cub Prince within the faith. This *cult,* as you call it, is well on its way to becoming the state religion. My advice to you, would be to get used to it."

A knock at the door interrupted the conversation. A uniformed mongrel runner entered without invitation, handed Zabit a piece of paper, and then quickly left.

The Singa commander opened the note and sniffed the message, before lowering his arm with a weary sigh.

"It appears that there are several hundred Bailian officials and others holed up in the Air Station. The station's commander is claiming diplomatic protection because the air station and adjoining embassy is technically Valdurian soil."

Jo-Rakk watched Zabit's face grow taut and he crumpled the paper in a clenched fist.

"I want that air station cleared!" Zabit said with a scowl.

"Once again Zabit, not one of your more stellar ideas."

"And what would Ambassador Jo-Rakk suggest we do?"

"Nothing."

"I beg your pardon!"

"Wait them out," Jo-Rakk flatly offered. "You've got the air station quarantined. Thanks to one of our assets, the remaining air fleet is still grounded. They're not going

194

anywhere. Besides, the Valdurian Ambassador is still in there, Valindra *Valdur* to be specific. If you go charging in there all heavy-handed, folks are going to get hurt or killed. Do you really want to take on the Valdurians too? I can assure you that is exactly what will happen if you set foot in that air station."

Zabit's sneer persisted. "I have my orders. This city will be brought to heel! Go and talk some sense into this Valdurian woman. The sentients in her care will disperse, one way or the other."

"It's too quiet down there," General Baag-Tar said, lowering the spyglass. "The entire oasis appears abandoned."

He handed the optical device to Commander Karga, standing next to him, and they peered out across the moonlit desert onto the Qua-Raman Oasis. The peaks of the Os'Ani Mountains loomed a short distance to the north.

The empty village of single-story structures surrounded three sides of a lake. A massive field of obsidian seemed to flow out of one side and onto the sand, forming its own body beside it. Six giant, circular star charts, etched in the black crystal, covered the surface.

A two-story tower with a simple box on top, stood inside a walled compound next to the obsidian field. A neatly manicured agricultural field, parceled out with rows of irrigation, filled the rest of the shoreline.

"Nothing going on down there, sir," Karga confirmed. "I'm betting they must have been warned."

The seasoned general found himself torn. They had been marching almost steadily now for seven lunas. His men were tired and hungry. They had been harassed by an unseen enemy the entire trek along the caravan route and everyone's nerves were raw. He liked the idea of an easy occupation, given the number of men he had lost along the way. However, something wasn't right.

"Well Commander, we know what we have to do. That oasis sits directly in the path of the only pass through those mountains. Take half of our forces around and push in from the west. I'll bring in the remainder from the east as soon as we secure that compound." He then quickly scanned the mountain range. "Have the Duma scouts been deployed?"

"Yes, sir, I sent a small team to reconnoiter the pass and mountains. I sent another west, towards the next oasis."

"Good, alright…"

The roaring, panicked cry of another soldier pulled beneath the sand cut short the general's order. Both senior officers helplessly lowered their heads and grimaced.

"Let's take the oasis while we still have an army to do it."

The visuals from the top of the dune proved correct and the entire oasis appeared abandoned. Commander Karga strode warily down the main street, his troops right behind. Lining the vacant thoroughfare, deserted shops and stores silently welcomed them. The wind whistled through the empty avenues and mini cyclones passed between the buildings.

"Find the lapidary's workshops," Karga said, indicating both sides of the sand covered street.

He watched his men fan out and warily approach the various store fronts. He considered calling out a word of caution, when the sky to the east erupted in a silent orange explosion, followed by countless anguished screams.

Another explosion happened up ahead where a four-man team just breached a building. A blinding orange flash and searing heat blasted out from the doorway they broke open. All four Singas fell screaming to the ground, their scorched black seared skin smoldering. The blast burned bystanders as far as twenty feet away. They ran about wildly wailing, their long manes burning halos around their heads.

Karga looked away, blinded by the flash. Even though he couldn't see, he could hear the cries of pain and smell the burnt fur and flesh up along the street where more buildings had been entered.

"STOP, EVERYTHING'S BOOBYTRAPPED!" Karga screamed, fumbling about in darkness.

General Baag-Tar looked around at the blackened bodies of his men lying motionless in the sand. Their charred faces locked in silent screams. A quick calculation told him he had lost well over a hundred men attempting to enter the lapidary's walls. By the flashes and shrieks coming from in town, Karga had been met in a similar fashion.

"Get to the water!" he barked. "Stay away from the buildings!"

When the two forces converged and reassembled around the calm lake, the orange Tiikeri general found himself mortified to see his commander and right hand being led with a cloth wrapped around his head, covering his eyes.

When he rushed over, grabbed Karga by the shoulders and started to question him, the large circular charts etched into the obsidian began strobing with a bright blue light. He barely had enough time to look over at them, when the strobes united in a giant blue flash.

In an instant, all fifty soldiers standing on the brittle, black surface promptly vanished. Once ferocious Singa warriors now milled about in confusion and alarm all around the area.

"Stay off the crystal! Move into the agricultural field!" the general ordered in an attempt to rally his troops.

After several tries, the large body of Singas assembled amidst the low rows of crops.

With Karga standing blindly beside him, Baag-Tar summoned what optimism he could muster and prepared to address his men, when the two Duma scouts returned. The humanoid cheetahs, faces steeped in unease, saluted.

"My general," one hesitantly began, "it's about the pass through the mountains."

A sudden gust of wind erupted from the normal flurries, sending the windchimes over the streets of Immor-Onn clattering symphonically. Demetrius scrunched his face and cocked his head at Okawa, who stood next to him. The wind-swept boulevards of the Bailian capital were almost always noisy, but a sudden outburst from the hanging Etheria above could overwhelm any clamor from below.

Demetrius wasn't sure he had heard her correctly, but he figured he would attempt a reply.

"What's wrong with where the sofa is right now?"

"It would look better against the far wall." Okawa replied, not taking her eyes off the bakery storefront across the street.

Demetrius congratulated himself on hearing correctly.

"You haven't even moved in yet and you're already rearranging furniture?" he jabbed playfully.

"What can I say, I'm a take charge kinda girl."

"So, I see."

A playful smile danced on Okawa's face. "Get used to it."

The smile disappeared when an old Bailian woman exited the bakery with a bag in her hand. "Okay, he's alone. I'm going to go have a little chat with Si. Usho. Wait here. Be ready just in case things go sideways."

"Sideways? What kind of sideways?"

"Just be ready fly-boy," she said, stepping off the curb.

Demetrius watched her saunter through the sparsely traveled avenue. The green jumpsuit she wore, while meant to be utilitarian and official, hugged her luxurious frame. He felt a twinge of arousal watching her navigate the chaotic flow of lizard drawn wagons. By now, the occupied Bailian capital slowly returned to life, however the numerous check points and patrolling mawls, reminded everyone, things were far from normal.

Okawa made it to the other side of the street and cautiously scanned both ways before entering the shop. Closing the door behind her, she flipped the sign hanging in its window from "Open" to "Closed."

Once inside, Okawa became struck by the warmth given off by the three ovens along the back wall. One of the furnace's doors was open and a middle aged Bailian man, in a full-length apron, removed a tray of buns and placed them on a cooling rack.

"I'll be right with you," he said, not bothering to turn around.

"I've been told you're the best baker in the city." Okawa said cheerfully.

"You have heard correctly," he replied, spinning and wiping his hands.

Eyeing the human and the closed sign, his pleasant demeanor turned suspicious.

"What's going on?" he asked, his smooth blue features pulled taut.

"I'm here to place an order, Usho." Okawa replied, keeping her pleasant deportment.

"You're not a marine," he said, scanning her uniform. "And you're not the usual one that comes for my payment. I mean, I know it's time…"

"You're right, I'm not a marine," Okawa said, cutting him off. "My unit is a little more *specialized*. What payment?"

"You know… protection."

Okawa's brow furrowed warily, just as the shop's door flew open and two Bailian's, in Valdurian Marine jumpsuits, boisterously barged into the room.

"Hey, hey, it's payday, Usho!" the lead private bellowed cheerfully.

His face immediately fell when he saw Okawa. "Uh, major, what are you doing here?"

Okawa drew and cocked her pistol crossbow in one swift, fluid motion.

"Arresting you," she replied calmly, pointing the weapon at them.

The gregarious one slowly raised his hands with a shocked look on his face. The other panicked and threw open the door, in an attempt to make a quick escape into the street.

He found himself met by Demetrius blocking his path with his pistol drawn. Giving a frustrated sigh, he raised his hands. Demetrius waved the barrel towards the door and the Bailian marine stepped back into the shop.

"On your knees, hands on your head!" Okawa gruffly ordered. "*Slowly.*"

The two complied and Okawa turned her attention to the visibly shaken proprietor. "I need some bakers twine."

The relieved baker heartily nodded and handed her a roll from a table next to the cooling racks.

"Talk about your bad timing and just overall crappy luck," Okawa said.

She bound the two together, single file, around their necks and hands. All the while Demetrius kept his pistol leveled ominously on them.

"You know, shaking down merchants is bad enough, but to do it in the uniform of the very ones supposedly protecting them?" Okawa paused and shook her head. "Commander Sandal is going to take a very dim view of this. Not to mention the Valdurian ambassador. I hear she can be quite the bitch."

"Now," she continued, pulling the two marines to their feet, "my associate over there is going to escort you to the air station. You'll note that I've got you boys secured single file. If you try anything stupid, one shot will be more than necessary to take out the both of you. So, behave."

She nodded to Demetrius, handed him the end of the leash and they departed with the two captives in the lead. Okawa turned her attention back to Usho's grateful smile.

"Now, where were we?" she said holstering her pistol.

"I... I don't know how to thank you," he said, still trembling. "This has been going on for quite a few grands."

"You're welcome," Okawa replied, "and I know just how you can thank me."

"Name it."

Okawa gave a sly smile. "You recently procured a shipment of Zeta Moth larvae. I need to know who your client was."

The Bailian's face went from grateful to worried. "I don't know what..."

"Cut the crap, Usho," Okawa snapped. "I know you're the best finder in the city. The only one in fact, with the connections to locate those short-lived little grubs."

The baker lowered his head and sighed. "I normally don't give up my clients names," he said sheepishly.

"But, because you owe me one, you'll make an exception this time." Okawa said, leading the conversation her way.

"One of my oldest bakery customers," he said, meekly peering up. "It was Ora-Kora, the old general."

"Okay, were even," Okawa said reassuringly, even though her mind raced at the discovery of the saboteur's identity. "I trust we're both going to keep this conversation between us, for much the same reason."

Usho meekly nodded.

"Good then," Okawa said, heading for the door. "Pleasure doing business with you."

It had only been two lunas since Queen Shula arrived in the Amarenian capital of Mostas and, even though the Amarenian's extended her and her entourage every courtesy, Phu-Suany, the queen's young Bailian handmaiden, knew exile definitely did not sit well with the Balian sovereign.

Her queen appreciated the city's round architecture and apparently liked her modest, three-story residence situated between the palace and air station in central Mostas. As of late, Shula even began mimicking the bare-breasted clothing style of the mostly female population. Each luna, however, she found her queen anxiously pacing while watching the moonfall in the west.

Phu-Suany gracefully navigated the stairs to the third floor, carrying the queen's evening meal in a covered tray. Understandably, the monarch didn't have much of an appetite of late, but she brought her food anyways and fussed at her for hardly touching her plate.

This evening, a surprised Phu-Suany found Shula not in her spacious apartment. The open beaded doorway accessing stairs to the roof beckoned and so she followed. The evening's pleasant temperature, accompanied by low clouds to the west softened the sun's rays. Perhaps the queen had decided to take her evening meal on the roof, she guessed.

Stepping through the beaded door onto the top of the building, the handmaiden could not have been prepared for what she found.

Akaa stood just to the right of the exit. The seven-foot-tall Outer Clan EEtah bodyguard glanced down briefly at Phu-Suany when she stepped through the door, but quickly returned his attention back to Shula who danced naked in the center of the roof.

Mu-Saeid, the other aide, stood off to the side also captivated by the solo dance. The older Bailian female had been at Shula's side for many grands.

The air on the rooftop was nothing short of electric. It took Phu-Suany's breath away and she felt her nipples stiffen. She could only stand and stare in wonder, watching her monarch sway and shimmy to a silent beat. Her undulating hips and swaying breasts frequently shifted from a slow, sensuous roll to a frantic, ecstatic cadence. Every so often, Shula raised her arms over her head and clapped her hands. Every time her palms met, an explosion of blue sparks erupted between them, showering the area and sending a ball of blue energy into the sky.

Mu-Saeid noticed her standing holding the tray and motioned her over.

"You might as well set that down," the elder Bailian said softly. "She's not going to want to eat until well after she's done."

"What is she doing?" Phu-Suany asked, setting the tray down, transfixed.

"Dancing."

"Why?"

"She said she couldn't just sit around while other people did the fighting for her."

"I don't understand. I had no idea she could dance like that. What does it do?"

"That," Mu-Saeid said, indicating the gathering storm clouds on the eastern horizon. "Long before she became queen, she spent time with a troupe of dancing shamans in the upper Goyan Islands called Merut Tribal Dancers. With our race's natural gifts for magic, she became very formidable. Some say her beguiling dance is how she became queen."

"How is it I've never seen her dance before?"

"You haven't been with her staff long enough. She's spent the last few grands ruling an empire. Now, she dances to help save it."

Shula undulated her extended arms at the growing storm. Lightning danced through the clouds, following the orchestration with her hands.

Phu-Suany's expression went from awestruck to serious. "Do you really think she can influence events a continent and an ocean away?"

The young handmaiden no sooner asked the question, when Shula clapped over her head, sending a large ball of blue energy towards the clouds. A shimmering tail, connected to her clasped hands, trailed the crackling sphere of psychic energy. Shula then began rotating her upper body in time to her dance. When her torso pointed east, she let go of the tail. The ball streaked across the sky eastward. It erupted in the distant storm, agitating and lighting up the clouds of the tempest over the Twilight Lands.

"What do *you* think?" Mu-Saeid asked resolutely.

Captain Bajec had taken a few moments to write another quick letter to his mate when he saw the Duma scouts return. The humanoid cheetahs rushed into the oasis on all fours and to the edge of the agricultural field, reporting to General Baag-Tar with their tails convulsing wildly. From the look on the general's face the news didn't appear good. When the scouts left, he heard his name being called and saw the general waving him over.

"Yes, sir," Bajec said, with a salute.

Baag-Tar briefly scanned his Singa army. The men were nervously peering about their agrarian prison, wondering where the next attack would come from.

"Bajec, we've got a problem," the general began. "The scouts have reported that the Tur-Qua Pass has been obstructed."

"Obstructed, sir?"

"Yes, they've apparently roped it off."

"Sir, they couldn't possibly think that would stop us?"

"No, but they obviously think it will slow us down. We also don't know if there's a force on the other side of the pass waiting for us.

Baag-Tar nodded towards the Commander beside him with bandages still covering his eyes. "With Karga unable to command, I'm promoting you to the rank of Commander."

"Thank you, sir!"

"I wouldn't thank me just yet, Bajec. I've got a job for you, and, because you're now a commander, I'll brief you on the operation's details."

"Yes, sir!"

"Its code name is Crystal Annex. Simply put, we're to commandeer the Etheria production in the Annigan for the Tiikeri Empire. General Ja-Wee is securing the Etheria fields to the north in the Barrens. We've been tasked with securing the oasis where the raw Etheria is processed. Another amphibious force is to take the City of Immor-Onn. With that city, along with our encampment at Gar-Yesh Point, we'll be able to distribute processed Etheria Crystals to any point in the Annigan we desire. Now, comes your job."

"Yes, sir?"

"Our grand strategic plan hinges on us controlling the harvesting and refining of the Etheria. That can't happen with Tur-Qua Pass blocked."

"Yes, sir, of course, sir!"

"We've got a little over four thousand men left. Take two thousand, clear and secure the pass. At that point, head west to Immor-Onn, where we'll all converge."

"General!" Karga sputtered. "Is splitting our army a wise move? Supreme General Jal-Pi ordered us not to deviate from the plan with our Worrg network down."

Baag-Tar's ears pinned and whiskers fluttered. "If we don't get that pass open, and under control, there is no plan!"

"Commander Bajec, you have your orders. I don't care how you do it, *but clear that pass*. Then, leave a small garrison at both ends. We'll rendezvous in Immor-Onn. You leave immediately."

"Yes, sir, I won't let you down, sir."

"See that you don't, commander. The success of this entire operation rests with *you*."

The Kan had just begun in the High Holy City of Zor. Instead of closing down as usual, the University of Marassa's main dining hall sparkled with light and hummed with activity. They removed the long dining tables, allowing for the crowd to easily mingle. A large selection of appetizing finger food covered the food tables against the back wall near the kitchen. Servers moved through the crowd, refilling glasses and tidying up.

A quinte ago, the Board of Regents sent invitations out to every Marassa, announcing a celebration of the two newest schools, including a meet-and-greet of their respective department heads.

Colonel Zekoff, soon to be Professor Zekoff, head of the fledgling School of Policing and Investigative Science, found himself unaccustomed to all the attention. His hand already started aching from being shaken so often and he had long since run out of small talk.

Across the room, Banavor de Moras, the other person of honor, stood amongst a small crowd of admirers. Zekoff marveled at the young man's ability to completely captivate those around him. At less than twenty grands old, Banavor now wore the red robes of a senior Marassa and had been promoted to head of the Banavor School of Economics.

Zekoff knew his meteoric rise to power in the Commodities Exchange didn't come without controversy. His reputation as a ruthless capitalist, surpassed only by his brilliant economic theories, now fueled an unprecedented fiscal boom for the entire Goyan Islands.

The old colonel realized he had not greeted his fellow honor recipient and made his way across the room. When he reached the outer circle of Banavor's well-wishers, he felt the overwhelming sensation of sexual attraction emanating from the youngster. It held everyone around him, effecting both male and female, but mostly the younger Marassas.

Zekoff felt it too, but because of his age and superior mental discipline, he easily shrugged it off. He had to admit, he found the teenager's smooth honey brown skin and curly hair extremely attractive, but not his preference.

Seeing the colonel's approach, Banavor's face brightened in recognition.

"The legendary Colonel Zekoff," Banavor said enthusiastically, extending his hand. "So good that we are finally able to meet."

Zekoff shook Banavor's hand, noting his weak grip and cold temperature of his skin.

"Well, I don't know about 'legendary,'" Zekoff said humbly, feeling himself blush a little.

"Nonsense," Banavor said, continuing his charm onslaught. "There's a reason they want you to pass on what you know. By the way, the robe looks good on you."

"Thanks," the old colonel said, self-consciously eyeing his robe which matched Banavor's. "It's going to take some getting used to."

Kasha had been working late but didn't want to miss the chance to congratulate Colonel Zekoff and get a look at the financial whiz-kid and youngest Senior Marassa. When she realized the time, she quickly locked up her office and made her way across campus from the Language Arts building to the Dining Hall.

She arrived to find the party in full swing. Several Marassas and their spouses immediately greeted her, all eager to express their well-wishes. She welcomed them warmly, but constantly surveyed the crowd until she finally spotted Zekoff. She felt fortunate he stood chatting in front of Banavor, eliminating the need to hunt him down too.

"It's been a while since I've seen this many red robes in one place," Kasha greeted cheerfully.

"Kasha!" Zekoff replied, offering her his hand. "I was hoping I'd see you this evening."

"I wouldn't have missed it," she said, giving him a firm shake. "It's not often we open two new schools here at the university. This is exciting."

The head of the Linguistics then turned her attention to Banavor. "And this must be the economic prodigy I've been hearing about," she said, extending her hand once more.

"Banavor de Moras," he said with a subtle smile, while accepting her greeting. "Thank you for your kind words."

An electric jolt passed through Kasha's body the moment she felt his icy touch, followed by waves of malice and greed. The spirit of Pa-Waga coursed through this young man and Kasha could feel the Tiikeri dark god's presence.

She inhaled sharply and tried to release her hand, but Banavor continued to hold on to it. His smile turned much more malevolent and knowing. Shuttering slightly, her mind flashed images of X's and I's, followed by a statue of a humanoid black cat, seated on a throne rising out of a sea of coins and gems. A slowly descending curtain of blood obscured her vision and she knew a paranormal assault when she felt it.

Fortunately, the Lolite in her ring acted as an effective psychic shield and the Carnelian gave her the inner strength to retract her hand away from the danger before her.

She realized that Banavor played an active role in Pa-Waga's attempt to contact her two cycles ago. By his arrogant smirk, she knew that he knew. Rapidly composing herself, she smiled at both of the new senior Marassas.

"I'm sure we'll be seeing more of each other," Banavor said, not relinquishing his sinister grin.

Kasha maintained her polite smile even though her stomach pitched and knotted. She realized she needed to distance herself from this strikingly diabolic entity.

"Yes, well, congratulations to you both," she said with a friendly nod, before moving off into the party.

Zekoff noted the odd exchange but didn't let on.

"Well, I think I'm going to go and see just how good university food is," he said, excusing himself.

Banavor nodded politely and watched him walk over to the buffet tables where Kasha stepped up beside him, filling her plate.

"What was that all about?" Zekoff asked, keeping his voice low and his attention on the food.

"I've got to talk with you," she said, clearly unnerved.

"Alright, let's find a quiet spot."

"Not now," she said, shaking her head. "Rafel's got to hear this too."

Zekoff paused and faced her. "Alright then, how's tomorrow morning's briefing?"

Kasha nodded her head and an immediate sense of relief flooded her. The feeling rapidly vanished, replaced by a chilling sense of dread.

She turned and met eyes with Banavor standing across the room. He stared directly at her and smiled rancorously.

True to her word, Kai opened the Whispering Zephyr to the officers of the invading Singa army. The lion men wasted no time in taking her up on her offer.

After only one luna, she had already gained valuable information, thanks to the large Larimar disk embedded in the ceiling. They placed the Etheria communication stones in all public buildings several grands ago, on order of Queen Shula, and the people generally loved the freedom of broken language barriers.

From her private table, she and Tam-Eez watched the tavern full of Singas getting drunk. Part of their agreement limited each mawl soldier to a two-drink maximum per visit. However, for the Singas, unaccustomed to Bailian hard liquor, two drinks proved more than enough for them to get sufficiently inebriated and their tongues wagging.

By directing her attention around the room, she had learned that they called the ribbon woven into the right side of their mane, "Sharits," with their different colors indicating rank. Some wore multicolored commendation beads suspended in their mane, below the chin, called "Cena." All handy intel for spotting the more important invaders.

From yet another group she discovered there were actually two armies marching their way across the northern and southern halves of the continent. None could be sure of their arrival time, because the mawls' communications network wasn't functioning for some reason.

The table she concentrated on contained the Singa with the distinctive white patch on his chin. His green Sharit indicated his rank as sergeant and the six red and gold Cenas, hanging from his mane just below the patch of white, identified him as a decorated soldier.

Kai scowled at his obnoxious manners which seemed crude, even for a Singa. The other Singa sergeants seated with him called him Gunahkar but Kai didn't care. This moonless would be his last. The children were ready.

When Gunahkar loudly announced he had "to take a piss," then stood and began to open his trousers, Kai bolted from her seat.

"YOU!" she screamed above the din, pointing directly at him. "TAKE IT OUTSIDE!"

The volume level in the room plummeted and all eyes focused on Kai and Gunahkar. No one noticed Tam-Eez inconspicuously getting to his feet and slipping out the door.

"What?!" the Singa said innocently, realizing he now commanded everyone's attention. "I was just gonna take a piss!"

Kai remained defiantly adamant. "Not in here you're not!"

Now, it became a matter of pride for the Singa. The small human called him out in front of his peers.

"Yeah," he said with a scowl. "Who's gonna stop me?"

Kai smiled confidently. "We'll see what Lord To-Nok has to say about it. He *personally* guaranteed his men would behave."

"Sergeant!" came a stern reprimand from a captain seated the next table over.

Gunahkar glanced over at his commander then back at Kai. His tail drooped behind him, thoroughly humiliated. Giving an obstinate growl of protest, the indignant Singa closed his pants and headed for the double front doors.

"Don't come back," Kai warned, just before he exited. "You're no longer welcome here."

Gunahkar awoke with a start to searing pain in his neck and head. The last thing he remembered, was trying to remain standing while he emptied his bladder against the alley wall behind the Whispering Zephyr. He recalled noting to himself how drunk he had become with just two drinks. The blow to the back of the head came when stuffing his cock back into his pants and all went black.

The Singa sergeant blinked and looked wildly around. He still found himself in the alley, but securely tied to a thick post, with his hands and legs wrapped around the pole exposing his head and torso. A swath of cloth, drenched in a sickeningly sweet perfume making him want to gag, had been shoved in his mouth.

A sea of children, mostly Bailian, with some humans and several crossbreeds, stood before him. The young faces stared at him grimly with hate burning in their eyes. Without a word they stepped closer. Catching glints of light, he saw each of the street urchins brandish a medium bladed knife. Thrashing wildly against his bonds, he tried to call out but quickly discovered speech and escape impossible.

The first to step up to him, happened to be a young Bailian girl, barely six, in a tattered, ill-fitting blue dress with a wicked gleam in her eyes. At four feet tall, her head came up to just below his chest. Her beautiful racial features contorted in anger. She glared up at him, meeting his gaze, as she raised the knife over her head.

"For Jetim!" she said scowling, before plunging the blade into his abdomen.

Gunahkar felt the knife enter his body and the accompanying pain. However, as a seasoned veteran of many violent, bloody campaigns, pain, fear and brutality had become a way of life for him. He snarled defiantly when the girl stepped away, leaving her blade lodged in his body.

A thin and sickly Human lad of about twelve immediately replaced her. His sneering face also displayed a look of mania uncommon for someone his age.

"For Jetim!" He drove his blade into the Singa's chest.

As with the girl before him, he stepped away leaving the knife wedged in place. No sooner had he stepped aside, when another of Kai's children, dagger at the ready, marched up and plunged it into the cat-man with all his might.

Tam-Eez purposely went last. He stepped up to the Singa, and unlike the other orphans who stood around watching, he had enough height to look him in the eyes. The mahogany haired teenager calmly surveyed the twenty-three knife hilts adorning his body and the rivulets of blood from each of the puncture wounds. He then met the Singa's weakened, yet still insolent, gaze.

"I'm so glad you waited for me," he coldly said with an evil smirk. "I really wanted you to see this before you die."

Reaching out, he gripped the Singa's mane with one hand. With the dagger in his other hand, he roughly cut the Sharit rank ribbon and Cena commendation beads from his dark brown mane.

Gunahkar could do nothing but look on in horror and shame, while the boy stripped away the proud symbols of his rank and status. Through waves of agony, he watched Tam-Eez bring the knife to his throat. The veteran Singa managed to get off one last muted, rebellious growl before the young man drug the blade slowly across the front of his neck. The last sensation he felt was the warmth of the blood torrent flowing down his chest and soaking his fur.

The last sound he heard was the young man's menacing voice, "For Jetim!"

Kasha, still rattled, finally made it back to her small two room apartment on the university campus. She gave a relieved sigh when she turned the lock behind her and promptly poured herself a glass of wine to steady her nerves. She had barely slipped on her sleeping gown, when she heard the emergency whistles coming from outside.

Peering out the window, she could see Jezik Square shrouded in Kan fog just across the street. Off to her left she caught the distinct glow of a fire and heard the throng of city guards noisily rushing around to put it out.

She closed the window to shut out the cacophony and settled into her favorite chair. Just after her first sip of wine, the front door burst open with the crash of splintered wood. Kasha cried out and dropped her glass. Her eyes widened in dread when the two EEtahs, Luft and Nagrada, stepped through the now open doorway.

"How come I'm always the one that has to breakdown the door, Naggy?" Luft asked innocently, ignoring the screaming woman.

Before Nagrada could form a sarcastic reply, Banavor entered after them and shot a dirty look their way, silencing the bickering duo.

"Oh, do be quiet," Banavor calmly said to the hysterical scribe. "With all the noise going on outside no one will hear you, besides, I'm just here to talk."

"Talk about what?" Kasha asked through subsiding sniffles.

"Right to the point, I like that!" Banavor said, stepping over in front of her with an evil leer.

The young man leaned over the seated woman until his face was inches from hers. His expression took on a sultry quality when his long tongue snaked out of his mouth and licked her lips. Kasha cried out in surprise and recoiled against the back of the chair.

Banavor paused for a brief moment, genuinely perplexed as to why she hadn't become beguiled. He quickly surmised something must be blocking his Etheria Crystal. With seduction now no longer an option, his sly smile returned and he stood up.

"I would very much like to know what you and Colonel Zekoff spoke about at the party?"

Kasha's face hardened. Her eyes bore into the attractive young man with androgynous features and short curly hair.

"I'm not going to tell you anything!" she said defiantly. "I know who your master is! I would never help you!"

Banavor sighed forlornly. "That's unfortunate."

Looking back at the EEtah's he motioned towards Kasha. "Make sure the Marassa remains seated throughout our little chat."

The EEtah's exchanged uncertain glances before Nagrada nudged his partner.

"Me?" Luft protested, walking over behind the seated Kasha. "Why am *I* always the one to hold them down?"

Banavor gave the whining EEtah another dirty glance before removing a thin bladed knife from under his tunic. Luft pinned both of Kasha's shoulders, while Banavor knelt in front of her.

"Last chance for this to be a more pain free conversation," he said, placing the tip of the blade just under her kneecap.

When greeted with silence, he shrugged. "Suit yourself."

He plunged the blade straight down into the tendon. Kasha screamed and thrashed about, but Luft held her securely in place. Banavor then withdrew the dagger and slowly pushed it into the tendon on the other side. He stood and smiled down at the woman writhing in agony and crying.

"You can let her go. She'll never walk again."

Banavor leaned over and gently waved the blade before the sobbing Kasha. "But that doesn't matter. Do you know why? Because you're going to tell me everything I want to know. And then... well... my friends haven't eaten all day."

An air of sullen stillness laced with an underlying sense of dread enveloped the city of Immor-Onn. It had been three lunas since the mawl invaders occupied the Shining Jewel of the East and they wasted no time in placing the populace firmly under the heel of the Tiikeri Empire.

Cha-Rod and Oro' Korra made their way along the city's main boulevard heading towards the docks. The occupying mawls' imposed lock down, until the city's residents could be "properly processed," greatly reduced traffic on the streets and walkways.

Up ahead, Cha-Rod could see six Singa warriors blocking the road, in one of the many checkpoints set up throughout the city. Their long manes partially obscured the round shields slung on their backs. A double-edged short sword rested sheathed at their sides.

Drawing closer Cha-Rod winced at the smell. He couldn't quite put his finger on what it reminded him of, but they all carried the same stench.

The group silently observed their approach and three broke away from the rest to face them.

"Letrat!" one growled confrontationally.

The Bailian duo didn't need a translator. The demand for their identification papers couldn't have been more obvious. Fortunately, they had gotten theirs yesterday at Oro' Korra's insistence. The former general had used his position to arrange for them to be one of the first issued so they could move about.

They reached into their pockets and both produced a folded, seemingly blank piece of paper. The Singa, who stood two feet taller than the Bailians, snatched the documents. Sniffing both in turn, he gave a begrudging nod, before returning the papers with a suspicious stare.

Cha-Rod's face betrayed no emotion when he accepted it, but Oro' Korra managed a weak smile. The Singas then stepped aside and the two Bailians got on their way.

"I have to hand it to the mawls," Oro' Korra admitted, "they're efficient and orderly. There's something to be said for law and order."

Cha-Rod merely grunted but remained silent. Directly in front of them stood the former royal palace, which the invaders now used as their headquarters. Out front at the main gate, more Singas stood guard over a long line of citizens. The mostly Bailian crowd snaked out the double doors of the palace, down the lawn and into the street.

Across the wide thoroughfare, they had turned the Palace Park into a killing field. The Bojo-Vat master scowled at rows of impaled sentients. Here they sent the ones who opposed their occupation, the troublemakers, the impure.

"You disapprove of their methods?" Oro' Korra asked seeing the disgusted look on Cha-Rod's face.

"To say the least," Cha-Rod grumbled.

Oro 'Korra laughed. "I seem to remember you bludgeoning to death quite a few impure in *your* younger days."

"Those were different times."

"Well, it would seem the old days may be returning."

Cha-Rod scoffed loudly and considered commenting, when one of the palace doors flew open. Two Singas, flanking a male Bailian/human mix, burst out into the moonlight. The Singas tightly gripped each arm, muscling him across the street in front of them. A white Tiikeri in bright blue robes trailed regally behind them.

"Another half-breed," Oro' Korra said contemptuously, watching them lead the struggling sentient over to an empty spike jutting seven feet out of the ground.

The pair paused and watched them move a twelve-foot-tall frame and center it over the spike. The Singas secured the captive's hands in wrist restraints attached to the inside of the frame's vertical side beams and winched his struggling body up, suspending him above the spike.

With a nod of the Tiikeri's head, the Singas let go of their ropes and the body plunged down onto the stake. The velocity of the falling body, combined with the needle-sharp tip, impaled the male between his legs. The thin pole drove through the torso and emerged out of the mouth. His body stopped its descent a few feet off the ground. He convulsed while blood and excrement began running down the pole.

Cha-Rod briefly looked away in revulsion, before turning his attention back to the Tiikeri.

"Who's that?" he whispered.

"Lord To-Nok," Oro' Korra replied. "He's the Empire's spy master and right now, the highest-ranking invader."

Cha-Rod stared malevolently at Lord To-Nok while he returned to the palace to resume processing the populace.

"He radiates cruelty," Cha-Rod said in disgust. "That is the difference between them and the Racial Purity Movement we lent ourselves too, so long ago. We did what we must. He enjoys it."

"You just might be right old friend."

"If perhaps, he could be... *removed*... it would serve a threefold purpose," Cha-Rod said hauntingly. "It would deny them a leader, demoralize their troops and there would be one less cruel bastard in the world."

"What you're suggesting is bold, indeed. Would your other contacts be involved? How do you propose we do it?"

Cha-Rod shook his head, deep in thought. "Let's split up and watch his movements for a few lunas. A plan will come to us."

Recognizing Kasha's private on-campus residence, Zekoff's heart sank when he saw the smashed door at the end of the hall and a small cluster of city patrol guards.

"This doesn't look good," Rafel said, picking up the pace to match his superior's.

A newly promoted Captain Vanir stepped out through the smashed door and nodded grimly at their approach. Zekoff felt thankful Vanir would be taking over the investigative duties when he retired to join the teaching staff here at the university. Fall semester started in a few quintes and he definitely would not miss visiting fresh crime scenes.

"It's a mess sir," Vanir reported, nodding towards the room he just exited.

"That's what the dispatch said," Zekoff said hollowly.

The small, twin room apartment, composed of a small bedchamber attached to a completely decimated larger living area. Blood and unidentifiable bits of body parts covered almost the entirety of the walls and floor.

Kasha's head rested in the seat of a chair close to the room's lone window. They had gouged out her eyes and ears and removed her tongue.

The old colonel felt a deep wave of sadness pass over him at the plight of his colleague. She had been through such a few rough grands and yet proved to be a real asset in recognizing Tiikeri culture and habits.

"She was eaten," Vanir said, stroking his red beard and indicating the head.

"It started in that chair," he continued, pointing out the large two-foot-wide bite out of its upholstery. "By the bite radius, I'd say it was an EEtah, maybe more than one. Notice the severing wound on the victim's neck? It was bitten off with serrated teeth. This has all the classic signs of an EEtah blood frenzy."

"Any witnesses?" Zekoff asked, looking around.

"Nope," Vanir answered, running his hand through his long red hair. "Gasata's patrol guys just finished interviewing people, nothing."

"Wait," Rafel said, clearly unconvinced. "You're telling me an EEtah or two smashed through that door, tortured, killed, then ate the victim, and no one saw or heard anything?"

"They set a fairly large fire down the street as a distraction," Vanir explained. "There was a lot of commotion to cover things up."

"She was targeted," Zekoff confidently proclaimed. "I saw her last Kan at a party and she told me she had something important to tell the three of us. She was supposed to be at this morning's meeting."

Vanir exhaled loudly. "Well, that goes a long way in explaining the mutilation of the head. Eyes, ears and tongue removed. This was a warning to anyone about reporting to the authorities."

"I didn't think EEtahs were that sophisticated," Zekoff said, staring at Kasha's mutilated face.

"They're not," Vanir morosely replied, reaching for his flask.

The tension had been building and it had finally reached a palpable level. Valdurian Marine Sergeant Riggio de Aris could feel it. It only made sense. Things in Immor-Onn's quarantined air base couldn't remain this way much longer.

Already food and supplies were running low. There still remained over a hundred Bailian and human refugees crowding the flight deck of Air Station East. Caring for these many needs while effectively being held hostage definitely tested the station's preparedness.

It started during the moonless. Flight mechanics began work on the few remaining airships, making sure all of their stabilizers were freed of the destructive moths and fit to fly.

At moonrise, Riggio watched both Commander Sandal and Ambassador Valdur organize things and personnel in the main hangar. When an Outer Clan EEtah marine joined them and they started shuffling around the Bailians, the Valdurian marine sergeant shifted his crossbow anxiously.

Riggio caught more movement off to the side of the wide doorway and noticed several heavily armed marines positioning themselves behind what few crates remained. He raised an eyebrow questioningly, when a human lieutenant, and yet another EEtah with a heavy crossbow, joined them.

"Marines," he heard the officer say softly, "you have new orders. You are to hold this door and fall back when ordered. If you understand, just nod."

All three nodded and the lieutenant joined the marines hidden from the view of the two Singa guards thirty feet away. The two large mawls at the end of the neutral zone hallway were both armed with spears and eyed the activity suspiciously.

One peered over at the other to mention the strange goings-on, only to see his comrade's mouth drop open in stunned surprise.

Quickly looking back, he gasped also. The side of a giant transport ship filled the opening to the outside, floating mere feet from the hangar. The Singa could clearly see the massive craft lowering its wide side hatch and Bailians herded towards a spot where the ramp would fall, preparing them to board.

The Singas found themselves at an absolute loss as to what to do. Their orders were to allow no one in or out of the air station from the city. Nothing in their directives mentioned airships and they had been strictly forbidden to enter what was recognized as Valdurian territory. Clearly, they needed direction.

"Get Zabit and To-Nok," one of the Singas directed.

Nodding, the other took off and the one giving the orders stepped forward. His action prompted three loaded heavy crossbows to be aimed in his direction.

The moment Kai saw To-Nok storm through the front door, she knew the nature of the visit. The late morning bells in the Turine just outside the twin harbors echoed through the city and she realized a Singa patrol had found the body just after moonrise. The assassin and priestess of Orad knew the Singa's death would probably cause some heat, but no one killed her children with impunity.

Two female Singas followed behind the white Tiikeri spymaster. They both sported the same crossed bandoleros loaded with sickle shaped blades and grim expressions.

"Lord To-Nok," Kai coyly greeted, before taking a sip of tea. "I see you've decided to join your men. This neighborhood has been quite popular this morning."

To-Nok stopped in front of Kai's table and glowered down at the one-armed human female.

"Were you aware they found the body of one of my men this morning behind this establishment?"

Kai calmly returned the mug to the table. "No, but I'm aware now. That also explains your people swarming all around here."

"He was found tied to a pole with twenty-three knives stuck in him and his throat slashed."

Kai scoffed. "Sounds like a lot to go through just to kill someone. Maybe someone was trying to send a message."

"I want answers!"

"What are you yelling at me for? I didn't do it!"

"You were seen arguing with him last moonless in this very room!"

"You mean the ass with the white tuft on his chin?"

"Yes. Sergeant Gunahkar."

"I didn't catch his name. I threw him out for being obnoxious. He wasn't going to leave until one of your senior officers made him go."

"Yes, I heard."

Kai scoffed again, this time more loudly. "So, what's this all about To-Nok?! If I had everyone killed who acted up in my place, this city's population would be a lot smaller than it is."

The man-tiger sneered threateningly. "Then you either know who did it or you can find out."

"You are giving me *way* too much credit here, To-Nok."

The Tiikeri's sneer turned into an evil grin. "Oh, I don't think so. You have until this time tomorrow to get me the responsible party or parties. If not, ten of your citizens will be executed at random. From now on, for every one of my men murdered, ten of your people will be publicly killed and eaten. My men are getting tired of eating rations."

Kai sneered, about to respond, when the front door flew open and a Duma runner stepped in off the street. The humanoid cheetah appeared slightly out of breath and his face held a serious expression.

"Lord To-Nok, you're needed immediately. There's trouble at the air station."

To-Nok and Commander Zabit arrived in front of the beset air station at the same time. The Singa commander had a contingency of thirty male Singa warriors in tow and he did not look happy.

At the entrance to the flight deck, they encountered the lone Singa guard, his tail thrashing nervously. He pointed his spear at two EEtahs and a human dressed in green jumpsuits aiming loaded crossbows back at him. Across the hangar, the throng of Bailian refugees streamed up the ramp and into an immense transport airship.

"I knew I shouldn't have listened to Jo-Rakk!" Zabit snapped, then spun to face the warriors. "Take this station! No quarter. Feel free to feed."

With a roar the Singas charged. The first three through the doorway were struck mid-chest by crossbow bolts. The heavy, barbed projectiles catapulted the lion-men back into their companions, allowing the marines time to reload their weapons and fall back. The Singa warriors recovered quickly and continued their charge with renewed fury over the deaths of their three comrades. The next six met a similar fate when they entered, coming under fire from the marines off to the side, hiding behind the crates.

Riggio drew his short sword, ready to charge the disoriented Singas, when he heard Commander Sandal's voice ring out across the flight deck, ordering them to fall back to the ship. Peering back, he saw Ambassador Valindra Valdur, her youthful face taut and serious, spurring the last of the Bailians up the ramp and into the ship.

"You heard the man," Riggio bellowed. "Let's get the fuck outta here!"

The ship floated fifty yards away and Riggio knew full well they would not be able to outrun those Singas. The six marine crossbowmen fell back in waves of three, with one set retreating and reloading, while the other fired.

Riggio quickly sheathed his sword before retrieving his crossbow from the floor and loading it.

"Form up with them!" he ordered the retreating EEtahs, pointing towards the shifting teams of crossbowmen.

The enraged Singas weren't stupid. One look at the disciplined methodology of half the group firing while the other half loaded gave them pause. They already lost half their numbers and knew they couldn't get to the retreating marines without losing the rest.

"STAND DOWN!" Lord To-Nok thundered across the besieged flight deck.

The Singas halted, glancing around at each other in confusion while the marines continued their orderly withdrawal. Commander Zabit spun and furiously glared at the Tiikeri spymaster. Too angry to speak, all he could do was tremble with clenched fists. To-Nok continued staring at the marine's orderly advance into the craft, ignoring the irate Singa commander.

"How many more men were you willing to sacrifice on such idiotic orders?" Zabit demanded.

The white man-tiger finally glanced over at the humiliated and fuming Zabit. "Jo-Rakk was right. We were hoping to avoid direct conflict with the Valdurians. Your little tantrum just now could very well have cost us dearly."

The Kan fog slowly rose in the Shallow Sea bringing all but the most daring of sailor's maritime activities to a standstill. With the promise of immanent fog cover, sixteen large Ves-Lari ships of the Tiikeri Empire exited from the Ocean Deep onto the Goyan Rise and headed towards the southernmost islands of the Tellasian Chain.

The mongrel rowers, twenty to a craft, stroked silently and quickly through the choppy water, taking full advantage of the lack of shipping activity. When the jagged peaks of Dal Island, the outermost island in the chain, came into view, the fog had almost consumed them.

In the lead craft, an older male Singa and Yagur stood beside the rudder operator, watching a herd of Kells take off from one of the mountain tops, guided by several Avions with long spears.

"Thirty degrees to port," the Singa ordered, watching the squawking herd of flying lizards bank to their left and assume a similar course.

"I don't like this," the Singa said, shaking his head. "If we're spotted..."

"Stop worrying, Gauna," the Yagur said nonchalantly. "The winged people don't care about the affairs of those on the ground."

"We shouldn't be here in the first place," Gauna replied. This operation is ill-timed and ill conceived. If we should be doing anything, we should be assisting our forces in the Twilight Lands, not making a raid so deep in Lumina."

"Our operative in Otomoria says that any forces that could oppose us are fragmented and weakened. This surprise attack will be a great victory for the empire and the lord."

Much like the bulk of the traditional military commanders, Gauna distrusted the clerics of this new religion that had taken hold of his king and people. The King deployed Yagur priests with every military unit, serving as spiritual advisers. With their god being one of greed, the taking of spoils seemed to be their main concern.

Kerani, the Yagur cleric standing next to him, happened to be just such a holy man. Ever since they embarked, the Pa-Waga priest appeared practically giddy, rambling on about the riches which could be seized from this fertile land they stood poised to attack.

Another thing bothering Gauna was half his rapidly slapped together force remained untrained. True, the mongrels had been bred bigger, stronger, and didn't need eye protection, but that didn't take the place of experienced fighters. The other half of his force consisted of the remaining two Singa prides, leaving the homeland virtually undefended.

The Singa commander sincerely hoped the cleric had been right, they needed divine intervention and soon.

High above Dal Island, Udana, a female Avion Kell
tender from House Eacher, watched a rogue Kell break away
from the herd and head out over open water towards the
advancing fog bank. When it veered away, she marveled at
the sunlight playing off the lizard's multicolored wings.

Sighing in frustration, she took off after it. Catching the
beast could not have been more important. Each of the
creatures represented a substantial investment in time and
effort not to mention profit for House Eacher. Once it
became enveloped in the Kan fog, it would be lost.

She saw the strange ships the moment she caught up with
the stray Kell. Unlike the crafts she became familiar with,
these appeared to be large and open-topped with rowers on
both sides. She counted sixteen of them before they
disappeared back into the mist, but not before she saw the
heavily armed cat people occupying them.

Climbing the wide stairs leading up to the Imperial Bank
of Zor, Vanir de Tuath realized he knew virtually nothing
about commodities trading. From the small amount he did
know, it appeared to be little more than an elaborate form of
gambling. Not that he had anything against gambling,
trading commodities just seemed like a more complicated
way to separate men from their money.

The red headed investigator rolled his eyes at the cynical
musings and nodded to the EEtah guard outside the

elaborately carved double doors. Inside, the clammer of the street faded away, replaced by a reserved silence. A half dozen large desks dotted the lobby, occupied by stern faced men and women studiously sliding beads back and forth on elaborate abacuses.

The door on the far side of the room led to the offices of the Zorian Monetary Council. A haggard looking, overworked young man carrying a stack of files greeted him there.

"I'm Captain Vanir of the Zorian Guards. I would very much like to speak with Lord Banavor."

"His office is right over there," the young man said, indicating a nearby door.

Nodding his thanks, he knocked and waited. When a very young sounding voice bid him enter, he paused wondering if he had the right office.

Vanir wasn't exactly sure what to expect. This would be their first meeting. He had been apprised of the economist prodigy's age, or lack thereof, but he smirked involuntarily when he first saw Banavor, surprised at the slight person who rose from behind his desk to greet him.

The wildly provocative way he dressed proved even more of a surprise. He wore a one-piece outfit, consisting of tight, Kel skin pants, cut high on the sides of his thighs, and high pointed fabric, turned into wide, suspender-like straps over his shoulders. Vanir's eyes drifted down the smooth, hairless body to the front of his pants where the extreme V cut ended just above his genitals, revealing the red bellybutton jewel as well as the top of his folded penis.

The lad seemed barely twenty, if that. His light coffee brown skin and alluring facial features accompanied a head of short, curly brown hair. The investigator now appreciated the fact he held the title of the youngest Marassa in the history of the university, with his own school of economics no less.

In stark contrast to his size and demeanor, two eight-foot tall EEtahs stood against the wall behind him, staring forward.

With the introductions, Banavor demurely offered his hand. When Vanir took it, he almost winced from the cold touch and the erotic charge shooting straight through his arm and down to his crotch. This struck him as odd. His preference had always been women, but there seemed to be something undeniably captivating about the young man.

"So, what can I do for the Zorian Guards today?" Banavor asked lyrically, in a slightly suggestive tone.

When Vanir felt the beginnings of an erection, he figured he better get down to business. "Well, I wish our initial meeting was on a more pleasant note. I'm afraid I have bad news. One of the university's Marassa's was murdered last night."

Banavor's eyes went wide and he covered his mouth dramatically with both hands. "By the gods, no!"

"I'm afraid so. It was after the party in your honor."

"That's terrible. Do you have any idea who did it?"

To Vanir this first question seemed odd. He wasn't interested in who had been killed or how they died, which constituted the normal first queries.

"No, it's early in the investigation. I'm just conducting interviews with any who might have interacted with Kasha at the event."

"I'm so sorry I can't help you captain," Banavor said, coming out from behind his desk. "I saw her there, but we didn't meet."

Vanir felt his erection returning, pushing at the front of his trousers when Banavor stepped close. He felt relieved his tunic covered his growing state of arousal, which almost caused him to look past the lie he just heard.

Zekoff already informed him Banavor and Kasha spoke at the party and she seemed unnerved by the conversation.

He also knew about Kasha wanting to meet this very morning. This young man's story just didn't add up.

Another jolt of raw sexual energy pulsed through him when Banavor gently touched his shoulder.

"It must be terrible having to deliver this kind of news to people," Banavor purred and softly stroked down Vanir's muscular upper arm. "I feel so bad for you."

All thoughts of the case now vanished from Vanir's mind, replaced by the wanton urge to bend Banavor over the desk and fuck him.

"It's definitely not my favorite part of the job." Vanir heard himself saying, watching Banavor step over to the door.

His eyes followed the V cut which accentuated his shapely buttocks, revealing the top of his ass-crack. The garment also revealed an engraved X and I on either side of the base of his spine.

"Please contact me if you can think of anything else that may be helpful." Vanir said when Banavor opened the door.

"Oh, I will," Banavor said huskily, offering his hand once more. "Perhaps our next encounter will be of a more *pleasurable* nature?"

Another jolt hit Vanir when he grasped the petite, icy cold appendage and he felt the warmth of his ejaculation against the front of his pants.

"Perhaps," he replied weakly.

A newly promoted Commander Bajec peered back over his shoulder at the columns of Singa warriors marching behind him. The Tur' Qua Pass lay a short, half luna's trek from the oasis, but it had not been easy. He could tell they were close because the ground beneath him slowly transitioned from soft desert sand to firmer ground. From their current position, the Os'Ani Mountain Range wasn't visible yet, due to a low bank of clouds which arrived with the rising moon.

"I've decided I don't like this land," the Singa captain to his left said.

Bajec nodded, about to agree, when a roar of surprise and shock rose up from the rear of the formation then went quickly silent.

They had gotten another one of his men.

Bajec closed his eyes and scowled but kept going. The inhabitants of this inhospitable land could move beneath its surface and strike with almost complete impunity. So far, his men had only managed to catch one of the underground assailants. They appeared no different than the other Gilas in the oasis, but their tan colored outfits made it all but impossible to see them even above the ground.

In order to minimalize casualties, he ordered his men to keep moving, no matter what. The sooner they could get out of this damnable desert the better.

When the sand gave way to hard packed rocky ground, Bajec felt a cool breeze blowing from the north and he knew the pass lay just ahead. A half mile later, the breeze picked up considerably. It blew away all of the low clouds, revealing a tall mountain range jutting straight up from the desert. The granite tops were still obscured by clouds but now at least they could see their destination.

The sight caused all to stop and stare in disbelief. The Tur' Qua Pass, the only way through the Os'Ani Mountains, appeared immense. Easily two hundred yards wide with the tops of each side high in the clouds.

Determining the depth proved all but impossible, due to the thick strands of spider webbing stretching completely across it. Individual strands of webbing crisscrossed each other all the way up, stopping just below cloud level. The spacing between each of the silk ropes revealed that a small humanoid could carefully navigate it, but not much more.

"By the gods!" Bajec found himself blurting out. "What could do that?"

"And why?" the captain asked in disbelief. "Surely whoever did this couldn't possibly believe it would stop us?"

"This wasn't meant to stop us," Bajec said confidently. "It was intended to slow us down."

"Not by much," the captain said, convinced of the mission's ease.

"Alright, Captain, we've got our orders. Position a first line of a hundred men with long swords. They'll be responsible for cutting through those ropes. Make the following lines fifty across. Let's clear this pass!"

The Turine in Makatooa's harbor was ringing thirteen bells, through a pervasive Kan fog, when Gre-Nor knocked on the door of Hanara's office. The orange Tiikeri didn't wait for a response before he opened it and stepped in.

"You wished to see me, Lord Hanara?"

The Hammerhead EEtah stood up from his desk and smiled. "Yes. Let's take a walk. There are things to discuss."

"A walk?" Gre-Nor asked, puzzled by the odd request.

"I need to clear my head." Hanara said, moving towards the door.

They waited until they were well away from the main house before starting a conversation. The Tiikeri agent surmised that the Lord of the Manor, eager to avoid unwanted eavesdropping, sought privacy.

"So, have you heard any news about your people's operations in the Twilight Lands?" Hanara asked, leading him into the gardens.

Gre-Nor paused in surprise. *How did he know?*

"Lord Hanara, I'm not sure what you're referring to."

"Come now Gre-Nor, no need to keep up appearances. An amphibious fleet has occupied Immor-Onn and I'm getting reports of Singa armies in both the Dark Waste and The Barrens. If it's the Etheria production and distribution markets you're trying to corner, I want a piece of the action."

The Tiikeri's stunned reaction told Hanara all he needed to know.

"There's very little that takes place upon the high seas that I'm not aware of." Hanara added, answering Gre-Nor's unspoken question. "I take it you were unaware?"

"Not entirely," the Tiikeri finally admitted. "Our communications network is not functioning and all parts of the operation were ordered to operate independently. What you just told me, was the first progress report I've received."

Hanara stopped and stared dumfounded at the Tiikeri. "Your leaders started a war with the West, without a way to communicate? Are they insane?! You're dealing with Bailians, which means you're dealing with humans. These aren't primitive tribes you can just fold into your empire!"

"I'm just following orders," Gre-Nor defended weakly.

"And what exactly *are* your orders?" Hanara asked, resuming his walk.

When Hanara received no reply, he stopped once again and sighed deeply. He raised his hand, snapped his fingers and five men suddenly stepped into view from behind the bushes on each side of them.

Four of them aimed loaded crossbows directly at the man-tiger. The remaining unarmed man, who measured almost as tall as the Tiikeri and had burn scars covering his entire face, silently stepped alongside Hanara.

Gre-Nor tensed when he saw the armed men and threw Hanara a look of panic and shock. "Lord Hanara, I hardly feel this is necessary!"

The EEtah mob boss ignored the protest. "You know, I couldn't figure out for the life of me what your reasoning would be to arm and set the Cul-Ta against each other. Then I started getting the reports and I asked myself; if I wanted to plunge the second largest seaport into chaos, how would I do it. I imagine there are more of your people over here in Lumina causing similar mischief as a distraction from your main objective. I've heard whispers from Otomoria, but I'm sure there's more."

Hanara paused and studied the Tiikeri's face. He had him, and Gre-Nor knew it.

"Normally, Cul-Ta killing their own wouldn't concern me," Hanara calmly continued, "but I spent too much money backing this reconstruction to have it jeopardized now that things are getting back to some semblance of normal. Your plan was starting to work too. The wild Cul-Ta killed a wealthy shipping client of mine the other Kan. That makes it, and *you*, a problem that needs fixing. Speaking of which…"

Hanara motioned to the human at his side. "Have you had a chance to meet my newest associate, Silovik? He has replaced my last *fixer* who went missing. Silovik is special. He worships a particularly unforgiving fire goddess who has bestowed on him certain… *gifts*."

Silovik smiled and snapped his fingers which produced a shower of sparks.

"Fire," Gre-Nor said, attempting to sound calm. "Not a very humane way to kill someone."

"You wound me," Hanara said with mock indignation, then motioned around at the armed men. "*They're* the ones who are going to kill you. *He's* going to make sure there's nothing left of your body. Goodbye Gre-Nor. I'll leave you all to the business at hand. Besides, I detest the smell of burning fur."

The basement, turned temple, of the Banavor manor felt cool and damp, with a cloying metallic aroma of dried blood. The space was empty, except for a large beam with hooks running along the center of the room's ceiling. Vast, intricate fields of X's and I's covered the walls.

Banavor stood nude, poised before Stryder, who rested motionless on a riser as an effigy of Pa-Waga. He stared out at three commodities traders, two men and a woman, also nude, kneeling facing him in the center of the room. Three naked, bound, and gagged beggars squirmed futilely, suspended by their feet from the beam, one above each of the candidates. They all had long since stopped struggling and now their eyes darted about fearfully.

"Do you accept the word of the lord as taught by the Proffitt?" Banavor asked in a solemn tone.

"We do!" they chanted in unison.

"Do you embrace the principles of avidity and reject the ideology of penury?"

"We do!"

"Do you reject the precept of charity and benevolence and swear to strike it down when encountered?"

"We do!"

"Will you spread the word of the Lord and Proffitt so that His prosperity will sweep across the land?"

"We will!"

"You will now receive the Mark of the Lord," Banavor said, moving behind them.

Starting at one end, he used his sharpened fingernail to carve an X and an I on either side of their spine at the base of their skulls. Banavor then stepped around to the first of the kneeling traders. From where he stood, he looked down on the heads of the new acolytes and directly into the horror-filled eyes of the suspended beggars.

"Repeat the words of the Proffitt," he commanded.

"Productivity is the only path to prosperity!" the man said enthusiastically.

"Welcome to the bosom of the Lord," Banavor said, before slashing the beggar's throat.

Arterial spray shot out from the neck, spotting Banavor's light brown skin with flecks of red. A veritable waterfall of blood gushed from the open wound, drenching the man kneeling below.

The remaining two vagrants witnessed what surely would be their fate and thrashed in vain against their bonds, too panicked to notice Stryder's eyes opening.

"Arise to a new life in the service of the lord."

Banavor reached down and assisted the blood-soaked man to his feet. He guided him off to the side and cut the restraints, allowing the body to fall.

He then moved over to the next trader and repeated the gruesome ritual. Once all three had been initiated, Banavor laid down on the gore sodden floor, amidst the three bleeding corpses. He writhed about, fondling his rigid member with a lust filled stare.

"Come," he said seductively, opening his arms to the latest disciples. "Let's consecrate your new bond before these bodies get cold."

Apolo watched the Kan fog envelope Staghorn Plantation as she had so many times before, from the window of whatever room designated as the nursery. Now, under the new lord, and with this child, they designated one of the guest cottages for that purpose.

The wetnurse didn't really mind. She preferred keeping her distance from the Tiikeri overlord. He turned out to be stern and often cruel. The mawl smell also proved very unpleasant. Lord Bo-Lah preferred a sharp, piercing aroma all the humans in his service hated.

When the manor house finally disappeared into the thickening mist, she pulled her gaze away from the window and peered down at the baby suckling away contentedly at her breast. It pained her that Lord Bo-Lah hadn't given the little boy a name. With a sad smile she caressed the top of the baby's head, allowing one of her fingers to lightly trace along one of the grey stripes. She would give him a name if the master wouldn't. It would be her own secret name.

I will call you, Ume," she said softly, "and I will love you even if your father does not."

The thought of the child now having an identity made her smile. She softly hummed a children's song from her home, when the door suddenly opened, interrupting her lullaby.

Two female Singas, Bo-Lah's bodyguards and killers, entered the room with the dampness of the intruding fog. One stood by the open door while the other approached.

"Lord Bo-Lah wishes baby," she said tersely in broken common.

"Of course," Apolo answered, relieved the Lord of the Manor finally took an interest in his son. "He'll be done feeding in just a bit and…"

"Now!" the Singa demanded.

"Well… alright. Just let me get some things together and…"

"No. You stay. We take!"

"This is not right," Apolo said firmly. "The child is under my care. You can't take a baby out in that kind of dampness without proper…"

The Singa abruptly slapped her across face. The blow slammed her head to the side, almost knocking her unconscious. The Singa then grabbed the baby by the leg and yanked it violently away from the nursing teat.

Not wanting to let go of its meal, the infant's teeth bore down, tearing away Apolo's nipple and part of the large brown areola. She wailed in pain and wept watching the Singa hold the flailing infant casually by its leg, totally unphased by its savagery.

Blood and milk poured down the front of her and she heard herself screaming through the fog of agony and over the ringing in her ears. When the Singas started to leave, she found herself begging and pleading for the child, but they remained silent. Both gave a final dispassionate look at her before stepping back out and disappearing into the Kan.

Through the still open doorway, she could hear baby Ume's panicked wailing growing fainter in the distance until she could only hear her grief filled sobs. She knew she would never see Ume again.

To Banavor de Moras, seduction and sex had evolved into merely a means to an end. He had already experienced more than anyone's share of carnality in his young life.

Born the youngest of ten siblings into a financially destitute family, the androgenous young man's father deemed him not manly enough. He sold him to the brothels, in his home city of Moras, at the tender age of ten. There, he was well trained in the ways of pleasing both sexes.

He quickly and enthusiastically excelled at virtually every aspect of lubricity and quickly established a large group of well-to-do clients. Eventually, the brothel sold him to Dolan Aramos and now, at the age of nineteen, he found himself in service of a mighty god.

Thanks to Stryder Aramos, he now fucked whoever he wanted, for whatever reason he wanted. The power felt good.

He had been dominated and desensitized the moment he entered brothel life. Morasian Puff Boys, especially the new ones, didn't have a say. However, those days were over. He now had money, power and skills.

This latest strategy emerged as only the beginning to the building of his empire. The brash young man wasn't going to let anything get in his way, least of all a common investigator for the city guards.

Captain Vanir obviously must be dealt with, but these things needed to be handled delicately. He couldn't just turn him over to his EEtahs, like the linguist the other Kan. No, in this instance, seduction was called for. Their encounter, the other day, proved that between his sensual abilities and the Etheria jewel which adorned his bellybutton, it would be just a matter of time before the prying redhead would succumb to him.

He even prepared the instrument of the captain's demise; a slow acting poison called the creeper released from a lubricant suppository. Once absorbed into the head of his cock, it would slowly kill Vanir a full cycle after fucking Banavor, apparently naturally of the pox.

Banavor would also be poisoned, but he had the antidote, in the form of a yellowish brown Etheria Crystal called Xenoti, which negates poisons and parasites.

Now, all that remained to do was coerce Vanir into having sex with him, and the chance for that happened sooner than even he expected.

The Grand Turine in the Zorian harbor rang five bells, which reverberated out across the city. The Kan would be starting soon, and classes would be ending for the day. Banavor, dressed in the red robes of a senior Marassa, had just left a mind-numbingly dull orientation meeting for new Marassa's, when he saw Vanir approaching down the wide crowded hallway.

"Lord, or should I call you, Marassa Banavor?" Vanir formally asked.

"You may call me anything you wish, Captain."

Banavor stepped up close to place a hand on Vanir's broad chest. Vanir felt the cold touch through his shirt and tunic. At the same time, a wave of almost debilitating lust swept over him. In an attempt to clear his head, Vanir struggled to focus on the reason for his visit.

"I was hoping to revisit some of your statements from our last conversation?" Vanir said, noticing he involuntarily reached out to touch his arm.

The moment his hand made contact, his erection returned and began to ache. Unlike before, where he had made every effort to disguise his arousal, he desperately wanted this young man to know it. Stepping in close he pressed his hardness against Banavor's thigh. The new Marassa responded with a knowing, lecherous grin.

"I'd be happy to oblige any way I can," he purred. "Let's take this up in my new office."

Once the door closed, Banavor leaned against it and smiled seductively.

"So, what do you think? It's kinda small but it's all mine."

"It's very nice, Lord Banavor." Vanir grasped to keep his feelings straight, but powerfully salacious thoughts flooded his mind. "Now, about your statements last cycle...."

Banavor gave a sexy pout and stepped close to him. "Do we have to talk about that boring stuff? I thought this meeting was supposed to be *pleasurable*."

"Uh, well, yes but..."

"Yes," he said playfully, reaching down and rubbing Vanir's erection through his pants, "we can talk about my *butt*, if you want."

"You know, I don't have anything on under these stuffy old robes," Banavor confessed, rubbing his nipples through the stiff red fabric. "It makes me feel so... *naughty*. Do you want to see?"

"Well, um..."

"Here," he said, undoing the sash, letting the robe slip off his shoulders and onto the floor before Vanir could answer.

The investigator stared at the beautiful, hairless, young man. His heart pounded and his rigid organ tested the buttons on his pants.

Banavor peered down at his own small, but rampant, erection and returned his aroused gaze back to Vanir. "Oh look, someone's excited to see you."

Vanir could take no more. He grabbed Banavor, pulled him in and kissed him passionately. When their lips met and their hardness rubbed against each other, Vanir grew lightheaded and single minded. In that very moment, the idea of fucking this beautiful young man consumed him.

I've got an idea," Banavor said breathlessly when they separated. "Let's christen this office. I want you to be the first one to fuck me in here."

Vanir hardly needed to be asked twice. He pushed his tunic to one side and quickly unbuttoned his pants until his weeping cock leapt into view.

"Very nice," the young man said, running his hand down the long shaft. "I need this inside me, right now!"

Banavor bent over the desk, wiggling his ass invitingly, while reaching over and opening the top drawer. He retrieved the oval shaped lube suppository and slowly inserted it in his pink, puckered anus, so that Vanir could see every aspect of the wanton display.

"This will make things nice and slick." He invitingly pulled both cheeks open and arched his back. "Fuck me. I need it now!"

Vanir hovered his cock head just outside Banavor's quivering asshole to plunge into the insistent youth when a vigorous knocking on the door broke the licentious spell.

"WHAT?!" Banavor demanded insistently.

"Marassa Banavor," came a meek voice outside the door. "The Head Regent needs to speak with you immediately."

Banavor gave a frustrated sigh and looked back at Vanir. The investigator hurriedly straightened his clothes and attempted to shove his still rigid member back in his pants.

"I'll be right there," the Marassa said defeatedly, while grabbing for his robe.

He turned his attention to Vanir heading for the door. "Oh Captain, do drop back by soon. There's still the matter of a christening to attend to."

Commander Bajec grew more nervous with each degree the moon fell in the western sky. Progress through the Tur' Qua Pass moved much slower than any could have anticipated. The webbing ropes, which completely clogged the only passage through the mountains, turned out to be very tough and coated with an incredibly sticky substance. Initial slices from the sword wielders proved partially successful, however the blades quickly became coated with the webbing, robbing them of their slicing ability, rendering them into ineffective clubs.

The new Singa commander solved that dilemma by making two alternating rows of choppers. The lead row of swordsmen hacked away while able, then fell back to clean off their blades while the second line took over.

With progress still painstakingly slow, Bajec did not want to be caught in this pass during the moonless. Fifty yards ahead, however, he caught the glittering dancing of moonlight through the crystal trees of the Barrens.

Smiling, he gave a hopeful sigh. "Come on men. We're almost there!"

A horn sounded from the rear of the army and Bajec relaxed a little more. The last column of his men had now entered the pass and were finally out of the desert. The Singa commander's relief proved to be short lived, however. From up and down their stony confines, the sound of surprised then terrified roars echoed off the steep walls.

Bajec no sooner spun to see the nature of the disturbance, when several large, webbed nets dropped from the tangled lattice above. The sticky, permeable blanket narrowly missed him, but entangled both lines of sword wielders. From the screams and shouts emanating down the pass, he imagined a similar scene playing out across his entire force.

He drew his sword in an attempt to free his men, when he saw thousands of black, hairy spiders, easily measuring two feet across, flooding down from the webs above and rapidly crawling out from behind rocks. The startled Singa had never seen spiders this large and he gasped, astounded at how fast they swarmed over his troops.

Bajec bellowed in defiance, slashing across a pair of large arachnids when they jumped at him. The two cleaved bodies dropped to the ground, twitching and spilling out their murky, grey innards.

As he prepared to chop at another, a white sticky rope shot down from above, entangling his sword hand and handle. Bajec glanced upward to see a male Cevot reach down and pull the web cord loose from the tip of its thorax. Its horrific human torso, set atop a large spider body, yanked the three-hundred-pound man-lion off his feet and up into the webbing above.

Unable to use his sword to free himself, Bajec attempted to sever the line with his other claw, only to have that appendage also trapped. He thrashed, kicked and roared when he felt himself adhere to the silken netting. His aggressive attempts at freedom only served to entangle him even more.

With a hungry leer, the Cevot quickly scampered over beside the rapidly tiring Singa. Bajec's curses became screams of terror when the Cevot hissed something in its language and pulled back its lips, revealing a pair of four-inch fangs. Drops of venom had already formed on the pointed tips. With a quick lunge, he bit the Singa commander on the arm. Then, beginning at his feet, the Cevot began encasing him in a white silky shroud.

Bajec immediately felt a heady, euphoric feeling wash over him. His outer extremities, beginning with the bitten arm, went numb when the powerful neurotoxin quickly took effect. He could do little more than watch the energetic man-spider pump out strand after strand from its thorax, encasing his body.

When halfway swathed, the Singa's throat began to tighten and he could just barely hear the sounds and cries of his men in the midst of combat. Slipping further into unconsciousness, his mind drifted back to his mate, Quadin, and their life together on the Rovina plains. He missed the grasslands of home and felt a twinge of guilt about being away from her for so long in the service of the empire.

Bajec's last thought before succumbing to the poison was that he hadn't eaten today.

For some reason he found that funny.

Zaad heard the lone baying howl in the distance. It echoed over the crystal trees of the Barrens, reverberating off the regions hard unforgiving terrain.

"Onay scouting party coming in," he said to Lazio, who faced the rising moon, stretching and yawning.

The EEtah reached down, picked up a handful of snow and shoved it in his mouth. He shuddered then swallowed.

"Now I remember why I hate this place," he said, wiping his mouth on his sleeve. "Too damn cold, I mean ya gotta eat a drink of water."

The Singa chuckled watching the man-shark's discomfort. "You get used to it."

"Ehh, not sure I want to." Zaad said, walking over behind a nearby red crystal tree. "There's something I've been meaning to ask you."

"Sure," Lazio said over the rushing sound of the EEtah relieving himself.

"Seeing how we're up against…you know. I guess what I'm asking, is it hard fighting your own kind?"

Lazio thought for a moment, watching Zaad come back around the tree, closing his pants. He finally shook his head.

"No, the various prides fight amongst themselves all the time. Especially the males. It's always something, usually land or women. You?"

"Nah, EEtahs are a cranky lot by nature. The Sunal's even have a creed they recite to each other about fighting beside each other one cycle and facing them in combat the next." The EEtah shrugged. "Eh, the life of a mercenary."

"But not you?"

"Hardly, I'm Outer Clan. I've spent practically my whole life around humans."

"You prefer their company?"

"Some of them. Humans can be a devious lot, but I've been fortunate. Captain Maluria treats me like family. The pay's not bad either. Of course, we're almost always either aligned with, or fighting against a ragged bunch of rowdies, like these folk."

Zaad nodded towards the pack of thirty wolf-men who rushed into camp on all fours rolling, tumbling and nipping at each other when one got too close to the other.

The unruly Onay filled the clearing and eventually stood up and shuffled around anxiously. Long Snout and an older female headed their way, while a young male slung two decapitated female Singa heads suspended on a rope over a low branch.

"We're taking heads now, Long Snout?" Lazio said disappointedly.

"We ambushed a hunting party of five. Some Ghorn helped us. They let us feed on those two, they said they had plans for the other three..."

The Onay leader suddenly assumed a defiant, superior tone and snarled. "So, our ways trouble you lion man? Perhaps you cannot stomach what must be done!"

Zaad contemplated snatching the brash Onay up by the scruff of his neck and shaking him, when the older female with grey and black fur stepped forward. Zaad had seen her around the Onay camp performing divination with small bones and doing other shamanistic duties.

"Enough of this!" she snapped. "The situation is dire! The invaders now occupy the Handiena Mount."

At the mention of the Singa's actions the Onay began angrily growling and yipping. Zaad and Lazio traded confused stares.

"It is the most sacred site to all the hordes!" she said emphatically. "They must be driven from it!"

This set the pack into a yelping frenzy, pushing and snapping at each other.

"ALRIGHT, ALRIGHT!" Zaad roared above the agitated group. "I get it! It's important!"

With the EEtah's acknowledgement the Onay quieted into an uneasy rumble.

"You can't just go charging in there like an undisciplined mob." Zaad said commandingly. "You'll be slaughtered."

Lazio brought his attention back to the female shaman. "What do they call you?"

"I am Smoke Through the Trees."

"Alright Smoke Through the Trees, how many are now guarding your sacred mount?"

"More than a hundred," she said confidently. "The main force of their army moved off to the east."

Lazio's eyes narrowed and he nodded. "I think I see their plan now. They're taking the Etheria fields while the bulk of their army heads for Immor-Onn. What do you want to bet there's another army moving across the Dark Waste to the south taking the oases?"

"We care nothing about the desert!" Long Snout spat arrogantly. "We must kill the ones who desecrate the sacred mount!"

The declaration set off another round of frantic howls and chaotic aggressive behavior.

Lazio gave Zaad a concerned look. "I can see maintaining discipline is going to be a task."

Zaad peered around at the restless Onay and shook his head. "They're going to attack no matter what. If we don't help them out, they're going to get killed for sure."

"Agreed," Lazio said with a weary sigh.

"ALRIGHT LISTEN UP!" Zaad bellowed.

To his surprise, the mob of wolf-men quickly calmed.

"We'll hit them during the upcoming moonless, but we gotta do it smart!"

The pack mumbled their agreement, placated at the plan of attack.

"We're gonna need a lot more forces than this," Zaad continued. "You say this site is sacred to all the hordes. Then all the hordes have a stake in this. You've got this luna to rally as many from each of the three hordes as possible. We'll converge on the mount shortly after moonfall. You have to do this without howls. This must be a surprise. Do you understand?"

Long Snout and Smoke Through the Trees lowered their tails and reluctantly nodded before they went about instructing the pack. Then they left as abruptly as they arrived, scattering in all directions to rally their normally fractured peoples.

The good thing about appearing as a doddering old person is you become virtually invisible on the streets. No one pays attention to the elderly man hobbling along aided by a cane. You are perceived as harmless and non-threatening.

That was exactly how Cha-Rod liked it.

As a lifelong member of the Order of Bojo-Vat, the Bailian stick fighter knew the royal palace in Immor-Onn well. His people had been enlisted as bodyguards and security by Bailian royalty for thousands of grands.

He and Oro' Korra watched the palace for the last two lunas, assessing how the mawl invaders used the annexed property, especially noting the comings and goings of the Tiikeri spymaster, To-Nok.

Now, while the moon fell over the occupied city, Cha-Rod hobbled past the front gate of the palace and paused. The plan had been formed and now the hour had arrived. The guards' shift change approached and the ones still on duty would be eager for their watch to be over and less observant.

Oro' Korra had gotten a head start and accessed the building from the rear. Their target occupied a private bedroom suite on the second floor. The plan seemed simple enough, Oro' Korra would cause a diversion around back, allowing him to slip in the front. After that, it came down to locating the spymaster's room and quickly dispatching him.

Across the street, Demetrius invisibly observed Cha-Rod stop at the front gate. He and Okawa had been taking turns watching the palace, using their shrouding crystals to conceal them. The pilot couldn't hear the commotion, but he saw the guard at the front door suddenly look to his left and then rush around the building.

As soon as the Singa moved out of sight, Cha-Rod cautiously looked around, and using the round Etheria head of his cane, he tapped the lock on the gate and it swung open.

Demetrius then saw the formerly feeble looking, old Bailian slip gracefully through the wrought-iron barrier, onto the palace grounds and up to the now unguarded front door. Using the cane again on that door's lock, he crept inside the spacious mansion and out of sight.

Interesting, Demetrius thought. Okawa would be along shortly. He decided to wait and see what she wanted to do.

Quietly closing the front door, Cha-Rod winced at the dank smell of ammonia permeating the air. His heart sank when he looked around at the once beautiful interior, now marred by claw marks and soiled furniture.

250

Heading up the wide staircase, he couldn't help but notice that the two ornate Ukko wood pillars extending from floor to ceiling—a gift from the Valdurian government—had been reduced to scratching posts. They shredded away most of the elaborate carvings and their shavings littered the floor.

On the second-floor landing, he looked down the hall and saw another guard looking out the window, presumably at the disturbance Oro' Korra had created. Bojo-Vat moved swiftly and silently up behind him, using the stealth walk technique. A sound rap to the back of the head sent the Singa toppling to the floor.

The door he guarded appeared slightly ajar and Cha-Rod peered through the crack. The suite contained three rooms. In the main living area, he could see the white Tiikeri, To-Nok, also staring out the window.

Thankfully, the door made no noise when he opened it just wide enough to slip through. To-Nok did not move when Cha-Rod raised his cane and started across the room. The Bojo-Vat master reveled in his good fortune on how the mission had, so far, gone without a hitch.

"Master Cha-Rod," To-Nok said, continuing to stare out the window. "I've been looking forward to meeting you."

The Bailian froze in mid-stride and watched the Tiikeri turn to face him with a gloating smile. No wonder it had gone so smoothly, it had been a trap. *But how?*

The door to the hallway suddenly flew open and three Singas armed with short swords entered and glowered menacingly.

"Oh, I had a feeling you would be dropping by," To-Nok said stepping closer. "I've been keeping tabs on you practically since our arrival. You see, we have a mutual friend."

Almost on cue, the side bedroom door opened and a smiling Oro' Korra stepped into the room. Cha-Rod's eyes went wide and his jaw dropped open.

"Y... you!" he stammered.

"Don't look so shocked," the old general said haughtily. "You see my philosophies are much more aligned with the Tiikeri's than with that weakling queen we had. They *understand* racial purity and are not afraid to embrace it."

"I see they also embrace traitors!" Cha-Rod spat.

"Traitor is such a subjective word," Oro' Korra said reflectively. "Personally, I thought Queen Shula committed an act of treason when she opened up this city to foreigners and allowed the races to mingle. Those unforgivable actions endangered our sacred bloodline! WELL, NO MORE! Under Tiikeri rule, the purity of the Bailian race will once again thrive!"

"You'd rather live in a vassal state, under the thumb of these heartless overlords?"

"I would hardly call them heartless. You see, I've been promised the position of regional governor. So, the answer is yes. Discipline and purity are returning to this city."

"So, now that all our intentions are clear," To-Nok said, moving across the room to the door on the other side. "Let's discuss your new friends that are sculking about the city."

"I don't know what you're talking about," Cha-Rod said. "I'm quite alone."

"I had a feeling you might be reluctant," the Tiikeri said, opening the door. "No problem, it's just a matter of time before we get them. So, I brought by some of your *old* friends for a little reunion of sorts."

From the now open doorway, a dozen middle-aged Bailians, formally dressed in tri-tailed jackets, paraded in and circled Cha-Rod. All carried canes of various sizes with heavy bulbous heads.

"I'm sure you remember your old Bojo-Vat comrades. They've been eager to see you."

Cha-Rod peered around at the dozen murderous stares.

"So," he said stoically, "you get your gauntlet after all."

The lead Bailian scowled and raised his cane. "You annulled the gauntlet by not returning to face the charges against you. That was your second and final insult."

Without waiting, he brought the head of the cane down hard on Cha-Rod's head, to be followed by another, and immediately joined by the others.

With a determined yank, Sentima stripped the last bit of flesh off the large hind quarter, then tossed the bones aside.

"The *only* good thing about this land is that there's plenty of meat around," he said still chewing.

"And with our hunters gone, it's a good thing they're easy to catch too," another replied.

Sentima swallowed the last morsel and looked out at the waning rays of moonlight filtering through the crystal trees of the Barrens. His meal now finished, he licked his hands and washed his face, hoping this wasn't going to be a long-term deployment. He hated the constant cold and snow.

Mostly he hated the lack of soft ground to lay on. Everything encountered in this forbidding place seemed hard and unyielding. Even the things passing for vegetation were composed of crystals. By the way the rest of the two hundred Singa force complained, they felt the same way.

He had to admit, as far as missions went, he really liked its ease. Their orders so far, were to hang out and protect the large mound of crystals they found themselves camped on.

Sentima suddenly snapped out of his melancholy trance when one of the perimeter guards yelled, "Hey, the hunting party's back!"

Quickly getting to his feet, Sentima and several others rushed over to the lone sentry. Peering into the gathering darkness, they could make out the shapes of three female Singas headed their way.

"There's only three," the sentry noted. "I wonder what happened to the other two?"

"Well, they don't have a kill with them," Sentima replied. "And they're walking funny. I bet they got attacked."

"HEY, ARE YOU ALRIGHT?" the sentry called out.

The females remained silent and kept up their advance.

"They must be hurt," one of the others said obviously concerned. "I better go get the shaman."

The young male took off running towards the middle of the mound, where the main body of troops were stationed.

Another approached the returning females, asking if they needed any assistance. One of the females lashed out, grabbed him by the throat and lifted him off his feet. The startled lion-man's brief roar of surprise reverted to a sickening gurgle when abnormally strong hands crushed his thick neck.

Sentima found himself inadvertently crying out in shock when the female casually tossed the corpse to the side as if it were a doll. The three females continued lumbering towards the alarmed Singa force.

Sentima and the sentry got a good look at them when they got close enough. All three had vacant, unblinking stares and appeared to have fatal wounds. One's throat had been chewed open, the other two had entrails dangling from wounds in their abdomen, but no blood could be seen. They all bore the same strange runes carved in their chest.

Armed male Singas rushed at the female revenants, but they showed no sign of intimidation in spite of being vastly outnumbered. A sentry lunged forward and ran one revenant through with his spear. The weapon made a sucking sound when it plunged through her body and exited out her back. The sentry frantically pulled on the lodged polearm, trying to free it, when she grabbed him by either side of his head and violently wrenched it.

Sentima heard the loud crunch when the sentry's spine snapped. He swung his short sword at the one plodding towards him. The heavy blade bloodlessly sliced across her rune filled chest but had no effect. Ducking to the right, he barely missed being raked by her claws.

The three undead females seemed completely unphased when swarmed by dozens of males roaring in rage. The scene beside the crystal mound plunged into total chaos. Brutish males with their manes flying tried everything they could think of to bring down this newest threat. Strikes and blows showed no signs of stopping them as they continued rending apart any Singas they could get ahold of with their unnatural strength.

A pile of crushed warrior corpses surrounded the Singa revenants. Even with their bodies riddled with lodged weapons, they seemed unstoppable. Suddenly, all three ceased their attack and their heads fell backwards, bobbing around aimlessly. They teetered and then collapsed.

Sentima heard chanting coming from behind him. He spun and saw the Yagur shaman with a crystal leaf in each hand. He closed his eyes and waved the leaves in a scissoring motion, while softly repeating ancient incantations.

It took a few moments for the commotion to die down. With ragged breaths, Sentima stared down at the female Singas lying motionless in the snow.

"Those runes on their chest," the shaman said, shaking his head and discarding the leaves in his hands. "The magic of the dead."

"I *really* don't like this place now," Sentima said, drained of any hope.

Before anyone else could comment, a baying howl rose up from the forest to their right. Immediately a yelping on their left answered the call. Soon after, hundreds of Onay howls filled the air.

The Singa troops milled around frantically in all directions, desperately searching for the source, which seemed to come from every direction."

"We're surrounded boys!" the commander announced defiantly. "That means we've got them just where we want them! DEFENSIVE POSITIONS NOW!"

"I SAID NO NOISE!" Zaad screamed in frustration.

All around him, the force of several hundred Onay began picking up on the rallying cries from the two other groups of wolf-men, poised and eager to attack. It began as random yips, quickly growing into a cacophony of howling, eventually working themselves into a frenzy.

Zaad and Lazio could do little more than watch while the force they were supposed to lead worked themselves up into a berserker charge. Finally, responding to some unspoken cue, the pack of Onay bolted, charging in mass towards the occupied Etheria mound a hundred yards away.

"Well, we're in it now!" Zaad said, drawing Bowbreaker.

The former Singa general pulled his blade and gave the EEtah an uneasy look. "I just hope those reckless bastards don't get us killed."

"I heard that!" Zaad said, taking off behind the unruly horde with Lazio trailing.

By the time they made it to the clearing around the besieged hill, they found it already littered with the bodies of scores of the wolf-men. The battle wiped the trodden ground clean of snow, revealing the cold flat crystal forest floor covered in blood.

The Singa force formed disciplined ranks on and around the snow-covered mound, with archers near the crest, a ring of pikemen below and finally short swords men at the base.

The main Onay force which made it past the archer's initial volleys, found themselves engaging the defensive frontline of Singa sword wielders. The few packs that broke through the line were individually picked off by the pikemen from the high ground above.

Zaad broke out across the clearing full of bodies. He reached down in midstride, grabbed a dead Onay by the scruff of its neck with his free hand and held it out in front of him as a shield. The EEtah no sooner raised the corpse barrier, when three arrows punctured through the body, their tips poking out the back.

To his right, Zaad caught a glimpse of Lazio engaging the frontline. The Singas appeared surprised to be fighting one of their own and Lazio took full advantage of their hesitation.

The Singa swordsmen also reeled in shock, having never seen an EEtah before. They fell back, away from the bellowing man-shark with the immense sword who stood a full two heads taller than them.

Zaad raked Bowbreaker against the three directly before him. Torsos followed severed limbs to the ground when the great sword cut its path of destruction. The enraged EEtah then spun to his left, tossing his cadaver shield, peppered with arrows, into a line of four. The group recoiled and Zaad capitalized on the distraction, slashing Bowbreaker across their upper torsos.

The thunderous reverberations of the conflict echoed through the crystalline forest. The clash of arms, roars from both the Singas and Zaad, as well as the growls and barks of the Onay, assaulted Lazio's ears.

He saw two pikemen running up behind Zaad while a couple swordsmen kept him engaged. Lazio tried to call out a warning, but realized the EEtah couldn't hear him and began slashing his way over to his friend.

Lazio could clearly tell the EEtah had entered a blood frenzy. He brought his great sword down with such ferocity that it cleaved a Singa before him in half. The force of the blow sent his comrade next to him reeling. Zaad arced his blade around to strike the other, when Lazio saw the spearmen plunge their weapons simultaneously into the EEtah's back.

Lazio screamed in horror and frustration watching the polearms plunge through the man-shark's body. The incensed Singas continued to push their spears into Zaad's back until they erupted from his chest, where the tips extended two feet out in front of him.

Lazio knew EEtahs in a blood frenzy didn't really feel pain, only an overwhelming sense of rage. Zaad initially didn't even acknowledge he had been mortally wounded. His next strike however, missed its killing objective and merely knocked the short sword from the Singa's hands. Finally, glancing down at the two bloody spear tips jutting ominously from his chest, he roared furiously.

Dropping Bowbreaker, he lashed out, grabbing the Singa by the mane on both sides of its head. With a powerful and savage tug, Zaad drove the Singa onto the protruding spear tips, pinning the two together. Zaad opened his mouth, preparing to bite down on the dying Singa's head, when his knees buckled and both toppled to the ground.

Lazio made it to them as the spearmen attempted to dislodge their weapons. He cut both down with a single blow from behind.

The fiercest fighting had now moved to the far side of the hill. With ragged breath, Lazio paused, staring down at his dead friend and then peered around at the fight still raging.

The Onay easily had a three to one superiority and should have been handily winning. Instead, they were just barely holding their own, due to their natural impetuousness.

Lazio now saw the folly in their plan. These wolf creatures could never be molded into a regimented fighting force. Their strength had always been in numbers and the sheer ferocity of their attack. They now paid the price for their ego in thinking they could change the creature's nature.

Keeping his sword on guard, he grabbed Zaad and dragged the body into the forest and away from the fighting. Once he decided they had made it to a safe distance, he sat down next to Zaad's body with his sword laying across his lap. He heard battle still raging a short distance away while he continued staring at Zaad.

When he felt something gently touching the top of his head he mournfully peered around.

It had started snowing.

Demetrius didn't know how much of a charge remained in the PSI battery on his belt, but once it ran out, the shrouding stone he carried stopped working and left him visible. It had been nearly a deci since he witnessed Cha-Rod slip into Immor-Onn's occupied palace and Okawa still had not returned. He began to worry.

The moon had just recently fallen and mawls left the Tiikeri Empire's temporary headquarters. Deciding not to wait any longer, Demetrius crossed the windswept street. If Cha-Rod needed his help, it would be best if no one could see him.

Approaching the broken gate, he made sure to open it just enough to slide through. The guard, a bored mongrel private, slammed the gate back shut, mistaking it for the wind.

He paused by the front door, knowing he wouldn't have long to wait. Just as he had been witnessing, the door opened and two orange Tiikeri exited, quietly talking. Making sure to stay clear of the exiting mawls, he sneaked inside the door before it closed.

Demetrius stood in a large foyer with two halls stretching out in both directions and a staircase. They had converted the ground floor to accommodate official business and, at this late hour, appeared deserted. Everything smelled dreadful and in a horrible state of disrepair.

He heard a door open on the second floor and quickly slipped into a corner. Standing quietly, he watched twelve Bailian males, dressed in formal suits with tri-tail jackets, descend the stairs. Demetrius' stomach knotted when he saw their blood splattered faces and shirts.

As they passed, he overheard them complaining about having to get their clothes cleaned to get Cha-Rod off them. His pulse quickened when he heard Cha-Rod's name and he bounded up the stairs dreading what he might find.

There were several doors running the length of the lone hallway, but only one had a sentry. Demetrius flattened himself against the far wall and slid along it until he reached a position opposite the mongrel guard.

The fawn colored mawl stood armed with a short sword at his side. From six feet away, Demetrius reeled at the aroma of ammonia and wet fur. The guard also warily sniffed the air. He peered around suspiciously, unfamiliar with a human's scent.

Thinking through his options, Demetrius instinctively moved away from the door just when it opened and an orange Tiikeri stepped into the hall. Through the open door he could see To-Nok, the white Tiikeri spymaster and General Oro' Korra standing over the badly mangled and bleeding body of Cha-Rod. Demetrius didn't have time to register the shock and horror of seeing his comrade dead.

"Get a clean-up squad in here immediately," To-Nok said, nudging the dead Bailian with his foot.

"Yes, Lord To-Nok," the orange Tiikeri replied, stepping near Demetrius.

"And have someone bring me my evening meal."

"Yes, Lord To-Nok."

Demetrius suddenly felt a tingling coming from the PSI battery at the small of his back. It quickly spread across his body as he became visible. The orange Tiikeri standing beside him jumped in surprise when the human appeared. It gave a roar of shock and backhanded Demetrius on the side of his head.

The blow rocked Demetrius and he staggered, almost falling. The Tiikeri grabbed him and, through a fog, he saw To-Nok and coming to the door.

"Well, well, what have we here," To-Nok said in an amused tone.

"Cha-Rod's accomplice," Oro' Korra said flatly.

"Do tell," To-Nok said, looking him over. "Human huh? I must say, that's an intriguing ability you've got there."

To-Nok then gave an evil smile to the orange Tiikeri. "Get him inside my quarters."

"Yes, Lord To-Nok."

"And you can cancel that order for my evening meal. My dinner will be served fresh."

"Yes, Lord To-Nok."

"And tell the cleanup squad to take their time. They can get the remains of both when I'm done."

"Yes, Lord To-Nok."

Okawa hated being late, but in this case, it turned out to be unavoidable. She could only hope Demetrius would be where she left him. By now, his PSI battery had probably gone dead, but fortunately the moon had set, which should offer some cover.

"Can't you go any faster, Sitsa?" she asked anxiously, watching the Os'Tor Forest give way to agricultural fields on the outskirts of Immor-Onn.

"Negative," the Tinian replied calmly, concentrating on the controls. "I am only now getting used to this craft. Each acceleration in speed, increases the chance of mishap by twenty percent."

Okawa exhaled loudly watching the skyline of Immor-Onn draw closer. Sitsa slowed the craft when the *Attila* arrived at the city's western gate. Okawa reached up to the overhead console and activated the shrouding stone. In an instant, the airship disappeared, allowing it to move unnoticed above the streets of the occupied capital.

When they neared the palace, Okawa once again accessed the overhead panel. This time, she touched the Larimar talking stone.

"Demetrius? Do you copy?"

Silence.

"Demetrius, can you hear me? Where are you? We're almost on top of your last position."

Her efforts once again were met by silence.

"There appears to be some sort of commotion at the palace." Sitsa said in her usual monotone.

The Tinian slowed the craft just over the spot where they had left Demetrius and hovered. It began to rain, but the inclement weather didn't deter a small, curious crowd of Bailians, flanked by Singa guards, from gathering around the palace gate.

Okawa and Sitsa looked out at an orange Tiikeri addressing the group. Neither could make out what he said, but his speech turned out to be short and then he opened the mansion's double front doors.

A white Tiikeri stepped out onto the landing. Okawa immediately recognized him as To-Nok, the Tiikeri spymaster she had encountered in the Worrg pits of Hai-Dar. Blood stained the white fur around his mouth, chest and hands red. The crimson taint ran down his torso when the raindrops washed over him. In each hand he carried a severed head.

General Oro' Korra joined him and the two strolled triumphantly to the gate. Okawa felt a sickening knot forming in the pit of her stomach when To-Nok mounted the heads on the posts flanking the gate. A single horrified gasp escaped from her mouth when she recognized the faces on the heads were Cha-Rod and Demetrius.

They stared lifelessly out into the crowd while the rain soaked them. The older Bailian's skull had been crushed in several spots and Demetrius' face appeared contorted in a silent grimace. Both of their necks appeared to have been chewed through.

Okawa found herself frozen in her seat, unable to take her eyes off the gruesome spectacle. No words or sounds came from her taut, trembling lips and a steady torrent of tears streamed down her face. She finally looked away when To-Nok raised his face and fists to the sky for a victorious roar.

A feeling of numbness descended on the Valdurian agent and she finally sat back in her seat, staring vacantly into space. Deep within her, a bubbling cauldron of rage began to form. A furor, which would sooner or later erupt into an orgy of violence, to rain vengeance down on all involved, rocking the Tiikeri Empire.

Throughout his grands of service in the Zorian Guards and during his apprenticeship under Colonel Zekoff, Captain Vanir had learned a great many things. The chief of which taught him to control his temper and tongue by not taking events happening on the job personally.

Early on, this proved a real challenge for the fiery red head with a temper to match. Looking back on his sometimes-shaky recollection, he couldn't remember a time more frustrating than right now. Yet, he marveled at how amazingly serene he felt.

The lobby of the Imperial Bank appeared moderately busy with the lifting of the Kan, and he calmly, but determinedly, trekked back to the offices of the Zorian Monetary Council.

"Can I help you with something, Captain?" a female clerk asked, in an attempt to intercept the unexpected visitor.

"That's alright," he said nonchalantly with a wave of his hand. "I know where I'm going."

'But Captain..."

Vanir passed through the doors to the council's offices with the protesting clerk trailing behind.

"Captain, I really must insist..." she called out.

He opened the door to Banavor's office, without knocking, and stepped inside. Both EEtah's tensed and Banavor looked up from some paperwork on his desk, obviously surprised at the unanticipated guest. His expression quickly turned from surprise to delight when he saw the head investigator.

"I'm sorry, sir," the flustered clerk said from the open doorway, "but he wouldn't stop."

"Quite alright, Josie." Banavor said, coming to his feet. "Why Captain Vanir, what a pleasant surprise!"

Vanir found himself taken slightly aback at the youth's appearance today. Completely nude, Banavor only wore a delicate male chastity cage covering his small, limp penis.

Vanir knew the finance prodigy liked to dress provocatively but this stretched things even for him.

The dark cleric genteelly offered his hand, but a smiling Vanir ignored it and, without being invited, sat down.

"I like your outfit," he said, settling back in the seat.

Banavor slowly sat back down and a mischievous look crossed his face. "I decided on simplicity today and if you've come for that christening, I'm dressed for it, but this is the wrong office."

With the suggestive statement, Vanir felt the sexual energy in the room build. However, his frustration, along with not touching the sensual youth, kept his libido in check.

"Actually, I'm here to congratulate you," Vanir announced cheerfully.

Banavor's demeanor shifted from sultry to pleasantly surprised. "Congratulations! Why, I'm pleased of course, but whatever for?"

"Yesterday evening, just before the Kan, I got called before the Zorian Security Council. The council suggested, *in the strongest terms*, that I turn my investigative gaze away from you and pursue another avenue of inquiry. So, congratulations, my investigation is now over. You apparently have won this one. I just wanted you to be aware, that I know you had a hand in Kasha's death."

Banavor kept his pleasant smile. "Why, Captain, do I look like a dangerous person?"

"No, you look like a slut."

Banavor's look grew salacious once more and he slid forward in his chair. "Why, Captain, I usually only hear that kind of language when I'm getting fucked. However, it is accurate that I am a slut. It comes in handy more often than you might think. I can't see letting all those grands of training go to waste."

In an instant, Banavor's demeanor changed again to friendly but serious. "Honestly, Captain, what did you expect. I'm the head of the Zorian Monetary Council at a time when the Goyan Islands, as a whole, are experiencing unprecedented prosperity. Who in their right mind is going to want to rock that boat?"

"You're not above the law," Vanir said seriously.

The mischievous smirk returned and Banavor playfully fluttered his eyelashes. "Apparently, I am."

"One day, I'll have you," Vanir promised through a resolved smile.

Banavor leaned forward onto his desktop, staring at Vanir with an aroused expression. "Captain, I thought my intentions were abundantly clear. You can have me anytime you want. I'm a slut, remember?"

Shom Eldor's face went somber and he scowled after reading the dispatch Attina handed him.

"I saw the seal from Avion House Eacher," Attina said, noting the foreboding expression on her sovereign's face. "What is it?"

Shom glowered and held up the paper. "Apparently one of Eacher's Kel herders spotted a fleet of sixteen large, open-top ships full of armed cat-people entering the waters of our eastern agricultural islands. I believe we're being invaded."

"What?!" Attina gasped. "I thought their forces were engaged in the Twilight Lands!"

"Well, you can't say the Tiikeri aren't an ambitious lot. How old is this information?"

"It was fast tracked through channels, so I'd say two cycles."

Shom nodded solemnly. "Alright, they've got a head start on us. Get over to House Nur immediately. Let's see how much EEtah muscle we can throw together on short notice. We need to call for assistance from House Valdur and Calden. Then get gulls flying to the regional governors. Hopefully they'll have time to call up the lancers. We might also want to get the scribes working on a formal letter of thanks to House Eacher. We owe them a debt of gratitude."

Attina nodded, staring off into space.

"You have something to add my dear?" Shom asked when he saw her pensive look.

"Warning letters to the governors is a good idea to be safe," she said confidently, "but I'm pretty sure I know where that mawl fleet is heading."

Lazio sat for the longest time watching the snow fall on Zaad's body and listening to the battle wind down in the distance. He didn't even move when he heard the Onay in a full panicked retreat rush past him in the forest, only scoffing loudly at the undisciplined rabble's frantic route.

When he and the EEtah first met in the tunnels of No-Zan, he remembered calling him "puny for an EEtah." Now, he lay dead before him.

Shark man fought well," came a crackly voice from behind.

"Obviously not well enough," Lazio said, not bothering to look up.

"Not your fault," the voice said, moving around in front of him. "The Onay are fierce, but stupid."

Lazio finally peered up at an old Bailian man standing by Zaad's body. He appeared frail, bald and badly hunched over. Lazio thought it odd that someone would wander the forest alone carrying no weapon save his crude pilgrim's staff. His rope belt, with three skulls suspended from it, held closed a loose hanging, simple black robe.

"We should have had them," Lazio said forlornly, shaking his head. "We outnumbered and outflanked them."

"Like I said, fierce but stupid."

"We were the stupid ones. We arrogantly believed we could change their nature and my friend here paid the price."

The Ghorn gazed down at the dead EEtah being slowly dusted by the falling snow. "I can return him, if you wish."

"Thank you, but no," Lazio said, returning his gaze to the body. "I've seen what happens when the dead return. Let him rest. I'll remember him as he was."

"As you wish," the Ghorn said, before he turned to go.

"One thing you can do, if possible?" Lazio said, when the necromancer started to walk away.

"Yes?" he asked, peering back over his shoulder.

"I would like to take him home for a proper funeral. Is there any way the body can be preserved?"

Zau peered down at the mass exodus of sentients plodding westward across the sands of the Dark Waste. The full moon above cast a creamy luster across the rolling dunes stretching to the horizon. The hurried migration of the oasis' noncombatants cast dark, shifting shadows against the desert. They resembled a river of marching ants to the crew of the *Haraka*.

"This doesn't look good," Zau said with a touch of dismay.

"It sure as fuck doesn't!" Mal confirmed.

The domed roof tops of the Asaro-He Oasis in the distance, and the immense lake it sat on, rapidly came into view. To the east of the city, only a few miles away, the moonlight clearly revealed a large force advancing on the desert community.

"This is gonna be close," Mal said, noting the proximity of the Singa forces.

The *Haraka* banked out over the lake and circled low, towards the walled compound of lapidary, Istan-Le. Mal peered intently out the side window and scowled when she saw the open gate in the outer walls to the city.

"And I really don't like the fucking looks of *that*!"

"Perhaps they have already left," Alto suggested.

"It's no good any fucking way you look at it," Mal said firmly. "Kumo, put her down in the same spot as last time."

"Yes, Captain."

Kumo brought the airship in low to the previous landing area and settled in, putting the lapidary's fortress between them and the city on the other side.

"Alright, Alto," Mal suggested, "let's see if we can sneak around to the front…"

"You don't have to do that, Mom," Tally said, pointing to the rear expanse of exterior wall. "We can get in there."

"I don't see anything," Mal said, staring in vain at the seemingly blank barrier.

"Neither do I," Alto agreed. "Are you sure little one?"

"Sure, I'm sure. Come on, I'll show you!"

Bounding to the side hatch, she looked back expectantly at her parents. Mal and Alto traded resigned looks and then joined her.

"Kumo, drop the side hatch. Once we're out, take her up to about thirty feet and keep a lookout. If that army, or anything that looks dangerous, gets too close, make sure they regret it, and then get us the fuck out of here."

"Yes, Captain."

"Zau, you're with us. Let's go."

When the hatch opened, Mal felt almost refreshed by the motionless cool dry air. Scanning the immediate area and seeing no one, she looked down at Taleeka.

"Alright, young lady, you're on."

Taleeka excitedly rushed past Mal and stood by a blank space of wall. "It's right here."

She traced a large oblong shape in the air in front of the wall. Reaching into her pocket, Taleeka retrieved her folding utility knife and opened a small flat blade. Starting down at ground level, she worked the tip of the blade into a small hairline crack. With surgical precision, she worked the blade upward. With each passing of the knife, sand fell away and the outline of a door began to take form.

"Well, I'll be dipped in shit!" Mal said, placing her hands on her hips.

When the ten-grand-old reached as high as her arms would allow, Alto lifted her so she could complete the upper sides and top of threshold.

"Sand got in the cracks making it hard to see," Taleeka reported proudly.

"Good job kid," Zau said, nodding in approval. "How do we open it?"

"Over here," Taleeka said.

Using the blade, she scraped the sand from an area three feet off the ground, to the door's right. Once she removed the caked-on sand, it revealed an inset circular knob.

"I can't turn it," Taleeka said, pointing her tiny finger at the latch.

Alto stepped up to assist, stood off to the side of the door and slowly turned the knob.

"You want to stand over here," she warned Zau and Mal, moving nearer the parked *Haraka*. "That notch on the top of the knob means it's trapped."

They joined her and when Alto rotated the knob a full circle, they all heard a loud whooshing sound, followed by stones grinding against each other. The moment the door slid open, a roar sounded and jets of Trinilic Etheria fire shot out thirty feet. The prolonged burst proved so intense it fused the sand into glass everywhere it touched.

"Good call, kid," Zau said, watching Taleeka fold her blade and put it away.

They could now hear the sound of rushed confusion from inside the compound. The four quickly entered and flattened themselves against the back wall of the main structure.

"Sure would like to know what the fuck's going on in there," Mal said, looking up at a row of windows a dozen feet up, mid-way below the domed roof.

"I can find out," Taleeka said confidently.

Before the Spice Rat could protest, Taleeka had already scrambled up the sheer wall. Mal held her breath and watched her daughter peer through the windows. She heaved a sigh of relief when she shimmied back down a few moments later.

"There are four lady-Singas," the young burglar reported in one breath with wide eyed excitement. "One is pointing a sword at two people. They look scared. The other three are taking crystals and piling them up outside the front door. There are a bunch of dead lizard people laying on the floor."

"Looks like those fuckers had the same assignment as us," Mal said tensely.

"Yes, but something tells me we would not have been quite so heavy handed about it," Alto replied. "We must stop them before their comrades arrive. I'll go around the front to draw them out."

"You got anything on that belt that can help?" Mal asked Zau.

The Singa flipped the seventh shell on her belt with a sneaky grin, reached down and grabbed a handful of sand..

"I've got something that will slow them down."

"Then time's a wasting, let's go," Mal ordered. "Tally, you stay here."

None of the three had time to see Taleeka's pout. Alto already disappeared around one side of the structure. Mal and Zau headed out of sight in the other direction.

Alto turned the corner at the front of the building, where he spotted two female Singas carrying out armloads of multicolored, polished Etheria rods. They carefully added them to an already sizable stack. When the two stood back up, they finally noticed the swordmaster's casual approach.

"One would think stealing was an act beneath the dignity of such a noble race," Alto said disappointedly.

Both Singas crouched and hissed threateningly. Each reached for a sickle shaped throwing blade from the bandoleers crossing their chests. The one to his left drew two first and propelled them at the brash human.

With his left-hand, Alto drew his short sword and raised its handle upward. Sweeping it in front of him, the repellent properties of the Ukkonite pummel sent the blades spinning off harmlessly. He then tossed the sword straight up, caught the blade near the tip and flung it at the attacking lioness.

The two-foot-long diamond Etheria blade plunged into the Singa's chest just above where her bandoleers crossed. The force launched the humanoid lioness four feet away and she landed dead on her back.

Zau ran around the corner in time to see the other Singa lifting her arm to throw her blades. She rubbed the exposed rune on her belt and blew the sand in her outstretched palm. The air magic spell sent the white powder sand blasting directly at the Singa.

The miniscule grains travelled at an unnatural velocity, shredding away the fur and flesh from the attacker's face and upper body. The Singa screamed and dropped to the ground, writhing about in agony.

Mal calmly walked around the corner just as Alto retrieved his blade from one attacker then plunged it into the other, ending her suffering.

"*Now* it's a party!" she said, not bothering to conceal her bravado.

The Spice Rat then looked down at the three-foot-high pile of Etheria crystal rods.

"Not a bad haul," she said with an appreciative nod. "Let's go get our two passengers."

Unconcerned with stealth, Mal drew her pistol crossbow, cocked it and led the group through the smashed open door into the besieged workshop of Istan-Le. They found the interior completely trashed, with overturned shelving, broken items, and, as Taleeka had reported, four dead Gila bodies oozing on the floor.

The two other Singas stood near the center of the room. One pointed a sword at a very frightened human female. Her attractive features contorted with fear, watching the tip of the blade circle dangerously close to her face. Tears streamed down coffee-colored cheeks, and her silver hair, which normally would have been piled high, fell loosely around her shoulders matted with sweat and blood.

"Marassa Sutayse, I presume?" Mal asked rhetorically.

The other Singa held a bald, middle aged Bailian out in front of her as a shield, her claws poised at his throat.

"Come any closer and he dies!"

Mal gave her a bored smirk, nonchalantly raised her pistol and without looking, fired at the one wielding the sword. The bolt struck the lioness in the right upper back, violently flipping her to the ground. The human female cried out and rushed over to Alto and Zau.

"Bullshit!" Mal cocked the pistol once again, raised it and pointed it at the Singa's head. "Without him to show you what to do with them, those Etheria you're trying to boost are almost worthless."

The Singa gave a cunning smile. "If we can't have him, no one will. Besides, my brothers will be arriving soon."

Mal knew she was right. The Singa army would be upon them at any moment. Time definitely wasn't in their favor.

At that moment, Mal caught movement from behind the captured Bailian lapidary. Taleeka had surreptitiously pried the window open and climbing inside.

"They won't be able to help you if you're dead," Mal said, in an attempt to keep the lioness distracted.

Suddenly, an explosion reverberated from outside, which Mal assessed to be near the eastern edge of town. The army had arrived and Kumo now held them off.

One loud report followed another, providing just enough to cover for Taleeka to finally slip through the open window and drop to the floor.

"Sounds like your boys have run into my little welcoming committee," Mal said.

Taleeka drew her knife and cautiously approached the unaware Singa from behind.

"Give up the Bailian and we're gone," Mal said, keeping the lionesses' attention on her. "Best of all, you get to live."

"I would gladly give my life in the service of the empire!"

Another explosion, closer this time, rattled the objects in the room and for the first time a crack appeared in the Singa's confidence.

Sensing movement behind her, she turned her head to look, but she noticed far too late. With a face full of grim determination, Taleeka slashed the foot long blade of Eldorian steel horizontally across the tendons in the back of her knees. The Singa roared in pain and began to fall.

Her exposed claws thankfully pulled away from her captive's throat, but still managed to rake across his right upper chest on her way down. The Bailian screamed and clutched his wounds. Blood soaked his robes and he dropped to one knee.

Zau and Alto rushed over to the wounded lapidary while Mal hovered over the prone Singa. She sneered up at Mal with pain and hatred.

"You should have taken my offer," Mal said, before firing a bolt into the humanoid lion's skull.

"I didn't mean for the blue man to get hurt," Taleeka said remorsefully.

Mal looked down at her daughter's blood-spattered face and gave a reassuring grin. "You did good, my little Tally."

Alto desperately tried stopping the maimed Bailian's bleeding by applying pressure to the three slashes using a nearby rag.

"How bad?" the Spice Rat asked.

"Bad enough," Alto replied. "I don't think it would be wise to move him."

"We don't have a fucking choice! That army is almost up our ass! Zau, can you do anything?"

Zau knelt by the head of the Bailian who drifted in and out of consciousness. Flipping over the eleventh shell on her belt she rubbed the rune on the opposite side with one hand. The other replaced Alto's on the temporary bandage. Zau closed her eyes and softly chanted until the bleeding slowly subsided. Sighing, the navigator wearily sat back on her haunches and glanced over at Mal.

"It's temporary. He really shouldn't be jostled around."

"Not an option," Mal said curtly. "We can't let this sentient fall into the hands of the Tiikeri Empire. If he dies along the way, he dies, but we have to get the fuck out of here *now*! Can you carry him?"

The lioness lethargically nodded her head.

"Good, let's go!" Mal ordered.

Alto, who stood watch by the door nodded. "All clear."

"Alright Blade Slinger, you're in the lead. Zau, you're carrying the Bailian in the middle with the Marassa. I'll take up the rear. Tally, you're in front of me, stay close."

The young girl looked up at Mal with eyes narrowed in a defiant stare.

"Don't worry mom," she said, raising the knife over her head. "I'll protect you!"

Mal smiled and patted her daughter's head. Then with the swordmaster leading the way, they started out into the hallway. They only made it a few feet before another explosion rocked the building again.

Peering around the corner to his right, Alto could see out the broken front doors onto the streets of the city, filled with burly male Singas rushing past, their long manes sweeping out behind them with every stride. Their thickly muscled bodies reminded Alto of their formidability.

"Our avenue of escape appears to be blocked," Alto said exasperated.

"What are we going to do?" the Marassa asked timidly.

Heaving a frustrated huff, Zau's eyes shifted nervously back and forth searching for an answer. Suddenly she froze when an idea came to her.

"My people, especially the males, don't like heights," she said excitedly.

Mal's head snapped around at her navigator. "Upstairs! The balcony!"

"Without waiting, Mal bolted to the narrow stairway. Pausing by the first step, she motioned the others over.

"Same order as before," she said, examining the stairway's entrance. "And it's nice and narrow up there. If they want to get to us, they'll have to do it single file. Come on!"

The group filed past the Spice Rat, who fell into the rear.

"Will whatever you're planning even work?" the Marassa asked anxiously when passing Mal.

276

"We don't have a whole lot of options," Mal replied, taking two steps at a time. "I just hope to fuck that Kumo's paying attention."

They passed the second-floor landing, which housed another Etheria processing center with large cutting and polishing devices. They found the personal quarters on the third floor under a tall, domed ceiling with four skylights placed strategically to light the bedchambers. Alto began throwing open doors until he discovered the one with the balcony overlooking the city.

"Over here," he said, motioning them into the chamber.

The room measured twenty feet square with six sandboxes covered with rugs on top. A wooden trunk rested at the foot of each bed.

"Out onto the balcony," Mal said, indicating the multipaned doors leading outward. "Alto, the trunks!"

The swordmaster nodded and began sliding trunks to blockade the door. Everyone else filed out onto the balcony.

Just down the street, Mal spotted the *Haraka*, suspended thirty feet in the air. It shot a weak fireball at a large group of Singas who took shelter around the corner of a nearby building. By the burnt corpses littering the intersection, Mal surmised there had been several unsuccessful attempts to escape the airship's reach.

The next attempt met the same fate, but Mal could tell by the weakened fireball that the ship was running out of PSI to power the Trinilic fire rods.

"We've got to get Kumo's attention," Mal said, desperately looking around for anything that might help.

"Zau, you got anything that can get Kumo looking this way?"

The Singa set the unconscious Bailian down. "I think I've got one more trick in me, but after that I'm not going to be able to carry him."

"Don't worry about that, we'll get him on the ship."

277

"You know that any signal I give will betray our position?" Zau said, drawing her dagger."

"Just do it!"

Flipping over the fifth shell on her belt, Zau rubbed the fire magic rune. She then ran the flat of her dagger briskly across the balcony railing. The shower of sparks ignited the blade which began sparking on its own. Zau then held the pyrotechnic knife aloft and waved it.

Alto could hear the rumble of them battering the door over the roar in the streets. He rushed back into the room just as door crashed open and an enraged male Singa appeared. Running past the beds, the swordmaster reached down and grabbed a handful of sand and one of the carpets.

The Singa soldier bellowed in anger, struggling to get past the barricade of trunks. Alto saw a long, single file line of impatient shock troops waiting to enter right behind him.

When the swordmaster reached the besieged doorway, the Singa slashed out at him with an extended claw. Staying just out of arm's length, the swordmaster threw the sand into the lion-man's face, before tossing the carpet over its head.

The Singa roared and frantically rubbed his eyes under the covering. Quickly drawing Defari, Alto plunged the growling blade through the carpet. The soldier gave out a howl of pain. Withdrawing the sword, Alto shoved at the rug where a red patch formed. The mortally wounded Singa toppled backwards into his companions.

Using the longsword's reach, Alto lunged forward, taking full advantage of their disoriented state, stabbing the second in line.

Mal wrenched her head back and forth, keeping an eye on Alto's situation and the *Haraka's*, which just released another round of chain shot from one of its ballista pods. The deadly missile chewed up a half dozen shock troops attempting to enter their building.

Mal could see Zau growing weaker with each wave of her outstretched arm. The sparks grew dimmer and the lioness' eyes appeared to grow heavy, when the *Haraka* turned toward them. Mal and the Marassa motioned furiously, when the Spice Rat saw Taleeka bolting back into the room.

"TALLY NO!" Mal screamed.

"Gotta help dad!" she proclaimed waving her knife above her head.

Alto engaged with a Singa who had pushed past his fallen companions, swinging his short sword. Taleeka ducked to the floor beside her father and hacked at the Singa's foot, severing three toes. The Singa's eyes bulged in shock and he roared in anguish, just before Alto ran Defari's tip through its open mouth.

The Singa dropped on top of his other dead comrades adding more of an obstacle in the single path line of berserker lion warriors. Alto looked back at the *Haraka* floating beside the balcony with her side hatch dropping.

"Tally, the ship!" he called out over frustrated roars.

Taleeka broke and ran for the craft. Alto backed away from the door and cast Defari into the air. The possessed Etheria sword hovered in mid-air, growling menacingly.

"Guard!" he ordered, just before bolting for the balcony.

Mal had successfully loaded everyone onto the ship and was assisting a very weak Zau up the ramp. When Alto paused to pick up the Bailian, he saw two Singas climbing over their dead companions on all fours.

Defari gave a blood curdling howl, before slashing across both of their chests as they attempted to rise to their feet. The simple-minded lion soldiers froze at the door, unsure of how to deal with the autonomous blade.

Alto carried the limp Bailian onboard to the sound of arrows bouncing off the ship's lower hull. When the *Haraka* began to pull away from the landing, Alto stretched out his arm and whistled loudly. The faithful sword streaked across the room and into her master's outstretched hand, leaving behind several frustrated and bewildered Singa warriors.

Mal did a quick head count. "Alright Kumo, good job. Now get us the fuck outta here!"

A scowling General Baag-Tar stared forlornly at the pile of Etheria rods and the two dead female Singas.

A Singa with a blue captain's ribbon woven into his mane briskly approached and saluted. "There's two more dead inside and fifty burnt and chewed up bodies just down the street. The lapidary is nowhere to be found."

"He probably got away in that airship we saw leaving a short while ago. What about the inhabitants?"

"Mostly gone, we're still searching. This is a big place."

The general nodded then glanced back at the Etheria rods.

"Get these and any others you find in a wagon. Have a detail take it south to the coast. Get an Ash-Ta aloft and have it locate our nearest ship, then rendezvous with this shipment and get it back home."

"Yes, sir," the captain said, saluting and hurrying away.

From his third story apartment window, Master Na-Ruu looked down on the Singa general overseeing the city's takeover with an entertained grin. The eighth level Bailian Kinjuto Dominator stubbornly refused to evacuate with the rest of the oasis' population. He had been expelled once before, from his home city of Immor-Onn several grands ago, by their sickeningly sweet queen.

This time, he wasn't going anywhere. Besides, he still had work to do and now, a whole new batch of furry sentients to play with.

"I do believe your colleagues down there are stealing all of my friends Etheria," Na-Ruu said, crossing his arms in front of his thin nude frame, still maintaining his vigil.

He continued watching while a lizard drawn wagon, filled with multicolored rods sped away. Scoffing loudly, he saw the mass body of invaders begin entering the various buildings and set up sentries.

"The moon will be setting soon," he said, turning back into the room and his several guests. "It appears you all will be spending the moonless with us, *splendid*. It will give us time to arrange a proper celebration for the next luna."

One of the Singas charged with conducting an initial search for inhabitants whimpered in pain. The team of three encountered his trap the moment they opened the door to his workshop abode. The initial pain inflicted on the first Singa to step through the door turned out to be more than enough to send a surge of PSI into the advanced torture mage. His subsequent fear spell set all on their knees cowering in dread from the Kinjuto's potent magic.

The unfortunate lion-men hung bound and gagged, suspended from a beam in the ceiling by a wire around their necks. They fought to stay on their tiptoes to avoid strangulation. The thin filament cut into their throats and they moaned in pain through their gags, forced to watch one of their numbers receive the Kinjuto's full treatment.

The unlucky recipient found himself bound securely to a thick wooden cross. He couldn't respond even if he wanted to, with his mouth filled with rags, forcing it open as wide as the jaw would allow.

On a pile in front of him lay his severed tongue, tail, scrotum and penal sheath. His long pink penis dangled vulnerably in front of him above a small puddle of urine on the floor.

A pile of long, dark brown hair, once his mane, littered the floor next to his amputated body parts. The bald, humiliated soldier, now devoid of his people's primary symbol of rank and status, could only peer around in terror. Dozens of scabbed over nicks dotted his pale wrinkled skin where the blade had slipped.

Through the haze of pain, the Singa private watched his captor slowly approach. He had not seen a Bailian before but felt certain this one had to be an aberration. His captor appeared tall and thin, with pale blue skin setting off a head full of rust red hair. His piercing blue eyes radiated a methodical cruelty which truly frightened the man-lion.

Most disturbing were the slits of various sizes cut into his skin, forming flesh pockets all over his nude body. From the lumps inside, he knew they contained concealed objects.

Na-Ruu paused just in front of the Singa, examined his work and nodded in satisfaction.

"I'm sure you'll agree, stealing is quite rude," he said calmly, "and while I'm in no position to stop them, I think a suitable punishment is in order. You and your friends hanging over there are going to help."

The Singa's dread filled eyes followed the Bailian across the room where he took hold of a free-standing full-length mirror and moved it in front of the bound captive.

"What do you think?" he asked, turning it so both reflections could now be seen.

The Singa could now view himself and he gave an anguished scream. All that it meant to be a Singa male had been removed. No longer concerned with his pride, he wept and wailed through the gag.

The tortured Singa's mental anguish sent a wave of ecstatic power coursing through Na-Ruu and he felt the beginning of an erection.

"Don't make me remove your eyelids," he warned, when the Singa looked away. "You keep looking at your handsome face while I give your people a little something to ponder."

Listening to the three mawls' muffled anguish with an enraptured look, he walked over and opened the window. A cool gentle breeze cascaded over his exposed flesh and he felt the psychic power building with the intruders every torment filled moment.

When it reached a peak within him, he extended both arms out the window and closed his eyes. The wind immediately picked up, slowly building until it reached gale force. In the distance, a massive cloud of sand filled the horizon and began swirling towards the city.

Na-Ruu remained motionless until the cyclone force winds swept down every street, sandblasting anyone outside. Closing the window, he smiled, acknowledging his accomplishment and then turned back to the Singa.

"Now, what did I tell you about looking away," he scolded, reaching into one of his skin pockets and pulling out a small flaying knife.

When Mal saw the fog bank ahead, she knew they had come off of the Ocean Deep and would soon be over the Goyan Islands.

"Good thing we're coming in during the Kan," Mal noted. "The university should be mostly vacant and finding a spot to land should be easy."

Zau, sitting next to her in the navigator's chair, nodded and peered around the cabin. Kumo stood at the helm's wheel. Alto napped in a seat across from the two passengers they rescued from the oasis. Taleeka slept on a bedroll in the cargo area beyond, hugging a sheathed Defari. The canine in the blade softly snored in the child's arms.

"We'll be there fairly soon, should I wake them up?" Zau wondered aloud."

"Nah, let them sleep a little while longer," Mal replied. "I have a feeling they're going to be putting us to work as soon as we drop off our passengers."

Zau gave a resigned sigh. "Back to the Twilight Lands I imagine."

"That's where the action is," Mal said. "I just hope Zaad and Lazio got the fucking Ghorn and Onay to stop killing each other long enough to fight the armies baring down on their asses."

The same moment they entered the Kan fog the Larimar communications disk began blinking on the overhead console. Mal reached up, touched the Etheria crystal and listened to the message.

"It's Lazio," she mouthed to Zau.

As Mal listened, her eyes glazed over in shock and her face grew steadily paler. When the Spice Rat's lower lip began trembling, Zau knew something was wrong.

"Okay," Mal said defeatedly. "Hang tight, we'll be there."

When the connection finally broke, Mal slumped back in her seat with a shocked, vacant stare.

"Captain, what is it?!"

Mal didn't respond, gazing blankly out the windshield.

"Captain?"

Mal slowly faced her navigator. "Zaad's dead."

Zau reeled in disbelief. "By the Goddess, no!"

"There was a battle in an Etheria field," Mal recounted, sounding hollow and empty. "Two Singas speared Zaad from behind. According to Lazio, the Onay were fucking worthless. Lazio's put his body on ice. As soon as we drop off our two passengers, we're going back for them."

They sat in grief-stricken silence until the outer Goyan Islands appeared below them.

"I'll wake everyone up," Mal volunteered. "They should hear it from me."

"This isn't going to sit well with Alto," Zau said warily. "He already has no love for the wolf-men of the Barrens. Shom and Zaad were also close. Angering the Eldorian king is never good. Wars have been started for less."

"Alto and Shom are big boys," Mal said, getting to her feet. "They've lost comrades before. It's the little one in the back I'm worried about."

General Oro' Korra woke suddenly with a splitting headache. The newly appointed regional governor remembered coming home to his recently acquired luxury suite in Immor-Onn's royal palace at moonfall. He no sooner stepped through the door when everything went black.

He found himself naked, gagged and securely tied to a heavy wooden chair.

He inhaled sharply through his gag when he saw Okawa seated on a sofa across the room staring at him. Her eyes appeared sunken and burning with hatred.

"I've been sitting here, debating how to kill you," she said low and menacingly.

The old general made a futile panicked struggle against his bonds while mumbling a frenzied explanation through the gag.

"Save it!" she growled, getting to her feet. "You and your cat buddies took someone *very* dear to me. I'm here to make sure *you all* pay. Starting with you."

He shook his head and looked on in wide eyed horror at the Valdurian agent crossing the room. She stopped directly in front of him and peered down. Her cold stare radiated mercilessness. Reaching over to a nearby table, she picked up a short iron club.

"I finally decided how, just before you woke up. House Valdur took the time and trouble to train me so you can trust it'll be slow and painful. I just can't decide where to start."

She suddenly lashed out with the baton smashing the tiny bones on the back of his hand. The Bailian gave a muffled scream, thrashing against his bonds. Through the tears welling up in his eyes, he saw the human female staring dispassionately at his agony.

"Hey, what do you know? I finally decided," she said icily, raising the club again.

The rising moon brought with it an intense squall. Sheets of rain blew sideways, inundating the covered streets of Immor-Onn. For the sixty Balians assembled in one of the many covered squares in the city, the moonrise brought only terror when they had been rounded up at random.

Some had been rousted from their beds, others were snatched from the streets when they began their morning routine. Now, chilled and wet, they shivered and peered around anxiously at the Singa abductors surrounding them.

To-Nok appeared and slowly stepped to the front of the crowd of Singas, ears flattened against his head, ignoring the deluge. The sound of rain pelting off the clear crystal coverings above drowned out the nervous murmurs passing through the gathering.

The white Tiikeri stood silent for a moment studying the fear-ridden faces. He then held up a large piece of paper and gave out a roar to both intimidate and quiet everyone.

"These notices have been placed all across the city," he declared above the pounding downpour. "Ignorance is not an excuse. Quite simply, it states that for each one of my men murdered, ten of you will die. Last moonless, we found one of my men dead. Today, you will pay the price."

He nodded to the Singas behind him. They fanned out through the terrified assembly and gruffly strong-armed ten panicked Bailians into a line. Some stood silently, paralyzed with fear, others cried and pleaded. To-Nok stood facing the frightened crowd with a dispassionate expression. The spear wielding lion-men then took up positions directly behind those in line.

"Do not worry," To-Nok continued mockingly. "Your fellow citizens will not have died in vain. For after their execution they will be used to feed my men. You will be a witness to this. If you look away, you will join them."

With another nod from the Tiikeri, the Singas drove their spears into the backs of their victims until the tips erupted from their chests. When they wrenched the spears free, the Bailians dropped at their killer's feet.

Screams and cries erupted from the group and one woman looked downward in revulsion. To-Nok lunged forward, grabbed the woman and sliced her throat open with a single claw. Blood erupted, coating the Tiikeri's white fur and several Bailians standing nearby. He tossed the woman beside the other corpses.

"Permission to feed, Lord To-Nok?" a Singa executioner asked, saliva pooling at the corners of his mouth.

The blood spattered Tiikeri kept his gaze on the terrorized group of Bailians. "Permission granted."

The Singa executioners dropped their spears and pounced onto the freshly killed Bailians. They ripped limbs and bodies open with a sickening chorus of snapping, tearing and chewing rising above the drumming rain.

The disgusted throng, remembering what happened to the woman who looked away, stood staring in silent horror while the Singas feasted on their fellow citizens and neighbors.

The rainwater ran red under the Tiikeri's feet and he nodded his head in satisfaction. "Remember what you witnessed here. Go back and tell everyone. Defying us carries a price. The Tiikeri Empire is not to be trifled with.

"Now go!"

The crowd quickly dispersed, eager to escape the horrific scene and a lone Duma with a troubled expression quickly approached To-Nok.

"Lord To-Nok, your presence is urgently requested in the palace. There's been a body found."

"Show me," he demanded, taking off for the Tiikeri headquarters.

They led him to the second story living suite of his newly appointed regional Governor Oro' Korra. Dripping wet and blood stained, To-Nok stood staring at the badly beaten body of his Bailian ally.

The old general had been gagged and bound to a chair. An inspection of the body revealed almost every bone in his body methodically broken and the entire top of his skull bashed in. The iron bar responsible for the pummeling lay on the floor beside the chair.

A folded piece of paper protruded from inside his mouth full of broken teeth. To-Nok glanced around at the apprehensive Singa in the room before removing the paper and opening it.

The message was brief and written in flawless Rasmi, the formal language of the Tiikeri court.

To the white Tiikeri scum,
You are next...

Okawa eyed the front of the Whispering Zephyr from her hidden position in a doorway across the street. The Valdurian agent heard rumors that the human owner of the tavern had connections to the resistance and right now, she sure could use a friend.

Even though her shrouding stone afforded her invisibility by bending the light around her, she still had a physical presence. While the Kan greatly reduced the traffic on the streets of Immor-Onn, she didn't want to chance a collision with a stray passerby. She froze when she saw twelve spear wielding lion-men, led by To-Nok, sauntering towards the tavern as if they owned the city.

Okawa watched the Tiikeri with a hatred she had never known before. To-Nok paused at the mouth of the alley just before the tavern, and directed half his men down the side street, sending them around to the back. The remaining six followed him to the front door.

Sensing an opportunity, Okawa unholstered her Mark Three pistol crossbow and cocked it. She checked to make sure nothing barred her way and crossed the street. The Singas noisily entered the tavern and she surreptitiously slipped in behind them.

Inside, only a few older, haggard looking Bailian patrons nervously nursed their morning eyeopeners in the virtually empty dining area and bar. A shockingly thin Bailian barkeep arranged glasses behind the bar. A short one-armed human female sat at a nearby table speaking with a mahogany haired, Bailian/human hybrid. Both bolted to their feet when the mawls entered.

"My regional governor is dead!" To-Nok said accusatorily, while pointing a finger at Kai. "Either you had something to do with it or you know who did!"

The Tiikeri now advanced toward Kai with two Singas following. Two blocked the door, while the other two moved into flanking positions in the room. Okawa, remaining undetected, stayed beside To-Nok.

"I'm taking you into custody until I have the guilty party," he said, prompting the two flanking Singas to move in so as to grab her.

"And, as promised, for every one of my people killed, ten of yours will die," he said calculatingly. "In this case I think we'll make an example of ten of your orphans. Would you like to choose, or shall I?"

At the threat of harming her children, the assassin scowled menacingly as a long blue ethereal blade erupted from the stump of her missing arm.

Okawa stood a few feet from To-Nok's side and pointed the pistol at his head. She trembled with loathing and tears of rage streamed down her face. The immediacy of the moment, and the overwhelming wave of vengeance, swept away any sense of strategy or nuance in the distraught agent.

"I told you that you were next, you Tiikeri scum!" she yelled, each word dripping with malice.

To-Nok's threatening demeanor vanished and he frantically looked around for the voice's origin. When he turned towards her, she pulled the trigger. The Tiikeri's head exploded, disappearing into a fine red mist coating everything within a five-foot radius, including Kai, all four Singas and Okawa.

The resulting shock at seeing their leader die right in front of them gave a now partially visible Okawa time to chamber another Na-Kab Carbon bolt and fire at the nearest Singa. His torso exploded in much the same manner as his leader's head, adding to the macabre painting of the room.

Kai took advantage of the stunned mawls and ran the nearest one through. The ghostly blue blade crackled when it passed through the Singa's chest and he exhaled whisps of smoke when he dropped.

Kai vaulted onto the nearest table and swung at another Singa. Tam-Eez and the bartender dove for cover behind the bar. Okawa flipped a table over and ducked behind it just before a door guard's spear embedded in it.

She popped back up and got off a quick shot at the one who hurled it. The bolt exploded through his torso and passed through his disintegrated body, shattering the glass door behind him.

Kai had just sliced through the head of the Singa she had engaged with when Okawa saw the other door guard rear back and launch his spear at her. The diminutive assassin looked up in time to see the barbed projectile hurtling her way. The heavy polearm struck her in the chest and exited out her back. The force launched her backwards into the air and onto the floor amongst the dead Singas.

Now unarmed, the only remaining mawl in the room charged Okawa. Backing slightly and using the table as a barrier, Okawa quickly cocked and fired her final round. The bolt caught the lion-man in mid-air as he vaulted over the table at her. He too exploded, showering the room crimson.

"There's more in the back!!" Okawa yelled at the two hiding behind the bar. "Run!"

She took off towards the entrance and made it through the shattered door, when she heard the back doors leading to the orphanage burst open and the remaining Singas pour through. The Valdurian felt a twinge of guilt at not checking on Kai, but there would be no time to grieve. An angry throng of Singas would be right behind her.

Okawa broke to the right in a dead run. Behind her, she heard her pursuers' growls and curses. Quickly ducking into the next alley, she shimmied up a drainpipe and onto the one-story flat roof. Hiding behind a low lip on the building's edge, she peeked down into the alley. From her vantage point, she saw the perplexed Singas searching in vain, while the children streamed out the back of the orphanage.

Okawa plopped down cross-legged on the roof and caught her breath while changing out her pistol's magazine. She sat staring into space while listening to the Tiikeri swarm around and through the Whispering Zephyr.

She had avenged Demetrius, but still felt a burning rage, along with a profound emptiness. An emptiness she decided, while cocking her weapon, that only a body count would fill.

Commander Gauna looked out past the receding Kan fog and onto the southwestern shore of Otomoria, then down the line of ships beside him. He had ordered his flotilla of sixteen ships to lineup side by side.

The orange Tiikeri leader's plan involved his force landing in a single massive wave, over running any opposition. From there, they were to march inland where they would meet up with Bo-Lah and his human allies.

He didn't like it.

The empire's forces had been stretched way too thin, and he didn't think he could rely on these untested mongrels. His tail anxiously lurched from side to side watching the shore.

"It will be a glorious victory for lord and empire," Kerani, the Yagur cleric of Pa-Waga, said giddily, peering down the line of ships.

Gauna glanced over at him and sneered. "Maybe, if everyone is where they're supposed to be and does what they're supposed to do."

"Where is your faith, Gauna?" Kerani asked, leaning on the railing letting the sea breeze ruffle the fur on his face.

"I leave faith to the priests and holy men. I just wish they left strategy to the military."

Kerani kept facing into the wind, ignoring the obvious jab. "It is written, 'only the foolish ignore the council of the lord.'"

Gauna scoffed loudly just before a loud cracking noise arose from amidst the ship. The sound of wood breaking immediately preceded the hull exploding in a shower of splinters when the barbed tip of a Yudon harpoon erupted through the bottom, impaling one of the mongrel fighters. It quickly retracted and the ship began taking on water.

The Tiikeri commander, an excellent swimmer, watched the mongrel fighting force, unaccustomed to water, descend into chaos. A quick glance down the line of ships revealed similar scenes on each Ves-Lari vessel in his fleet.

"Get that hole plugged!" he ordered in an attempt to rally the fighters.

A massive explosion of water next to the sinking vessel immediately followed his command. A twelve-foot EEtah with harpoon drawn breached the surface of the sea. Bellowing, he landed amidst the scrambling mawls slashing and biting.

The vessel now rocked violently, throwing frightened mongrels overboard, where they flailed about, unable to swim. The ones left on board while the craft dipped further under the waves, were easily slaughtered by the massive man-shark, who thrashed about in a blood frenzy.

Gauna and Kerani could do little more than stand frozen in terror and reverential awe at their first encounter with an EEtah. The Tiikeri shook his head in disbelief. Yes, it massacred his men, but the militaristic side of him couldn't help but marvel at this perfect killing machine.

Gauna knew all was lost when he caught sight of a dozen Calden warships approaching from the east along the coast. He drew his short sword and brought it down hard on the Yagur's head.

"This is your doing!" he screamed.

The Pa-Waga cleric toppled to the deck just before a harpoon impaled the chest of the Tiikeri. His last thoughts, before being yanked off his feet and into the sea by a tug on the lanyard, concerned the folly of allowing priests to dictate military matters.

The Fifth Eldorian Lancers had been on the move for three cycles straight, heading west towards the coast. Commander Cavus drove them hard, stopping only to rest the horses. An invasion fleet from Nocturn neared their shores and there was no time to waste.

When Cavus saw plumes of smoke rising in the distance he knew they had gotten close. The rolling grasslands of southern Otomoria soon flattened out to meet the Shallow Sea. Drawing closer, the lancers saw Valdurian airships ducking in and out of the smoke and heard the sounds of combat echoing through the hills.

Stopping their mounts on the crest of a row of foothills, they could see the ground gently sloping downward for half a mile until the knee-high grass met the narrow beach. Smoke rose from a multitude of burning ships just offshore. A dozen Calden war ships circled firing burning ballista bolts into their hulls.

In the churning water, EEtahs and sharks feasted on cat-people desperately trying to make it ashore. The bodies of mawls who found no respite on land littered the thirty-foot-wide sandy beach.

On the field before them, Cavus could make out the waving standards of Volga, Kenyev, Vladof, Donyeb and Booshka—the remaining Lords of the Western Fork—

actively engaged with a substantially smaller force of Dreeats, EEtahs and Valdurian Marines. Cavus guessed their numbers to be over a thousand. Valdurian Airships peppered the river lord's forces with arrows from above.

"Would ya look at that," Cavus said to his patrol sergeant riding next to him. "Well, we were going to have to kick them off the land anyway. You know the river lords weren't going to leave without a fight. May as well do it now while we've got the help."

The lancer commander then gazed down the double line of mounted troops.

"Alright lads!" he shouted. "Looks like we got here just in time. Someone's trying to cheat us out of a fight! Lance Up!"

"LANCE UP!" they called back in unison, drawing their lances from their saddle holsters.

"CHARGE!"

ACT THREE

Endgame

General Ja-Wee heaved a sigh of relief when they exited the Os-Tor Forest and saw the snowflake shaped spires of Immor-Onn. The Tiikeri's Singa army of five thousand had been cut down to a little more than two thousand, hardly an effectively sized force.

After leaving a small garrison in the large Etheria field in the Barrens, they performed a forced march and were harassed every step of the way. The crystal forest of the hard and unforgiving Barrens proved to be the worst. Bailian necromancers and packs of wolf-men killed hundreds in the bitter cold. Finally, in the Os'Tor Forest, huntsmen archers picked away at them with seeming impunity, disappearing into the thick jungle.

The entire ordeal left his men jumpy and demoralized. He certainly hoped General Baag-Tar had an easier time of it in the south or this operation would be in serious jeopardy.

By the time his procession made it to the former palace, now field headquarters, Commander Zabit and Ambassador Jo-Rakk waited outside the gate for them. The orange Tiikeri general stared in shock at the heads of Cha-Rod and Demetrius on the poles flanking the gates. Slowly his gaze fell on the rows of rotting impaled bodies in the park across the street.

"What in the name of the empire is going on here?!" he incredulously asked, ears pinning with anger and tail thrashing furiously behind him.

296

"Lord To-Nok's idea of bringing the city to heel," Jo-Rakk answered, unable to disguise his contempt.

"I see. Zabit, get those bodies down. Speaking of To-Nok, where is the sneaky shit?"

"Dead sir," Zabit replied.

Ja-Wee sighed in frustration. "If this was his idea of how to run a city maybe it's for the best. The bodies, Commander?"

"Yes, sir," Zabit said, saluting and heading off.

"Alright, Jo-Rakk," Ja-Wee said, "you were obviously the calmest head around here. What's the situation?"

"Well..." The white Tiikeri exhaled loudly and rubbed the back of his neck. "We're holding the city, just barely. The population hates us and is growing bolder in their resistance."

"Can't really say I blame them," Ja-Wee said, watching mongrel slaves taking down the impaled bodies under the direction of a Singa sergeant.

"We've got room for your men on the docks in the air station," Jo-Rakk said, eyeing the depleted troop strength. "I would have thought you would have brought more."

"I started that way." Ja-Wee said grimly. "What about the air station?"

"Zabit took it, sir. There was a bit of a dust-up with the Valdurians."

The Tiikeri general closed his eyes and exhaled again loudly. "Casualties?"

"No Valdurian casualties. We lost half a dozen."

"No human dead, that's a plus. We might be able to smooth this over. The last thing we need right now is to pick a fight with the humans."

Rafel threw himself into his work and it helped to heal his broken heart. It had been almost three grands since Hoyt's murder and Zekoff had been right. Every day it got a little better. Of late, he adopted a more hands on approach to information gathering, by accompanying his operatives in the field.

The Kan fog seemed thicker this time and the Zorian spymaster could barely see the edge of the roof fifty feet away, much less the three-foot-long cylinder near its edge.

"Sir, are you sure?" One of the two city guards beside him whispered.

"She didn't put that up here for no reason," Rafel whispered back, indicating the cylinder. "Just be ready."

With that admonishment, both guards checked their crossbows and continued their vigil from behind the stairwell's housing.

Rafel raised his forefinger to his lips when he heard the erratic beating of wings. A brief moment passed and the fog pushed clear around the tube as an Ash-Ta landed with a soft thud. The fog surrounded the bat creature when he folded his wings and knelt down to grab the cylinder.

Rafel nodded and the two guards stepped out with weapons pointed. The Ash-Ta looked up and gave a panicked screech, just as one of the bolts struck him in the chest, launching him close to the edge in a heap.

The three Zorians cautiously approached and, on Rafel's command, one fired a second bolt into its head. Now, certain of its death, Rafel picked up the cannister. He opened it and examined the five sheets of paper with a satisfied nod.

"Alright, toss its body over the side," he ordered. "The Vurr cleanup crews will find it in the morning. Let's go and get the sentient who left this here."

Rafel knew her as a half human and half Duma mawl who went by the name Karışım. Mostly human in appearance, she proved all but invisible on the diverse Zorian streets. She had escaped the mawl expulsion last grand by her appearance and by not living in Tiger Town.

She claimed to be an artist and could be found every day on the Zorian wharf with sketch pad open, drawing furiously. She was in fact a Tiikeri spy. The cannister full of detailed sketches of the docks, along with a record of military ships' schedules, proved her guilt, as did the Ash-Ta who came to retrieve it.

His people had been watching her small apartment by the northern docks and Rafel saw the room's solitary light cast her silhouette on the window coverings. The androgenous spymaster hated heavy-handed tactics. There appeared to be only one way in or out, so he stepped up to the door, made sure his guards were ready, then knocked.

"Who is it?!" came a terse hiss in common from inside.

"City guards, Karışım," Rafel said calmly, not wanting to cause any alarm. "Please open the door."

"What do you want?"

"I want you to open the door so I can talk to you."

"We're talking now. What do you want?"

Rafel sighed. "Look, I don't want to kick this door in any more than you want me to, Karışım. So, why don't we do this the civilized way. I've got some questions. Will you please open the door?"

Rafel heaved a sigh of relief when he heard the latch turn. The door opened just far enough to get a glimpse of her. Karışım stood just a little over five feet tall and wore a simple green tunic, contrasting her bright reddish-orange hair. Her face indeed looked mostly human, with subtle cheetah markings around her cheeks, nose and mouth.

Without waiting, the two guards pushed the door all the way open and forced their way in. Karışım cried out in surprise and backed up, protesting loudly. Rafel casually

299

followed them inside and she licked her lips nervously when she saw him carrying the cylinder.

"I thought we might have a chat about ships," Rafel said with a confident smile.

"I don't know anything about ships," she said defiantly. "I'm an artist."

"Yes, I've seen your artwork," Rafel replied, indicating the canister. "It's a shame your Tiikeri bosses' won't have the chance to appreciate your attention to detail."

With a sudden hiss Karışım launched herself into the air, well over the men's heads. Both guards fired, but she moved entirely too fast, seizing the element of surprise. Both bolts lodged harmlessly in adjacent walls.

In mid-air, Rafel saw a dagger appear in Karışım's hand and she slashed one of the guards across the face. He dropped his crossbow, screamed and covered the wound, blood pouring from between his fingers.

She landed in a crouch and immediately lunged, driving her blade into the chest of the other Zorian.

By now, Rafel had managed to pull his pistol crossbow. He brought it up to fire, when she lashed out with her free hand striking him on the wrist. The distinctive sound of cracking bones and Rafel's cry of pain preceded the pistol flying from his grasp.

The pistol clattered noisily across the floor, well out of his reach. Karışım turned her full attention, and dagger on the now unarmed spymaster.

Rafel backed up, desperately looking for anything he could use as a weapon, when he tripped and fell onto his back. The mawl spy grinned maliciously, crouching to pounce, when she stopped suddenly and swatted at the back of her neck. In an instant, her face froze in surprise, her eyes rolled back in her head and she tumbled to the floor.

The most handsome man Rafel had ever laid eyes on stood filling the open doorway behind the now fallen attacker. He easily stood six foot three with a broad muscular frame accentuated by the skintight, grey Valdurian Ghost Suit he wore. Rafel guessed his age to be mid-to-late thirties by the touches of grey in his short jet-black hair and neatly trimmed beard. He stepped over her body deftly and twirled a miniature blowgun, before slipping it into one of the several utility pockets on the one-piece suit.

"You *did* want her for questioning later, right?" he asked with a mischievous grin.

Rafel managed a stunned nod of the head, enchanted by his deep baritone voice and captivating, good looks.

"Good, she'll be out awhile," he said, reaching down and offering Rafel his hand.

Taking it, the spymaster felt a jolt of excitement he hadn't felt since Hoyt. Once on his feet, Rafel's hand instinctively ran up the mystery man's taut, bulging upper arm and rested on his broad shoulder for support.

"I was following her, too," he explained, not seeming to mind Rafel's hand on his shoulder. "You and your men stayed behind, waiting for her contact and I stayed with her. Sorry about your men by the way."

Still speechless, Rafel couldn't take his eyes off his striking rescuer. The pain of his broken wrist finally brought Rafel back to the present and he winced. Reluctantly removing his hand from the man's shoulder, he let it trail back down his bicep then cradled his wounded appendage.

"I'd have someone look at that right away," he said, peering at Rafel's wrist and then back to the unconscious spy. "As for our artist over there, something tells me she could be a wealth of information."

"Who are you?" Rafel finally choked out.

The stranger ignored the question and smiled. "I should go. It was good working with you."

Without another word, he slipped back out the door and disappeared into the thick fog.

Tiikeri general Baag-Tar felt glad to finally be out of that accursed desert which claimed so many of his men. His army now numbered only a little more than a thousand strong and very demoralized. He could still hear the screams of his men they pulled beneath the sand, never to be seen again.

Licking his hands and washing the dirt off his face, Baag-Tar contemplated the high cost the oases extracted from his army. The effort seemed hardly worth the elusive reward. He sincerely hoped the garrisons he left back there would be enough, but the haunting voice inside him said otherwise.

Eventually, the soft sand beneath him turned hardpacked with scrub. That terrain then gave way to rolling hills of waving, knee-high grass, starkly illuminated by brilliant moonlight. The wind definitely picked up and he could see a faint glow on the western horizon.

"The Plains of Taka-Vir," he said to the young Singa colonel beside him. "Beyond these grasslands lies our destination, the City of Immor-Onn. By now, Commander Zabit should have the city well under control. This should help your men feel a little less homesick."

The newly promoted officer nervously nodded. "They need *something*, they're uneasy."

The ground rumbled and the sound of whinnying off to the left caused both mawls to smile. A herd of twenty horses galloped into view, running in loose circles with the males clashing to decide dominance.

"A good meal would also go a long way," the Singa conceded.

"I agree," Baag-Tar said hopefully. "How many female hunters are left?"

"Four, sir."

The surprised look on the general's face at the sparce number appeared obvious, but he nodded his acceptance.

"Send them, and any Dumas left, around on the other side of that herd and drive them this way," he ordered. "It will be the first decent meal we've had since arriving."

The Singa colonel took off behind their position and ordered the approaching army to crouch down in the tall grass, ready to ambush.

From his elevated location Baag-Tar watched the remaining four Singas and two Dumas circle around behind the herd. The young colonel returned and squinted at four lone figures on a distant hill.

"Sir?" he said, pointing.

The general retrieved his spyglass, opened it and peered through it. The Tiikeri had never seen anything like it before. The creatures had the bodies and heads of horses, but with humanoid torsos.

They appeared to be manipulating thin white strands, glinting in the moonlight and stretching upwards. Following the strings, he could see they were attached to large brightly colored kites, circling and dancing high in the air.

"What's going on sir?" the young colonel asked, struggling to see.

"I'm not sure. Perhaps an elaborate signaling or communications system."

The moment the female Singas and Dumas rose up to drive the herd, the answer to the officer's question became clear. The On'Dara manipulated the battle kites in progressively larger, faster circles, dipping them close to the ground. One large kite swept past the Singa nearest the horses and, for the briefest instant, the large rectangle of cloth obscured him from view. When it swept up and away, Baag-Tar gasped in shock when he saw it cleaved the Singa neatly in two with a Darian silk cord.

The strike happened so quickly, the upper portion of her torso toppled into the tall grass and disappeared, but her legs kept running, propelling the bottom half several more feet before pitching over.

"By the gods, they're weapons!" the general barked. They've got to get out of there!"

For the unfortunate mawls, however, the answer came much too late. The other three kites now joined the first, slashing through the cat-people. When one kite easily sliced through two of the Duma scouts, the remaining two Singas dove to the ground and attempted to crawl away.

This proved futile. They sailed the kites just above the top of the grass. The string acted as a scythe, mowing down the grass and anything hiding in it. Baag-Tar couldn't see the victims, but by the geysers of blood erupting over the pasture, he knew the kites completed their deadly task.

"Sir, how are we going to get past them? They'll cut us down before we even get close!"

"Get the men ready to attack," the general ordered. "We'll put the spearmen out front to entangle those kites."

"Sir, I don't think that's going to be enough, LOOK!"

Baag-Tar raised his glass once more and peered back at the distant hills. Lines of On'Dara archers filled the two grassy mounds flanking the kite wielders.

Captain Rafel had just returned to his office from his usual morning meeting with Colonel Zekoff. The Zorian spymaster found himself feeling rather nostalgic about their twice-a-cycle briefings now that the colonel had announced his forthcoming retirement.

He brushed his hand over the stack of reports on the top of his desk and prepared to sit down when a gentle knock on his open office door interrupted his thoughts.

Standing just outside the doorway' a smiling Pierce Calden nodded his way. The Calden Ambassador's baby face and trimmed youthful beard radiated authority and confidence.

When Rafel saw who stood beside him his heartbeat quickened and he broke into a wide grin. It was the handsome, mysterious stranger from the last Kan. However, instead of a skin-tight Valdurian Ghost Suit, he wore the blue waistcoat and grey trousers of a Calden naval officer.

"Sorry to disturb you," Pierce said apologetically.

Rafel forced himself not to gawk at the bearded officer and concentrated on the ambassador. "Not at all Si. Ambassador, come in. I was just getting my cycle started."

Both entered and Rafel caught himself staring again.

"Rafel, I'd like to introduce you to Senior Lieutenant Mukavar de Oris," Pierce said officially. "He's been assigned to the Societies Calden Desk here in Zor and I'm sure you'll be working together."

"You!" Rafel beamed, unable to conceal his delight.

Mukavar smiled broadly. "How's the wrist?"

Rafel held up his wounded appendage. "Better, thanks, the Clerrias did a pretty good job fixing it up. It's still a little sore though."

"You two know each other?" Pierce asked grinning curiously.

"We met last Kan. Lieutenant Mukavar was responsible for the capture of the spy." Rafel's tone and demeanor immediately softened and he found himself staring again. "As well as saving my life."

"Anytime," Mukavar said, returning the gaze. "And please, call me Muuky."

Rafel felt his face flush under the lieutenant's attentive scrutiny. "I certainly will, *Muuky*."

"Lieutenant Mukavar served on the same ship as my brother, Blyth," Pierce continued. "In fact, they both earned their Brightstar certification on the same Innaca Run."

Rafel allowed his eyes to drift down to the coveted star and swan pin resting above a double row of ribbons on the breast of his waist coat.

"Brightstar, very impressive," Rafel said on the verge of cooing. "I must say, when I saw you last, you wore a Valdurian Ghost Suit, so I naturally assumed…"

"House Valdur and Calden have been working a lot more closely since the Ukko Wood incident." Pierce explained.

"I see," Rafel said, now not caring if anyone saw him staring. "Well, Muuky, I must say, you cut a striking figure in that ghost suit."

Mukavar gave a shy smirk. "Thanks, I'm still getting used to it. The *clingy* part that is."

Rafel felt a brief touch of guilt, almost as if he had betrayed the memory of Hoyt. He just couldn't help himself. This man seemed just his type, tall, rugged and drop dead handsome. He had to come to terms with the fact that Hoyt had long been gone and he had to get on with his life.

Summoning his courage, Rafel knew this could be his chance to make a move. "Well, Muuky, speaking of the spy and working together; I was just going to have a little chat with her and wonder if you'd like to accompany me?"

Mukavar's face lit up and turned almost seductive. "I would be honored. Your organic methods of information extraction are legendary in the Society."

"Keep that up and you're going to make me blush."

"Perhaps afterwards, we can get a drink?"

"Muuky, you were reading my mind."

Okawa watched them from the second story rooftop of an adjacent building, her face permanently frozen into a contemptuous sneer. Down below, a Tiikeri general, two high ranking officers and a half dozen in their entourage casually passed through the checkpoints which seemed to be on every street. They chatted casually while strolling past Execution Park, which up until recently, contained row upon row of impaled bodies. When they entered into the fenced courtyard of the once royal palace, the Tiikeri did most of the talking.

The Valdurian continued her vigil until she saw movement in a second story window. Confident of their location, she calmly strode back to the *Attila,* parked on the other side of the roof.

Once seated inside, she glanced over at Sitsa who stood behind the wheel. The humanoid moth stared expectantly at her through large compound eyes.

"The palace," she coldly stated facing out the windshield. "Second story, mid building."

The Tinian pilot wordlessly nodded and turned on the Etheria engine, which hummed softly when it came to life. Reaching up to the overhead console, she engaged the Shrouding Stone and the now invisible Valdurian Resistance Class Cruiser lifted off.

They hovered for a moment over Execution Park while Okawa stared through the window with hate filled eyes at the mawl war council.

"Time to cut the head off this beast," she said icily, not taking her eyes off the window.

"You do realize I will not be able to maintain our invisibility?" Sitsa's words slowly translated in Okawa's head from its complex Coxeter language.

"I don't plan on staying long."

Still maintaining her death stare, Okawa reached up and tapped once on either side of the orange disk. They heard a loud crackling sound, followed by the smell of combustion and two fireballs, the size of oversized melons, blasted from the Trinilic rods on each side of the airship. They exploded upon impact, blowing out the second story of the building with a thunderous roar and flash of light.

"Ten degrees down on the bow," she curtly ordered.

The nose of the craft dipped and she fired another two rounds at the front gate and doors. The explosions sent dead mawls flying and left a smoldering hole for an entrance.

The sparce population in the streets gasped in shock, pointing at the *Attila* and the burning Tiikeri headquarters. Two Singa guards, at a nearby checkpoint, couldn't even nock an arrow before the ship rose up beyond the rooftops of Immor-Onn and streaked away.

Okawa peered down at the gauge on the console. With just a little over half a charge left in the *Attila's* Obsidian PSI battery, she realized she must now be judicious in her use of the Shrouding Stone, as well as her choice of targets.

Rafel had never felt this excited about an interrogation before. Now, he had someone to share his passion with, a handsome kindred spirit. He stole a peek at Mukavar walking closely beside him when they exited the Zorian Forum. The morning was already sultry and the spymaster knew the summer months were upon them.

"The secret to breaking mawls is their fur," Rafel said, leading the Calden agent to a nearby building. "It's a source of pride and identity to them. So, in preparation, I've had my prep-people start the process by completely shaving her."

Prep-people?" Mukavar asked.

Rafel gave a sadistic giggle and took the opportunity to caress his shoulder. "Oh yes, I've got a team of three. Every interrogation is unique. Fear more often than pain is what gets a sentient to talk. One must learn what your subject fears and begin with that. It's because of my unusual methods that my playroom must be altered to account for each guest. It's this attention to detail that gives me my success."

"And reputation," Mukavar praised and playfully rubbed his shoulders.

The larger man's physical contact sent a jolt of arousal coursing through Rafel, settling between his legs.

"Trying to make me blush again, Muuky?" Rafel teased sensuously.

Mukavar gave a lecherous smile, but said nothing, prompting Rafel to continue.

"So, as you can imagine, it can be a labor-intensive set-up, break down, disposal of the body and clean up. I have other duties, so…"

"A team," Mukavar finished his sentence.

"Yes," he said, unlocking the door to a small, single-story building. "In her case, being mostly human, there was only short, fine fur to shear. The challenge on this one was the set up."

Rafel led him inside. The building contained only two rooms, both windowless, except for a huge picture window in the wall of the outer room looking into the inner chamber.

Mukavar couldn't help but peek through the window. They secured the hairless female spread eagle on the floor. The Calden agent noted that for a mongrel mawl she definitely looked human, with the exception of the few cheetah markings on her body and her six small breasts.

Six badgers, three on each side of her, snarled and snapped at the bound sentient, held just out of reach by a chain around their necks. The ferocious creatures strained against their bonds to get at their next meal.

The mawl prisoner jerked her head back and forth in a panic. Her fear filled eyes darted from one creature to another every time they lunged at her.

"I see what you mean," Mukavar said, obviously impressed.

"Well, I better get to work," Rafel said, opening the door. You can watch it from here. It might get messy in there."

"I don't mind messy," Mukavar said, panting slightly, still staring at the bound captive.

Rafel paused in the open doorway and peered over at him with wide-eyed excitement. "You sweet talker. Watch through the window. It'll be like you're spying on me, but much naughtier. I'll leave the door open so you can listen."

The Calden operative nodded, staring through the glass.

"Hello!" Rafel greeted her cheerfully, stepping into the room. "I see you've met my little friends. It's Karışım isn't it? At least that's what you've been calling yourself of late. It really doesn't matter *now*, does it? I think I'll call you meat. That's all you are to these little fellas."

Karışım said nothing but continued her frightened stare at the Zorian spymaster. Her eyes followed his every move when he picked up a small pail placed by the door.

"These are blood Badgers," Rafel said, while playing with the handle of a brush in the pail, "and this is blood."

He lifted the brush and revealed its red stained bristles. The sight and smell of the blood set all six badgers snapping and tugging harder at their collars.

"As you can see, they're quite ferocious, but, because of their short legs they can't catch their own prey. So, they let the more mobile predators take down the quarry. Then they swoop in and drive them off after the kill and blood has already been spilled, hence the name. I must tell you, the smell of blood drives them wild, as you can see."

Stepping over to her arms he knelt down and painted the tips of her fingers with the crimson liquid. He then moved over to a set of levers and pulleys attached to the chained animals. Moving one of the levers, the tension on the leash of the badger nearest her arm relaxed and the creature lunged at her hand.

Rafel yanked it to a halt, inches from the painted digit. Karışım screamed when she felt the creature's breath and snapping jaws so close to her fingertips.

"Now, let's discuss what the Tiikeri have in mind for the Zorian harbor."

Rafel peered down at Karışım's partially eaten body and marveled at another job well done. He had what he needed, and it hadn't taken that long. She lasted through having the fingers on both hands devoured, but when he painted a broad bloody stroke on her vulva, she broke and began talking.

Amazingly she was still alive, whimpering in pain, when Rafel pulled the master lever, releasing all the badgers to the full extent of their leashes. The screaming renewed when the beasts pounced on her, ripping and tearing at her flesh. Rafel nodded in satisfaction, then stepped out of the room and closed the door.

The spymaster paused in stunned, lurid surprise. Mukavar stood half naked in front of the window. His pants were down around his ankles and his large rigid cock in his hand. He gave Rafel a helpless stare as he masturbated furiously.

"Why Muuky," Rafel said seductively. "This takes appreciating my work to a whole new level."

Dropping to his knees in front of him, Rafel looked up at him with a blood-stained face and lustful stare.

"I hope you weren't planning on wasting this?" Rafel purred over the screams coming from the next room.

By the time General Baag-Tar led the remnants of his decimated southern army through the eastern gates of Immor-Onn, the orange Tiikeri felt profoundly weary. He tired of marching across an unforgiving land and he tired of losing good men, but mostly he tired of this fool's errand he had been sent on.

They heard the explosion and saw the smoke the moment they entered the agricultural fields, just outside of the city. Following the billowing column led them to the badly damaged palace still burning. Dead and severely burnt Singas lay about the small courtyard and street, some with their fur still smoldering. The other Singa soldiers stood around totally disoriented, watching their former headquarters go up in flames.

"You there, sergeant!" Baag-Tar called out to a Singa limping away from the corpse of a comrade.

The dazed mawl stared blankly back at the Tiikeri, chattered away senselessly and attempted a weak salute.

"What in the name of the empire happened here?!"

The sergeant shook his head in a daze. "Some sort of flying thing that shot fire."

The general paused, assessing what he had just heard.

"Where's your commander?"

The Singa pointed to the burning building. "Dead."

"All of them?!"

"It was the morning officers' briefing."

Baag-Tar sighed in frustration realizing he now had inadvertently become the sole commander of a shattered army. He had to get control of the situation before discipline dissolved and chaos set in.

"Rally the men and get some water over here. We've got to get that fire out."

The sergeant stood motionless, his face blank.

"Dammit man, get a grip on yourself! The men need leadership, lead!"

Carrying an air of confidence, Baag-Tar watched the junior officer hobble around doing as ordered, but deep down, his faith in this operation had already dissolved.

The only way anyone could tell Colonel Zekoff occupied the room would be the scent of evergreen pipe tobacco. He sat in a corner of his crowded office puffing away contentedly, while Vanir ran the morning briefing from behind his wide desk. The commander of the Zorian guards would be retiring in three Quinte and he wanted his protégé to be able to take over effectively on day one.

"So, I take it that the interrogation proved fruitful?" Vanir asked, pouring whiskey from an unlabeled bottle into a heavy bottomed tumbler. Glancing around the room he held out the bottle offering a drink.

Rafel and Gasata waved their hands, no.

"A little early for me," Mukavar proclaimed.

The red headed captain shrugged his acceptance, corked the bottle and placed it back on the corner of the desk within easy reach.

Rafel gave a sly, confident smile. "Yes, Captain, they always talk. This time around, the news is disturbing to say the least."

"I have a feeling I'm going to need this," Vanir said, downing a healthy gulp.

"Probably," Rafel replied. "Last cycle, Lieutenant Muuky, I mean Mukavar and I were independently following a mawl/human mixed breed suspect on the wharf. We caught her attempting to pass on detailed plans of the docks, as well as shipping schedules, to an Ash-Ta."

"One of my morning patrols came across the body, just before the Vurr cleanup carts picked it up for disposal," Gasata said, stroking his perfectly trimmed moustache. "I was going to bring it up, but you beat me to it."

Vanir took another sip of whiskey. "Well, it's a safe bet that if we're dealing with Ash-Ta, the Tiikeri are behind it."

"It gets worse," Rafel continued. "Under questioning, our spy revealed there is a sleeper cell of mawl/human hybrids, even more passable than her and they're poised to strike."

"Prepared to strike at what?" Vanir asked. "And how passable?"

"Virtually indistinguishable from humans," Rafel replied grimly. "And their intentions are unknown."

"Most of the ship schedules Captain Rafel recovered were of a military nature," Mukavar said, finally joining the conversation. "That's why House Calden wants me involved."

Rafel nervously cleared his throat. "Yes, the lieutenant and I will be working very closely on this one."

Zekoff appeared calm, but inside he smiled watching Rafel and Mukavar interact. He saw the way they looked at each other and Rafel's demeanor appeared much the same as when he romantically partnered with Hoyt. He inwardly rejoiced the spymaster had finally found someone.

Vanir took another gulp from his glass, nearly draining it. "How in the name of the gods were they able to replicate humans so exactly?"

"Remember those Whitmar slave ships hijacked by the Tiikeri last Grand?" Rafel asked, sitting back in his chair.

All nodded yes.

Rafel gave a wry chuckle. "Those slaves they stole weren't bound for a Tiikeri auction block. They were headed for their breeding center. They wanted passable saboteurs. This invasion must have been in the works for a while."

"So quickly?" Gasata wondered. "It's only been a grand."

Rafel shrugged. "That's about all I got out of her."

"I'll put extra patrols on the docks," Gasata offered.

"Have them check out anything unusual," Vanir said, picking up his glass once more. "No detail is too small."

"Any remote idea what to look for?" the patrol captain asked hopefully.

"None," Vanir replied, before draining the glass.

Well past moonfall, the clouds parted and a sparkling blanket of stars adorned the sky over the Tiikeri capital of Hai-Darr. From his position atop the wall surrounding the city, Pahak could clearly see across the hundred-yard clearing and the dark shapes of the triple canopy jungle of the Dasos region beyond. The orange Tiikeri leaned on his spear and watched the light bugs flicker amongst the trees, sometime blending with the faintly glowing pockets of bioluminescence scattered throughout.

"Daydreaming again," came a friendly voice off to his right. "Don't let the captain catch you, or they'll take away that promotion."

"The captain doesn't come up on the wall during the moonless, Vordur," Pahak replied. "He's probably fucking some cute mongrel whore right about now."

Both chuckled but knew it to be true. Leaning over, he gave his comrade a friendly lick on the arm before joining him at his post.

"You're lucky," Vordur said, joining his friend peering out into the moonless. "After the ceremony tomorrow, you won't have to stand watch anymore."

Pahak scoffed. "If I was truly lucky, I'd be in the Twilight Lands right now fighting and gaining glory."

"Eh, the generals were probably right," Vordur rationalized. "Why not let the Singas do the fighting and take the risks."

"No risks, no glory."

"Wow, you really are taking this promotion thing seriously."

Pahak gave a dismissive glance and said nothing.

A mischievous look crossed Vordur's face and he reached inside his tunic. "I've got just the thing to relax that serious attitude of yours."

He pulled out two stalks of Maudo grass and proudly held them up for inspection. "Something to celebrate your promotion, *Sergeant*."

"I'm not a sergeant yet, and we're not supposed to be doing that on duty!"

"Yeah, I can see how you'd want to stay on your toes with all this activity going on around here," Vordur said, handing him the foot long stalk with delicate blue flowers.

Pahak reluctantly accepted the offering and grinned at his friend.

"To Sergeant Pahak," Vordur toasted tapping his stalk against the other.

Both popped the stalks into their mouths and stripped off the flowers. The subtle blue petals quickly dissolved on their tongues and they sighed as euphoria swept over them.

"There, that'll make your shift go better," Vordur said, before watching Pahak's face go serious.

"What?"

Pahak held a hand up for silence while straining to listen.

"Did you hear that?"

Vordur listened for a brief moment, then shook his head. He could hear nothing but the chorus of insects from the forest beyond.

"There it is again. A clicking sound."

"I heard it," Vordur said, pointing off to their right. "It's coming from over there."

"No, it sounds like it's right in front of us."

The rapid clicking sound grew louder and more numerous. Both guards gripped their spears and looked around in confusion. When the racket seemed right on top of them, the two friends were in a state of panic, frantically searching around for the source of the noise.

"What is it?!"

"I don't know! I don't know!"

Before either could ready their weapons or cry out, a massive wave of Do-Tarr swarmed over the top of the walls.

Pahak now realized the sound they heard was Mantis feet scaling the wall. He could see thousands of Do-Tarr scrambling over the parapets at an alarming speed.

"THEY CAN SEE US!" Vordur's terror filled screams resonated out over the sleeping city. "THEY'RE NOT SUPPOSED TO BE ABLE TO…"

A Do-Tarr bounded off a rampart and buried a mining hammer into his skull, cutting short the Tiikeri's cries of alarm. Blood splattered all over Pahak as he watched four more mantises grab his friend by his arms and legs, tearing them away from the torso with a nauseating ripping sound.

Pahak had no time to lament his comrade's fate because dozens now streamed over the wall right in front of him. Through the throng of humanoid bugs surrounding him, he could see many more streaming into the city and hear the shocked cries of its citizens.

He looked into the black, emotionless eyes of his people's mortal enemy, readied his spear and lunged at the nearest Do-Tarr. The tip pierced the exoskeleton with a crack and the humanoid mantis gave out a high-pitched squeal of pain.

317

When he tried to pull it out, he found the barb securely lodged. He had no time to contemplate anything else before half a dozen of the quickly scurrying mantis creatures covered him.

Pahak felt the humanoid hands grabbing at his limbs with unimaginable strength. When his right arm tore away from his body, he felt thankful the Maudo grass he ingested earlier would greatly reduce the pain of his demise.

Alvo knew he and his friends were different, he just wasn't sure why. The thin young man with a head full of unkempt black hair remembered that they had found themselves on the shore of Narian Bay, just outside Zor, several quintes ago with no recollection of their prior lives.

The dozen human teenagers of both sexes all appeared around the same age. All shared blue eyes, blue birthmarks on their necks and felt mysteriously linked, even though they had no remembrance of each other.

Naked and with no means of support, they turned to the only vocation which seemed to come naturally, stealing. Now they had clothing, food to eat and a bit of money in their pockets, but no answers as to their origin.

They learned quickly that the high holy city did not tolerate gangs. This meant each acted independently during the Kan, returning to the alley they called home to pool their acquired loot just before the fog receded.

The Grand Turine in the harbor now rang fifteen bells, the Kan would be lifting soon and the young miscreants had returned home one by one. Alvo watched the last straggler, a girl of about fourteen, slip into the alley and place her bag of ill-gotten gains with the others in the center of the narrow thoroughfare. He smiled in satisfaction. This had been a good haul. Everyone had returned with something.

He opened the first bag to begin sorting, when all their attention turned to a flapping noise at the end of the alley. Strangely, no one seemed surprised when an Ash-Ta landed and folded back his long leathery wings.

The bat creature stood five feet tall with a conical shaped head and large eyes. It wore a simple tunic with several deep pockets and he carried a metal cylinder, four inches in diameter and two feet long. Standing the tube upright on the alley floor, he beckoned the young thieves over and they curiously approached without hesitation.

Once they all had gathered around him, he removed a cap from the end of the tube. All could see it filled with a clear liquid. The Ash-Ta then struck the small shard of Trinilic on the ground and it began to glow. Beckoning them closer, he dropped the Trinilic into the liquid.

By the time the youths gathered tightly around the canister, it began to emit a thick cloud of green gas. The billowing smoke enveloped the youngsters, obscuring them completely. When the fumes cleared, they all stood staring blankly outward while the mawl part of their brain awoke and their genetic programming kicked in.

The bat creature reached into his pocket and produced a large blue leaf.

"Smell it, all of you," the Ash-Ta croaked out, handing the leaf to Alvo.

The young man sniffed it then passed it on. It had a sweet earthy odor with metallic highlights.

"Remember the smell," the man-bat said, watching each of the youths pass the leaf around. "There is nothing like it in Lumina. All your targets are marked with that scent."

With tail lowered, General Baag-Tar slowly walked between the rows of exhausted Singa soldiers standing at attention in the park across from the burnt-out palace. The wounded sergeant hobbled beside him, easily keeping up with the depressed senior officer.

"How many men are left?" Baag-Tarr asked peering from side to side at the once proud Singa warriors staring vacantly off into space.

"Five hundred and twenty-seven," he answered promptly. "Besides yourself, I am the only officer left."

The general shook his head in disgust. "Nowhere near enough to hold a city of this size."

When they reached the end of the row, they surveyed the temporary encampment.

"You say you're the only officer left?" the general asked.

"Yes, sir."

"Very well, what's your name?"

"Alnaaji, sir."

"Alnaaji, I'm giving you a field promotion to captain, effective immediately."

"Thank you, sir!"

"Save your thanks. I'm also pulling the plug on this disastrous operation. I want you to get all five hundred and twenty-seven men down to the docks. We're going home."

"Yes, sir!" Alnaaji said, obviously relieved.

The new captain saluted and spun, about to leave, when shrieks came from the skies behind them. Two Diaemus Clan Ash-Ta landed in the deserted street and walked briskly up to the mawl officers. Diaemus Ash-Ta were the most intelligent of all the bat-creatures, capable of tasks deemed too complex for the others of their kind. They also possessed the best verbal skills.

"General," one began in broken Tiikeri. "We have dire news!"

Baag-Tar remained silent and suspicious, the grim expression on his face turning even more dour.

"It's gone," the Ash-Ta continued.

"What's gone? Spit it out!" The general asked, clearly losing patience.

"Everything," the man-bat said remorsefully. "Your cities have been leveled. Your people are dead."

The news struck the Tiikeri like a blow to the stomach, and he paused for a moment in stunned silence. The home he ordered his forces to return to didn't exist anymore.

"What! How?!"

"Do-Tarr, many of them. They killed all Tiikeri and any other mawls in the city. Then they destroyed all buildings."

"What of my people?" asked an anxious Alnaaji.

"Only Tiikeri cities," the Ash-Ta answered simply.

"What of the king and the Cub Prince?"

"All dead."

With this revelation, two things became painfully evident to the stunned general. Tiikeri's had always emitted a pheromone rendering them invisible to the mantis creatures. Something drastically changed. Secondly, he now commanded whatever remained of the once mighty Tiikeri Empire.

"Have your people fly to the remote places we are stationed," Baag-Tarr said, sadly nodding his head. "Tell any non-Tiikeri their contract with the empire has been fulfilled and they can return to their lives. All Tiikeri, whatever is left of us, are to rendezvous in the Unaligned City of Shun-Dra. It's time to see what's left."

It had been at least three grands since Kem Aleki visited Zor. The last time, the Calden Intelligencer traveled to the high holy city for pleasure. This time, business brought her to the largest metropolis in the Annigan.

The trip also marked her first airship ride. The partially constructed air station in Makatooa offered limited flights and she caught the first one available. She had to admit, even though initially reluctant, the flight proved exhilarating.

Kem nodded while passing two female EEtahs of House Nur in a conversation with an Avion in white flowing robes. Everything else about the city seemed just as she remembered it.

The oversized architecture impressed her the most. They fashioned doorways, corridors and rooms to accommodate every known form of sentient life. The Zorian Forum personified the spirit of inclusion.

Her destination happened to be the office of Colonel Zekoff for a much-needed meeting. Normally, information passed between the Society of Whispers was handled by coded dispatch, but this she needed to convey in person. She felt fortunate to be able to finally meet the legendary Head of the Zorian Guards before he retired to academic life.

As usual, she caught the scent of evergreen tobacco wafting out into the hall through the open door. She also noted the colonel had visitors.

Knocking, Kem poked her head in and noticed the red headed man seated behind the colonel's desk. The commander sat off to the side puffing away on his pipe. A thin androgenous man, with a shadow of facial hair, sat in front of the desk. She assumed he must be Captain Rafel, another legend. A man she knew well, Senior Lieutenant Mukavar de Oris, sat beside him.

All stood when she entered.

"Intelligencer Kem," Rafel said, extending a hand. "I've read many of your dispatches, so it's good we finally meet."

"The pleasure is all mine, sir," she said, shaking his hand.

"Knock off the 'sir' crap, I'm Rafel."

Kem's golden brown skin flushed, and she smiled awkwardly. "Yes, sir... I mean Rafel."

"Zekoff de Corab," the colonel said, nodding. "Behind my desk is my soon to be replacement, Captain Vanir."

"Yes, sir, its truly an honor to meet you, sir," Kem fawned. "My boss, Commander Velitel, is scheduled to take your class next grand."

"It will be good to finally meet my counterpart in Makatooa," Zekoff said, before bringing the pipe up to his mouth once more.

Kem finally turned to Mukavar and a broad grin crossed her delicate features. "Hey Muuky! I heard they stationed you here in Zor. Killed anybody yet this cycle?"

Mukavar chortled and offered his hand. "Nah, but then, the cycle isn't over yet either. You still fucking the mayor?"

Kem, taken slightly aback that he knew about the affair, quickly recovered. "Somebody's got to, his wife's never there."

"Alright, Intelligencer Kem," Rafel said, attempting to start the meeting. "What is so important that you decided to visit our fair city in person instead of sending a dispatch?"

"I must say my first-time flying was quite something," Kem said, chuckling slightly. "Anyways, last cycle I had an interesting conversation with Lord Hanara, one of our wealthier citizens."

"Spice Islands Trading Company?" Rafel asked.

"The same. Turns out, Lord Hanara had secret dealings with what he *thought* was a Tiikeri gem merchant but turned out to be a Tiikeri agent saboteur. He whipped up two rival factions of Cul-Ta trying to throw the docks into chaos."

"You all just rebuilt and expanded your wharf," Zekoff said, obviously concerned.

"That's right," Kem confirmed. "And Hanara footed the bill for it. When he found out about the plot, he had the Tiikeri killed. Now, we're mopping up the Cul-Ta problem."

"Probably a distraction from their invasion of the Twilight Lands," Vanir offered from behind the desk.

"More than that," Kem replied. "With the expansion, Makatooa now has the second largest wharf in the Annigan. The only one larger, is right here in Zor."

"And you think they might try something here?" Vanir pressed.

"It only makes sense," Kem replied. "We have the only two systems of docks capable of launching an amphibious or naval operation against them."

Rafel held up a piece of paper. "Speaking of the Twilight Lands; Here's a little piece of information that will probably make everyone smile. I just got this, the Tiikeri forces in the Twilight Lands are in full retreat."

The Zorian spymaster paused. "And hold onto your hats for this; Word from the Avion scouts say that the Tiikeri Empire has been *crushed*. No survivors, their cities raised to the ground."

A moment of dumbfounded silence descended on the room with everyone staring in disbelief.

"What? How?!" Vanir stammered.

"The Do-Tarr," Rafel said, on the verge of giddiness. "The blocker worked!"

"Don't get me wrong, I'm happy," Vanir said, shaking his head, "but what are you talking about?"

"It's good you didn't know," Rafel said exuberantly. "It means the tight security worked. This was a secret operation and a gamble. The Marassas over at Clerria House got ahold of a dead Do-Tarr and took it apart. They developed a pheromone blocker from one of its glands. This allowed the Do-Tarr to finally see the Tiikeri. We had Mal and her crew deliver it to the Do-Tarr. There were probably less than six people who knew what was going on. AND IT WORKED!"

The joyous moment turned out to be fleeting.

"That just leaves the Tiikeri sleeper cell, here," Zekoff said grimly.

Kem spun in surprise to the colonel. "So, they *are* here too!"

"Yes, but we're not dealing with Cul-Ta," Rafel said. "They've placed a cell of mawls that look like humans."

"What do you think they're up to?" Kem asked.

"Unknown," Rafel replied resolutely, "but you can bet it's not good."

"Hold on here," Vanir said quizzically. "If the Tiikeri Empire is destroyed, why are they keeping up hostilities?"

"I can answer that," Kem replied. "The Tiikeri agent revealed to Lord Hanara that their Worrg communication network went down."

"We've got House Valdur to thank for that," Rafel interjected happily.

"Each part of the Tiikeri plan was to be carried out independently with little to no contact between their players," Kem continued. "The operatives in your city are operating in the cold, with no way to contact anyone. They don't know they've been beat."

"Zekoff's mouth fell open in astonishment. "The Tiikeri attempted an operation of that size and complexity *without* communication?! That's insane!"

"The Tiikeri were always an overconfident lot." Rafel said. "And this time they paid for it."

"Well, empire or not, we've got twelve leftovers of the war to root out before they cause trouble." Zekoff cautioned, tapping out his pipe.

Lord Julius, former Ambassador of Avion House Pyre to Immor-Onn watched the line of Singas marching to the harbor from his high balcony. Towering beside him stood Dak, his EEtah seneschal.

They're leaving, thank the gods, he thought. So many questions plagued him. *Why did they invade? Furthermore, why occupy a city just to retreat?* But mostly he questioned the gods on the death of his dear friend, Kai.

He remembered they didn't start out as friends, but quite the opposite. He and his sister Drucilla encountered the petite assassin when their respective paths crossed at the base of Mount Goya. She had been an initiate to the Hand of the Wind on her first assignment to kill the leader of a bandit gang. Trust did not come immediately and it wasn't until they saved her life that a bond formed.

They had been through much together over the grands and Julius didn't seem surprised when Kai and Drucilla fell in love. It turned out that their forbidden love got his sister expelled from House Pyre, but the two refused to separate.

When Drucilla died, Julius felt his sanity start to crack and slowly slip away. The Avion prince felt fortunate Kai decided to stay by his side. Her bow and dagger skills proved invaluable in his various travels and adventures.

During one of those adventures in the Twilight Lands, Kai decided to stay in Immor-Onn. Julius beseeched his father to be appointed House Pyre's ambassador to the Bailian Empire.

Now his good friend and anchor in reality was gone.

"I grow weary of all of this," he said hauntingly.

"Weary, sir?" Dak queried.

"Mortality, it holds no more allure to me. If anything, my connection to Mount Goya, and the Na-Kab below it, have grown stronger."

"Are you leaving again, sir? You *just* arrived."

"I only returned when I had the vision about Kai. I no longer belong here."

"But sir…"

"As a Harbinger of Balance, the neutrality of the insect races appeals to me. The Na-Kab's motives are pure, honest... and ever since their queen was restored, peaceful. It is with them I will dwell, always watchful for an imbalance in the Annigan."

"Will I ever see you again, sir?"

"Perhaps. These quarters are now yours. Keep them up in case I do visit. I'll arrange to provide you with regular funds. You should want for nothing. With the invaders leaving, the queen should be returning from exile. I know you love her and she loves you, protect her."

"I'll miss you, sir."

Julius peered up at the humanoid shark's melancholy expression and patted him on the arm.

"I know."

Captain Vanir scowled when he, Rafel and Mukavar halted outside the doors of the Zorian Monetary Council.

"I just want to say that I am against this plan," the investigator snarled. "We should be taking the little shit into custody, not coddling him!"

Rafel gave a frustrated sigh. "I know! You've made yourself abundantly clear on a number of occasions. We both know that isn't going to work, so we'll try this."

Vanir gave an annoyed grunt of acceptance, then followed his two colleagues through the door.

The receiving area seemed just as busy as his first time here with clerks scurrying about carrying stacks of papers.

"His office is right over there," Vanir said, pointing the way.

"All right," Rafel said, leading them forward with a determined stride. "Let's get this over with."

The Zorian spymaster gave a brief formality of a knock, before opening the door. Banavor, seated behind his desk, looked up and smiled. The two EEtahs standing behind him tensed, but quickly relaxed seeing their boss' demeanor.

"Why Captain Vanir, you've returned to me," he beamed standing.

In his traditional flamboyant and provocative style, the youth wore a white fishnet bodysuit which left nothing to the imagination. Vanir felt a slight tingle of Banavor's sexual emissions sweeping over him, but this time he came prepared. Kasha's ring, safely nestled in his pocket, warded off the licentious spell. He inwardly thanked Zekoff for giving him the Etheria bauble when they learned of Banavor's special ability.

Rafel and Mukavar did not fare as well. Both stood staring in enraptured arousal.

"And I see you brought friends," Banavor said, coming from around the desk. "You must be Captain Rafel. I keep hearing about you and your special skills. And who is this handsome fellow?"

"This is Senior Lieutenant Mukavar," Rafel said, trying to sound calm.

"Senior Lieutenant," Banavor purred. "That would make you Calden navy."

"You know the Calden navy?" Mukavar said, blushing.

"Intimately," he said playfully, rolling his eyes. "Very intimately. Calden sailors were always some of my favorite clients. Now, what can I do for the Society of Whispers?"

"We have a proposal for you," Rafel said huskily.

Banavor leaned back against the edge of his desk and locked eyes with him.

"I like the sound of this already," the youth said, his tone matching Rafel's.

"We would like your assistance in preventing a potentially damaging event which we fear will be of great detriment to this city."

Banavor shrugged. "What can I do? I'm just an economist."

"I've seen your marks," Vanir said, unaffected by the young man's sexual bewitchment. "You worship that mawl god of greed."

Banavor gave the investigator a sensuous pout, spun and stuck out his butt. All could clearly see the X and I marked on either side of the base of his spine through the fishnet.

"You mean these?" he said, slowly running his hands over the markings then down around his shapely ass cheeks.

Rafel and Mukavar became completely ensorcelled by the brazen display, but Vanir remained unchanged.

"Yes," he said coldly, temporarily breaking the spell.

"You're correct, Captain," Banavor said, leaning on the desk's edge. "The Lord guides my hand in gaining prosperity for myself and all believers. Others prosper just by being in the Lord's presence. How does that matter?"

"So, you understand mawl thinking," Vanir said hopefully. "Perhaps you and your god can assist us?"

Banavor shook his head. "The mawl races, more specifically the Tiikeri worship Pa-Waga differently than humans. Tiikeri have no need for commerce. They take what they want. Tiikeri are interested in increasing their empire and the glory that comes with it. Humans are interested in accumulating wealth."

Vanir retained his businesslike demeanor. "Be that as it may, there is a Tiikeri plot about to unfold on this city's docks which will cripple the economic growth of this community. Can you help us stop it?"

"Perhaps," Banavor said, smirking. "What's in it for me?"

Vanir nervously cleared his throat. "Well, despite the fact that any Tiikeri plot would seriously affect your income, the Society of Whispers is prepared to ignore certain ventures you might attempt in the future, provided they're not calamitous to the capital."

"Why Captain Vanir, I would never do anything to undermine the prosperity of this city. How can I help?"

"We captured a Tiikeri spy mapping out our waterfront. Under interrogation she revealed there is a sleeper cell of twelve specially bred mawl hybrids virtually undetectable from humans. We don't know who they are or their plans, only that they exist."

"And you think that through me the Lord can help you?"

"We were hoping."

"Your words have swayed me. I believe I can help. I accept your offer. Now, who was present at the interrogation."

"Captain Rafel conducted the interrogation," Vanir said, happy that the sensuous youth no longer held power over him. "Lieutenant Mukavar was also present."

A mischievous grin crossed Banavor's face and he wiggled a forefinger at the Calden Intelligencer. "Well, in that case, Senior Lieutenant Mukavar, I need you to take off your clothes."

Mukavar found himself taken aback at the request, but with Banavor's lustful enchantment permeating the room, he quickly complied.

With a satisfied smile, Banavor dropped to his knees in front of the muscular sailor, his face directly in front of Mukavar's growing erection.

"Now, let's see what we can find out," Banavor said lubriciously, peering up at Mukavar's chiseled frame and lustful stare.

Using his long, sharpened forefinger, he pricked the tip of the forefinger on his other hand. The blood began to flow immediately and he painted an X, then and I, on either side of Mukavar's hairy abdomen while giving off a low chant. When he finished painting, the Calden agent's cock jutted rock hard, inches from the young man's face.

"Now, Senior Lieutenant Mukavar, I want you to remember the interrogation. Run it over in your mind with as much detail as you can remember."

With those simple instructions given, he deftly slipped his mouth around Mukavar's rigid member and began slurping and pumping away with greedy abandon.

Rafel surprisingly felt no jealousy, only blinding arousal, watching his lover being treated to an enthusiastic blowjob by another man. Vanir turned out to be not so affected. He turned away and took a quick hit from his flask.

The oral onslaught lasted only moments before Mukavar grunted and released his load into Banavor's mouth. The young man continued sucking until Mukavar went soft. He then sat back on his legs in contemplation, while swallowing the last of the agent's seed.

Banavor then stared back up at Rafel and Vanir with a thin ribbon of white liquid still dotting the corner of his mouth.

"They're young, barely teens," Banavor said ominously, all hint of salaciousness gone. "You will know them by their blue eyes and blue birthmark."

"What's their plan?" Vanir asked expectantly.

The young man's face turned bleak, and he wiped the cum from the corner of his mouth. "Destruction and disruption."

The moon rose over the eastern Twilight Lands as the *Attila* cleared the Os'Ani Mountains, streaking over the thin peninsula of land leading to Gar-Yesh Point.

Since leaving Immor-Onn, Okawa spent the entire trip alternating between uncontrollably weeping and pacing up and down the airship in a rage. Sitsa watched her from the pilot's seat while the Valdurian screamed and pounded her fist into things, and finally dropped into the seat beside her, quietly sobbing.

If the Tinian seemed confused about human behavior before, this only deepened her bewilderment. She had mated, meeting at the birthing stone and allowing all the males of her pod to share their seed with her. She couldn't understand the human's strong attachments to a single individual. A bond so strong, that the death of one could spark another emotion foreign to her, vengeance. The humanoid moth, unsure of what to do, decided her best course of action was to stay quiet and still, concentrating on piloting.

The look on Okawa's face when she saw the structures on Gar-Yesh Point truly worried Sitsa. The human grew eerily quiet, her crying and outbursts ceased, and her face became a mask of controlled malevolent fury.

"Take her down," she ordered through taut lips.

From the windshield, both could see the compound that once bivouacked the Singa army had now grown into a mixed mawl community. The center of the village contained the enclosed single-story dwellings used by the Tiikeri and their mongrel slaves. The outskirts of the village consisted of clusters of the open sided huts favored by the Singas.

The interior of the town bustled with activity. Mongrels were in the process of constructing more buildings, while Tiikeri females and cubs moved up and down the three main streets on their morning errands.

Okawa's mouth turned upward in a sadistic sneer, not bothering to note the absence of warriors. The only males visible, both Singa and Tiikeri, appeared advanced in age.

"Take her over the center of town," Okawa ordered again in a menacing growl, "just above the rooftops."

The Tinian pilot did as requested, and Okawa, with eyes locked on her target, reached up to the overhead console.

When they reached a hundred feet from the first Singa huts, the Valdurian began tapping on the orange Trinilic disk embedded there. Fireballs shot out from under the hull of the *Attila* as fast as Okawa could tap. The melon-sized, glowing orbs exploded on contact with deafening roars and large columns of flame.

Okawa continued her onslaught, sweeping across the center of the town, painting it in a swath of explosions and fire. Mawls screamed and ran, while the strange and terrible thing from the sky destroyed their new homes.

"Bring her around again," Okawa ordered coldly when the airship had cleared the far side of the hamlet.

Sweeping around, Okawa caught sight of a crowd of females and cubs attempting to flee town running down one of the side streets.

"There," Okawa said, pointing at the escaping mawls.

The *Attila* swept in low again and this time Okawa placed her hand against the orange disk and held it there. A tendril of continuous flame erupted from both of the exterior rods, engulfing the entire street in a rapidly travelling inferno.

It overtook the fleeing women and children and they were caught up in the magical blaze. Their screams quickly died away, with their flesh and fur rapidly seared from their bodies. The *Attila* sped past the carnage, leaving a street full of blackened humanoid mawl corpses.

"Again," the Valdurian ordered.

"Okawa, our PSI battery for the armaments is nearly empty," Sitsa warned.

"Again!"

The Tinian banked the craft around and brought it over the only strip of town not burning. Okawa continued shooting until the rods stopped raining fireballs. The airship then ascended and circled the burning scene of devastation.

"Okawa, I do not understand the nature of this attack," Sitsa said, while both surveyed the destruction.

"I wouldn't expect you to," Okawa said hollowly. "But I'm just getting started. We're going to need more firepower. Let's get to Landagar."

"What exactly are we looking for, sir?"

Mukavar smiled sympathetically into the puzzled face of the young Zorian guard. "You heard the briefing, 'Young, blue eyes and birthmark, acting suspiciously.'"

The morning bustle of the Zorian wharf swirled all around the two and the young man pushed back a lock of long brown hair, anxiously eying the crowd. Carts full of goods clattered on the street, to and from the docks. All the while, a steady stream of various sentients, including Piceans, EEtah and Otick, mingled with their human counterparts. All worked steadily, conducting the business of the high holy city and commerce hub of the Goyan Islands.

"You mean like that?" the guard asked.

He pointed out a young woman hovering around the doors of the Harbormaster's and Quartermaster's offices. Mukavar guessed her to be no more than thirteen, dressed in a shabby grey tunic with long black hair. She nervously glanced around at the passing crowd to see if anyone observed her and then began sniffing at the front of the building.

True to Banavor's vision, they could see her striking blue eyes from across the street and when she turned, the blue birthmark on her neck caught their attention.

"Exactly like that," Mukavar confirmed. "Good catch."

The young guard beamed with the compliment, then looked to his superior for direction. Mukavar nodded his head down the street and both crossed at the same time.

The young woman had stopped sniffing and now looked around nervously. Reaching into the pocket on either side of her tunic, her eyes darted back and forth until she saw the Zorian Guard headed her way. She immediately halted and began a brisk pace in the opposite direction.

Her determined trek brought her directly into the arms of a much taller and stouter Mukavar who she had paid no attention to because of his everyday clothing.

She hissed and screeched, while wildly thrashing against his tight grip around her. People stared when they passed and began to gather. The uniformed guard rushed up to assist Mukavar with the struggling suspect.

"Watch out for her pockets!" the guard cautioned when within ear shot over the busy street. "She's trying to reach in her pockets!"

With the warning, Mukavar concentrated on keeping her arms pinned. When the guard finally caught up to them, Mukavar motioned for him to see what she had reached for. The search proved far from easy with the woman's thrashing and inhuman screeches. The Calden Intelligencer finally ran out of patience.

"We can do this with you conscious or not," he growled. "You decide."

The ultimatum went unheeded and the woman increased her wrestling against his grip.

"Suit yourself!" Mukavar violently headbutted her and with the crack of one skull against the other, the young female went limp in his arms.

The guard then easily searched her pockets and retrieved two palm sized orange disks. Mukavar's eyes widened when he saw them.

"Trinilic!" he said, gasping. "No wonder she had them in separate pockets. Keep those disks away from each other!"

The young man anxiously glanced at the Etheria crystals in each hand. He held his arms out to his sides to keep them further apart.

Mukavar easily tossed the unconscious woman over his shoulder. "Alright, let's get her and her destructive toys to Captain Rafel.

Poma awoke abruptly with a splitting headache and a large lump on the side of her head. The mawl/human hybrid attempted to move and noted the thick leather straps securing her to a chair. Even though she was held firmly in place, they bent her torso slightly forward, allowing her arms to be extended outward from the arm rests.

The room in which she found herself had a wide window on one wall which looked to another room. She saw the man who captured her peering through the glass.

Rafel stood across the otherwise empty room, beside a large, chest high slatted wooden box. She could see winged insects buzzing around inside, moving in and out of the slats.

"That's a nasty bump you've got there," Rafel said.

The young woman hissed loudly at him and struggled against her bonds.

"My colleague in the next room says that you were about to cause mischief down by the docks. Let's discuss that, shall we? And while we're at it, let's also talk about your friends and their plans to cause trouble."

The woman spit at him which missed by several feet.

The spymaster sighed and opened the box to reveal a massive beehive. Thousands of bees swarmed across the vast array of honeycombs.

"My good friends the Toma monks were kind enough to loan me some of their little friends," Rafel cheerfully explained. "You see, the interesting thing about *these* bees is their alchemistic wax and their incredibly painful sting. Luckily, they are quite docile… unless you disturb the hive."

Rafel then slid the bustling hive within inches of her hand. The woman squirmed in fear, staring at the throng of insects mere inches from her.

"Now, where were we?" Rafel said with a broad grin.

Airlord Osip de Deros had been at the forefront of the Valdurian airship program since its inception. Always a forward thinker, it was he who pushed the Valdur family to invest in research and development. He also became instrumental in the building of the place he now called home, the balloon city of Landagar.

Landagar became more of a remote outpost than an actual city. Accessible only by air, the six massive balloons were connected by a driverless shuttle system and under the strictest security.

Osip nervously stroked his gray beard and stared out the window at the snowcapped Atarian Mountains from one of those driverless shuttles, pondering how such an egregious breech of security happened. Joc' Valdur, seated beside him, appeared just as worried, watching them approach the balloon designated Weapons Research.

"The Dwarf said it was only a few items," Osip said, finally breaking the silence.

"Depending on the items, this could be catastrophic," Joc' replied apprehensively.

The two immediately exited the small craft when it came to a stop on the enclosed landing pad and swept past an EEtah guard who briskly saluted. The Valdurian officials wore red badges on lanyards around their necks, granting free access through all the color-coded security regions.

The green color-coded Weapons Research balloon rose three floors in height, with offices on the top floor and two massive workshops and test areas below. They designed the main armory on the bottom floor with the most security, and for good reason, the Landagar Group designed the most sophisticated weaponry on the Annigan.

Upon arriving, they saw the man who summoned them, Tresnat de Warton, code named "The Dwarf." Standing at just under five feet tall, Tresnat made up for his diminutive size with his intensity and brilliance at his craft of Magitech—the very heart of the integration of Etheria Crystals and mechanical objects.

An EEtah sentry guarded the secured armory door behind Tresnat. The Dwarf held several sheets of paper in his hand while speaking with his head armorer, who appeared to be doing more listening than talking.

"How bad is it?" Osip asked, getting straight to the point.

Tresnat sighed and adjusted his round goggle style glasses. "Bad enough. As far as the number of items taken, it was very small. They just happened to be some of our latest and most deadly weaponry."

"You got a list?" Joc' asked hesitantly.

Tresnat nodded and consulted one of the sheets of paper in his hands. "Looks like two Mark three pistol crossbows, along with a thousand rounds of those Na-Kab Carbon bolts. Also, about a dozen Trinilic grenades, but the worst thing missing is a Griesbach 200 sniper rifle."

Joc' rubbed his temples and exhaled loudly. "How did this happen?"

The armorer swallowed nervously. "Sir, it's like I was telling Commander Tresnat, it was Major Okawa. She has clearance and she outranks me by a lot. She always checks weapons out, so I didn't see anything that seemed out of place. But I just gotta say, she did not look good."

"It gets worse," Tresnat said, holding up a second sheet of paper.

Joc' gave a weary sigh before turning his attention back to the Airlord.

"It looks like she had *The Attila's* PSI battery fully charged."

Joc' shook his head in dismay. "She probably emptied it destroying the settlement at Gar-Yesh Point last cycle. Tiikeri forces have been retreating for a while now. That mawl encampment contained mostly females, children and the elderly. She technically committed a war crime. Those were non-combatants."

"From the equipment she took, it appears she's not done," Tresnat said ominously.

Joc' nodded with a bleak expression. "Vengeance is a driving obsession. Since the death of Demetrius, her methods have become, unsound."

"To say the least," Osip agreed.

"Well, it's a safe bet to say she's heading for the Land of Mists. It's a target rich environment. We can't have one of our rogue agents out there randomly killing sentients with the latest weaponry we've developed."

"Not to mention the *Attila* itself," Tresnat added. "That's either got to be brought back or destroyed. We can't have that kind of Magitech fall into the wrong hands."

Joc' nodded in agreement but remained silent.

"Should we order her terminated?" Osip asked reluctantly. "It seems such a shame. I just promoted her."

"Not yet," Joc' said, shaking his head. "Let's try and bring her in. We owe her that much."

Tresnat gave Joc' a perplexed look. "But if she's over in Nocturn, sir?"

"I've got a team that's used to working in Nocturn," Joc' said grimly. "They'll find her."

"I don't know what they need us for, Sarge, there's enough guards on these docks to repel an invasion force," Dawria de Ruros said, adjusting her sword belt and peeking down an alley to her right.

Patrol Sergeant Rontu de Bogat chuckled, crinkling the laugh lines on his naturally jovial face. "I thought you liked the smell of day-old fish."

"Very funny," Dawria said, scrunching her nose. "I liked it just fine where we were. The university's a lot cleaner and smells a lot better."

"Yeah, and those academic types cause a whole lot less trouble," Rontu added. "Relax, it's temporary. Whatever's going to happen, the powers that be think it's going to happen soon."

"They sure didn't give us a lot to go on," Dawria said, pausing at a fish merchants stall to examine a row of small red and grey fish.

"That's because they didn't have a lot to go on. 'Young, blue eyes and birthmark' is all we know."

"Don't forget 'acting suspicious,'" Dawria teased. "Very important."

"That covers half the sentients we've come across this morning."

Both laughed and the pair of Zorian Guards continued their rounds, turning the corner onto Beach Drive which paralleled the southern docks and beyond.

Rontu liked his young partner. She was cute, feisty and boy could she fight. He once saw her breakup a six-man bar brawl by herself, after they had knocked him to the ground. His wife, Naine, even liked her and insisted she frequently join them for dinner. Rontu guessed she reminded Naine of her little sister who died several grands ago.

They had stopped again by an Otick pearl vendor and Dawria called over a nearby Picean to translate. After a brief conversation, inquiring if it had seen anything unusual, and alerting the humanoid crab to be vigilant, they set off again.

The duo traveled another twenty yards passing various vendors and nodding a greeting when Dawria suddenly paused.

"Hey, Sarge, you see what I see?"

Rontu stopped and looked in the direction his partner indicated. A young teenage boy in a dirty grey tunic skulked down the docks nervously peering around. A hood covered his head but both guards could see his bright blue eyes. He headed towards dock sixteen, where several large transport ships had been moored, waiting to be unloaded.

Rontu put his hands on his hips and huffed. "Well, I'd say that fits the description of suspicious. Let's go."

They started out at a trot, easily coming up on the overly cautious teen.

"You there!" Rontu called out. "Hold it right there!"

The youth looked over in a panic and then took off running down the street, away from the wharf. The guards trot now became a dead run. Both marveled at how fast the youth could move.

Passing a diagonal side street, Dawria peeled off on an intersecting path, leaving Rontu in direct pursuit. Rontu decidedly had more trouble keeping up. The youth not only possessed astonishing speed, but being even a small part mawl, could leap remarkable distances navigating around the various street vendors they encountered.

The chase ended abruptly when Dawria lunged full speed from the interconnecting street, tackling the swift young man and knocking him to the ground.

The boy leapt to his feet first, followed by Dawria, just as Rontu arrived. The youth now crouched aggressively in front of a recessed doorway, trapped by the Zorian Guards. His eyes narrowed to mere slits and he hissed angrily. The hood got pulled back in the tumble and they could clearly see a large bright blue birthmark on his neck and abnormally long canine teeth. Both guards pulled their swords and slowly advanced on the aggressive youngster.

"Just calm down," Rontu said calmingly. "We just want to ask you some questions."

"Yeah," Dawria added. "We're not going to hurt you."

The young man ignored the assurances. His eyes darted about wildly looking for an avenue of escape. Finding none he hissed again and feinted a lunge at Dawria but backed off immediately when they raised their blades.

"Come on, don't make this any harder than it has to be." Rontu pleaded, watching the teen back into the deeply recessed doorway and reach into both his pockets.

"Let's start with your name," Dawria calmly said, while slowly closing the distance.

When the duo got within ten feet, he gave a defiant hiss and pulled his hands from his pockets. Each contained a palm sized orange disk. Before the guards could take another step, he hissed again and clapped his hands together, striking the disks against each other.

The massive explosion blasted through the side street out into the main thoroughfare, where it obliterated one vendor's stall and set two others on fire. Both Zorian Guards died instantly, but their deaths were not in vain, for now the Tiikeri endgame plan had definitively revealed itself.

Suicide bombers.

The temples of EEtah House Nur grace the waterfront of almost every major seaport in the Goyan Islands. Their gently sloping shark fin arches are a beacon and gateway to any who seek official contact with the EEtah people. They serve many purposes; spiritual solace for the EEtah race, administrative duties, and on this occasion, funereal.

Taleeka had been sniffling since the moment they arrived and she saw Zaad's body. He lay in repose on the immersion platform overlooking the water in the rear of the main temple. The precocious ten-grand-old had not left Mal's side since they entered the sanctuary.

Now, standing on the funeral landing, she hugged her mother's waist, peeking out at the large man-shark lying so still and lifeless. At this moment, she wished more than anything, to be bouncing joyfully on his knees or practicing her skill at learning his language. But now, it came time to say goodbye and she couldn't stop the tears.

Mal had been unusually quiet and sullen all morning. She had barely spoken two words since embarking for the service. All knew to give her some space and time to process the loss of her longtime friend.

Alto stood stoically beside them and also stared at Zaad's motionless form. He held his hands clasped behind him, the normal twinkle in his eye missing. Behind him, Zau, Lazio and Kumo kept a silent vigil. Their races may have been unfamiliar with profound grief, but they understood the solemnity of the moment.

The purple robed priestess gathered herself, about to start the service, when two men at arms, wearing the uniforms of the Eldorian Guards, stepped briefly onto the landing, peered quickly around, and then left. A brief moment later, Shom Eldor and his seneschal, Attina, stepped through the doors and for the first time this cycle. A smile, all be it a sad one, erupted on Mal's face.

"You came!" she said as they embraced.

"I can imagine nothing on my schedule so important which would cause me to miss this," the royal replied sadly.

He then turned his attention to the little girl clutching his friend's waist. "And who might this be?"

"This is my daughter, Taleeka," Mal said, gently touching the top of her head.

"Well, Taleeka, I'm certainly glad to meet you," Shom said, crouching down eye level with her. "I just wish the circumstances were different."

Taleeka sniffled again and stepped over to the Eldorian Sovereign.

"You can call me Tally," she said dolefully. "I loved Zaad. Were you his friend, too?"

"*Very* good friends," Shom replied gently. "He, your mom, dad and I got into lots of trouble together."

"He died in the war with the cat people, and I really miss him." She said, her eyes welling up again.

"I'm going to miss him too," Shom said softly.

With that confession, Taleeka threw herself into his arms. Shom Eldor, a man hardly known for his tolerance of children, embraced the child warmly. When they separated, he smiled reassuringly before she returned to Mal's side.

Shom greeted the rest of his friends and former adventuring companions before the EEtah priestess approached.

"We should begin," she said softly. "Do any of you wish to speak?"

Mal, Shom and Alto searched each other's faces until Shom gave a resolute nod.

"I guess that duty should fall to me," he said, then stepped over to the body.

Clearing his throat, he peered around at the people Zaad considered family.

"What can I say about Zaad?" Shom somberly began, chuckling mournfully. "I could tell you about his humble beginnings as an Outer Clan EEtah. From those modest roots came his meteoric rise to the rank of commander in the Valdurian Marines.

344

"I could mention that he was a loyal friend and comrade. At one time or another in our travels, we all owed our very lives to his valiant actions.

"Then, there was his wit. I know it may be hard to believe an eight-foot-tall sentient, who could rend you in two, could be funny, but he possessed a subtle dry wit, most didn't see. In fact, the entire time we knew each other he only called me by my proper name once. I was always, 'the funny little man.' And every time I would correct him, he would always respond the same way, 'I know.'

"I also would wish you to know of his compassion, risking his life to save those intent on doing him harm.

"Now, as we're about to give our final goodbyes, these are the things I can say about Zaad, and, most of all, how very much he will be missed."

When he finished and stepped away, the only sound penetrating the profound silence were Taleeka's sobs while she clutched Mal's waist. The Spice Rat stared stoically at the body of her friend, rare tears flowing down her face.

The EEtah priestess gave Shom a questioning look, making sure he finished, before stepping over to the lever which released the body. She reached over about to pull it when the approaching sound of marching boots interrupted the ceremony.

All looked up to see ten Sunal EEtahs parade through the temple and onto the landing. When they reached Zaad's body, the procession broke in two, with five EEtahs on either side of the foot of the immersion platform.

"We of Dakor Sunal have come to pay our final respects to this fallen hero," the EEtah at the head of the far line proclaimed gruffly. "For even though he was Outer Clan, his deeds are that of legend. We can think of no higher tribute."

He then addressed his comrades. "Dakor Sunal, present arms!"

In unison, all the EEtahs deftly unslung their Yudon harpoons and extended them outwards, forming an arch until their tips clacked together as one when they touched.

The priestess, once again, extended her arm, ready to pull the lever, when a weeping Taleeka broke away from Mal's side and rushed over to Zaad. She threw her head down on his chest and continued her innocent lamentations.

Mal let her have a moment before going over and gently touching her shoulder. "Tally, sweety, it's time."

"Goodbye Zaad," Taleeka tearfully choked out, stepping back in her mother's arms. "I love you."

The priestess finally pulled the lever and the platform tilted towards the sea. Zaad's body gracefully slipped down the archway of steel and under the waves of Narian Bay for the last time.

Alvo slipped through the thick Kan fog while listening to the Grand Turine in the Zorian Harbor ring seven bells. He could only see a few feet in front of him, but sight did not guide the mawl/human mix. This time, the sense of smell led him to his target.

The pungent musky aroma of the Miris leaf lingered in his senses. It conjured up images of a night sky full of stars and the triple canopy jungle of the Dasos region in the Land of Mists. It comforted and guided him in this strange world of perpetual sunlight. It led him to his target.

He kept to the shadows of the buildings along the wharf. He couldn't afford to be captured. They had already lost two of their numbers and the humans were now on guard, with stepped up patrols on every dock. It became obvious his initial plan of single random attacks designed to terrorize hadn't worked. One massive blow must be struck, and the time had finally arrived.

All across the Zorian waterfront, the ten remaining members of his cell moved in on their targets. Alvo had abandoned his originally designated target and instead chose the one his companion had died trying to destroy, the offices containing the Harbormaster and Quartermaster. He knew the importance of this target to be paramount. Its destruction would plunge the shipping trade of the capital, and most likely the entire Goyan Islands, into chaos.

He considered the fact that they all died completing this mission irrelevant. The glory of the empire was all that mattered now.

Catching the familiar pungent odor, his heart quickened and he picked up the pace, enthusiastically following the olfactory trail. When the smell grew overwhelmingly strong and he thought he might pass out, Alvo knew he had arrived.

The small building, one of many, rested on the side of a hill overlooking the docks. Alvo smiled with satisfaction and started reaching in his pockets for the Trinilic, when he heard from behind him the distinctive sound of a crossbow bolt being pulled back.

"Keep your hands up where I can see them," a male voice ordered.

Alvo froze and slowly extended his arms outward from his sides.

"Now, turn around... slowly."

Alvo complied and saw three human males. Two wore city guard's uniforms and aimed medium crossbows at him. The leader, a human with red hair and beard, stepped forward armed with a pistol crossbow.

"I figured you were using scent markers when we caught one of your pals sniffing around here," the red headed man said. You mawls just love to use scent. But you know who else is good at sniffing things out? Hounds."

Alvo's heart already thundered in his chest and now, with the thought of their plan being thwarted, he felt his mouth go dry and a wave of lightheadedness sweep over him.

"Don't worry, we've got welcoming committees at all your locations. So, you may as well give it up."

They stood for an extended moment staring at each other. Alvo honestly didn't know what to do. If he went for the Trinilic he would be dead before his hands got inside his pockets.

"Look, the game's over," the red head continued. "The Tiikeri Empire has been destroyed. There's nothing left to fight for."

"LIAR!" Alvo yowled in indignant disbelief.

Vanir paused briefly, considering his response, when a giant explosion erupted in the middle of the bay. It rocked the entire wharf and sent a fireball soaring several hundred feet into the air.

Immediately following the deafening roar, a tumultuous cacophony of bells rang out as the burning Grand Turine toppled into the bay. The essential edifice disappeared below the gentle waves and the hiss of flames interacting with water closely followed. The liquid, however, had no effect in extinguishing the magical fire and the bay gave off an eerie orange glow where the giant time piece submerged.

A blanket of silence covered the calamitous racket, amplifying the ringing in everyone's ears. Capitalizing on the distraction, desperate to do something, Alvo plunged his hands into his pockets. He just managed to grab both disks when several crossbow bolts struck him at the same time.

The force of the blows knocked Alvo back against the building wall and he slowly slid down the wall to the ground, leaving a large swath of red on the surface behind him.

The mawl, semiconscious, still tried to get the Trinilic out, when he felt a boot pinning his wrist to the cobblestones. The Tiikeri sleeper agent faded from consciousness hearing explosions going off down the wharf and he greatly feared they missed their targets.

Vanir walked up to the dead mawl, putting his pistol away. He stared at Alvo's body for a moment before glancing over at his men.

"He sure looks human," Vanir said in morbid appreciation. "Let's get this body over to the university. Maybe the Marassa surgeons can take him apart and see what the Tiikeri have done here."

The Unaligned City of Shun-Dra lies in the eastern foothills of the Kel-Raku Mountains. In the city center, beside the river sharing the name of the mountains from which it flows, is the compound known as the Agora Den. For ages it served as a neutral meeting place where business deals could be forged and where rival mawl factions could meet to work out their differences.

The city earned the reputation as a safe haven for any mawl on the run from the Tiikeri Empire or rival Singa pride because violence was not tolerated there. No one dared defy the two simple laws strictly enforced by a mysteriously pervasive magical mist: no theft and no acts of aggression.

In an ironic twist of fate, it now served as the last true refuge for the remaining Tiikeri from their Do-Tarr enemies.

"How many of our brothers and sisters arrived last luna?" Jo-Rakk asked from the head of the table.

The white Tiikeri and former ambassador to the Bailian Empire appeared weary. He leaned his elbows on the table and glanced around at what was, in fact, the new leadership of the once mighty empire. Lazio and Baag-Tar sat on either side of him, and Alnaaji sat next to Karga, who sat blindly staring into space.

"Ten, sir," the Singa and former sergeant replied. "Less and less each luna."

"How many total?"

"Somewhere around five hundred, sir. An exact count is difficult with the new arrivals."

Jo-Rakk gave a mournful sigh and his ears flattened. "A mere one hundredth of our former population."

"And no bodies found in the ruins of any of our cities," Alnaaji said sadly.

"Carried off by the Do-Tarr," Lazio said disgusted. "You can bet the bugs feasted that moonless, as did their children in the maggot pits."

"What about housing for the new arrivals?" Jo-Rakk asked hopefully.

"We've started building on the north side of town, sir," Alnaaji reported.

Jo-Rakk nodded his approval and Baag-Tarr stood. The once proud orange Tiikeri now carried a humbler bearing.

"The Tiikeri military is no more," he said dolefully. "No one is sadder than I at that fact. So, I think it's time we dropped the military manner in which we address and deal with each other. We are all brothers and sisters and I propose we adopt that as our new identities."

"Here, here," Lazio said enthusiastically.

Baag-Tar glanced around the table. "Agreed?"

Agreed!" came the unified reply.

Baag-Tarr sat back down and Jo-Rakk stood.

"I would also propose taking this a step further," he said. "The old ways did not serve us in the end. We must repurpose and rededicate ourselves."

"How?" Karga asked, finally joining the conversation.

"We must abandon this notion of Tiikeri superiority. With the opening of Lumina to us, we are going to encounter many worthy races that we can work with."

"You're referring to the humans?" Karga warily asked.

"Among others," Jo-Rakk confirmed. "We now have a chance to reinvent ourselves from a place of safety. A charter for our governance must be drawn up and agreed to by all. We must abandon our ways of unfounded superiority and naked aggression. After all, it is those things which led to our downfall."

Baag-Tar huffed. "Brother, those things may have been a contributing factor, but we all know what caused our downfall, it was that accursed religion. The moment the king started listening to the clerics instead of the generals, we were doomed."

"I agree," Karga said emphatically. "Every major defeat we suffered happened because the priests of Pa-Waga beguiled the king. I personally blame them for our empire's fall and wouldn't mind seeing the cursed religion wiped from the face of the Annigan."

Once again, all nodded in agreement. Lazio sat back and smiled. He could now happily report back that the Tiikeri matter had been finally settled. It had been a wise move by Rafel to implant him here to keep an eye on the Tiikeri survivors and their future plans.

"Something to ponder once we get settled," Jo-Rakk said thoughtfully, "after all we've only been here less than ten lunas. Perhaps something to add to our charter?"

Jo-Rakk had just sat down when the door to the meeting room flew open and a young male Tiikeri rushed in.

"Sirs, you need to come see this," he panted. "It's a miracle!"

All exchanged curious glances then got up and followed the enthusiastic young male. He led them to a row of tiny humble shacks near the southern edge of town. A small, excited crowd of orange and white Tiikeri stood gathered around one of the hovels open front door.

Pushing their way through Baag-Tarr and Jo-Rakk stood in stunned amazement. The simple one room dwelling contained only a bed, table and three chairs. Seated in the chair by the bed, Taa-Je sat nursing her newborn infant, a black Tiikeri."

"How can this be?! Baag-Tar blurted out. "King Kar-Gor and the Cub Prince were killed when Hai-Dar was overrun."

"I don't know sir," Taa-Je said frightenedly. "When I heard the Cub Prince had been born, I knew my baby would be killed, so I ran."

"This is also Kar-Gor's son?" Jo-Rakk asked in amazement.

Taa-Je weakly nodded, unsure if she could be in trouble. "Yes, I was one of the king's consorts."

By now, Lazio led the sightless Karga in to join them.

"What's this?" the Singa general asked quizzically. "There is only supposed to be one Cub Prince!"

Karga looked in the general direction of his companions which he could not see and smiled.

"And now there is."

The wind gusted through the empty hangar of Air Station East, blowing Tam-Eez's long mahogany hair all about. Through the giant opening he could see the armada of twenty airships hovering just outside.

The queen was coming home.

A large crowd of Bailian citizens murmured excitedly when the large transport ship entered. It landed off to the right side of the hangar and a detachment of Valdurian marines came pouring out. The crossbows strung across the back of their green jumpsuits clattered noisily and they formed two long lines standing at attention.

A smaller transport ship arrived just behind it and parked next to its larger counterpart. With a barrage of clicks and squeaks, a work team of twenty Do-Tarr scrambled down the ramp. The humanoid mantis creatures, eager to get back to work, scurried past the crowd and into the city.

One by one the airships landed and the hastily evacuated officials and city workers disembarked, greeting loved ones which could not escape.

A crackle of energy seemed to course through the crowd when the last ship finally landed carrying the queen. They were forced to wait a moment longer, however, watching the Valdurian Ambassador Valindra Valdur, Commander Sandal, Quadar, as well as her ladies in waiting, Phu-Suany and Mu-Saeid exit first. The anticipation became virtually palpable when the queen's personal bodyguard, Akkaa stepped onto the ramp. The massive EEtah barely fit through the hatch and, out of habit, he cautiously scanned for threats.

The queen immediately followed, and the crowd went wild, cheering and rejoicing that they had their beloved sovereign finally back amongst them. The petite, blond Bailian royal, in a sheer floor length dress slit up the side with a deeply plunging neckline, smiled and waved at the crowd. In her arms, her pet Cheepa, Manar, peered around at the excitement with wide eyes.

The queen stepped onto the ramp and continued waving regally with her free hand. The marines all snapped a salute, holding it until she passed through their ranks.

"Welcome home, Your Majesty," Tam-Eez greeted. "As you can see, everyone's delighted you've returned."

Shula smiled gratefully and gave a relieved sigh. "I'm so glad to be back. How bad a shape did they leave my city in?"

"Surprisingly, not too bad. The Tiikeri didn't want to plunder it. They wanted the city intact to act as a distribution point for their stolen Etheria. The palace, however... well, let's just say they made themselves at home."

Shula nodded then glanced over at the still excited crowd.

"Here, watch over Manar for a moment," she said, handing him the purring Cheepa.

The queen then extended her arms and strode into the jubilant crowd which closed in around her. Everyone seemed eager to touch or be near the cherished sovereign and she smiled and caressed them in return.

"My people," she beamed, "you have suffered much in these past few lunas, but that suffering is over. You honor me with this greeting, and I decree that this luna will be set aside as a time of celebration from here on out! Let us take time to revel in our liberation. I hereby decree that all taverns, eating establishments, entertainment venues, and the like, offer up their goods and services with the cost to be borne by the crown!"

This news set off another round of cheers and revelry.

Making her way back through the joyous throng, she took Manar back from Tam-Eez and smiled sadly.

"Kai?" she asked.

The new spymaster grimaced and lowered his head. "She was devoured by the Singa's that killed her. That's what they did to most of our people they killed. I've constructed a temporary memorial with some of her personal items. Just until the Do-Tarr can build a permanent one."

Still maintaining her woeful smile, she brushed the cheek of the only other sentient who loved Kai as much as she did.

"Take me there."

The *Haraka* came in low over the foothills of the Kel-Raku Mountains. Up above, a brilliant full moon and blanket of stars illuminated the waving sea of grass below them.

"And there it is," Mal said triumphantly, when the partially concealed *Attila* came into view.

"That's amazing!" Zau said, staring out the window from her navigator's seat. "How in the name of the Goddess did you know where to find it?"

"This was an easy guess," Mal said, carefully examining the *Attila* laying half buried in the tall yellow grass. "Shun-Dra is only a few miles from here. Now, it's the Tiikeri, or what's left of them, being hunted. Shun-Dra's the only safe haven for them. So that makes it an ideal hunting ground for those with an axe to grind."

Taleeka had now joined the two, standing between the command chairs, munching on a dried meat stick and watching the abandoned craft below, while the *Haraka* slowly circled above.

"She looks like she's sealed up pretty tight," Mal noted aloud. "Tally honey, do you think you can get us in that thing?"

The ten-grand-old took another bite and chewed the fibrous delicacy while carefully analyzing the ship beneath them.

"Sure mom, it's almost exactly like the *Haraka*."

"Good enough," Mal said playfully tussling her hair. "Kumo, put us down next to her. Let's see what's going on."

"Yes, Captain."

The *Haraka* landed twenty feet away from the abandoned craft and floated inches above the ground. When the side hatch dropped Mal, Alto and Taleeka exited and made their way over to the partially concealed Resistance Class Cruiser. Zau followed to stretch her legs and Kumo scampered off, disappearing in the grass on a hunting expedition.

Standing by the *Attila's* side hatch, Taleeka pointed to a spot in the edge of the door near the top.

"That's where the main latch is," she said, reaching in her pocket and pulling out her folding utility knife. "Dad, can you give me a boost up there?"

"Of course, little one," the swordmaster said, picking her up by her waist.

Alto lifted her into position and she extended a thin bladed flat edge from the tool's many options. Taleeka slid it into the door crack where she indicated, jiggled the tool. With a brief moment of effort, a loud click came from within and the hatch began to drop, converting into a ramp.

"See, easy! she said, beaming back at her parents.

"Well done!" Alto praised.

Their exuberance proved short lived. The overwhelming stench of body odor and human waste escaped from the opening, causing everyone to turn away in disgust.

"That smells horrible mom," Taleeka whined.

Mal sorrowfully shook her head. "Smells like someone who's given up."

The Spice Rat observed the revulsion on her family's faces and heaved a sigh. "Alright, wait back at the ship. There's no reason for anyone but me to go in there."

This time, no argument came from Taleeka as to wanting to accompany her. Alto led their daughter back to the *Haraka,* when Kumo emerged from the grass with a large unidentifiable carcass wrapped in a silk cocoon.

"Kumo," Mal called out and the Makara paused at the back hatch.

"Yes, Captain?"

"Be ready to take off as soon as you see me exit this craft."

"Yes, Captain," she said, before disappearing into the *Haraka* with her prize.

Mal then exhaled loudly and started up the *Attila's* ramp. The bare interior turned out to be just as bad as imagined. The command chairs reeked of body odor and urine. She navigated around dried pools of vomit interspersed randomly on the cabin floor. The stench of human waste drifted up from the rear cargo area.

Mal worked quickly, stepping up to the center overhead console. A small hatch covering the rear of the panel caught her attention and she pried it open with her dagger. A single orange ring loomed ominously inside the shallow compartment. Reaching up, the Spice Rat gave it a firm pull.

The ring connected to a three-inch-long pin which easily came loose in her hand. Immediately the orange Trinilic disk in the console began blinking. Wasting no time, Mal bolted from the craft as fast as she could run.

"Go!" she shouted, after bounding through the *Haraka's* open side hatch.

Kumo lifted off and closed the hatch at the same time. The airship had reached fifty feet away when the *Attila's* self-destruct device went off. Everyone watched from the safety above while the Trinilic rods mounted underneath the craft began to glow and sputter orange sparks. Within moments, the Ukko Wood hull of the craft became engulfed in one of the few things which affected it, Etheria fire.

"Alright," Mal said, shaking her head. "One problem solved. Now for the hard part."

Of late, Farrag felt a mixture of being lucky to be alive and safe, along with a profound sense of survivor's guilt. The orange Tiikeri and his small family had been at sea, returning from a holiday, when an Ash-Ta landed on the bow of the recreational ship and told them there was no home for them to return to.

Everything had been taken from them; the empire's three magnificent cities, both he and his wife's extended families, as well as all their friends.

He now took solace in his family's daily walks along the newly expanded boarders of Shun-Dra. He felt it ironic that he considered a city he never had the chance to visit before now his home. The moon had risen only a short while ago and the misty foothills glittered with dew. His pregnant wife, Baarga, walked slowly beside him carrying the child conceived on that fateful holiday, while their young son, Daagar, frolicked just ahead of them.

"Aren't you afraid of being late?" Baarga asked concernedly. "I mean, we did get a bit of a late start this morning."

"I won't be late," Farrag replied. "Besides, it will be hard for them to draw up any kind of charter without their scribe."

"Do you think we as a people can even survive with such few numbers?" Baarga asked genuinely concerned.

Farrag smiled reassuringly, reached out and touched her extended belly. "I'd say we're off to a good start. We'll be safe as long as we stay here. Slowly our ranks will grow, but we have already determined that we will probably never be a nation again."

"Yes, you mentioned that last moonless when you came home. Instead of empire it was…what did you call it?"

"The Order of Kaplan," Farrag said ceremonially. "A rather regal name, don't you think?"

"If we're not going to try and rebuild the empire, what will this Order of Kaplan be?"

"We're sorting that out. The miracle that the Cub Prince is among us has given us real hope for the future. The only thing clear at this point is we must bring about the destruction of the Pa-Waga religion and its followers."

"How do you destroy an idea? I've heard it's taken hold and spreading amongst the humans in Lumina."

Farrag smiled and gazed over at the Kel-Raku Mountains in the distance. "One thing at a time, my dear. One thing at a time."

While her husband stared wistfully into the distance, Daagar spotted movement up ahead. A rabbit crossed the road and slipped into the grassy fields. Young Daagar gave a roar of delight and took off after the hare. The mother gasped in shock. They had lectured the impetuous child about the dangers of straying outside of town.

"Daagar, no!" Baarga called out, which snapped Farrag out of his trance.

"Daagar, get back here this instant!" Farrag scolded.

With the sound of his father's stern tone, the young Tiikeri stopped and spun back to face his parents.

Farrag started to call out again, when his son's body suddenly and silently exploded, showering the waving grass around him in a fine red mist. Baarga screamed in horror and took off running towards the blood-stained grass.

"BAARGA NO!" Farrag yelled in a panic, but the young mother could think of nothing but getting to her son, or what remained of him.

"BAARGA COME BACK, PLEASE!" he screamed just before his wife's torso blew apart, sending her head flying. Her legs remained upright for a brief moment before toppling over, disappearing into the tall, misty grass.

Farrag stood paralyzed in horrified disbelief. He tried to cry out, but no sounds escaped and he became aware of the tears running down his cheeks. He fought the impulse to go to her, realizing that they were gone and certain death waited on the other side of the road where he stood.

Two hundred yards away on the crest of a hill, laying prone in the tall grasses, Okawa took aim on the lone Tiikeri and waited. She had been more than pleased with the Griesbach 200. It proved to be everything the Landagar Group claimed. The range was incredible and the new vertical rail sights made missing all but impossible.

"Come on, you furry bastard," she softly said aloud, while keeping a bead on her target. "Go to them. You know you want to."

When the Valdurian agent heard movement behind her she dropped the rifle and rolled onto her back while drawing her pistol crossbow. She relaxed when she saw Mal standing a few yards away.

"That was some good shooting," the Spice Rat said calmly, walking up to her and sitting down cross-legged beside her.

"Three this morning so far, if you count the pregnant one as two." Okawa said mercilessly.

Mal barely recognized the once beautiful Valdurian. She appeared shockingly thin, with bloodshot eyes sunken into her head and she smelled awful.

"Damn, Okawa, you're a fucking mess! And by the smell of that hole over there you've been shitting in, it's a wonder you haven't been spotted."

"I suppose they sent you to bring me in?" Okawa asked, sitting up.

Mal gave a business-like nod. "More the airship, but yes."

Okawa stared down at the rifle straddling her lap. "So, now what?"

"That's up to you."

"You don't understand!" Okawa said, breaking down and sobbing. "They stole someone from me! Someone good, and decent. One of the few I've met in my life."

Tears now streamed down the agent's face and she could barely choke out the words. "He didn't even swear, can you believe it?! The man wouldn't say shit if his mouth was full of it! I mean... besides my father, he was the only man I've ever loved. Did you know that after the war we were going to move in together? Now... now the only thing that brings me any satisfaction is when I kill a Tiikeri."

"I know how you feel."

"How could you?"

"A few grands ago we lost Alto in the Dark Waste. I thought he was dead. Then last grand my little girl was kidnapped, also in the Dark Waste, rat-men: I was ready to kill all of them. Believe me, I get it."

Okawa's face softened. "I didn't know you had a little girl."

"It's a long story. Look, I'm not going to bring you in, but you can't keep this shit up."

"Wait, you're *not* going to try to bring me in?" Okawa asked, clearly confused.

"Fuck no, we've been through too much shit together. Personally, I don't give two fucks how many of the fleabags you kill, but you're making House Valdur look bad. You gotta look at it from their perspective. You're an asset, just like the equipment you boosted from them to go on this little killing spree.

"The big thing for them was the ship. I set off the self-destruct protocol in the *Attila*. They won't like losing it, but it should appease them knowing it didn't fall into enemy hands. I'll go back and tell them we destroyed it in battle and you died on onboard. It's the perfect opportunity for you to disappear. Go far away, where no one knows you. Start a new life. Allow yourself time to grieve."

Okawa's sobs had changed to sniffles and she patted the rifle. "I grieve by killing Tiikeri."

Mal scoffed loudly. "You can't kill them all!"

"I can try. I've still got plenty of ammo."

"Sure," Mal countered, "but I guarantee, If I go back and tell them I got the ship but not you, and you keep up this wholesale slaughter with Valdurian hardware, they'll put out a contract on you with the Hand of the Wind."

"That might not be so bad," Okawa bemoaned. "I'm not sure I want to go on. Maybe just see what kind of a body count I can rack up until the Hand catches up with me."

"Talk about a colossal fucking waste! Come on, Okawa, no man is worth that! You've already killed a shitload of them. I'd say Demetrius has been well avenged. We've all lost someone dear to us in this war. You're being handed a gift, take it for fuck's sake! Come on, my ship is just behind the next hill over, we'll take you wherever you want to go.

Okawa sat hunched over for a few moments, her tears subsiding while she contemplated Mal's offer. "Anywhere?"

"Anywhere," the Spice Rat confirmed. "Make up your mind quickly. We've got another run to make from the university back here."

"I'm keeping one of the pistols and some ammo," she defiantly acquiesced. "Where *I* want to go, I'm going to need it."

Fine!" Mal compromised. "Keep the pistol. One thing though."

"What?"

"The river is right over there. You've gotta wash your ass before you get on *my* ship."

The moon slowly rose over the triple canopy jungle of the Dasos region in the Land of Mists. The *Haraka* exited from a cloud bank and descended on the multi-colored treetops.

"There should be a break in the jungle about a mile from here," Zau said, pointing to a spot on the three-dimensional map being projected from her eye.

"That's good," Mal replied, staring out at the dense foliage streaking by just below, "because we're sure as shit not going to be able to get through all that mess down there."

The stirring of her nine passengers caused the Spice Rat to peer back into the ship's cabin. The three middle-aged, female Marassas yawned and rubbed their eyes. Two wore the purple robes of Clerria House medical researchers. The other wore the traditional red robes of a senior Marassa from the Etheria Studies Department.

The six-man security team blinked and took in their surroundings. The patch on their arms identified them as part of the newly formed Foreign Protection Detail of the Zorian Guards. A burly sergeant, with a ruddy clean-shaven face and thick arms, led the detachment.

"We're almost there," Mal reported to everyone.

Just as when they boarded, the sight of the *Haraka's* crew took the humans by surprise even though they lived in the most diverse city in the world. It wasn't every day you got to fly, much less with a Singa, a spider creature from another dimension as well as a legendary swordmaster and fixer.

"How close can you get us?" the sergeant asked stepping up to the command chairs and peering apprehensively at the jungle below rushing by.

"Unless there's some serious obstruction, we'll put you down right by the front doors," Mal said confidently.

"Good, I really don't like the idea of humping all those boxes through the bush. Then, if the place is all locked up, we'll have to kick the doors in."

"Nah," Mal said with a smirk. "My kid back there will get you in without having to break anything."

The Zorian Guard stared back at Alto running Taleeka through her knife drills back in the cargo area between the boxes of equipment and provisions. The young girl practiced an intricate knife kata. The blade sliced through the air as she gracefully maneuvered up and back in the tight quarters, all under the swordmaster's watchful eye.

"She sure is something," the sergeant noted, clearly impressed.

"Yeah, she's a handful."

"She looks pretty deadly with that blade," he assessed. "Of course, with her teacher, I'd expect nothing less."

"Who, that bum?" Mal playfully teased.

"You are aware I can hear you, are you not?" Alto spoke up from the rear of the craft.

"Does he always talk like that?" the sergeant asked, nodding towards the swordmaster.

"All the fucking time," Mal replied with a broad grin.

"Okay," Zau alerted, pointing to another small spot on her translucent map projection. "We've got a small clearing coming up here. Kumo, bubby, you might want to slow her down just a bit."

"Slowing," the humanoid spider confirmed meekly.

True to the warning a hundred-foot-wide break in the trees appeared. The *Haraka* stopped over the clearing, hovered for an instant then descended into the thick foliage.

Once on the forest floor, the passengers looked on in amazement when the tint on the airship's windshield changed to orange and the heat signatures in the jungle around them glowed.

"That's some neat trick," the sergeant said appreciatively.

"Courtesy of the research folks over at House Valdur," Mal said, turning her attention to the view in front of them. "It's fairly new. This feature used to be only available with glasses, but it was a pain in the ass taking them on and off.

"Okay, Kumo, there's the trail. Keep it slow and steady. We're a long way from home and we don't need to be running into shit."

"Yes, Captain."

They moved cautiously a few feet above the forest path. Vegetation now encroached upon the once heavily travelled wide avenue.

"And here we are," Zau finally announced, lowering her eye patch which extinguished the map.

The area wasn't open to the sky and a double layer canopy of trees, about fifty feet above the single-story U-shaped structure, covered the large clearing, blocking out the sky.

Much like the trail that led them there, the jungle had rapidly reclaimed the area.

The *Haraka* easily cleared the six-foot-high wrought iron fence and Kumo set the craft down in front of the entrance to a grotto in the center of the once well-manicured courtyard. Breaking in proved to be unnecessary as the double front doors had already been smashed open.

"So, this is the Kharry Institute," Mal said to Zau. "A lot of bad memories from this place I'll bet."

"Too many," the Singa replied woefully.

The side and rear hatches dropped open, and the security team grabbed their crossbows and exited the ship. They fanned out across the grounds, making sure the area was safe for non-combatants. When the sergeant reappeared from the grotto entrance and gave the "all clear" sign, the Marassas began unloading the cartons from the cargo area.

"All right," Mal said when they finished. "We'll be back to get you in a cluster. I hope you find some good shit."

"We're bound to," one of the Marassas said, before the hatch closed. "The Tiikeris, in their own way, were pretty sophisticated."

"Not sophisticated enough to get past their own fucking egos," Mal muttered to Zau once the hatch sealed shut.

It had been three full cycles since Kesis had entered the vision lodge. For the followers of the earth god Toma, having their high priest enter the round structure in the center of their village by himself was hardly a unique event. Staying confined in meditation for this long, however, seemed highly irregular. Still, all had faith in him. For he alone appeased the angry god Elmos when the forest of Zer had been stolen.

By the end of the first full cycle, a few of his clerics had gathered around the lodge's entrance, chanting and watching the smoke trail upward into the skies over Goya from the tiny opening in the top of the structure.

The smoke turned blue on the second cycle and a small crowd had gathered. Now, as the Kan fog set in on cycle number three, the smoke finally stopped and the entire village, except one, crowded around the sacred edifice curiously speculating as to what had transpired.

Young Saghira had better things to do. He sat nude, daydreaming on a grassy hillside overlooking the Zorian waterfront and Narian Bay.

He, as well as all of the followers of the earth god Toma, enjoyed the feeling of the ground against their naked bodies. Clothing would only be worn during the winter. Now in the summer no one wanted anything to get between their bodies and their god.

Saghira didn't need a Vision Lodge to commune with Toma. Why should he need any physical trappings? Even with the few ceremonies he attended in his young life he already had three evergreen sprigs sprouting from the top of his head. Thin and supple, they grew down to his shoulders and proudly swayed when he walked.

Down below, in the harbor, workers rebuilding the Grand Turine had just finished up for the cycle. He hoped they would complete it soon. He missed the sound of the bells tolling across the waves and countryside, dutifully marking the time.

His wishful musings were interrupted by his friend, Lorna. The sun shimmered off the sweat on her golden-brown skin as she bounded excitedly up the hill from the village. He felt a twinge of arousal watching her youthful breasts bounce when she ran.

One day soon, they both would mate for the first time, but it would not take place in the Vision Lodge in accordance with tradition. No, they would take each other under the warmth of the sun, on the fertile ground and in the bosom of Toma.

"Saghira, Saghira," she called out, finally reaching him. "Come quickly, the smoke has stopped!"

She knelt down beside him out of breath and he reached up and ran his hand across her sweat soaked chest.

"Why would I care?" the rebellious young monk said nonchalantly. "Come, lay with me and enjoy the day. The Kan will be upon us soon."

Lorna trapped his hands in between her breasts with both hands. "You saw the blue smoke. This is important, come!"

Standing, she kept hold of his hands and tugged. Saghira reluctantly got to his feet and the two walked back to the village holding hands.

They arrived just as Kesis parted the covering to the lodge's entrance and stepped out into the daylight, followed by a cloud of residual blue smoke. The unnaturally colored fumes enveloped the high priest, causing an excited murmur to pass through the crowd. The geometric patterns painted upon his nude body when he had entered, now ran down his sweat drenched form. His head full of sprigs hung limp against his back down to his waist. He immediately fell to his knees and pressed his forehead on the ground.

"The bosom of Toma," he said, rising back up on his legs and extending his hands into the dirt.

"The bosom of Toma," the crowd chanted their reply.

As usual, Saghira became the first to speak. "What was your vision, Kesis?"

The high priest gave the inquisitive youngster a sad, knowing smile. He accepted the youth's sometimes impetuous attitude.

Saghira's lack of attendance at ceremonies could also be overlooked because of his skill in tending the hives, as well as collecting sacred wax and honey. He worshiped the god in his own way and the sprigs already growing from his head revealed Toma's affirmation.

"Long did I confer with the gods," Kesis said solemnly. "They revealed many things to me, but all of my visions pointed to one thing. The anger of the gods!"

With that ominous statement, a nervous murmur went through the assembly.

"Tell us, what vexes the gods this time?" Saghira's tone bordered on flippant.

"One of their numbers has crossed over and walks among us." Kesis said, ignoring Saghira's inflexion.

"Don't the gods walk amongst us all the time?"

"No," Kesis said, coming to his feet. "The Middle Realms are the home of the gods. They exert their influence through various vessels here in the Annigan. Now, one of them, a god of greed, has stepped into this realm. His actual presence here now makes him the most powerful of all the gods."

"Did they reveal to you what gods are angry?"

Kesis' eyes bore into the brash young man.

"All of them."

Banavor's blood-spattered nude body quivered in excitement and his erection grew so hard it actually felt a bit uncomfortable. This would prove to be his crowning achievement in spreading his lord Pa-Waga's influence across the city, continent and eventually the entire Annigan.

The naked street person dangling lifelessly upside down in front of him had erupted blood when he ceremoniously slit his throat. The bowl beneath his head quickly filled and that was all that mattered.

Banavor dipped his finger in the blood and he traced an X and I on his forehead. He then picked the bowl up and placed it at the feet of Stryder's metamorphosized cat statue.

Backing away, he knelt, lowered his head and began chanting as he masturbated. When he climaxed, several ropy streams of ejaculate arced into the bowl of blood and the crimson liquid began to churn.

Slowly, the blood and semen mixture overflowed the rim of the bowl and pooled around the base of the statue, where it immediately became absorbed. When the vessel finally ran dry, the black humanoid cat statue began to strobe with fields of X's and I's. The very fabric of the statue began undulating and changing shape.

When it stopped, the black statue no longer resembled a humanoid cat but a man in fancy robes with a stern face and scraggly beard. There were three lines of Yassett now engraved in its base.

OLDMAR CALDEN

FOUNDER

3868 P.A.

This would now be taken and placed on the trading floor of the commodities exchange where its prosperous influence would eventually be felt by all.

Zekoff had been gone only a few cycles and his former office seemed all but vacant. An empty desk and bookshelves along with a few chairs and the lingering scent of evergreen were all that remained. Vanir set the box down on the desktop and stroked his red beard while looking around. He almost felt guilty that he would be rearranging his mentor's office he occupied for so long, but Zekoff had his own new office at the university, and he knew they would stay in close contact.

A knock on the open door brought the new Chief Investigator of the Zorian Guards back to the present.

"Just dropped by to see how you were settling in," Rafel said, stepping into the room and gazing around at the spartan appearance.

"Just getting started," Vanir said cheerfully, turning his attention to the open box. "I probably won't be moving any of the furniture around. The rest I'll customize as I go."

Rafel watched with a touch of amusement at Vanir removing a handful of partially filled bottles of whiskey and two tumblers from the box, setting them on a bookshelf behind his desk, within easy reach of his chair.

"Drink much?" the spymaster poked.

Vanir paused and assessed the bottles in front of him.

"Now that you mention it, capital idea! Care to join me in a celebratory snort?"

The Pride and the Fury

GLOSSARY

Spoiler warning: The following is a master glossary for all the books in this series. Reading beyond a specific word or phrase searches could result in spoilers.

Adad Sunal – EEtah war collage belonging to House Bran, specializing in conducting internal security for House Bran.

Agress – A green Etheria Crystal with red striations which opens and closes doors, windows and hatches, negating any locks but not traps or wards.

Aiken – Semi-sentient clouds sent out across the Annigan from Mount Ghas-Tor, recording everything they witness on the ground and in the air. They are indistinguishable from other clouds against the backdrop of a blue sky. Aiken constantly send visuals back to the mountain, but recent images remain in their limited memory. Those possessing psychic abilities can access their recent memories by flying through and communing with them.

Akina – Humanoid fox creatures native to the Barrens in the Twilight Lands. Often sly and excellent thieves.

Amarenian – Female human race formerly noted for their hatred and slavery of men and piracy.

Angona – Roasted eel on a stick. Sold from vendors' carts all over the City of Immor-Onn.

Annigan – The name of the world which is the setting for the various stories in the Tales of the Annigan Cycle. It includes the two hemispheres of Lumina and Nocturn separated by the Twilight Lands.

Anointed Sister – The title for the Amarenian Queen.

Aquamarine – Pale blue Etheria Crystal which reveals something's true nature.

Ara-Fel Party – Political party of Amarenian farmers.

Arapa Fish – A large fish native to the back waters and tributaries of the Otoman River. Their tough scaly skin is coveted among the Dreeat as armor. The scales by themselves are so abrasive they are also sold as nails.

Ash-Ta – Avion term (winged monster) for the widespread colonies of humanoid bats inhabiting the rocky crags stretching across of the Spine of the World. Avion scholars record six tribes: the Molossi, Acero, Chiro, Ptero, Diaemus and Desmodus. The Ash-Ta allied with the Tiikeri due to their shared enemy, the Do-Tarr.

Astute Sister – Amarenian title for high level politician.

Aur-Quaz – Iridescent Etheria Crystal stimulating energy.

Available Regions – Uninhabited areas of Immor-Onn waiting for the residents displaced by the recent Black Pearl Revolution to return and inhabit.

Avion –Proud sentient rulers of Lumina's sky. Incredibly beautiful and graceful to behold and unabashedly elitist, especially towards their distant cousins, the Humans. Avions refuse to wear any armor and yet have led the way in almost every major war fought. Their scholars contributed a great deal to the knowledge of Lumina. Their four Great Houses occupy the airspace and mountain tops of the Goyan Islands.

Avion Great Houses:

House Azar - Avion House inhabiting the City of Mitar, on the Island of Dal, in the Tellasian chain, ruled by Queen Averin. Their territories include the skies over the Tellasian Chain, Otomoria, Zer-Tal Twins, and the Zerk Atoll. They are known for their healing Clerics of Neami and their beautiful music.

373

House Eacher - Avion House inhabiting the Island of Wou, City of Picon & surrounding airspace. Ruled by King Sindil.

House Solas – Smallest of all the Avion houses. They inhabit the city of Adean on the Island of Temil in the Outer Zerians and control the surrounding airspace.

House Pyre - Eldest, largest, and most powerful of all the Avion Houses. They inhabit the skies above the Island of Goya. Their city stronghold, Darmont Keep, sits on the north face of volcanic Mount Goya. Unlike the other Avion Houses who utilize Air Magic, they mastered Fire Magic drawing their power from the volcano.

Awal – First of the ten Quinte Grand Cycle, Spring.

Azurite – Purple Etheria Crystal which connects to the Middle realms.

Bailian – Predominate race of the western Twilight Lands. Descended from the Piceans, they are a beautiful humanoid race with pale blue skin and large eyes.

Banja – The seventy-seven Amarenian noble families, eleven for each of the various seven provinces called Dors.

Banok Atoll – Island ring in the Southeastern Ocean of Lumina housing one of the largest permanent Flavian portals. Its psionic ripples extend out hundreds of miles and affect the entire southeastern Deep Ocean of Lumina.

Banok Run – The final test for admittance to the elite Brightstar Sailors where they must navigate a tight circle around the turbulent seas surrounding the Banok Atoll without being pulled into its giant Flavian portal.

Bespoke Lords – Members of prominent families who have Bespoke Names and serve as advisors to the sovereign in a respective noble human house in the Goyan Islands.

Bespoke Names – Honorary family names only bestowed by a Goyan Island governor or higher as reward for exemplary service to the crown.

Black Mural – A magical record of the Annigan located deep in the Rod-Ema Trench in the Ocean Deep of Nocturn. It slowly grows in size as it records every act of imbalance on the planet. If it grows too large, it will penetrate into the planet's core, killing all life and allowing it to start anew.

Black Talon – Special forces of the Aramos Army, the Fosvara Guard.

Boustian Mage – Bards who perform magic by singing, playing music and storytelling, found predominantly in the larger cities of the Goyodian Chain of islands.

Brightstar – Elite sailors of House Calden qualified to sail the Deep Oceans and the storm-tossed seas of the Twilight Lands. Captains in the Calden Navy must be Brightstar qualified. Brightstar only allows acceptance to their ranks upon completion of the treacherous Innaca or Banok Runs.

Brom – Horse size dragonflies inhabiting the steep southern foothills of the Amaren Mountains.

Calcite – Clear Etheria Crystal which aids in navigation.

Caldani – Privateers hired by Human House Calden to patrol their waters.

Calden Intelligencer Service – House Calden's elite spy agency and secret police. They draw recruits mostly from the Calden Maritime Legion.

Calden Maritime Legion – Marines for House Calden

Calisma – Main library in the University of Marassa.

Cali – Branch libraries and scriptoriums in the five Human capital cities in the Goyodian Island Chain.

Carbana – Chewing tobacco rolled into a tight tube.

Cavernite – A pale green Etheria Crystal with pink striations that can increase the physical dimensions of the interior of any structure it is placed within. The size increase depends on the amount of Cavernite used and the level of PSI used to power it. Without a constant supply of PSI power, the dimensions revert back to their original size. Often used with an Obsidian PSI battery backup.

Centi Elipse – Called a Centi for short. Unit of time in the Goyan Islands equaling a minute.

Celot – Amarenian term for a priestess.

Cevot – Large sentient spider creatures known for their silk, inhabiting the Os-Oni Mountains of the Twilight Lands.

Ched – Seventh of the ten Quinte Grand Cycle, Autumn.

Chanakans – An ancient race of sentient octopoids dwelling in vast underwater cities in the Ocean Deep of Nocturn. They worship the ancient ones of the abyss and practice a powerful water magic.

Cluster – The name for ten cycles, the Annigan's version of a week. There are five clusters to a Quinte (month).

Cobalcite – Deep pink Etheria Crystal used for healing.

Code of Tisina – Mobster code of silence in the City of Zor. Because of Zor's zero tolerance for organized crime, the various independent criminals adopted a "no cooperation" rule with city officials. The slightest violation of this code is punishable by death.

Common – The Common Tongue, a spoken only language used mostly by humans and those in business with them.

Cocoonessa – Cocoon city of the Tinian Moth people on Mount Natal in the Land of Mists. Also called the Silk City.

Corporal Reach, The –The prime material plain of the middle realms where the Annigan resides.

Coxeter – Both the language and magic system of the Tinian race based on a complex form of three-dimensional geometry. The written language is made up of cryptic mathematical notations using lines and dots. Tinian minds perceive all math as the three-dimensional mapping, best displayed in their silk weavings of intricate geometric patterns. When combined with Etheria Crystals, these patterns can be used to perform spells.

Croquis – Magitech mapping devise projecting a scalable three-dimensional holographic image of a desired location, including the other planes of the multiverse.

Cub Prince – A rare black tiger heir to the throne of the Tiikeri Empire. Once every generation, the Tiikeri king must breed an heir. All prominent Tiikeri families offer their most eligible daughters for breeding, but only one will conceive of a black tiger. All other cubs produced from this royal union are killed at birth. They move the complete family of the female who gives birth to the Cub Prince into the palace and considered them nobility. They immediately begin grooming the Cub Prince for the throne, and, when he comes of age, he must kill his father to take it.

Cul-Ta – Humanoid rat creatures found in almost every City in Lumina.

Cycle – Time period equivalent to a day.

Dag – Amarenian term for a common slave. A derogatory slang word for a male.

Darek Witch – Amarenian earth shamans acting as midwives and performing other shamanistic duties.

Darian Silk – High quality silk spun by the Cevot Spiders traded to the On'Dara.

Darwan – A cross between the Balians and the Fudomi, this race is the most prolific humanoid native to the Barrens. They situate their villages around Ghorn temples and must pay tribute to the Onay hordes of the region. Villages close to the borders of the hordes remain under constant threat. Darwans raise a herd animal called the Ng'Ombe which provides the major staple food in the Barrens.

Dasam – Tenth of the ten Quinte Grand Cycle, Winter.

Deci – Time unit equivalent to one hour.

Derde – Third of the ten Quinte Grand Cycle, Spring.

Diamond – Clear Etheria Crystal which transfers power.

Doggin – Derogatory term used for slave dock workers in the city of Aris.

Dolin – Etheria gem hunters, mostly of the Gila race, traveling the Barrens in small caravans and harvesting raw Etheria Crystals to sell to the Zadim lapidaries of the Oasis in the Dark Waste Desert.

Dor – Title of the seven various provinces in Amarenia. Taia-Dor, Denat-Dor, Mivira-Dor, Amoso-Dor, Kinning-Dor, Rackam-Dor, Durik-Dor.

Do-Tarr – Sentient, hive-minded mantid creatures from the Land of Mists in Nocturn. They comprise two large hives in the north and south with precise subterranean tunnels connecting them. They are expert builders and remain neutral in all forms of politics.

Dreamer in the Lake – Demi-God of the Os'Tor Forest and a Harbinger of Balance. She rests at the bottom of a large lake encased in mud and manifests herself on the lake's surface as a multicolored lotus. Her accolades, sentients from every race, sleep around the lake's shore, sending their ethereal bodies out into people's dreams and guiding them.

Dreeat – Humanoid crocodilians inhabiting the end of the western fork of the Otoman River in Otomoria. They grow sugar cane and make magical healing candies from it. They harvest river fish as a major part of their diet. For thousands of grands, ever since the arrival Human race, the Human families have tried to eradicate them.

Dronning Mare – Female horse chosen to breed with the On'Dara chief.

EEtah – Large, powerful and aggressive sentient humanoid shark creatures trained in martial schools known as Sunals to become the professional warriors of Lumina. After their egg birth in the hatcheries and their first year in the nursery, they are sorted into one of the various Sunals of their House. Females enter House Nur and the males go through a highly competitive Sunal scouting and recruiting process with the nursery's called the Garess. Sunals hire out bodyguards, sentries, mercenaries and virtually anything martial. This, along with weapon manufacturing and sales, provides the main revenue stream for the great houses.

EEtah Great Houses:

>   **House Nur** – This Noble house is female only. Co-ruled by a secular Queen Mother and spiritual High Priestess.
>   >   Temple of Drulain headquartered in the High Holy City of Zor.
>   >   Specialty: Scribes, Clerics, Healers, Politics, Domestics.

>   **House Crom** – Three Sunals in the Tellasian Chain.
>   >   Sedar Sunal on Roe Island. Specialty: Bodyguard.
>   >   Boril Sunal on Uma Island. Specialty: Crom Internal Security.
>   >   Zorod Sunal on Tel Island. Specialty: Castle and Town Defense.

>   **House Bran** – Four Sunals in the Goyodian Chain.

Garf Sunal on Quell Island. Specialty: Long term inland duty.

Tukk Sunal on Mobis Island. Specialty: Shipboard Security.

Adad Sunal on Creos Island. Specialty: Bran Internal Security.

Farak Sunal on Roust Island. Specialty: Bounty Hunter, Vengeance.

House Zed – Three Sunals in the Wouvian Islands.

Dakor Sunal on Owling Island. Specialty: Shock Troops.

Jut Sunal on Tor Island. Specialty: Zed Internal Security.

Morrak Sunal on Billow Island. Specialty: Police, Executioners.

Elipse – A unit of time equaling a second.

Ellie – Slang and abbreviation for an Ellipse.

Esteemed Sister – Amarenian title for Ambassador.

Etheria Crystal – Crystals containing magical properties mostly found in crystal trees in the Barrens of the Twilight Lands. Residents of the Dark Waste Desert harvest and process the oases' crystals. These crystals provide the primary form of magic in Nocturn.

Flavian Portals – Portals through space making different points in the Annigan instantaneously accessible by passing through the inter-dimensional Middle Realms. Each portal is different. There are several large, fixed portals on both Lumina and Nocturn and hundreds of smaller dedicated Flavians. Certain animals, intoxicants and magical items can open smaller portals.

Frozen Sea – The vast expanse of ice flows covering the majority of Nocturn and the largest centrally occupied area in all of Annigan. The ice ranges from a slushy mixture with icebergs near the land masses to several hundred feet thick in the eastern areas.

Forsvara Guards – A rank-and-file foot soldier army of House Aramos.

Fudomi – Sentient humanoid ram creatures inhabiting the western Os-Oni Mountains of the Twilight Lands. They steal and sell the Cevot Spider broods' silk and eggs, which they consider a delicacy.

Galeb – Sea Gulls with a psychic connection to a handler. They are used to transport messages across Lumina.

Garf Sunal – EEtah War college belonging to House Bran. Their specialty is long term inland duty.

Gar-Kal – Fish head humanoids living on the ocean floor of Nocturn. They are of low intelligence and aggressive.

Geta – Amarenian title for a master at a skill or craft, especially if they teach it.

Ghas-Tor – This is the tallest peak on the Annigan. It reaches upward 32,000 feet in the Os'Ani Mountain range of the Twilight Lands. More than a mountain, it is a sentient being and the epicenter of Air Magic in the world.

Ghorn – Necromancers of the Barrens in Twilight Lands.

Ghost Suit – A gray, skintight jump suit used mostly by Valdurian forces to blend into the Kan fog.

Ghosts of the Kan – Mariner's term for Rayth raiders. Due to their ghost white chalk covering their bodies and acting as camouflage when they attack during the Kan fog.

Gila – The main sentient race populating the Dark Waste. Hybrids comprising Bailian pilgrims and a now long-gone sentient lizard native to the region. They are an advanced race occupying the three large oases of the desert.

Golden One, The – Otick term for the Golden Avatar.

Goy-Ardia – Goyan fire mages trained at the University of Marassa.

Goyan Calendar – Method of time keeping found only in the Goyan Islands. It consists of a Grand Cycle (year) which is comprised of ten Quinte (months) named; Awal, Teine, Derde, Kvara, Peto, Sesto, Ched, Merve, Tisa and Dasam. Each Quinte is divided into fifty Cycles (days) with each cycle being divided into fifty Deci (hours) twenty-five in sunlight and twenty-five in Kan. Ten cycles equal a Cluster (week) with five Clusters per Quinte.

Goyan Rise – A 300-mile-wide sea mount in central Lumina acting as the floor of the Shallow Sea. Its volcanic vents fuel the volcano of Mount Goya.

Grand – Short for Grand Cycle. Unit of time equivalent to a year.

Grass Eater – Singa insult

Gustare' – Amarenian bath house and tavern.

Hackney – Etheria driven floating carriages found throughout the major cities of Lumina.

Hand of the Wind – The Assassin's Guild of Annigan. All members worship Orad, goddess of death. The upper levels are clerics of Orad.

Hakim – A judge in the High Holy City of Zor.

Harbingers of Balance – Sentient creatures of all types called to a secret society monitoring the balance of the Annigan and warning when something upsets it.

Hasteen – City of the Dreeat crocodile people.

Hill Sister – Hermaphroditic warriors inhabiting the northern foothills of the Amaren Mountains in Amarenia. Though they possess both male and female sex organs, they cannot procreate. Popular with Amarenian nobility as seneschal/bodyguards partly because they can have sex with them and not violate their "no man" pledge.

Hoon – Word used in Zor to denote a pimp or the manager of a brothel.

Howlite – Gray Etheria Crystal used for glamour, disguise and polymorphing.

Humans – The Human race descended from the Avion race. In 5070 PA, the rebellious Avions which joined Xandar the Mad's doomed Great Kraken Incursion had their wings severed as punishment before being banished and scattered to the Goyodian Chain. 171 years later the Seventh Avatar sang the "Song of Rebirth" evolving them into a separate race. They formed their Great Houses, spreading out across the Goyan Island Chain and beyond the Shallow Sea.

Human Great Houses:

House Aramos –The largest and wealthiest of the great human families directly descended from the First Men. The capital city of Aris is located on the Island of Vakai in the Goyodian Chain of Islands in the Northern Shallow Sea. They control banking and finance in Lumina and constantly hatch Machiavellian plots to expand their power over the other houses.

House Calden – This great house controls the seas with the largest military and commercial fleets. Their Capital City of Nader is on the Island of Tarla in the Goyodian Chain, but they command the island chain of the Zerk Atoll where their sailors are trained.

House Eldor – This great house controls virtually all the agricultural islands of the eastern Goyan Islands. Their Capital City of Rophan is on the Island of Tolle in the Goyodian Chain of Islands in the Northern Shallow Sea.

House Valdur – This house is known for their incestuous practices to keep the family bloodline pure. Their capital city of Dryden is on the Island of Atar in The Goyodian Chain of Islands in the Northern Shallow Sea. All but destroyed in a surprise invasion by House Eldor called the Unification War, only the discovery of lighter than air travel and a fleet of war balloons saved their home island. They lost the rest of their agricultural lands to Eldor. Their entire culture revolves around their powerful air guild, the Valdurian Air Service.

House Whitmar – This family runs the organized and sanctioned slave trade on Lumina from the City of Nier on the northern Goya coast. Their Capital City of Brinstan is located on the Island of Umin in the Goyodian Chain in the Northern Shallow Sea.

Immor-Onn – Large city known as "the Shining Jewel of the East" located on the western coast of the Twilight Lands. Home of the Bailian Empire.

Idonian Philosophy – The Avion prejudice that Humans are a scourge which should be wiped out. The driving belief of the Idonian Cabal of Avion House Pyre and Solas.

Innaca Deep – Giant whirlpool in the Northwestern Ocean of Lumina housing one of the largest Flavian portals. Its psionic ripples extend out hundreds of miles.

Innaca Run – The final test for admittance to the elite Brightstar Sailors where they must navigate a tight circle around the turbulent seas surrounding the Innaca Atoll without being pulled into its giant Flavian portal.

Ironmark – Brutal enforcers of the Quartermasters in the Goyan Islands of Lumina. Each island chain has their own Ironmark specializing in their own unique form of torture.

Itori – Insect Shamans found throughout the agricultural western Goyan Islands. Although they control mostly locusts, they can command any insect and are immune to all insect venoms and stings.

Jangwa – Elite desert commandos defending the outer parameter of the two civilized oases in the Dark Waste Desert. Capable of traveling under the sand and rapidly over the surface of the desert, they make frequent scouting missions to the untamed Qua-Raman Oasis and the Buried City of Nof-Saloom.

Kaefom – Traditional Amarenian breeding ritual overseen by the Darek Witches.

Kan – Period of the day in the Goyan Islands when the thick sea fog rises blotting out the sun, used mostly for sleep. It is an effect caused by geothermal activities only found in the Goyan Islands and Shallow Sea.

Kel – Flying lizards bred and tended by Avions for food and as beasts of burden.

Kharry Institute – Tiikeri medical facility located outside the Tiikeri capital city of Hai-Darr and run by the brilliant and ruthless Dr. Met-Ge, specializing in crossbreeding Mawl races to produce Mongrels for specific duties. The Institute created Cheepas and the Ves-Lari.

Kinjuto Dominator – Sex mage using BDSM techniques.

Konaleeta – Called the Island of the Lost. The entire island is caught in a permanent Flavian Loop. It bounces around from location to location across any of the planes of the Middle Realms, never staying in anyone place for very long.

Kusars – Mawl bandits from the Dasos region in the Land of Mists.

Kvara – Fourth of the ten Quinte Grand Cycle, Summer.

Ky-Awat – Sentient rat creatures of the Dark Waste Desert. They have bred them up from the Cul-Ta and are larger and more aggressive, but no smarter. Various factions use them as cannon fodder. They breed quickly and are plentiful, especially around the three main oases.

Land of Mists – The largest land mass in Nocturn. So named because the mixture of cold temperatures in the air combined with the warmth of the ground results in a uniform constant low hanging fog over the entire continent. Three distinct landscapes cover the surface of the land, separated by the Kel-Raku Mountain range and dimly illuminated by bioluminescence, outcroppings of Etheria Crystals and the moon and stars. The thick rainforest of Arboro lies to the north, and the vast savannah of Rovina runs to the south. They're connected by the Bor-Kaa Pass. The dense jungles and swamps of Dasos lie to the east.

Landagar Group – Research and Development Division of the Valdurian Air Service located in the balloon city of Landagar high in the mountain peaks of the Valdurian home island of Atar.

Larimar – The "Talking Stone," a milky white Etheria Crystal with blue striations, used for psychic communication between parties within proximity of the gem.

Learned Sister – The title given to Amarenian teachers, scribes & academics.

Legates – Suicide messengers hired through House Whitmar. Candidates are usually elderly or terminally ill. Upon their death, House Whitmar agrees to care for their surviving family for their remaining lifetimes.

Lor-Danta Oasis – The eastern most major oasis in the Dark Waste Desert. The large Obsidian field stretching from its shore contains six Tanum Charts of the skies used by the Arron-Nin Astrologers dwelling there.

Lumina – The hemisphere of the world in constant sunlight.

Luna – Term for the lunar cycle used by every culture in the Annigan except the humans in the Goyan Islands, who cannot see the moon.

Luroh – Bolo/sash weapon used by the Mahilia. The sash contains the person's rank and record. The two metal balls at either end become an effective weapon when twirled.

Magitech – The fusion of magic and technology. Mostly referring to the use of Etheria Crystals and specific mechanical items. i.e., Airship engines.

Mahilia – City guards in Mostar, the capital of Amarenia.

Makari – Inter-dimensional race of sentient spiders from the Pasture Plain of the Middle Realms. They seeded the Cevot race in the Os'Tor Mountains in the Land of Mists. The males resemble hairy wolf spiders, the females resemble black widows. The females have been known to allure any male of any race. They compulsively kill after sex.

Malachite – Light green Etheria Crystal, absorbs energy.

Marassa – A professor at the University of Marassa.

Masha – Amarenian for master.

Maudo Grass – Tall grass with a bright blue flowering tuft growing in the Land of Mists. The flowers are a favorite intoxicant for Mawls and especially coveted by the Tiikeri.

Mawl – Overall name for the humanoid cat races of the Land of Mists. It is also the term used for the common language they share.

Medikua – Medical officer aboard Calden naval vessels.

Merve – Eighth of the ten Quinte Grand Cycle, Autumn.

Middle Realms – Constantly shifting inter-dimensional plane between worlds. Sometimes referred to as the Fairy or Dream Realms.

Mongrel – The product of cross breeding between the Mawl races found all over the Land of Mists. Pure breeds mostly shun them and the Tiikeri use them for slave labor.

Moonfall – Period of the cycle when Nocturn's main illuminating body, the moon, dips below the horizon issuing in the Moonless

Moonless – The "night" period of the cycle when Nocturn's main illuminating body, the moon, orbits around to the Lumina side of the Annigan.

Mora – Term used for teacher or master in the Whovian Sword Schools of Rohina Takki.

Morasian Puff Boy – Male prostitute from the Port City of Moras on Goya's west coast. Known for their distinctly feminine demeanor.

Mostas – Capital City of the Amarenian Empire on the western shore of Amarenia.

Najuka – Amarenian emasculation ritual performed on all males except those used for breeding purposes in the Kaefom Ritual.

Na-Kab – One of the three insectoid groups originating from below the Land of Mists. They occupied the easternmost hive closest to Mount Natal. Their exoskeleton is made up of fire magic. Their tail has a penis shaped stinger capable of impregnating any living thing they sting.

Namesake – Term used for spouse when they share a bespoke last name.

Narrows, The – Remnants of an old iron mine forming the slums of the Hidden City of Toriss in Otomoria.

Nocturn – The hemisphere of the world in constant night

Nolton Boat – Ships made of Ukko wood in a secret shipyard on the Island of Zer, mostly used by Brightstar sailors. Hovering less than an inch above the water, their Ukko rudder guides and propels. The specific construction of the hull makes the boat unsinkable.

Noma – Poison from the Noma Viper.

Nurian Edicts – EEtah rules of conduct set down by House Nur forming the basis for all Sunal laws. The various Sunals add their own individual laws to this baseline.

Nyanja – Large seahorses ridden as sea cavalry by the Calden Navy.

Obsidian – Black Etheria Crystal storing psychic energy.

Ocean Deep – Name referring to any of the deep oceans of Lumina or Nocturn.

Ol'daEE – Person able to cast spells while having sex under the influence of Oldust.

Oldust – Hallucinogenic powder derived from the spores of the rare Impia Mushroom, increasing magical abilities and is essential for individual travel to the Middle Realms.

Onay – Humanoid wolf men of the Barrens, banding their various packs together in three distinct hordes.

On'Dara – Sentient horse creatures living on the Plains of Taka-Vir in the southeastern Twilight Lands. They raise and train horses, trading them for silk with the Cevot Spiders and selling them to the rest of the Annigan.

ooD – Shell worn on the back of the male Otick warriors as armor. They mark the warrior's rank and house on the outside of the shell and inscribe a record of their deeds on the inside. They place the ooD over the entrance to their homes in the sand.

Oracle of the River – Demi-God who dwells in the cypress swamp at the end of the western fork of the Otoman River for thousands of grands. It appears as a partially submerged giant catfish with its many whiskers sunken into the water. These whiskers perceive anything happening in, on, or around the waterway.

Orad – Air goddess of death and predominate deity of the assassin's guild, the Hand of the Wind. Her creed: *She comes as the wind. And takes whom she wishes. Her name is Orad. And she is death.*

Orad Dex – Initiates to the Orad priesthood. Street/entry level assassins.

Orad Con – (Taker of the Divine Wind) These are full priests of Orad. Their special skills are the Kiss of Death, the Poison Breath and the Phantom Dagger.

Orad Sto – (Giver of the Divine Wind) High priests of Orad who can also restore life.

Otick – Humanoid crab people inhabiting the Shallow Sea. Among the first sentient creatures to rise from the ocean floor they evolved into a proud, deeply spiritual and noble race. Goya's volcanic warmed waters provide home to the Otick's prolific oyster beds littering the floor of the Shallow Sea. From these beds arose the five great Pearl Avatars, creation gods whose songs brought life and sentience to Lumina. Otick society is divided into a highly structured caste system: Worker Class, Warrior Class and Mother Class, and organized into two main categories: domestic and military. The Shelled Triad, the three Otick Great Houses, tend their own oyster beds and compete for the birthplace of the next Avatar.

Otick Great Houses:

> **House Awa** – Home of the last two avatars. Located in the Tellasian Chain, in the capital city of Hidet on the Island of Zod. Mother Class specialization.

> **House Pewa** – Located in the Goyodian Chain, in the capital city of Oniack, on the Island of Zak. Worker Class specialization.

> **House Sensu** – Located in the Otoman Group, in the capital city of Sunico, on the Island of Lakia. Warrior Class specialization.

Otomoria – Large Island continent in the western Goyan Islands. The main grain producing agricultural island.

Outer Clan EEtah – Humanoid shark creatures smaller in stature than regular EEtahs and cast out from the three great EEtah Houses hatcheries. The survivors band together into loose clans, contracting themselves out as deck hands or recently volunteering in the Valdurian Marines.

Padi – Regional demi-god of water worshiped in and around the High Holy City of Zor, associated with the peace and calming effect of water and represented by a calm pond.

Palu EEtah – Rare hammerhead EEtahs. They are as big as the Outer Clan EEtah but extremely intelligent. They tend to be reclusive loners.

Pappia – Members of the child street gangs of the Hidden City of Toriss in the slum section of The Narrows.

Pa-Waga – Lawful evil god of greed worshiped mostly by the Tiikeri. Its clerics practice binary blood rune magic comprised of the letters "X" and "I."

Peace Babies – Children born of a union between any of the five major Human noble houses.

Peto – Fifth of the ten Quinte Grand Cycle, Summer.

Piceans – Humanoid fish people of Lumina. Capable of breathing above and below the water and impervious to the ocean's depths. They have gill flaps large enough to fold over their ears and when the vocal sound waves pass through the membrane, it translates it. This makes them valuable translators in the seaports of the Goyan Islands.

Piety Watch – Militant, religious police faction of the Pa-Waga church. They arrest anyone caught begging, idle, or not being productive. Minor offences are punished by a beating with thin cane rods. They wear red shirts under black capes with high pointed collars resembling cat ears.

Pisar – Bailian title for a scholar.

Pomaku – Humanoid leopard people (Mawl) native to the Arboro region in the Land of Mists, Nocturn.

Protocol 13 – EEtah House Nur code phrase requesting a meeting between an intelligence asset and their handler.

Qua-Raman Oasis – An oasis in the central Dark Waste Desert. Due to its location just south of the Tur-Qua Pass, it serves as a major trading post for gems harvested in The Barrens to the north.

Quartermaster – Collector of taxes and tariffs in the Goyan Islands who use the Ironmark to enforce their rule.

Queen's Envoy Service, The – The Amarenian Empire's spy service and member of the Society of Whispers.

Quinte – Time period equivalent to a month.

Ramu – A gambling dismemberment game banned everywhere in Lumina, except the Free City of Tannimore.

Rayth – Pirate faction of the Amarenian people in open revolt and attempting to form their own nation.

Rod-Ema Trench – Massive abysmal fissure running along the equator in the western ocean floor in Nocturn. At its head is the Agar Goyot and the Black Mural is found on its north wall dipping into the ocean depths.

Rohina Takii – Sword school originating on the Island of Wou. Known for its strike while drawing technique.

Sardor – Amarenian title for a female warlord.

Salar Winds – Turbulent winds surrounding the peak of Mount Goya which must be navigated to enter the Avion City of Darmont on the mountain's northwestern face. Avion term of exasperation, "By the mighty Winds of Salar!"

Secor – Street name for the Imperial Gold Ingot equivalent to ten struck gold coins.

Sesto – Sixth of the ten Quinte Grand Cycle, Autumn.

Shallow Sea – The body of water surrounding the greater Goyan Islands covering the Goyan Rise. The depth is no more than thirty feet deep at its lowest point.

Si – The term for "mister" in the Common Tongue spoken in the Goyan Islands.

Sikari – Female Singa hunter/killer squads, traveling in groups of two or more. They arm themselves with crossed bandoleros covering their chests and filled with sickle shaped throwing blades.

Silent Partner – Seven cabals of organized crime families in the Goyan Islands.

Simikort – Round engraved coin acting as an Amarenian noble's calling card.

Singa – Humanoid lion people (Mawl) inhabiting the southern Rovina area of the land of Mists.

Skirting the Upwinds – Dangerous maneuver practiced by few airship pilots. It involves taking the airship up to the edge of the atmosphere and then plummeting down to your destination. Allowing long-distance travel in a short period.

Society of Whispers – The general intelligence cooperative of the five Human noble houses, the Zorian Spymaster, the Calden Intelligencer Service, Suusho, and the Queen's Envoy Service.

Spice Rat – Smugglers operating in the Spice Islands chains (Zerian Reef Chain and Outer Zerians) and occasionally in the entire western side of the Goyan Islands.

Spooks – Street term for spies and operatives in the Society of Whispers.

Strasta – Ancient prophet in the folklore of the Cevot spider people of the Os-Ani Mountains.

Sunal – EEtah war college specializing in martial skills.

Suusho – The Bailian Empire's spy service and member of the Society of Whispers.

Szoldos Mercenaries – One of several small private armies for hire on the Goyan continent.

Taking it Upstairs – Airship slang for skirting upwinds

Tanum Charts – Six maps of Nocturn's night sky. The Arron-Nin Astrologers use them for divination and sometimes the opening of Flavian portals.

Teine – Second of the ten Quinte Grand Cycle, Spring.

Ten/Fifty— Cliché phrase in the Goyan Islands referring to the ten cycles (days) in the cluster (week) and fifty decis (hours) of the cycle (day). The equivalent of 24/7.

Tenable Sister—Title given to Amarenian lawyers.

Tiikeri – Sentient humanoid Tiger creatures of the Dasos region in the eastern Land of Mists.

Tisa – Ninth of the ten Quinte Grand Cycle, Winter.

Trinilic – Orange Etheria Crystal, fire magic connection.

Turine – Tidal clocks used in the Goyan Islands.

Twilight Lands – Area between Lumina and Nocturn in constant state of Twilight. Due to converging hot and cold air masses its weather remains perpetually stormy.

Ukkonite – Bronze Etheria Crystal with natural repellant properties. It is the crystal equivalent to Ukko wood found only in Nocturn.

Ukko Wood – Magical wood from the World Tree, harvested only on the Island of Zer in the eastern Goyan Islands. Its natural repellant properties are used in shields, weapons, Brightstar Nolton Boats and used as currency.

Ulana – Chaotic evil sea goddess worshiped by a small sect of Amarenian Rayth in the province of Durik-Dor

Unification War – Conflict started by House Eldor in 2 P.A. against the eastern agricultural islands of House Valdur. It ended as quickly as it began when House Aramos forced them to the negotiating table by threatening to freeze both houses' accounts in the Imperial Bank.

Valorous Sister – Amarenian title for heroic acts which affected the realm.

Vedette – Small fast Nolton Boats crewed by a single ex-Brightstar sailor and used for fast, anonymous travel around the oceans of Lumina.

Velocomite – Pale blue Etheria Crystal with red bands, increases or decreases an object's speed travelling.

Veros Pearls – Highest quality pearl cultivated in the Otick oyster beds. They are capable of holding a magical charge.

Ves-Lari – Mawl mongrels bred by the Tiikeri for rowing and poling. They are a combination of Pomaku (leopard) and Duma (Cheetah). Crews can pole or row for hundreds of miles at a time without stopping.

Vurr Carts – Carts used by the Vurr Clerics to collect the City of Zor's dead and garbage. There are two types: stationary carts situated on every major street where citizens can deposit their waste and roving carts mostly dealing with collecting the bodies of the dead.

Vurr Clerics – Accolades of the Free God Vurr serving as waste disposal in the City of Zor. Once maintaining constantly pyres burning everything from corpses to ordinary refuse. The city upgraded the pyres to full crematoriums. Vurr clerics smell of smoke and generally work nude, wearing only a simple cloak.

Wraith – Deep cover agents for House Aramos drawn from the elite Black Talons unit.

Yagur – Humanoid jaguars (Mawl) from the Arboro region of the Land of Mists. They are seers, healers and shamans, serving all the various Mawl races.

Yudon – Harpoon with a rifled the shaft for throwing accuracy. The standard weapon of every Sunal EEtah.

Yupik – a.k.a. the Ice Clans, one hundred and sixty-five clans divided into three major groups. The nomadic wanderers of the Western Flows compete for resources while the Ash-Ta constantly hunt them as prey. The largest group inhabits the vast Eastern Flows with semi-permanent settlements surrounding the Ice City of Mos-Agar'.

Zadim – Lapidaries operating in the Dark Waste Desert.

Zerian Rangers – Woodsmen fighters belonging to any of nine different clans occupying the forests of the Island continent of Zer in the Goyan Islands.

Zoldak Group – A private mercenary army comprised of former Black Talons of House Aramos.

Zorian Monetary Council – A ruling body founded in 3850 P.A. controlling all banking in the High Holy City of Zor. The council coordinates with the Calden Commodities exchange to regulate the exchange of money, goods and services, and uses the Quartermasters Guild for the collection of taxes and tariffs.

MAPS

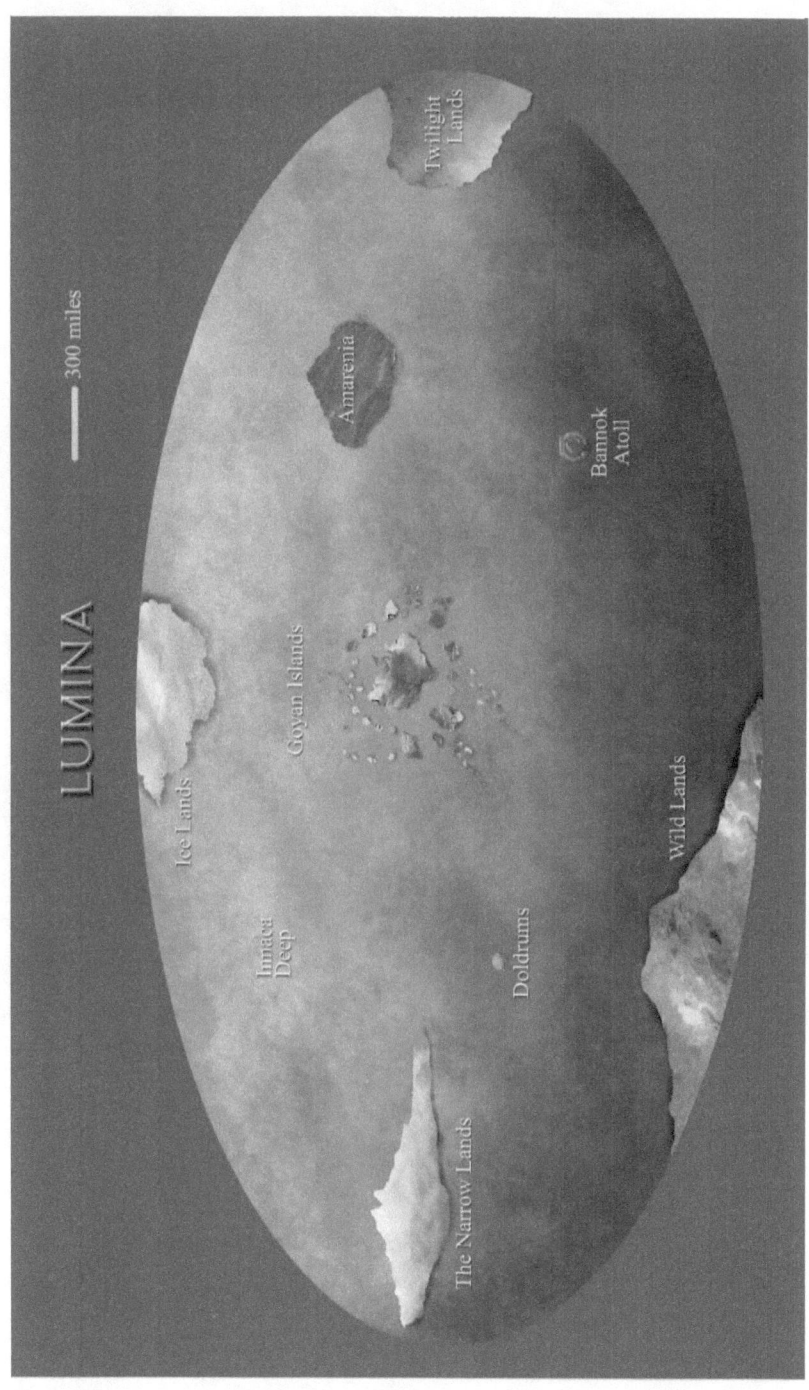

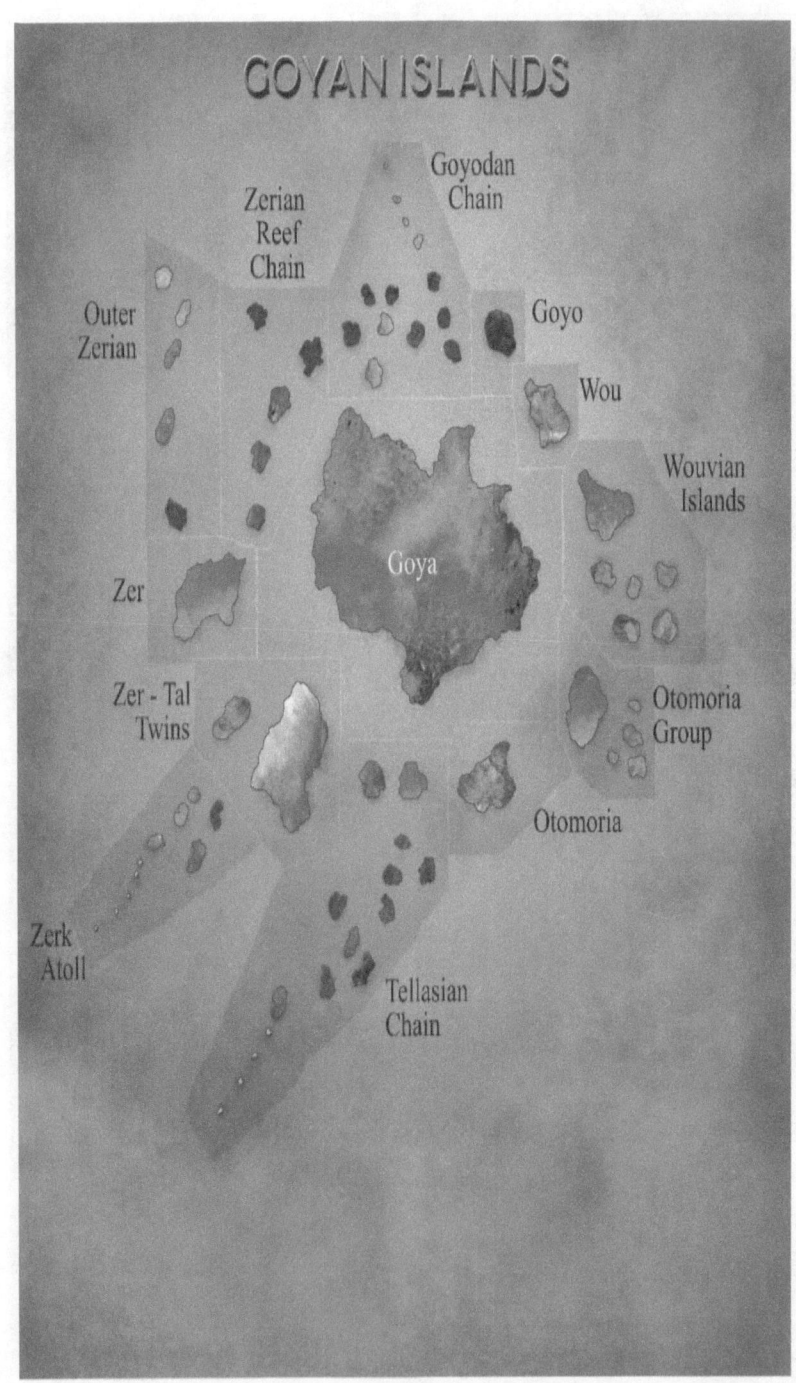

GOYAN ISLANDS

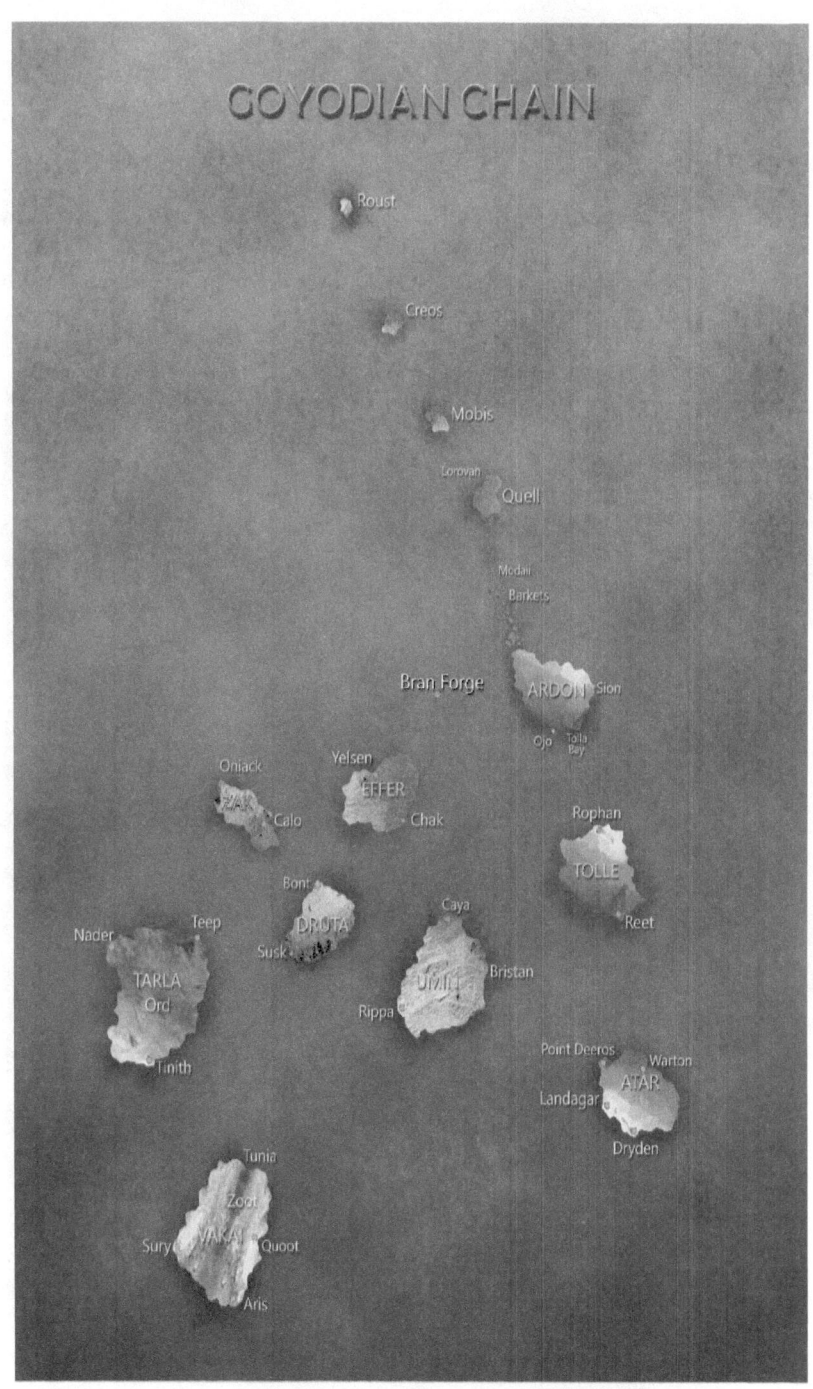

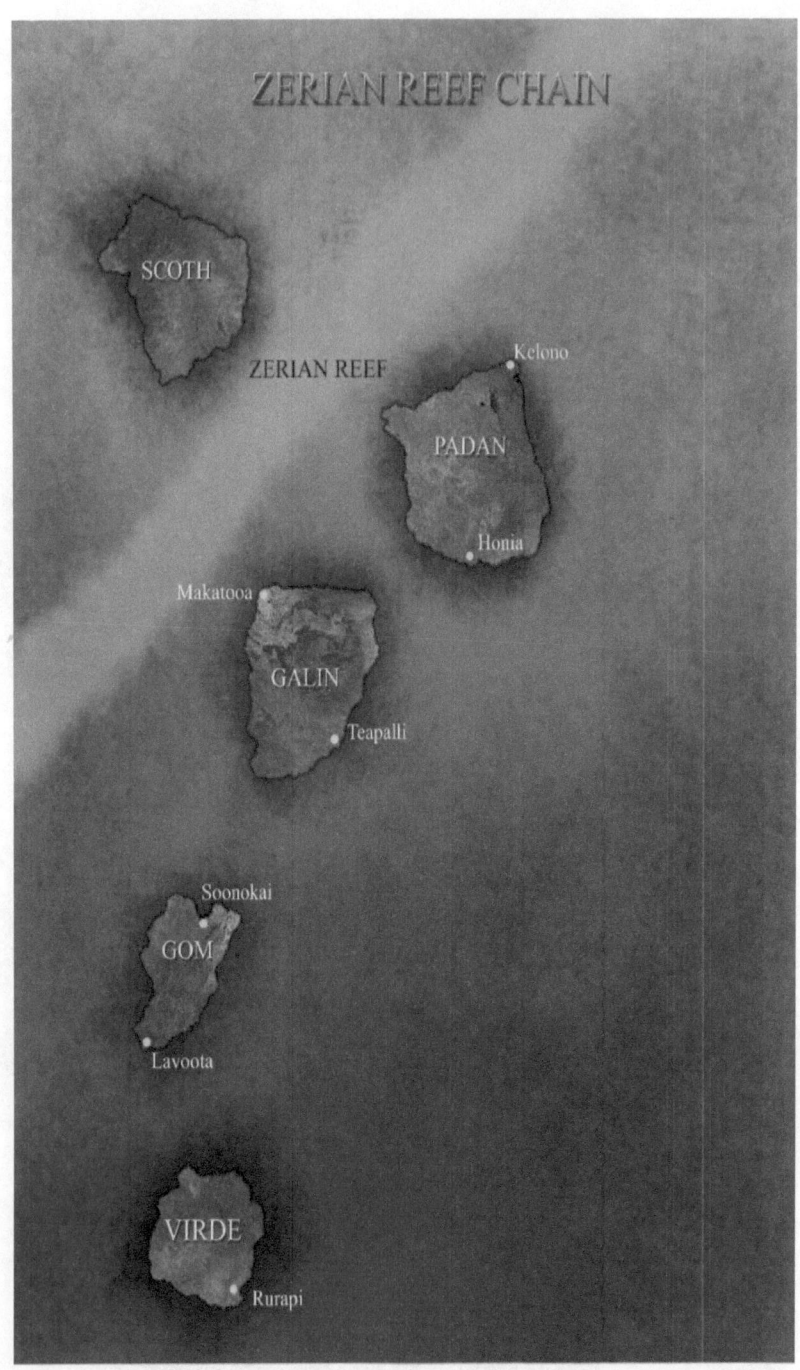

ZERIAN REEF CHAIN

SCOTH

ZERIAN REEF

Kelono

PADAN

Honia

Makatooa

GALIN

Teapalli

Soonokai

GOM

Lavoota

VIRDE

Rurapi

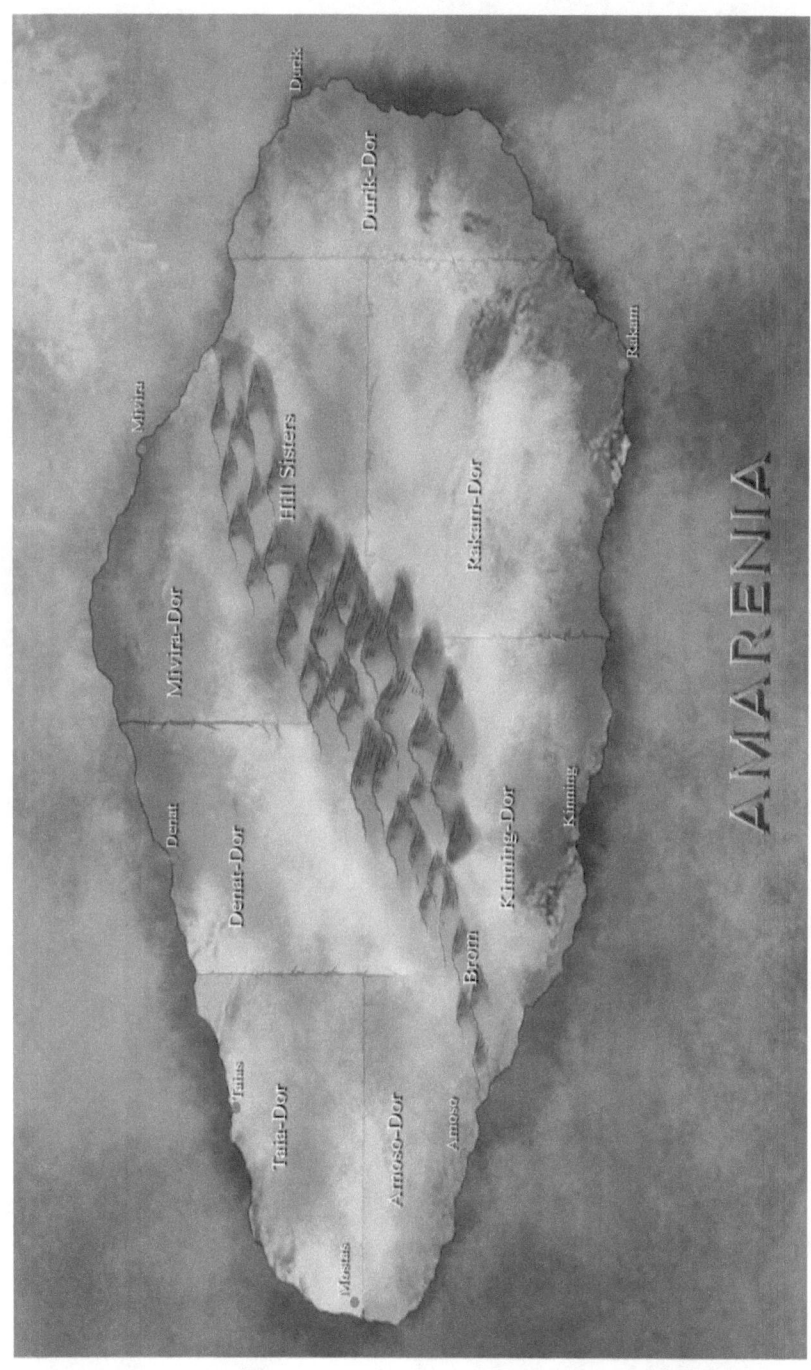

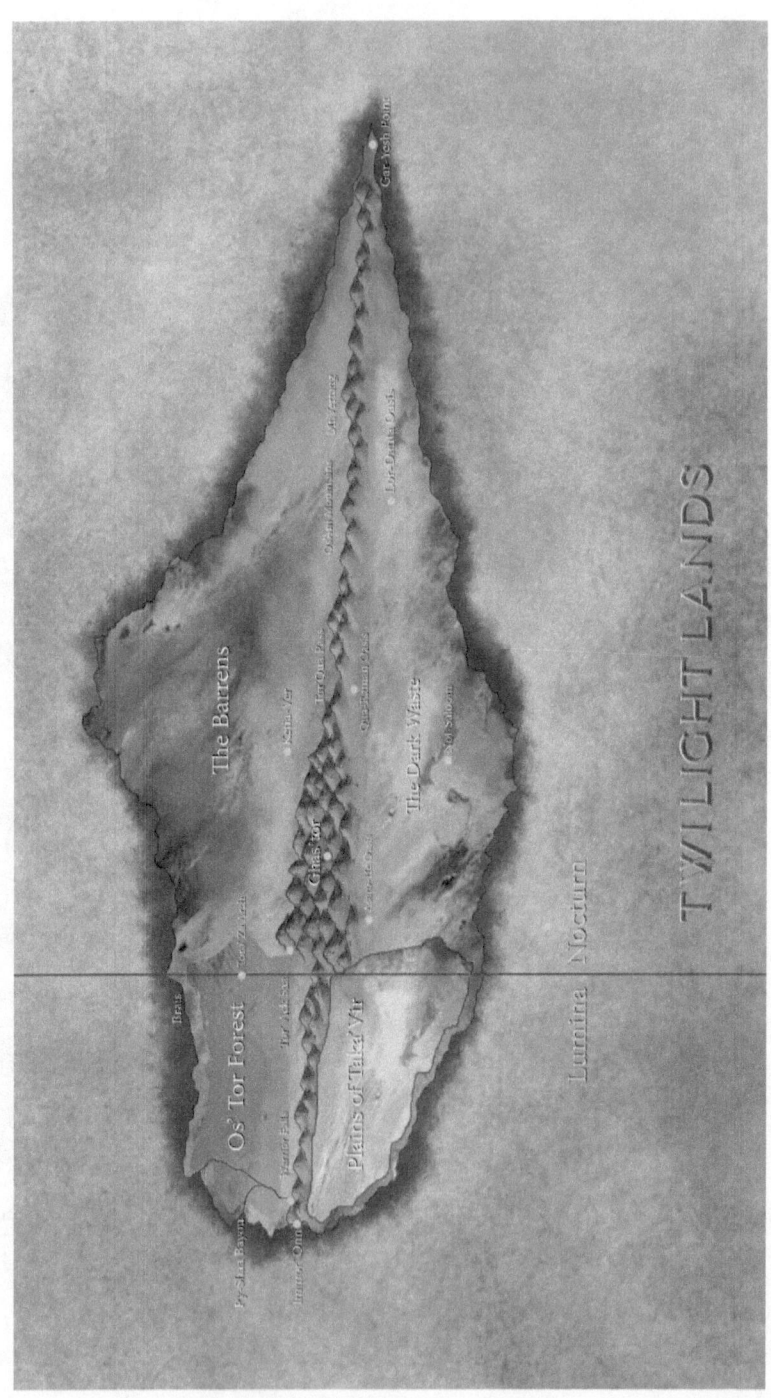

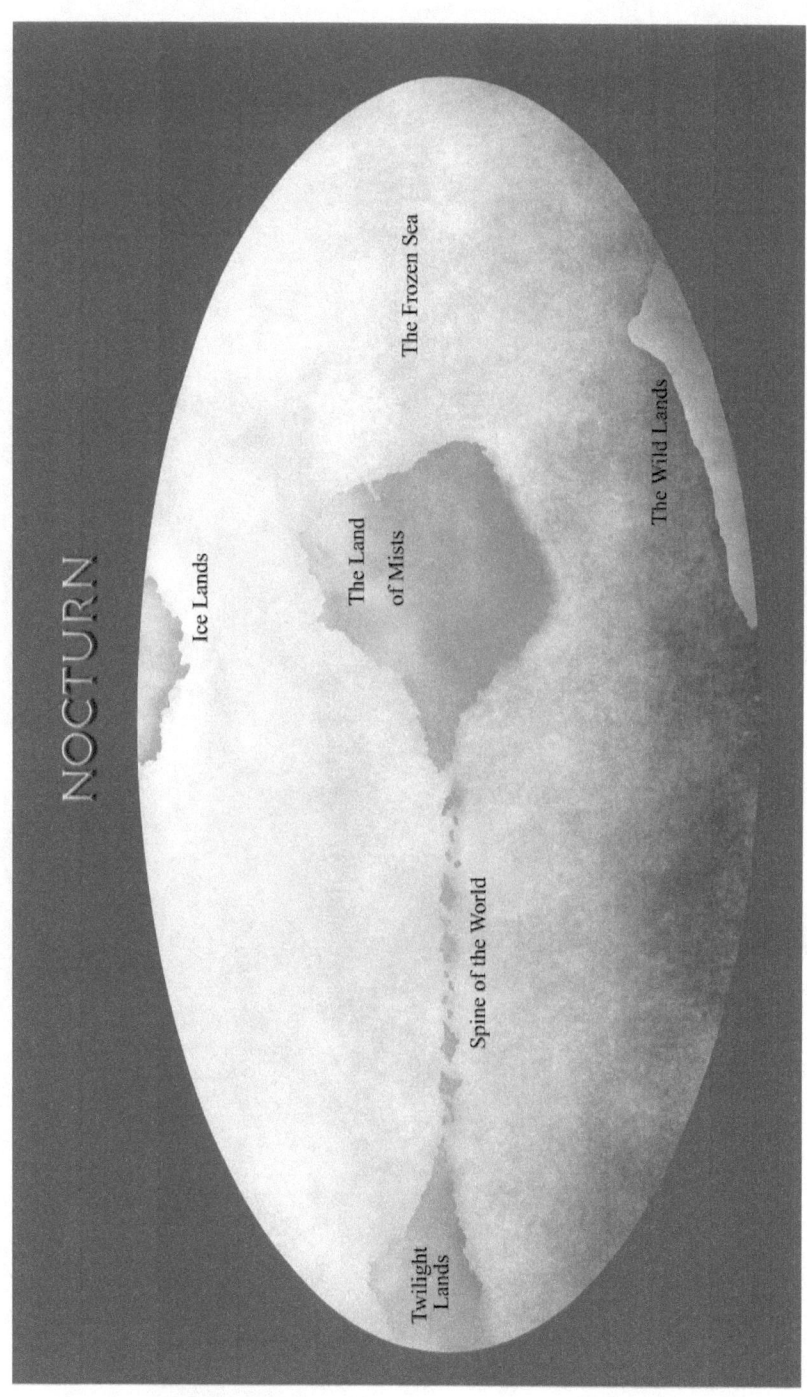

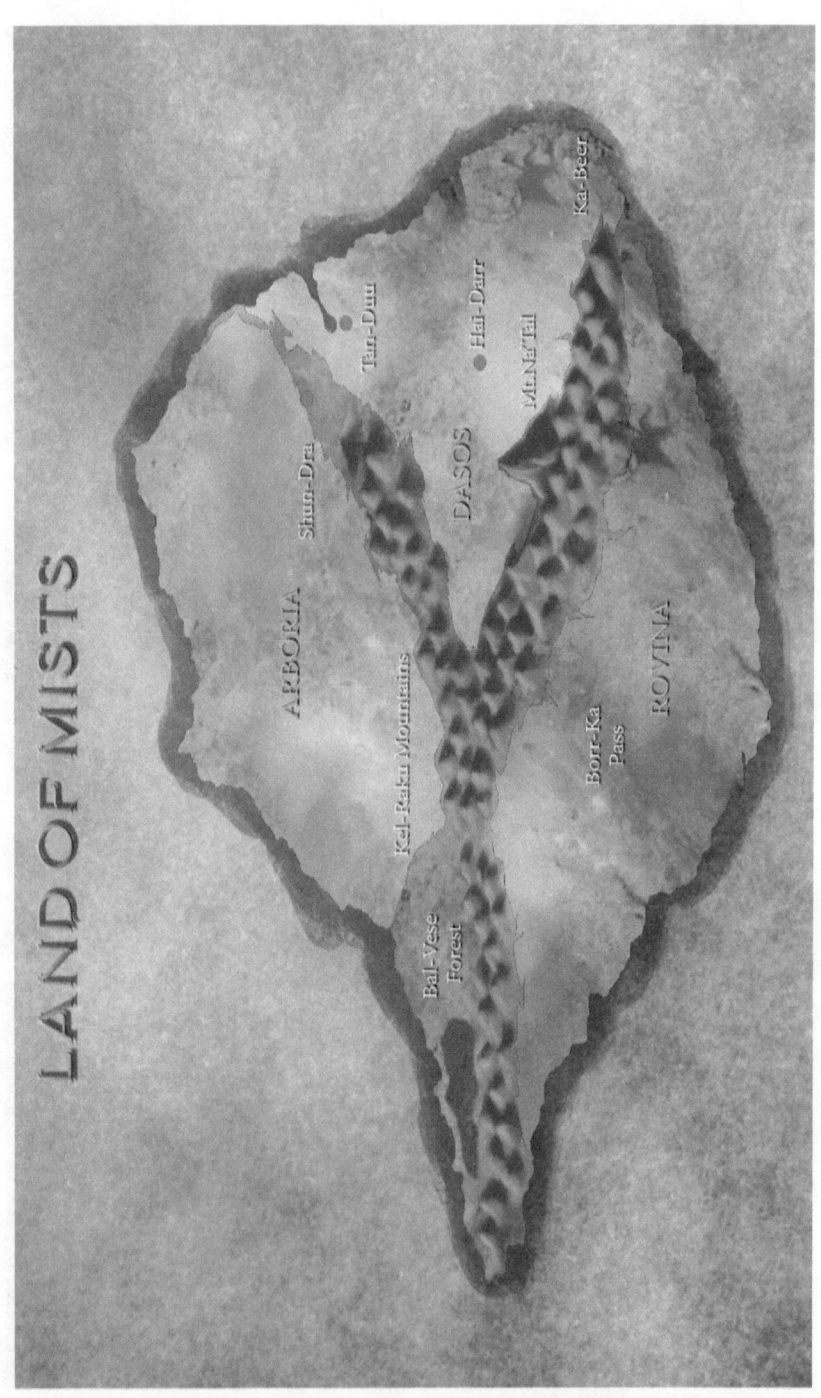

LAND OF MISTS

ABOUT THE AUTHOR

R.W. Marcus spent most of his life selling books. Along the way he managed to become a Falconer, 3rd Dan Black Belt in Yoshukai Karate, Freemason, Freelance Photographer, Ad Copywriter and WMNF Radio Disc Jockey. Marcus' radio commercials and freelance photography won numerous awards, including Best of Shows and Best of the Bay Addy Awards for work with Creative Keys and Laughing Bird Productions. R.W. Marcus was also Founder and Creative Director of United Game Masters, where he cowrote the UGM Universal Gaming System which he used to create and playtest a role-playing game based in the world of the Annigan Cycle. He formally held the title of Director

of Incunabula at Griffon's Medieval Manuscripts, where he penned his first nonfiction title, *The Ship of Fools to 1500*, which Amazon called "an authoritative guide to one of the most popular works of secular writing." Now retired, he created a new genre of fiction—Pulp Fantasy Noir—to exorcise the darker side of his good nature.

CONNECT
WEBSITE: https://AnniganCycle.com
FACEBOOK: https://www.facebook.com/noirrwmarcus/
TWITTER: @NoirRWMarcus
EMAIL: RWMarcus@yahoo.com

THE TRUE BELIEVER
TALES OF THE ANNIGAN CYCLE
BOOK SEVEN
FROM LAUGHING BIRD PUBLISHING